I0891476

THE POWER OF SYMPATHY AND OTHER WRITINGS

broadview editions
series editor: Martin R. Boyne

THE POWER OF SYMPATHY AND OTHER WRITINGS

William Hill Brown

edited by Jennifer Harris and Bryan Waterman

broadview editions

BROADVIEW PRESS
Peterborough, Ontario, Canada

Founded in 1985, Broadview Press is a fully independent academic publishing house owned by approximately twenty-five shareholders—almost all of whom are either Broadview employees or Broadview authors. Broadview is supported by a collaboration with Trent University, a liberal arts university located in Peterborough, Ontario—the city where Broadview was founded and continues to operate. Broadview is committed to environmentally responsible publishing and fair business practices.

Library and Archives Canada Cataloguing in Publication

Title: The power of sympathy and other writings / William Hill Brown ; edited by Jennifer Harris and Bryan Waterman.
Names: Brown, William Hill, 1765-1793, author | Container of (work): Brown, William Hill, 1765-1793. Power of sympathy. | Container of (work): Brown, William Hill, 1765-1793. Sans souci, alias Free and easy. | Container of (work): Brown, William Hill, 1765-1793. Occurrences of the times.
Series: Broadview editions.
Description: Series statement: Broadview editions | Includes bibliographical references.
Identifiers: Canadiana (print) 20240480643 | Canadiana (ebook) 20240480651 | ISBN 9781554812950 (softcover) | ISBN 9781770489585 (PDF) | ISBN 9781460408827 (EPUB)
Subjects: LCGFT: Novels. | LCGFT: Drama.
Classification: LCC PS715.B6 P63 2024 | DDC 813/.2—dc23

Broadview Editions
The Broadview Editions series is an effort to represent the ever-evolving canon of texts in the disciplines of literary studies, history, philosophy, and political theory. A distinguishing feature of the series is the inclusion of primary source documents contemporaneous with the work.

Advisory editor for this volume: Zubin Meer

Broadview Press handles its own distribution in Canada and the United States:
PO Box 1243, Peterborough, Ontario K9J 7H5, Canada
555 Riverwalk Parkway, Tonawanda, NY 14150, USA
Tel: (705) 482-5915
email: customerservice@broadviewpress.com

Broadview Press acknowledges the financial support of the Government of Canada for our publishing activities.

Canada

Cover design and typesetting: George Kirkpatrick

PRINTED IN CANADA

Contents

Acknowledgements

Jennifer Harris thanks the Social Sciences and Humanities Research Council for funding that supported research toward this volume.

Bryan Waterman thanks the Massachusetts Historical Society for an Andrew W. Mellon Fellowship that supported early research on this project. In addition, he thanks the research assistants who, over several years, helped with research or transcription: Cassandra Barney, Joey Bui, Angad Johar, Sachi Leath, and Scout Satterfield. He also thanks Jane Kamensky for many conversations about the Apthorp–Morton scandal and for sharing unpublished writing and archival findings on the topic.

January 22

Firſt *American* NOVEL.

This day is publiſhed, Price 9s. bound and lettered, and 6s. 8d. ſtitched in blue paper.

The POWER OF SYMPATHY: Or, the TRIUMPH OF NATURE. A NOVEL founded in truth. In two volumes 12mo. The firſt volume ornamented with a Copperplate Frontiſpiece. Dedicated to the Young Ladies of America.

Fain would he ſtrew Life's thorny Way with flowers,
And open to your View Elyſian Bowers;
Catch the warm Paſſions of the tender Youth,
And win the Mind to Sentiment and Truth.

The following is the Author's Preface:—

"Novels have ever met with a ready reception into the Libraries of the Ladies, but this ſpecies of writing hath not been received with univerſal approbation: Futility is not the only charge brought againſt it. Any attempt, therefore, to make theſe ſtudies more advantageous, has at leaſt a claim upon the patience and candor of the public.

"In Novels which *expoſe* no particular vice, and which *recommend* no particular virtue, the fair reader, though ſhe may find amuſement, muſt finiſh them without being impreſſed with any particular idea: So that if they are harmleſs, they are not beneficial.

"Of the Letters before us, it is unneceſſary to remark, that this error, on each ſide, has been avoided—the dangerous conſequences of *ſeduction* are expoſed, and the advantages of *female education* ſet forth and recommended."

Printed at Boſton, by I. THOMAS and Co. and ſold at their Bookſtore, No. 45, Newbury-ſtreet.

Introduction

In January 1789, a few months before George Washington (1732–99) became the first president of the United States, newspapers in Boston began to run advertisements for a curiosity: the "First *American* NOVEL." An anonymous, two-volume work, *The Power of Sympathy: Or, the Triumph of Nature* was "founded in truth"—that is, based on a true story or ripped from the headlines—and "Dedicated to the Young Ladies of America." Comprising anecdotes of betrayal, incest, and madness, moralistic advice on courtship, and denunciation of parents who abandon their responsibilities, the novel promised to be more useful to young female readers than other novels tended to be by illustrating "the dangerous consequences of SEDUCTION" and promoting "the advantages of FEMALE EDUCATION."

Many readers in Boston would have recognized one of the book's central tales—the suicide of a young woman who had been seduced and betrayed by her older brother-in-law—as based on a scandal that had roiled the city the previous summer, when a prominent lawyer and politician, Perez Morton (1751–1837), already the subject of some notoriety for extravagant living, had carried on an affair with his much younger sister-in-law, Fanny Apthorp (1766–88). A smaller number of people knew this had happened once already: Fanny had borne an earlier child by Perez. When the second pregnancy threatened to become public, Fanny took her own life by poison. The surrounding events, including transcriptions of her suicide notes, had been published in one of Boston's newspapers and reprinted in papers in several other American cities throughout the fall of 1788. The Boston paper that had first published those letters also took notice of the novel prior to its release: "We are informed that one of the incidents upon which the Novel is founded," wrote a contributor to the *Herald of Freedom*, "is drawn from a late unhappy suicide." Speaking for the *Herald*, this writer promised to "lay before our readers" additional details about "so truly Novel a work" as soon as they were able.[1] Like Fanny Apthorp's letters, the advertisement for this new "*American* NOVEL" gradually spread up and down the coast, from Portsmouth, New Hampshire, to Annapolis, Maryland, over the course of several months. North or South, the

1 "An American Novel," *Herald of Freedom*, 16 Jan. 1789, [3].

message to the novel's "fair reader[s]" was clear: what you read will determine your preparation for life. In this new nation, even novels—"a species of writing which hath not been received with universal approbation"—could be turned to the more "advantageous" purposes of moral instruction.

But what would these hoped-for moral effects of the first American novel look like in real life? What kinds of cultural work could a work like this hope to do in the face of the structural disempowerment that left young women in such peril? And what was it about the activities of people like the Mortons and Apthorps that led so many of their contemporaries to comment on them, in newspapers, in novels, and in the satirical plays also included in this volume? Our introduction draws on the experiences of three young American readers: Betsy Cranch (1763–1811), Abigail Adams Smith (1765–1813), and Nathan Webb (1767–1853), all of whom were contemporaries not only of Fanny Apthorp but also of the novel's anonymous author, William Hill Brown (1765–93). With these young contemporaries as guides, we examine how the novel and plays (and the scandals that occasioned them) affected individual audience members, how they contributed to Boston's faction-riven post-Revolutionary culture, and how they helped shape the idea of a national reading audience—and citizenry—whose virtue was regarded like the virtue of young female Americans: tenuous and imperiled. What roles might actual young women play in this new American nation? What was the "power of sympathy" in this political and cultural context? Was it strong enough to change a heart? To save a marriage? To bind a national citizenry? Who would be included in or excluded from its embrace? Who or what threatened it? Could it be misused or exploited? And, finally, why did some Bostonians think that the novel, still a relatively new and somewhat controversial genre, might prove to be a particularly useful vehicle to pose such questions? The materials included in this volume form a singularly rich case study for exploring these and other questions about the earliest US literature.

The epistolary novel consists of sixty-five letters, some of which include additional documents, such as poetry or other letters forwarded as enclosures.[1] Almost half the letters are from young Thomas Harrington to his friend Jack Worthy, who writes a much

1 Readers should note that parts of this Introduction reveal details of the plots of *The Power of Sympathy*; *Sans Souci, alias, Free and Easy*, and *Occurrences of the Times*.

smaller number of letters in return. The other principal characters are Myra Harrington, Thomas's sister and Worthy's fiancée, who corresponds primarily with a friend, the young widow Mrs. Holmes, who lives in a rural town called Belleview (today known as the city of Bellevue), roughly ten miles from Boston's city center. A few letters also turn up from other characters: Harriot Fawcett, a young woman of lower-class status who is the object of Thomas Harrington's romantic interest, writes a handful of letters to Myra and one to Thomas; and two members of the older generation correspond with each other (the senior Mr. Harrington, father of Thomas and Myra, and the Rev. Mr. Holmes, who is Mrs. Holmes's father-in-law). From these letters, collected and arranged by an unseen editorial hand, the novel's readers are able to piece together the story of ill-fated love between Thomas and Harriot, which culminates in both their deaths—one from consumptive grief, the other by suicide—after they learn that they are half-siblings, Harriot being the offspring of the senior Mr. Harrington through an illicit youthful affair. (After her mother died, the infant Harriot was raised as a serving girl by an acquaintance of the Harrington family.)

As in most eighteenth-century epistolary novels, much of the most important activity happens off-page in the reading and writing of the very letters that make up the novel. Letters convey the information that determines the twists and turns of the plot. When other activities are described, they also tend to revolve around the common activities of communal literacy: debates about appropriate reading, especially for young women; descriptions of reading preferences or current reading; or transcriptions of conversations that allow discrete anecdotes, often in the form of moral tales, to trade oral for written form, extending their circulation and social utility. The letters—and the poetry and various anecdotes they comprise—are occasions for readers not just to debate but also to rehearse and demonstrate sensibility or emotions, which they model for the novel's readers, sometimes by the negative example of unregulated or excessive feeling. The relationship between reading, writing, and enlightened emotions, then, becomes one of the novel's predominant concerns.

The novel's most dramatic narrative tension emerges with the nascent relationship between Thomas Harrington and Harriot Fawcett. In his first few letters, Harrington informs his friend Worthy of his interest in Harriot, but given her lower-class status he proposes to seduce her and keep her as a mistress, rather than to enter into a courtship leading to marriage. But Harriot's virtue wins him over quickly, so the tension shifts to the older Mr. Harrington's refusal to permit his son to marry "early," that is, before he has established himself professionally. As Thomas Harrington recounts the details of this conflict to Worthy, letters between other characters elaborate on the novel's topical concerns with female reading and the dangers of seduction. Harriot conveys to Myra the "story of Ophelia," a scandal among people within their acquaintance that is clearly modeled on the Apthorp–Morton affair. Worthy and Myra discuss a similar story of another tragic outcome of seduction. Mrs. Holmes writes Myra didactic letters on female education. Eventually, Myra's letters to Mrs. Holmes, in which she details her growing awareness of her brother's affection for Harriot, trigger alarm bells for the community's older members, who are aware that Harriot is secretly Thomas and Myra's half sister. Mrs. Holmes tries to end the romance, but the revelation of their blood relation arrives only after Thomas and Harriot have formed a deep attachment, the natural "sympathy" they would have enjoyed as siblings but diverted into an incestuous passion. Distraught, Harriot lapses into a depression and dies. Thomas, after sending a flurry of increasingly desperate letters to Worthy, resolves to kill himself. Worthy, who can't keep up with the rapid rate of Harrington's letter writing, travels to Boston hoping to intervene but arrives too late. His final letter, to Mrs. Holmes, gives an account of Harrington's funeral and includes a copy of the epitaph Harrington has written for himself and Harriot, at whose side he asks to be buried.

"Catch the warm Passions of the tender Youth," the novel's epigraph promises, and you will "win the Mind to Sentiment and Truth." *The Power of Sympathy* promised that novels, instead of inherently posing dangers to their readers, could be used to teach them moral lessons. But by modeling one of the novel's collected seduction tales on the Apthorp–Morton scandal, the novel also aimed, as the two short plays included here also did, to function as political exposé and warning: if the morals of the new nation's founding "fathers" were flawed, national virtue was already imperiled, without even a decade having passed since war with Great Britain had come to a close.

Scandal and Sympathy

What did it feel like to be a young American in the aftermath of the Revolution? Fatigue with the suffering and cultural dislocation occasioned by imperial crisis were adequate starting points.

Novels, some believed, might have an important role to play in reinstituting a broader sense of connection, even if they also posed some danger. The feelings caused by reading were evidence of the emotional ties needed to bind society. In keeping with the "community of love" imagined by the Revolution's leaders as a precondition for the new nation, the ideal reader in late eighteenth-century America was a sympathetic one, capable of "imagining oneself in another's position." Consuming literature this way, readers entered "a narrative model whereby readers could ostensibly be taught an understanding of the interdependence between their own and others' identities" (Barnes ix).[1] When the prominent Boston printer Isaiah Thomas (1749–1831) undertook to publish William Hill Brown's novel, he knowingly waded into a several months' long public scandal surrounding Fanny Apthorp's illicit pregnancies and suicide. How were readers supposed to feel about such a case? Who was to blame, and where would justice fall? What might such a case portend for the new republic? To understand how the novel imagined itself within such a chain of responses requires some understanding of the scandal's central players.

The previous August, some of Fanny Apthorp's neighbors in Braintree, Massachusetts, had an inkling that something was wrong. Among these neighbors was Betsy Cranch, the twenty-five-year-old unmarried niece of the Revolutionary politician and diplomat John Adams and his wife, Abigail.[2] Betsy's mother took tea with the Apthorps in mid-August and confirmed Betsy's fears that "Fanny [was] very unwell,"[3] an eighteenth-century euphemism for pregnancy. This wasn't the first time Fanny had been "unwell," though Betsy had made no explicit mention in her diary of Fanny's out-of-wedlock childbirth a year earlier. The Apthorps and their son-in-law, the prominent Boston lawyer Perez Morton, worked strenuously to conceal the event. But Betsy and her mother seemed to know, even if they kept it quiet, that Fanny's

1 This line of thinking draws on Adam Smith's (1723–90) formulation of imaginative sympathy in *A Theory of Moral Sentiments* (1759).

2 John Adams (1735–1826) eventually served as the second president of the United States from 1797 to 1801. In 1764 he married Abigail Smith (1744–1818), who herself became a politically savvy commentator on the Revolution and early national period. Elizabeth "Betsy" Cranch was the daughter of Abigail Adams's eldest sister, Mary Smith Cranch (1741–1811). "Fanny" was the nickname of Frances Theodora Apthorp.

3 Elizabeth Cranch Norton, Diary, 19–26 Aug. 1788, Jacob Norton Papers, Massachusetts Historical Society (hereafter MHS). Subsequent quotations in this paragraph are from this source.

brother-in-law, Morton, in whose home she had been living, was the father. While the first pregnancy was undeniably scandalous, it might be understood by friends and family as a momentary lapse in judgment. However, the second pregnancy was more troubling, as it suggested both a lack of genuine repentance and the inability to learn from mistakes, implying an ongoing threat. On 23 August, Fanny herself visited the Cranches' home, where Betsy's mother "made many enquiries of Fanny respecting Mr. Morton." Not long after, over breakfast with friends, Betsy participated in a conversation that apparently touched on Fanny's situation and "led to some observations—which gave me exceeding painful sensations—my peace wholly disturbed—and I pass'd the fornoon in a most disagreeable state of mind." She called on her future husband, Jacob Norton, to take her home, but she couldn't initially bring herself to confess what was bothering her. That night she "went to [her] chamber & felt all the distress that contention between duty & affection could produce." The following day Betsy's mother suggested she had made too much of things, but within hours the Apthorps' maid arrived with the shocking news that "Fanny Apthorp was dead—she had gone to Boston in perfect health yesterday morning—but she had taken poison—& died at night." Rushing to the Apthorps' home, Betsy found Fanny's parents rummaging through trunks, searching for anything that would explain their daughter's actions; what they discovered assured them, as Betsy noted in her diary, that "it was not an unpremeditated action—We were all much agitated—but the matter is dark and unfathomable! ——."

Betsy Cranch's account of this neighborhood tragedy, as it builds toward the climax of Fanny's suicide and the family's frenzied ransacking of her belongings, already feels like a scene from a sensational tale of seduction and betrayal: Betsy's dramatic flourishes become more and more literary as she goes on, suggesting that she experienced these events through the mediating frame of the popular seduction stories that filled domestic and imported magazines and had served as a basic template for the era's most popular novels. Just how unfathomable the situation was seems to be suggested by the despairing dashes into which Betsy's account devolves as it ends. But even these gestures feel conventional, as if this situation were all too predictable rather than truly shocking. Indeed, as the rest of her diary and correspondence bear out, Betsy obsessed over marriage, seduction, friendship, and deception, all staple elements of eighteenth-century fiction. In an April 1788 letter to her suitor, Jacob Norton, she refers to a friend,

Anna, possibly a pseudonym for Fanny, who has been deceived, she writes, but may look to the world like a coquette or a tease. How will she and Jacob know, she asks, that neither of them is deceiving the other?[1]

Betsy consistently presents herself in letters and her diary as a sympathetic reader of those around her, reacting to stories about her neighbor with the exquisite pain—and moral dilemmas between duty and affection—demanded by the cult of sensibility, the codes by which middling and upper-class eighteenth-century citizens of the Atlantic world demonstrated refined tastes and moral superiority over lower classes and supposedly uncivilized nations. She copied into her diary and letters snippets of advice to wives and passages from novels that dealt with marriage and sensibility, and she sympathized with fictional victims of seduction, including a youth named Benignus, whose "history"—a novel by the popular English writer Samuel Jackson Pratt (1749–1814)—taught her that "for want of resolution—the seducer could draw him aside—to every gratification that would tend to bring upon him disease dishonour poverty & death … & we can only lament—that virtue was not strong—."[2] But when Betsy's own novelistic narrative fails, leaving the matter of Fanny's death "dark and unfathomable," she lapses into religious explanations: "Providence does not permit these things but for some wise purposes," she wrote in her diary, resolving within minutes of receiving and writing about the news to make personal "improvement[s]" from the materials of this tragedy.[3] A little over a week earlier, she had written to Norton that her father had given her similar counsel, probably in response to her mother's initial news about Fanny's distress:

> My good Papa has just made an observation which pleased me—which reconciles me to some of the most painful sensations which I ever experience, from sympathizing with the sorrows & distresses of my fellow creatures. He says: "let us be content to weep with those who weep—& be grateful to the author of our being who form'd us with the powers and

1 Elizabeth Cranch to Jacob Norton, Apr. 1788, Jacob Norton Papers, MHS.

2 Samuel Jackson Pratt published dozens of works under the pen name Courtney Melmoth. Betsy refers to his debut novel, *Liberal Opinions*, which followed the moral travails and life lessons of a young clergyman.

3 Elizabeth Cranch Norton, Diary, 29 Aug. 1788, Jacob Norton Papers, MHS.

> faculties which enable us to do it—for tho that may be their employment here, yet when our spirits are assimulated [*sic*] with the just made perfect they shall only be the avenues & inlets to the joys and felicity of inumerable happy beings—& then answer the intentions of our benevolent creator—who has not form'd us with one faculty which, if we direct it to its proper object, will not encrease our happiness—tis by the perversion of them that they prove Evils."[1]

Betsy Cranch's father preached, here, a little sermon on the power of sympathy. Aware of his daughter's obsession over her innate capacity for "sympathizing," William Cranch—a self-educated English tradesman to whom his famous sister-in-law, Abigail Adams, attributed her own love for reading and writing—offers an interpretive key derived from his enlightened Congregationalist Calvinism: if such feelings come from God, they must lead to happiness. Otherwise, they must come from a different source. How, then, could one guard against the "perversion" of such "powers and faculties"? Could someone exploit our innate capacity for empathy or compassion, potentially leading us astray or manipulating our emotions? Betsy takes comfort in the idea that our capacity to feel others' sorrows would be compensated for by shared joys, in this life or the next. In the meantime, her father assured her, the best she can do is weep and stay watchful.

The concern shown by Betsy and her father for the relationship between emotion and imagination, especially for the sources and experience of fellow feeling, typifies a broader cultural fixation in the eighteenth century with humanity's capacity for sympathetic responses to suffering. Most major writers in the European Enlightenment had weighed in on the subject of sympathy. Theorists and critics of oratory, rhetoric, poetry, prose composition, the theater, and aesthetic response in general tried to explain emotional responses to art and eloquence; physicians rooted emotional responses in understandings of the body; moralists focused on the contributions of sympathy to social organization. Whether one believed, as the Scottish philosopher David Hume (1711–76) argued, that emotions were contagious, or, as the American reformer and physician Benjamin Rush (1746–1813) did, that fellow feeling could be exhausted or wasted on

1 Elizabeth Cranch to Jacob Norton, 17 Aug. 1788, Jacob Norton Papers, MHS.

fiction all while neglecting actual human suffering, enlightened thinkers seemed especially attuned to understand—and eager to experience—true feeling. One outcome, as the philosopher Adam Smith argued in his influential *Theory of Moral Sentiments*, is that the experience of sympathy helped confirm one's own virtue: that is, it could produce a feeling of pleasure grounded in a conviction that we have the capacity to feel deeply and appropriately with others (see Debes).

For her part, Betsy consistently presents herself in letters and her diary as a sympathetic reader of her acquaintances, reacting to neighborhood tragedy—and moral dilemmas between duty and affection—with a combination of exquisite, sympathetic pain and virtuous distance that made up what contemporaries referred to as "sensibility." In the words of a popular poem by the English writer Hannah More (1745–1833), widely reprinted on both sides of the Atlantic, those who possessed a high degree of sensibility or a sympathetic imagination could not help but feel acutely:

> ... [W]here bright imagination reigns,
> The fine-wrought spirit feels acuter pains;
> Where glow exalted sense and taste refin'd,
> There keener anguish rankles in the mind;
> There, feeling is diffus'd through every part,
> Thrills in each nerve, and lives in all the heart;
> And those, whose gen'rous souls each tear would keep
> From others' eyes, are born themselves to weep.[1]

To "weep with those who weep," as Betsy's father had glossed a key biblical injunction, was an experience that brought its own contentment through self-approbation. Her reactions to others' suffering, on this line of thinking, should have reassured Betsy that she possessed a refined taste and moral superiority that distinguished her from uncivilized or ungodly peoples. Sympathy, as the Cranches and others like them understood it, didn't necessarily mean equality. It could also confirm cultural hierarchies.[2]

1 For versions of Hannah More's poem published in the United States, see More, *Poems by Miss Hannah More* and *Sensibility*.

2 Andrew Burstein argues that after the Revolution, which had drawn liberally on the language of feeling and sentiment to mobilize a united resistance to British rule, many Americans came to believe, "once they began to define themselves in sentimental terms," that "republican sympathy" was not incompatible with "elite aspirations" (629).

This idea manifests in Betsy's diary in various ways. Like users of social media today who curate or repost relevant material, Betsy copied or "common-placed" various things she read into her own diary as a way to make them hers, placing advice to wives alongside passages from novels that dealt with marriage and sensibility, giving her opportunities not only to sympathize with fictional victims of seduction but also to use them to think through the world around her. Fictional characters and real-life friends were treated equally by the ideal reader when contemplating their fates, both in the sympathy they elicited and in the responses they inspired. Fanny Apthorp may have succumbed to evil forces, but in doing so she fortified Betsy's sense that she could do better.

Betsy's family may have been among the first to know of Fanny's death and something of the context, but they were by no means among the last to feel strongly about the case or to seek to fill in the blanks and assign various morals to the story. Within days, Fanny's final letters (included as Appendix A in this volume) made their way into newspapers in and beyond Boston, inviting thousands of readers who did not know her to join in speculation about these events and the individuals involved. As the scandal's audience widened and the media in which it was reported continued to proliferate, so did its meanings. These acts of an ostensibly private nature were, for many, clearly of public importance. A drama was unfolding on Boston's post-Revolutionary public stage. Who was the victim? Who was the villain? And what did these events portend, not just for Braintree or Boston but also for the future of the new nation?

While Fanny Apthorp's story may be unfamiliar to most readers today, anyone who has watched a scandal unfold over popular media recognizes the pattern: rumors and innuendos circulate privately; as the appetite for information grows, the gossip cannot be contained; eventually, events take on a life of their own, becoming public property in the process. People take sides. The more the public knows, the more the public wants to know. In our world this might mean a tell-all interview, a congressional hearing, an unauthorized book, a made-for-TV movie. These iterations, for better or worse, address the public's desire to make sense of what Betsy Cranch describes as the "dark and unfathomable" elements of a story. The stakes are even higher when the scandal involves political figures, as twentieth- and twenty-first-century scandals involving former presidents Bill Clinton or Donald Trump or Supreme Court justice Brett Kavanaugh attest. The powerful, on one hand, work to cover tracks and discredit news that might damage networks of partisan allies, not just the people involved. The powerless, too often, even when they gain a hearing, fail to gain adequate redress. Worse, they may receive the blame themselves for stepping forward. In the context of the new nation, freshly emerging from constitutional debates and busily preparing new federal institutions, onlookers couldn't help but ask: What kind of people should be at the helm of this government? What relationship would their private behavior have to their ability to lead effectively? Whose version of events should we trust? Who has the most to gain or lose? What becomes the accepted version of events often advances a sense of resolution or closure, however simplistic or false. In the process, a cautionary moral emerges: This is the moment when someone went wrong; this is how you can avoid his or her fate.

As politicians and ordinary citizens alike struggled to define the new nation, like Betsy Cranch, they monitored and commented on the motives and conduct of others, debated appropriate behavior, and judged others according to their adherence to what they perceived as republican virtues—that is, the moral code that would underwrite the new nation's experiment with self-governance. Perhaps not surprisingly, not everyone was in accord when it came to defining a national code of conduct, and in the post-Revolutionary period such disagreements would take on partisan political dimensions. This was one means by which reading might produce "sympathy" among an audience of observers: partisan lines harden in times of crisis as people throw their support to those they imagine best share their political sentiments. But the Apthorp–Morton scandal and the literature it produced also reveal that cultures of sentiment and sympathy were stratified by forms of identity and experience rooted in gender, class, race, and age. In the post-Revolutionary United States, elite young white women's sexual virtue came to stand, in popular political culture, for the moral virtue of the new nation. Thus the danger of any transgression could be contained through a story's reworking by the public as a meaningful lesson, whether or not guilt was actually determined or culprits were held accountable for their actions. And so the "first American novel" presented itself as an inoculation or remedy of sorts: "Intended to represent the specious CAUSES, and to Expose the fatal Consequences, of SEDUCTION; To inspire the FEMALE MIND With a Principle of SELF COMPLACENCY, and to Promote the ECONOMY of HUMAN LIFE," as its title page trumpeted.

Do the private activities of powerful people have a bearing on their public roles? Are the actions or feelings of ordinary young women really a barometer by which national virtue can be measured? Can private morality, in a moment of scandalous exposure, be transformed effectively into political propaganda? Such questions about the connection between private and public action guided the wide range of responses to this case in Boston and beyond. Some locals must have known that Fanny had borne a child out of wedlock in the winter of 1787–88, but initial print publicity for the Apthorp–Morton family's sordid affairs did not begin until Fanny's rambling suicide notes—some written as diary entries, some directly addressing people involved in the case—made a sudden and spectacular appearance in the first issue of a new biweekly newspaper, the *Herald of Freedom*, on 15 September 1788, roughly two weeks after Fanny's death.[1] "To morrow I mean to prove my *guilty innocence* (for I can give it no other name)," Fanny wrote, anticipating the debate that would occupy the public about her mental state and hence her agency and accountability for her death. "It will be called by some a rash step—yet a thing which has not been out of my mind for a fortnight, cannot be called sudden. It may be for the interest of some to call it Lunacy—yet, consult any physicians; ask them whether distraction was ever consistent. I felt, from the first, that this matter would go against me; I resolved not to live after it had" (Appendix A, p. 232). And so Fanny would have her own say about what she was thinking when she died. Betsy Cranch had seemed convinced, perhaps by the early discovery of these very

1 The supposed original of Fanny Apthorp's suicide note is in the collections of the MHS, Misc. Bound MSS, dated 20–27 August 1788; on the outer leaf it says the note was "[f]ound in a book bought in a second-hand bookstore, New York" and was given to the MHS by Harry Walter Roett on 9 September 1897. We believe this item is, most likely, not the original but a case of scribal publication, as similar copies of Fanny's notes appear elsewhere in the MHS's collections and in additional New England archives. See, for example, three contemporary manuscript copies/scribal publications, also at the MHS, filed as "Copies of Papers Written by the Unfortunate Francis Theodore [*sic*] Apthorp, the last weeks of her life," Price-Osgood-Valentine Papers, 1588–1910, Box 2 (1763–1788), Folder 1786–1788, MHS; Thomas Wallcut Papers, MS N-1720 (microfilm P-391, reel 2); and another contemporary manuscript copy filed as "Frances Theodora Apthorp Letter," A/A652, Schlesinger Library, Radcliffe Institute, Harvard University. The versions printed in the *Herald of Freedom* appear in this volume as Appendix A.

letters, that Fanny's suicide "was not an unpremeditated action." Who else would be called on to determine if she had proved her "*guilty innocence*," or what that phrase might mean?

Judging from the editorial decision to print Fanny's letters, Betsy wasn't the only one in Boston who wanted Perez Morton's crimes aired. Their publication feels personally or politically motivated, perhaps both. The infant *Herald of Freedom* was the only one of Boston's half-dozen newspapers to publish this material, but papers elsewhere—in New Hampshire, western Massachusetts, Connecticut, Rhode Island, New York, Pennsylvania, even South Carolina and Georgia—reprinted them over the next several weeks.[1] Names were redacted, the framing remained oblique, and the farther the story traveled the more it seemed an allegory of the times rather than merely an indictment of specific individuals. But blanks could be filled in by word of mouth or private correspondence, and in a few cases newspapers added their own details to assist readers in making sense of the materials. In Providence, Rhode Island, the *United States Chronicle* inserted a paragraph of its own to sum up "this melancholy affair," giving it all the excitement of a literary thriller: "a young lady of a very respectable family, by an illicit amour with her sister's husband, Mr. M______, was like to become a mother," et cetera. M______ denied "the connexion," as did Dr. and Mrs. P_____s, whose house had supposedly been used for the couple's secret meetings, and so Miss A______ resorted to "a large dose of poison." Offering its readers a way to interpret the story, as well as a rationale for reprinting it,

1 "J" to "Messrs. Printers," *Herald of Freedom*, 15 Sept. 1788, [2]. For reprints, see *Massachusetts Spy* [Worcester], 18 Sept. 1788, [2]; *American Herald and Worcester Recorder* [Worcester, then-recently relocated from Boston], 18 Sept. 1788, [2]; *United States Chronicle* [Providence, RI], 18 Sept. 1788, [3]; *New Hampshire Spy* [Portsmouth], 20 Sept. 1788, [2]; *Essex Journal* [Newburyport, MA], 24 Sept. 1788, [2]; *Hampshire Chronicle* [Springfield, MA], 24 Sept. 1788, [2]; *Hampshire Gazette* [Northampton, MA], 24 Sept. 1788, [2]; *Connecticut Journal* [New Haven], 24 Sept. 1788, [2]; *New-Haven Gazette* [New Haven], 25 Sept. 1788, [2]; *Newport Herald* [Newport, RI], 25 Sept. 1788, [3]; *Daily Advertiser* [New York], 25 Sept. 1788, [2]; *Pennsylvania Mercury* [Philadelphia], 25 Sept. 1788, [3]; *Connecticut Courant* [Hartford], 29 Sept. 1788, [2]; *American Mercury* [Hartford], 29 Sept. 1788, [2–3]; *Middlesex Gazette* [Middletown, CT], 29 Sept. 1788, [2]; *Litchfield Monitor* [Litchfield, CT], 29 Sept. 1788, [2]; *Freeman's Oracle* [Exeter, NH], 11 Oct. 1788, [4]; *Connecticut Gazette* [New London], 17 Oct. 1788, [4]; *State Gazette of South Carolina* [Charleston], 3 Nov. 1788, [2]; *Georgia Gazette* [Savannah], 4 Dec. 1788, [3].

the *Chronicle* both titillated its readers by inviting them to fill in the blanks in the names and turned the tragedy into a moral tale: "Thus fell, in the bloom of her days, a young Lady, who, had she not been led astray from the paths of virtue, might long have been a comfort to her friends and an ornament to her sex!"[1] The *New-Haven Gazette* appended more salacious intelligence: "It is further said that Miss A. was again pregnat [*sic*] when she put an end to her life by poison; just before which fatal accident the abovementioned letters were written."[2] Perhaps a member of the Coroner's Jury, assembled to rule on Fanny's mental state and culpability for the crime of self-murder, was the one who let the copies slip, but a family member could have as well. Granting Fanny's request to tell her own story and claim her own sanity, the letters' publication in manuscript and then in print also served to drag a villain from the shadows, signaling a desire to hold him accountable.

Days later, the *Herald of Freedom* continued its treatment of the case by publishing a long, lovelorn poem, also supposed to have been written by Fanny, though other newspapers quickly published alternative claims that it was the work of Elizabeth Whitman (1752–88), another purported victim of seduction who had died a month earlier in Danvers, a small town to the north of Boston.[3] (In a memorable scene early in *The Power of Sympathy*, the characters discuss the story of "the unfortunate Miss Whitman" as part of a multigenerational debate about novel-reading, in a letter that includes a long editorial footnote drawn mostly from the newspaper stories that circulated after her death. Whitman's case became the basis for another anonymously published novel, *The Coquette; Or, the History of Eliza Wharton*, a decade later.[4]) Subsequent newspaper commentary on Fanny's death included multiple elegies lamenting her fate and that of seduction victims in general.[5] A Coroner's Jury determined that Fanny had been in her right

1 "From the Herald of Freedom of September 15, 1788," *United States Chronicle: Political, Commercial and Historical* [Providence, RI], 18 Sept. 1788, [3].

2 *New-Haven Gazette*, 25 Sept. 1788, [7].

3 On the newspaper circulation of Whitman's story in Boston and elsewhere, see Waterman, "Elizabeth Whitman's Disappearance."

4 Our edition of that novel includes materials related to Whitman's life and death; see Foster.

5 For a poem on the incident popularly assumed to have been written by Sarah Morton (1759–1846), see *Massachusetts Centinel*, 27 Sept. 1788, [2], with a response in the 4 October issue, [3], included as Appendices B2 and B3, respectively, in this volume.

mind when she took her life, concurring with Betsy's early conclusion and Fanny's own claims. On one hand, this legal finding confirmed Fanny's guilt, under Massachusetts law, of the crime of self-murder, but on the other, it left room for speculation that she had been driven to this desperate act by other forces.[1] The ruling was not welcomed by Perez Morton, who had hoped a verdict that Fanny had been insane would have let him off the hook personally. But it was also a problem for the Apthorp family, since such a decision would have called into question Fanny's right to a Christian burial, something traditionally denied those who died by suicide. Hoping to shift the blame from his daughter, James Apthorp continued to hold Morton responsible; Morton, in turn, argued that it was actually Apthorp's paternal cruelty that drove Fanny to her death. Disputing the coroner's findings, Morton and Apthorp agreed to a private inquest by the former governor James Bowdoin (1726–90) and the well-known Massachusetts patriot John Adams, who had recently returned to Boston after several years as a diplomat in Europe. Accepting the request, and apparently seeking to keep the scandal and the family feud from intensifying, Adams wrote to Morton that he hoped that through their intervention "the late misfortune may be alleviated, and the happiness of the two families promoted."[2] Despite some initial public support for this intervention by "*characters*, in point of honour, knowledge, and integrity inferior to none in the State,"[3] Bowdoin and Adams sparked new controversy when they sided against the Coroner's Jury and declared their opinion that Fanny had been insane when she took her own life.

---

1 See "Bill of James Prince of inquest and burial costs for Theodora Apthorp," Suffolk County: Coroner's Inquisitions, Adlow Collection Selected Documents, MS Adl. C (33)—Suffolk Co., Mass. Coroner, Boston Public Library Rare Books and Manuscripts. Claiming to be in her right mind—begging forgiveness of God and family—Fanny wrote in her final letters that she would submit to divine judgment and, as she put it to Morton in an earlier letter, "die at the bar with the truth in my mouth" (Appendix A, pp. 230–31).

2 See *Massachusetts Centinel*, 8 Oct. 1788, [3]; *Herald of Freedom*, 9, 13, and 16 Oct. 1788, pages [3], [2], [2], respectively; John Adams to Perez Morton, 15 Sept. 1788, Adams Family Papers, Letterbooks, MHS.

3 This approving notice of an upcoming private investigation into "a certain recent, and melancholy event" appeared without a headline in the *Independent Chronicle*, 18 Sept. 1788, [3]; it was reprinted in the Worcester, Massachusetts, *American Herald* on 25 Sept. 1788, [3], and Philadelphia's *Pennsylvania Packet* on 27 Sept. 1788, [2].

As it continued to play out in print, the debate over the meaning of Fanny Apthorp's death suggests that the reading public would serve as yet another "bar" or jury in the case. The *Massachusetts Centinel* published the "happy" news that Adams and Bowdoin had found that "the accusations brought against a fellow Citizen"—the implication in her letters that Morton bore some responsibility for her actions—"have not been in any degree supported." Initially seeming to endorse the Bowdoin–Adams opinion, the *Centinel*'s correspondent expressed relief that the "only accountable cause" for Fanny's suicide could have been "an insane state of mind." But this led to new questions about the authority of the Coroner's Jury relative to the influence of these independent gentlemen. Was this merely a case of well-connected public figures letting each other off the hook? This commentary on the report, which appeared in three other Boston papers over the next two days, contained its own caveat: "[W]ere it not for the verdict of the Jury of Inquest to the contrary (for verdicts must always be respected), it would have been the wish of many" to concur with Bowdoin and Adams that Fanny had been insane.[1]

The *Herald of Freedom* joined its printing of the same notice with a series of forceful critiques that lasted for several weeks, including a letter from a member of the jury who demanded to know "whether there is such a crime in our laws as self-murder?" If Fanny were not insane, that is, what were the appropriate consequences of her suicide? Importantly, the jury's own sympathetic responses were on the table here. Was the jury supposed to have prioritized "the feelings of those interested parties who might or might not be hurt" and allowed "the principles of humanity to gain the ascendancy over their judgments"? That is, would sympathy for Fanny threaten public officials' ability to render judgment

---

1 "Boston, Wednesday, October 8," *Massachusetts Centinel*, 8 Oct. 1788, [3]. Reprinted in *Herald of Freedom*, 9 Oct. 1788, [3]; *Independent Chronicle*, 9 Oct. 1788, [3]; *Massachusetts Gazette*, 10 Oct. 1788, [3]; Portsmouth's *New Hampshire Spy*, 11 Oct. 1788, [3]; *New-Haven Gazette*, 16 Oct. 1788, [7]; *New-York Packet*, 17 Oct. 1788, [2]; the *American Herald and the Worcester Recorder*, 23 Oct. 1788, [1], omits the caveat and collects this piece with other reprinted commentary from Boston on the situation. The notice quotes from Adams and Bowdoin's report only the line about Morton's lack of culpability, along with their hope that "therefore there is justification for the restoration of peace and harmony between them." The correspondent only implies that their findings accorded with "the wish of many" that Fanny's "extraordinary conduct" had been "early attributed" to insanity.

on sin—or on the facts of the case as introduced into evidence? Couldn't everyone see that Fanny herself, as the suicide letters made plain, dismissed the idea of an insanity defense? That it had been impossible for jurors to "declare on their oaths a person insane, when full and clear evidence was adduced to the contrary?"[1] In the following issue, a letter signed by "A CITIZEN" even more directly charged eminent "PATRIOTS" among the self-styled "better sort" with setting a "dangerous" precedent: "for if such palliative measures are introduced, we may soon find it become very fashionable, in particular instances, to assemble a few private friends, in a private room, to review a matter after a legal decision by a Jury." Such a practice would amount to a "new judiciary mode" by which "our most fashionable vices may be wrapt up in private."[2] In the face of such responses, Adams and Bowdoin might have had reason to worry that they could end up being damned by too close an association with the likes of Morton, someone who had put his talents to the service of the Revolution but departed from a morality they would have approved. Had they been mistaken to try to protect him and keep the peace between him and his father-in-law?

Critics of the Adams–Bowdoin inquest asked important questions: If laws existed to regulate sexual morality or punish self-murder, how could these matters be rendered merely "private" affairs? And who had recourse to such extralegal protections? Over the course of the eighteenth century, it is true the public regulation of sexual behavior had been tempered in many ways.[3] But not all Boston's inhabitants would have been granted the same privileges. Members of middling and elite families were often allowed to resolve such things as out-of-wedlock pregnancies on their own terms, while the public regulation of sexuality

---

1 Letter signed "One of the JURY," *Herald of Freedom*, 9 Oct. 1788, [2]. For signs that other members of the jury were equally upset by the Adams–Bowdoin inquiry, see a notice in *Massachusetts Centinel*, 11 Oct. 1788, [3], in which the author of the original announcement of the decision underscores regret that the jury's verdict had been set aside. The *Centinel* seems more hesitant than the *Herald* to allow correspondents to call one another names. In a note on 4 October 1788, the editors explain, "We cannot see either sentiment, wit, or genius, in the epithets 'base, mean, low lived, rascally,' &c. nor in the terms 'villain, poltroon, debauchee,' &c.—and therefore, we cannot give place to [a submission signed] 'Retaliator'" ([2]).

2 Letter signed "A CITIZEN," *Herald of Freedom*, 13 Oct. 1788, [2].

3 On the gradual move, especially among upper classes, to address premarital sexual transgression as a family matter, see Dayton, ch. 4.

fell more and more on the poor and non-white people.[1] To some, money seemed able to cover a multitude of sins. This view had been voiced even prior to the publication of the Adams–Bowdoin decision by a correspondent to the *Herald of Freedom* who lamented the ability of "devils in human shape!" to defy both law and religion and "hug themselves up from the idea, that they are safe from publick chastisement." Having through their own "cunning, art, subtilty, and hell planned inventions" managed to avoid "the jaws of destruction," such "villains" and "wretches" would eventually encounter "vengeance" when eternal judgment was handed down at a divine tribunal.[2]

The *Herald*'s final commentator on the case that fall called attention to a more earthly arena for rendering justice. The press itself, this writer argued, was a "tribunal of the impartial publick." Just as villains could win a day in court, "knaves" also had access to newsprint and were capable of "publish[ing] their own shame" as a way to "silence all opposition."[3] Morton—unnamed throughout the piece—had indeed tried to control the public story not only by orchestrating a private tribunal but also by ensuring its results were made quite public. The *Centinel*'s original celebration of Adams and Bowdoin's decision in the matter, in this writer's view, "wound[ed] the publick" by silencing the law and shamelessly "blast[ing]" a seducer's actions "from New Hampshire to Georgia." The effort, this writer believed, would backfire as the "discerning" public came to recognize "iniquity" for what it was, regardless of whether eminent names were attached to the supposed vindication. Perhaps there was no "legal evidence" to assign Morton blame for the suicide, but the "learned" gentlemen had hardly acquitted him of his crimes. "Is not the cognizance of ____st still amenable to a jury," this writer asked, "at the presentation of the A______y G_____l?" That is, a crime other than suicide had been committed and not disputed: the crime of incest, as a relationship between brother- and sister-in-law would have been regarded by Massachusetts law. Shouldn't the state's attorney general call Morton before a jury on those charges? This was the closest a newspaper writer came to naming the full breadth of

1 On the roles played by popular media in producing new gender ideology in the wake of these transformations, see Ryan, ch. 6. For similar developments elsewhere in the new United States, see Lyons, ch. 5.

2 "Boston, October 6," *Herald of Freedom*, 9 Oct. 1788, [3]. This correspondent's words appear in the fifth paragraph.

3 Letter signed "Unappeased Justice," *Herald of Freedom*, 16 Oct. 1788, [2].

Morton's crimes. The process, to this point, had given "humanity" the upper hand. That is, sympathy for the survivors was preventing Morton from receiving the full force of law. But "the rest who does not know?" Everyone knows the rest, the writer implied: everyone in Boston as well as God on high.[1] The newspapers had helped to make sure of it.

Adams and Bowdoin's deliberations on the matter do not appear among the many references to the Mortons and Apthorps that are scattered among the Adams family's voluminous correspondence. Both had entered the arena desirous of an outcome that would reconcile the families, and their determination would have been welcome on both sides: Morton would be less vulnerable to charges that he was responsible for Fanny's death, while Apthorp would be able to bury his daughter in the family crypt at King's Chapel. If they leaned toward taking Morton's side, it may have been because his father-in-law was a suspected Loyalist who had even been declared detrimental to the town of Braintree a decade earlier, during the war.[2] They may also have hoped that a reconciliation between Morton and his father-in-law would de-escalate the damage and scandal: after all, the common good, locally or nationally, would hardly be served by fractious behavior and familial discord among Boston's political leaders, already under the pressure of partisan responses in the debates on the federal Constitution.

But other observers believed that sweeping these potential crimes under the rug would compromise the virtue necessary to

---

1 God's omnipotence is implied by two lines of poetry the writer cites in conclusion: "*But blast the villain, tho' to altars fled, / Who robs the living and insults the dead.*" The lines come from an English epitaph widely reprinted in the eighteenth and nineteenth centuries. It had appeared just a few weeks earlier, for example, as "An Epitaph on an Honest Man," *New-York Packet*, 3 Oct. 1788, [4]. The poem implies that (mortal) churchyards might shelter criminals beneath "pompous inscriptions" in cemeteries, but God's hand would reveal their crimes. As used by "Unappeased Justice," the lines may refer to Fanny Apthorp's burial at King's Chapel, an apparent act of "humanity," given that her death by suicide should have rendered her ineligible for a Christian burial (interment in a churchyard cemetery with her family).

2 Adams claimed to want peace between parties he respected and loved, but his stronger sympathies still seemed to be with Morton, though the Adams family privately used both Morton and his father-in-law to confirm their own moral superiority and republican virtue; see Butterfield 5:280n11. The Adams family letters are riddled with comments on James Apthorp's Anglophilia and erratic behavior.

maintaining a just and moral society. These members of the public were less inclined to forgive what they saw as Morton's arrogance and entitlement, as well as his abuse of patriarchal power, both in his domestic life and among the political elite. In an era before social media provided a venue for public excoriation of those in power, scribal publication and print media sufficed. Blistering commentary and satirical poems (with titles such as "An Admonition to the Fair" and "A Picture of Suicide") appeared in the local papers. Preachers invited their congregations to reflect upon the scandal's meaning and even warned against novels as one of the causes of such situations: "Do we not see [that] those unhappy Persons who ... have put a miserable end to their own lives ... have been great readers of Romances?," one prominent minister asked.[1] In decrying such behavior from the pulpit, the clergy helped to shape the public meanings and reception of these events. Like all other purveyors of media, they also whetted the public's appetite for more. In the case of the Morton scandal, this invocation of "Romances"—often a synonym for "novels"—would prove prescient, for the novel, like the newspapers, would present its case, engage its readers' feelings, and ultimately leave them to decide what kind of characters deserved sympathy or were fit to govern society.

Print and the Making of Perez Morton's Character

If Perez Morton still had friends in high places, he had also made more than a handful of enemies along the way. For half a decade, he had already been at the very center of debates over suitable social conduct in post-Revolutionary Boston. To the chagrin of some Bostonians, Morton and his family were a little too comfortable having had their behavior debated in print. Like their neighbors, the Mortons lived in relation to expectations of appropriate behavior, sometimes adhering to them, sometimes contesting, defying, or even flouting them. In doing so they occupied an in-between space where they might simultaneously set fashion and trends while also creating public outrage. We might recognize parallels in the scrutiny accorded a trend-setting tabloid couple today: we ask "was her performance too risqué?" while practicing the same dance moves at home; magazines criticize his luxurious or outlandish outfit while also informing readers where they can buy a

1 Jeremy Belknap, sermon dated 21 Sept. 1788, manuscript sermon book for 1788, Belknap Papers, MHS.

less expensive version. Fans and haters alike pay attention to celebrities' fickleness in romantic relationships, or debate their mental health, even as gossip writers feverishly speculate about their next partners. The same contradictions and considerations preoccupied the Mortons' world in Revolutionary Boston: Was playing one kind of card game harmless and another scandalous? Was it possible to throw a fashionable party that was also respectable? How could single men and women socialize enough to evaluate one another's true nature while also maintaining a proper distance? Was public theater immoral, but private or "closet" performances or readings of dramatic works acceptable? Where were the lines drawn, and by whom? The Mortons crossed all the lines at times and in the process found themselves the subjects of public scrutiny, even as they were heralded by many as Boston's social leaders. In diaries, letters, and newspapers, people debated, derided, and defended their conduct. As these debates intensified, the Mortons would find themselves censured and satirized in creative works, notably those republished in this volume. So who were the Mortons, and just what did they do to test sympathy's limits and earn such notoriety?

Perez Morton may have been immortalized by peers as a literary villain, but the early arc of his trajectory as a public figure suggests he might as easily have made an excellent hero in an eighteenth-century novel—or an important figure in national politics. Morton's social standing in late-eighteenth-century Boston exemplified the possibilities for mobility in the new nation, propelled to prominence by his own skill with words and his sensitivity to the dynamics of Revolutionary publicity. His father was proprietor of the White Horse Tavern on Boston's Newbury Street, a meeting place for the Patriot radicals who would later assume important positions in the new government (Carr-Frobose 93–94). Morton's education at the Latin School and Harvard University raised him above his father's profession, even as his tavern connections served him well: he read law with Josiah Quincy (1710–84) and served as deputy secretary of the Massachusetts Provincial Congress to Samuel Adams (1722–1803). As Morton succeeded socially, he also made gains financially, buying up inexpensively the properties of Loyalists, including those of some of his in-laws who had fled the country, or been chased out, following their siding with the British crown during the Revolution.[1]

1 For Morton's biography in general, see Shipton 555–61; Milford, "Boston's Theater Controversy" 71–73; Kamensky, *Exchange Artist* 39–45.

Morton's political celebrity began when, at age twenty-six, he delivered what the *Independent Chronicle* reported as an "ingenious and spirited Oration" at King's Chapel.[1] The occasion was the reinterment of General Joseph Warren (1741–75), a prominent Patriot who had been killed at Bunker Hill. The catalog of Warren's virtues, which goes on for a dozen pages, reads almost as a guidebook to Morton's own ambitions. In Morton's hands, Warren's apotheosis is as swift as Britain's fall will be; citing familiar lines from Shakespeare's *The Tempest*, he waxes prophetic in conclusion: "We will assert the Blood of our murdered Hero against thy hostile Oppressions, O shameless Britain! and when 'thy Cloud-Capp'd Towers, thy gorgeous Palaces' shall by the Teeth of Pride and Folly be levell'd with the Dust ... the Name and the Virtues of WARREN shall remain immortal" (10–13).

In sealing Warren's immortality, Morton also hoped to secure for himself a permanent association with the Revolutionary martyr and an enduring reputation as an orator. Abigail Adams, one of his auditors in King's Chapel, was impressed: she wrote to her husband, John, that "a young fellow could not have wished for a finer opportunity to have displayed his talents."[2] If Perez Morton understood the utility of patriotic eloquence, he also grasped the value of publication and publicity. Printed in Boston, Philadelphia, and New York, his oration remained a popular selection for schoolboys well into the next century, even as Morton's political opponents referred to him derisively as "the Orator," suggesting that his silver tongue wove flimsy fabrics of its own (Kamensky, *Exchange Artist* 41).

The first backlash against Morton's oratory came not from partisan opponents, however, but from Boston's female population. In a speech to his fellow Freemasons in late 1777, Morton asserted glibly that women would never be admitted to Masonic lodges because they were incapable of keeping secrets.[3] The charge cut against new understandings of women's place as avatars of sensibility and civilizing morality, and it came at a time

1 "Boston, April 25," *Independent Chronicle*, 25 Apr. 1776, [3]. For more on Morton's entry into public life, see Waterman, "'Heaven defend us'" 51.

2 Abigail Adams to John Adams, 7 Apr. 1776, in Butterfield 1:374–75.

3 Because Morton's text has not been preserved, it is impossible to know exactly how seriously to take the attack. Reactions from his contemporaries imply they varied in their interpretation of its sincerity. On Freemasonry's contributions to the political ties that bound the Revolutionary generation, see Bullock.

when many—Abigail Adams not least among them—were asking pointed questions about women's roles in the new society they were helping to usher into being. At least two poems were published in response to Morton's slight, defending the "female heart" as the "safest guard" a confidence could find. The longer of the two was structured as "A Trial" in which Morton's insults were shouted down by a round of female orators with fiery eyes and words; Morton himself is branded a hypocrite who knew how to "praise each charm" when he played the part of the "swain" but who, "for one sad word, / [would] Lose all the joys our sex afford!"[1] If this poem criticized, the other cautioned:

> You said Sir on a late Occasion,
> When speaking forth your fine Oration,
> Ladies could never Masons be,
> Alas! they fail in Secrecy.
> Then with your Brothers pass your Life, Sir,
> Without a Mistress or a Wife, Sir;
> Lawyers with Masons ought to dwell,
> For both have much unfit to tell.[2]

The final lines suggestively hint that the author may have information Morton would rather keep secret, and that Morton could do better to monitor his own conduct. If he has secrets unfit for female ears, in other words, perhaps they are unseemly, a sign of his own insensibility. Unfortunately, Morton failed to heed such warnings; a decade later, following Fanny Apthorp's suicide, Morton's moral failings confirmed for many his lack of true feeling.

Though this poetic skirmish may seem minor (especially in the context of an ongoing war with Great Britain), contemporaries remembered it and used it against Morton on occasion. That spring, another small scandal broke out when Morton was

1 "A Trial," *Independent Chronicle and the Universal Advertiser,* 15 Jan. 1778, [3]. Morton's name is not used in this poem; rather, he is referred to as Castalio.

2 "To the Lawyer Who Pronounced an Oration to the Free Masons on Saturday Last," *Boston Gazette, and Country Journal,* 29 Dec. 1777, [3]. A few weeks later the same poet wrote again, acknowledging that "the Lawyer" had "Resolv'd to be a Fool no more" and so had been pardoned by Boston's women, who "grant him Leave to take a Mate." See "The Pardon," *Boston Gazette, and Country Journal,* 12 Jan. 1778, [3]. As the author of "A Trial" makes plain, not all were as quick to forgive.

accused of accosting a neighbor in the street and demanding he free the enslaved members of his household. Again, Morton was portrayed as someone whose public morality might be merely an act, his advocacy for abolition nothing more than performing a sensible character. Morton published a lengthy defense, denying that he had done any such thing and submitting the facts "to the candid judgment of the public." Concerned to protect his "reputation," which he held "dearer than his life," he resorted to self-defense in newsprint, even though he acknowledged that some may have considered such a public venue inappropriate for airing private disputes.[1] Within weeks, several affidavits were published to counter Morton's claims of innocence, the first of which raised the prior issue of Morton's slight against Boston's female population. Morton was becoming accustomed to seeing his name in "the Gazette of late," this writer charged, since "the Ladies" had been placed "under the necessity to convince the world, that the reflection thrown against them, by him, was unjust, cruel, and testified him to be a man void of sensibility."[2] The association of Morton's public personality with concerns unbecoming a man of feeling seems calculated to damage his reputation and undermine his credibility.

This characterization of Morton as insensible appears to have taken hold. Abigail Adams, so recently Morton's admirer, by 1780 had developed a different view. Recalling the brouhaha occasioned by Morton's comments on female secrecy, she launched harsher charges against Morton in a letter to a young male relative. Warning her correspondent away from the insincerity of "[m]odern refinement and Chesterfieldian politeness,"[3] Adams invoked the controversial English nobleman Philip Dormer Stan-

1 Perez Morton, "To the Public," *Boston Gazette, and Country Journal*, 27 Apr. 1778, [3].

2 Henry Howell Williams, "To the Public," *Boston Gazette, and Country Journal*, 11 May 1778, [2]. The same page contains several other related items, mostly affidavits against Morton.

3 In 1774 the letters of Philip Dormer Stanhope, Earl of Chesterfield, were collected and published posthumously as *Letters to His Son on the Art of Becoming a Man of the World and a Gentleman*. The volume was popular in Revolutionary America, reprinted in New York in 1775. Adams's skepticism of Chesterfield's approach to social performance—particularly his attitude toward women, whom he saw as disposable pawns in larger contests for social and political power—was shared by her friend Mercy Otis Warren (1728–1814), among many others. See Appendices C1 and C2 for their writing in this context.

hope, Earl of Chesterfield (1694–1773), whose popular volume of advice to his son was seen by some moralists as shallow and advocating insincerity. She directly followed this attack on Chesterfieldianism with commentary on the upcoming marriage of Sarah Wentworth Apthorp and Perez Morton ("You know who publickly affronted the whole Sex"). How, Abigail wants to know, could such a "Lady [have] refused such a Gentleman and such a Gentleman—for a Gambling Rake"? Her indictment of Morton grew even more serious, by implying that he may even have consorted with prostitutes: "Can a Bosom of Sensibility and Innocence, accept a Heart hardened by a commerce with the most profligate of the Sex? a Constitution enfeabled, the fine feelings of the soul obliterated? What but disgust, suspicion, coldness, and depravity of taste, can be the consequence?" (Appendix C2, p. 246).[1] In Adams's mind, Morton's distrust of women as confidants should have been an early indicator of his insensibility and hypocrisy, just as his newspaper antagonist had warned. The oratorical prowess that had launched Morton's political career had, within a few short years, begun to seem suspiciously like a seducer's charms.

The Sans Souci Scandal

By the fall of 1784 Perez Morton had settled into married life with Sarah Wentworth Apthorp. Wedding Sarah raised Morton's capital, both financially and socially. No child of a tavern-keeper, Sarah hailed from a prominent merchant family, if one dogged by the specter of Loyalism. Sarah was remarkable on many fronts: her education exceeded that of most women of the age and she had established literary ambitions, apparently publishing anonymously before her marriage. If this were not enough, she was an acknowledged beauty who had, as Abigail Adams noted, turned down several suitors. That year, with their two children and numerous servants, the Mortons assumed occupancy of her

1 The editors of the Adamses' correspondence speculate that the couple Abigail mentions are Perez Morton and Sarah Apthorp, though they worry that the timing of the scandal seems off, given that this is still eight years ahead of Fanny Apthorp's death (see Butterfield et al. 3:377–79). Adams's reference to the slight on "the whole Sex," which the editors do not recognize as a reference to Morton's Masonic oration, would seem to confirm the identification. Adams's letter suggests more skeletons in Morton's closet than those to which scholars have been privy.

family's impressive State Street mansion, affirming their position as prominent members of Boston's most elite social circles. With the coming of winter, the Mortons and their friends established a social club, the Sans Souci. Coming on the heels of wartime austerity and amid calls for new national virtue, the club's activities were readily embraced by some and frowned upon by many others. While wagers were capped at a quarter, subscribers could play cards at one of forty tables. Dancing, an activity some Bostonians disapproved of, was encouraged. Refreshments such as tea, coffee, and hot chocolate flowed freely (wine, punch, and lemonade were available for purchase). Not only did the sexes intermingle with ease, but male subscribers were allowed to escort two ladies—the imbalance no doubt intended as a lure for those men who might not be able to secure female company on their own. Those attending ranged in age from sixteen years to the fifty-four-year-old Catharine Macaulay (1731–91), the famous English writer and defender of the American cause, who was a visitor to Boston that winter.

But many in Boston were not amused, and the Sans Souci was held up by critics as a hotbed of promiscuous gambling and undemocratic social climbing (see Warren; Davies, ch. 5). Republican detractors characterized the group's most vocal defenders as young and impertinent. To Samuel Adams, in his early sixties and one of the group's fiercest opponents, Perez and Sarah Morton, among the group's more prominent members, were part of the youth culture. (Perez was thirty-four in 1784–85. Sarah was almost a decade younger and had spent most of her twenties pregnant: the couple had four children before Sarah turned twenty-six.) Adams couldn't help looking on his former deputy secretary's endorsement of urbane politeness as irredeemably unrepublican. The club's defenders, on the other hand, felt such an institution would be "very useful in polishing the manners and promoting harmony and social intercourse in the town."[1] Young Harrison Grey Otis (1765–1848), who would go on to a prominent political career, worried his aunt, Mercy Otis Warren, herself an astute political commentator and friend of the Adamses, with his spirited public advocacy on the club's behalf. He claimed its members remained sufficiently patriotic and vowed that the group would continue to meet for its "innocent amusement" while the club's opponents huddled "in some sequestered

1 "Son of Candour," *Massachusetts Centinel*, 26 Jan. 1786, qtd. in Davies 221.

corner, brood[ing] over the virtues of the ancient Republics, and pin[ing] upon the contemplation of pleasures which [they are] not qualified to enjoy."[1] (A week later, Otis would more explicitly describe his opponents as being bitter over their literary failures.[2])

As writers traded barbs in the local papers, the publishers of the *Massachusetts Centinel* took things a step further by announcing the forthcoming printing of an anonymous closet farce, *Sans Souci, alias, Free and Easy: Or an Evening's Peep into a Polite Society*. Such "closet dramas," plays that were intended for private reading rather than public performance, had been a staple of Revolutionary Boston's literary landscape, with colonial governors and British officials coming in for a drubbing as stock villains, the secret facilitators of a conspiracy against the local citizenry. The publication of *Sans Souci* made it plain that such literary weapons would find a place in post-Revolutionary cultural debates as well. Almost immediately the publishers found themselves under attack, including alleged death threats from associates of the Mortons who had been portrayed as threats to public morality. This assault on the press occasioned another flurry of newspaper commentary from all sides, but the play was published and went into a second edition. The Mortons, satirized in *Sans Souci* as Mr. and Madam Importance, are portrayed as markedly snobbish. The latter considers her fashion sense evidence of her superiority and uses it to incite envy and create new social distinctions: fine dress "will be the most effective means to establish a *precedency*," she crows. "[W]e have for a long while been too much on a level" (p. 187). Her husband, meanwhile, chases fame and power, flattering women to gain social advantage, having learned his lesson, as another character reminds him, that "nothing is more fatal to a man of fashion than doing anything reflecting [poorly] on the ladies." Once in control of the club, he plans to use it to "soften" republican principles "in the school of politeness," the same way he and his set had already "modernized" "the old principles of religion—staunch Calvinism" (pp. 197–98).[3] In this way, he

---

1 *Massachusetts Centinel*, 19 Jan. 1785, qtd. in Warren 325.

2 "Sans Souci," *Massachusetts Centinel*, 26 Jan. 1785, qtd. in Warren 12.

3 The reference to modern religion indicates Morton's role in bringing Unitarianism and lay ordination to King's Chapel, where he was a vestryman from 1783 to 1788. Opponents of liturgical reform saw it as another sign of liberty becoming licentiousness. See Milford, *Gardiners of Massachusetts* 102–07.

embodies republicans' worst fears of the kind of man who could cavalierly seduce a female acquaintance: his taste for pleasure, artificial manners, and social approval would all undermine traditional New England morality and nascent national virtue. The play ends with the party engaged in a game of cards; Madam Importance and her friends deflect the efforts of their male companions to distract them from the game by offering flattering compliments; meanwhile, the ladies hope to use their charms to gain the upper hand. The characters are painted as shallow, grasping, vain, and in possession of latent Loyalist sympathies—in short, as unsuitable to lead a new nation.

Such closet dramas had served during the Revolution not simply to expose counter-Revolutionary politics but also to critique the ostentatious performances of polite manners on which they often depended. The Mortons, the play implied, hoped to establish their own fortunes, and possibly Perez's political career, by manipulating their public reputations in ways that many took to be part of the corrupt monarchical culture they had just thrown off. In a society that had not yet embraced the idea of theater, the very notion that society depended upon such insincere performances was heavily loaded. The farce's characters take on the names of highly gendered and ranked social types, suggesting performed roles rather than authentic individual identities. The men are divided, by age, into pairs such as Young Forward and Little Pert, obviously satirizing Otis and his peers, and sets of older male friends, such as Mr. Importance and Dr. Gallant, who conspire to put social pleasures and political influence alike to the service of making their fortunes. The women are divided into pro–Sans Souci pairs (Madam Importance and Madam Brilliant) and those who serve as the voice of republican critique ("Mrs. W——N," a stand-in for Mercy Otis Warren, long but wrongly assumed to be the playwright, and "Republican Heroine," meant to indicate Catharine Macaulay, who in all actuality was a supporter of the club). Women and men alike calculate their every move before an audience of peers and onlookers. Mr. Importance credits Dr. Gallant with "improv[ing] on Chesterfield" in his plot to use their calculated appearances at the public assemblies as a means to establish "importance" (p. 190). The result of all this social theatricality, the farce suggests, will be an upending of the supposedly "natural" social order: women will strive for undue influence over men, self-interested lawyers will supplant benevolent clergy in social influence, the "public lectures" will become a blanket occasion for inappropriate subjects and may even become an inroad to legalizing theatrical entertainments.[1]

Sans Souci also suggests that the threats to social order extend to society's lowest-ranking members: enslaved and free black men and women who served the upper classes. In a late scene, Jack and Cuffy, identified as "servants"—a word meant to distinguish them from those enslaved, but used here with some irony as they are reduced to racist caricatures—discuss how the late-night outings of "Massa and Misse" allow black members of the household to have their own fun. The scene is intended as comic relief, presented in heavily stereotyped dialect pandering to white prejudices about African American speech and competency. At the same time, the scene turns on the beliefs of Boston's elite that white members of a society, especially those, like the Mortons, who professed an opposition to slavery, had paternalistic obligations to black members of their household, still demeaned as racially incapable of self-governance. In allowing Jack and his friends to frolic at all hours, the white characters were—according to the era's racist logic—abdicating their responsibility to provide proper paternalistic oversight of black members of their household. If they can't govern their own houses, the play seems to suggest, how can they govern the nation? Given that white Bostonians feared criminal behavior or retribution from those enslaved or disenfranchised on the basis of race, Jack and Cuffy's "Massa and Misse" were also failing to ensure that black household members were closely monitored for the safety of their white neighbors. For racist white Bostonians, black freedom of movement would have been a genuine source of anxiety and fear, one that *Sans Souci*'s author obviously hoped to exploit.

Contemporary readers might be forgiven for finding themselves at a crossroads as they contemplate the criticisms leveled against the Sans Souci. The natural social order posited and upheld even by the club's republican critics is decidedly problematic to twenty-first-century readers. The assumption that women should be subordinate to men, and that like non-white people they will get into trouble unless sufficient oversight is exercised, is undeniably offensive. The ways in which the play presents those

1 The reference here is obscure now but quite pointed to contemporaries. As of 1781, Catharine Macaulay's brother-in-law, Dr. James Graham, a Scottish pioneer in sex education, gave lectures on conception in London, alongside an electrical "Grand State Celestial Bed," which he promoted as a cure for infertility; see Porter 159–66.

non-compliant women and black subjects are likewise offensive, grounded in gendered and racialized stereotypes that supported white men of the ruling classes. However, to the club's more fashionable defenders of the era, who were by and large white men and women of the middling and upper classes—or those who were striving to join these ranks—white paternalism or social hierarchies were not so much problems in and of themselves. These citizens of a new nation may have thrown off the monarchism of their Loyalist neighbors, but they certainly didn't aim to eliminate social distinctions. Even as we recognize the offensiveness of the republican confidence in an older moral order, or see their objection to gaming or dancing as distasteful remnants of New England Puritanism, we can also acknowledge the fairness of their fears that Morton and his peers sought to introduce new artificial conventions and fashionable, exclusionary practices that placed themselves at the top of Boston's social hierarchies. Neither side in these debates is progressive when it comes to the rights of women and racial minorities. After all, allowing women into a club to play cards isn't progressive if most of those women are treated merely as luxury goods. To twenty-first-century readers, neither Chesterfieldian politeness nor republican austerity offers a set of social values we would necessarily want to celebrate.

"I hope our Countrymen will be Wise enough to take warning": Novel-Reading and National Virtue

The Mortons survived their public lampooning as Mr. and Madam Importance and continued on their upward social trajectory, only to find themselves at the center of a much more serious private drama a few years later, the one with which we opened this introduction. In 1786 or 1787, Sarah's younger sister, Fanny Apthorp, came from Braintree to Boston to live with the Mortons. She had been overseas, probably to escape the uncertainties of the war. Young, attractive, and literate, Fanny offered her sister's family companionship after Sarah had given birth to the couple's fourth surviving child, in August 1786. Sarah was expecting another by the following spring. It was a cycle familiar to women of the era, dangerous and exhausting. But this time Sarah was not alone. Fanny was also carrying Perez Morton's child, giving birth late that year. This is the pregnancy the Apthorps so successfully concealed from friends and neighbors—but when it became clear that Fanny was pregnant again the next summer, the indiscretion was less easily forgiven. Family strain began to show, with Sarah's father apparently trying to force Morton to assume responsibility for his actions. Then, in late August, Fanny's suicide propelled the private family drama into the public realm. Less than a week before Sarah Morton's thirtieth birthday, her younger sister was dead and her husband had been exposed as the author of crimes far more serious than dancing, card-playing, or vanity. In eighteenth-century New England, seduction was a crime. So, too, were adultery and incest, which is how Fanny and her brother-in-law's relationship would have been understood.

As the scandal gained currency, Betsy Cranch was not the only family acquaintance who scrambled to make sense of it. Following the public exposure of Morton's role in the affair, Betsy's cousins, the children of John and Abigail Adams, took up the subject in their own correspondence, mediating the events as Betsy had through existing literary and religious frameworks. Writing from Jamaica, New York (present-day Queens), twenty-three-year-old Abigail ("Nabby") Adams Smith used the scandal as the basis of a secular sermon on the state of society in a letter to her brother John Quincy Adams, a recent Harvard graduate who was studying law in Newbury, Massachusetts. Nabby, already married for two years to her father's former secretary, responded to John Quincy's account of Fanny Apthorp's death in terms that were also recognizably literary: "the Tragical Story you relate has made much talk here as well as with you," she wrote. "[T]hat family seem to be devoted to misfortunes of every kind,—if there are any innocent—one cannot but regret that they should be doomed to suffer with those whose atrocity of Guilt is almost unparalleled—." But rather than demonstrating the intense personal sympathy and exquisite sensibility her cousin Betsy had when faced with the same situation, Nabby quickly refigures the Apthorps' "misfortunes" as a national allegory with economic overtones:

> I hope our Countrymen will be Wise enough to take warning from those instances they have recently had of the pernicious affects of Such extravegance, dissipation, and folly;—as have been exhibited to view these late years;—the fatal Consequences which thousands of Innocent Persons experience from the downfall of thease airry fabricks—and visionary Castles of splendor—aught alone to deter others from pursueing So fallacious a Plan of Life—[1]

1 Abigail Adams Smith to John Quincy Adams, 28 Sept. 1788, in Butterfield 8:299–300. The editors of the volume do not identify the (*continued*)

As is often the case with politicians caught in highly publicized domestic scandals today, Morton had personal failures that were read as indicators of potentially systemic political corruption. For Nabby Smith, the terms that best describe Morton's seduction of his sister-in-law ("dissipation" and "extravegance") have unmistakable economic connotations of overspending, waste, and conspicuous consumption, behaviors incompatible with republican virtue. And, as with land schemes that ruined dozens of investors after the Revolution (and made dozens of the founding generation, including Morton, extraordinarily wealthy), his "visionary Castles of splendor," once they began to fall, ruined not just his

Apthorps as the family being discussed in these letters. The lines Nabby cites bear a similarity to Prospero's from *The Tempest* (4.1.148–56):

> ...These our actors,
> As I foretold you, were all spirits and
> Are melted into air, into thin air:
> And, like the baseless fabric of this vision,
> The cloud-capp'd towers, the gorgeous palaces,
> The solemn temples, the great globe itself,
> Ye all which it inherit, shall dissolve
> And, like this insubstantial pageant faded,
> Leave not a rack behind.

But they also echo the conclusion of a frequently reprinted poem by Ambrose Philips, "Epistle to the Earl of Dorset" (1709), which itself draws on Shakespeare's imagery:

> Like some deluded peasant *Merlin* leads
> Through fragrant bow'rs, and through delicious meads,
> While here enchanted gardens to him rise,
> And airy fabricks there attract his eyes,
> His wand'ring feet the magic paths pursue,
> And while he thinks the fair illusion true,
> The trackless scenes disperse in fluid air,
> And woods, and wilds, and thorny ways appear,
> A tedious road the weary wretch returns,
> And, as he goes, the transient vision mourns.

Such references to castles in the clouds, which Morton had used in his anti-British oration for Joseph Warren, also became common figures for upward mobility—especially rapid upward mobility—in post-Revolutionary America. As Jane Kamensky has shown, variations on the phrase "cloud-capp'd towers" were applied liberally not only to fortunes built on dubious financial speculation but also to actual edifices erected on such "baseless fabric"; see Kamensky, *Exchange Artist* 248 and *passim*.

sister-in-law but all those who had given him their confidence or who had invested in him socially or politically. Rather than lifting his family upward, Morton has propelled them downward, Smith believes, trapping them beneath the moral rubble of scandal. In contrast with Betsy Cranch's anguished response to a neighboring family's grief, Nabby seems uncertain whether anyone in the family is innocent enough to warrant her sympathy.[1]

Nabby Smith's attack on the "pernicious affects" of luxurious lifestyles, perfectly consistent with her relative Sam Adams's attack on the Sans Souci club a few years earlier, offers a textbook example of the classical republicanism that underwrote much Revolutionary American rhetoric. Classical republicanism argued for the common good over individual self-interest or the interest of one class. Advocates of classical republicanism feared that seduction deprived a family and community of a woman's future contributions by rendering her and her offspring social outcasts; individual avarice and dissipation, then, could eventually drain the new nation's collective virtue. In Nabby's mind, Morton's lack of personal restraint was a contagion that threatened to poison anyone connected with him. This should hardly be a surprise coming from the child of John and Abigail Adams. But the invocation of staple metaphors for literary imagination (the "Tragical Story" of "airry fabricks" and "visionary Castles") introduces a literary register not often considered by historians of republican ideology. A week later she wrote to her mother, who had likewise sent her a version of the story, deploying terms that also foreground the influence of this specifically *literary* understanding on her allegories of national economy:

> The recent instance of perfidy and unheard of atrocity, which you mention in your letter, and which has made much talk this way, ought to brand with infamy the name and character of the author. Yet it seems hard that innocent persons, if there are any such connected with him, should

1 Nabby Smith had herself contracted an unsuitable alliance when, at the age of eighteen, she became engaged to Royall Tyler, a young lawyer who had lodged with Betsy Cranch's family. It was not a secret that he had spent several years indulging in dissolute behavior. Eventually Nabby ended the engagement, marrying her father's secretary in 1786. For a consideration of the Adams family that is extraordinarily sensitive to the cultural importance of sentiment and sympathy to the Revolutionary generations, see Barker-Benfield.

> suffer in their characters and reputations, by their affinity to this fiend of wickedness. This family seems devoted to misfortune of every kind, but I think that this instance must be the criterion of them.[1]

Morton is, at once, the subject of gossip (a "character" in the anecdotes being traded) and the "author" of nefarious plots against others. Understanding "character" and "author[ship]" in terms that move beyond moral nature to something like literary or dramatic performance, and casting the story as a domestic tragedy, Nabby turns this scandal into a cautionary tale that doesn't just test the neighbors' capacity for sympathetic response but also teases out the local and national political implications of Morton's behavior.

Epitomizing the national consciousness produced in the course of the Revolution, Nabby Smith's response reveals how this mindset was grounded and nourished in networks of print distribution. In the case of *The Power of Sympathy*, marketed so self-consciously as the first "American novel," the identity or intentions of the publisher may have been more important to readers than the identity of the anonymous author.[2] Isaiah Thomas, the printer who issued the novel at the start of 1789, had established his reputation as a Patriot printer during the war. His weekly, *The Massachusetts Spy*, which first appeared in 1770, helped pioneer the partisan rhetorical strategies that fueled the rebels' cause. Initially opening his paper to all parties, he soon found impartiality to be bad for business and adopted a style that made him seem trustworthy precisely because his political outlook was clear. A thorn in the side of royal officials, Thomas was brought up on charges of seditious libel. The attempt failed, and his vigorous defense of a free press helped entrench a popular commitment to freedom of expression and served as a model for others to follow. Still, fearing for his personal safety and worried that the British soldiers occupying Boston might destroy his press or types, he removed himself and his paper inland to Worcester in April 1775. Following the war, Thomas expanded his publishing catalog with several "instructive" or moralistic titles targeting young readers. A

1 Abigail Adams Smith to Abigail Adams, 5 Oct. 1788, in Butterfield 8:303.

2 Cathy Davidson makes a similar point about *The Power of Sympathy*, that "the novel results as much from the publisher's intentions as from the author's" (158), though in either case questions of direct intention remain mostly undocumented and implicit.

supporter of the federal Constitution in the late 1780s, Thomas reestablished the *Spy* in Worcester in April 1788, now aiming to provide "Knowledge of the World" instead of active resistance to tyrants. Soon after, Thomas resumed a portion of his business in Boston, where he opened a bookstore and printshop with his former apprentice, Ebenezer Andrews. Together they founded the *Massachusetts Magazine*, the first issue of which, dated January 1789, included excerpts from *The Power of Sympathy*, under the heading "BEAUTIES of 'The POWER OF SYMPATHY,'" purportedly submitted by a contributor under the cognomen Calista.[1] When, in mid-January, the *Herald of Freedom* announced that an American novel had gone to press locally, the notice didn't mention the title or publisher, but hinted that the novel would take "a late unhappy suicide" as its source material, declaring its intention "to enforce attention to female education, and to represent the fatal consequences of seduction."[2] Thomas seemed to take for

---

1 On Thomas and the *Spy*, see Buckingham 1:229–47; on Thomas's rhetorical style, see M. Stephens, ch. 1, and Pasley 36, 40; on his evasion of seditious libel conviction, see Warner 156–57. Eleven excerpts were published as "The BEAUTIES of 'The POWER of SYMPATHY,'" in the *Massachusetts Magazine* in Jan. 1789, pp. 50–53, falling under the following headings: Beauty, Novels, Female Study, Self Knowledge, Self Complacency, Sensibility, Tears, Ingratitude, Suicide, Conscience, Seduction. The heading "Female Study" included a portion of the book's treatment of "the story of Miss Whitman," illustrating the dangers of "desultory reading," or self-education without adequate structure. The final sections, "Suicide," "Conscience," and "Seduction," didn't directly address Fanny Apthorp's case, but anyone who had seen advertisements recalling the "late unhappy suicide" would have made the appropriate associations when reading the general indictment of those who violate "the sacred ties of connubial duty." Even though "a violation of those ties may be overlooked by the eye of justice, the heart shall supply a monitor, who will not fail to correct those, who are hardly enough to burst them asunder." The issue's date is misleading: it wasn't advertised until 12 February 1789. It was the first issue of Thomas's magazine. "Beauties" was reprinted in the *Vermont Journal* [Windsor], 4 May 1789; the format and general title of this selection are a conscious imitation of the widely republished and wildly popular volume *The Beauties of Sterne: Including all his Pathetic Tales, & most distinguished Observations on Life. Selected for the Heart of Sensibility*.

2 *Herald of Freedom*, 16 Jan. 1789, [3]. Reprinted in *New Hampshire Spy* [Portsmouth], 23 Jan. 1789, [3]; *New-York Packet*, 29 Jan. 1789, [3]; *New-York Journal*, 29 Jan. 1789, [3]; *Pennsylvania Packet*, 3 Feb. 1789, [3]; *Albany Gazette*, 6 Feb. 1789, [2]; *Vermont Gazette* (Bennington), 23 Feb. 1789, [3].

granted that his readers would know exactly what local situation was being incorporated into the novel he was putting to press and puffing elsewhere.

Thomas placed his official advertisement—identifying himself as publisher and his new shop as the best place to buy the book—in at least four Boston papers, beginning with the *Centinel* on 21 January. The advertisement reproduced the author's preface, which promises the book will both expose "the dangerous Consequences of SEDUCTION" and display the "Advantages of FEMALE EDUCATION," and quoted the poetic lines the novel took as its epigraph:

> FAIN would he strew Life's thorny Way with Flowers,
> And open to your View Elysian Bowers;
> Catch the warm Passions of the tender Youth
> And win the Mind to Sentiment and Truth.[1]

The verse makes clear the novel's view that young people's minds and passions were a contested field up for grabs. The next phase of the Revolution—a culture war—would be waged in print. Thomas's renewed interest in novel and magazine publishing at the start of 1789 indicates his confidence that the national character rested with young people and that popular print forms could be used to "win the[ir] mind[s]" before they fell prey to more seductive forces. In the second issue of the *Massachusetts Magazine*, another contributor, writing as "The Dreamer," underscored the novel's claim to address an important aspect of female education, by "put[ting] into her hands, those books which will give her an idea of the characters of men."[2]

---

1 "First American Novel," *Massachusetts Centinel*, 21 Jan. 1789; *Independent Chronicle*, 22 Jan. 1789; *Herald of Freedom*, 23 Jan. 1789, [3]; *Boston Gazette*, 26 Jan. 1789; *Massachusetts Spy* (Worcester), 29 Jan. 1789; *Pennsylvania Packet* (Philadelphia), 3 Feb. 1789; shortened advertisements in *Salem Mercury*, 3 Feb. 1789, with a note that the paper's printer is selling it; *Daily Advertiser* (New York), 4 Feb. 1789, with a note that it's being sold there by Robert Hoge; *Hampshire Chronicle* (Springfield), 25 Feb. 1789; *New Hampshire Spy* (Portsmouth), 9 Mar. 1789; *Pennsylvania Packet* (Philadelphia), 14 Mar. 1789, sold by Thomas Dobson; full advertisement in *United States Chronicle* (Providence, RI), 16 Apr. 1789, with a note that the paper's printer is selling it locally. Several of these publications ran the advertisements over subsequent weeks.

2 "The Dreamer—No. 2," *Massachusetts Magazine*, Feb. 1789, 101. Whether men were more (or less) stable than Brown's novel indicated

What did it mean to couch an attack on Morton in the form of a novel, and what was the "idea of the characters of men" the novel hoped to put forward? When Thomas released the novel, its unknown author may have become the new nation's first published novelist, but he wasn't inventing a new genre. For several decades, the most famous English and Continental novels, magazine sketches, and newspaper stories, many of which enjoyed wide circulation in the American colonies, had involved variations on the seduction plot. Many of them, like *The Power of Sympathy*, were epistolary—that is, they pretended to be letters written by the principal characters, collected and published after the drama of the story had already closed. These were tried-and-true formats, popular with readers for decades. In the most familiar iteration of the seduction novel, a vulnerable heroine who is steeped in the moral and cultural values of her era nonetheless becomes the victim of a cunning man who confounds her sense of right and wrong, tricks her into believing she is loved, and then impregnates her outside of marriage, before finally abandoning her—a fate which for many heroines led to physical debility and eventual death. Brown includes this convention in *The Power of Sympathy* through several set-piece sketches, including the story of Ophelia and the story of Maria Fawcet, the mother of Harriot. As readers repeatedly watched such scenarios unfold across various novels and periodical accounts, they gained a sense of seduction's inevitable outcomes, grounded in hindsight. We know how this will end, but we can't stop reading to determine how the characters get there, looking for clues to their downfall. By 1789, Americans had been active consumers of European novels of seduction for decades; indeed, the first novel printed in the colonies was Samuel Richardson's *Pamela: or, Virtue Rewarded* (1740), published by none other than Benjamin Franklin (1706–90) almost a half century earlier. Although *Pamela*'s eponymous protagonist wins the day—her would-be seducer, secretly reading the letters she has written to her parents, falls in love with her and ultimately determines to marry her—Richardson's other novels, including the eight-volume *Clarissa* (1748), pointed to more tragic ends for seduced maidens. (After being kidnapped, imprisoned, drugged, and raped by the villainous Lovelace, Clarissa slips into madness and then wastes away into death.) In choosing to end her life following an illegitimate pregnancy, Fanny Apthorp seemed to concede and confirm

---

remains the subject of some satirical contemplation through the remainder of The Dreamer's commentary.

both the veracity of the seduction plot and its compelling power for women who were faced with exceptionally few options.

Eighteenth-century American readers were preoccupied with the specter of seduction. Anyone could be seduced, men as well as women, whether by power, money, false teachers, or freedom, with significant costs for families and communities. Young people and other social dependents were especially vulnerable. Yet the female seduction novel came to inhabit a prominent place as the literary representation of such political and economic anxieties; characters who callously disregarded courtship and marriage rituals (which benefited families and communities) in favor of clandestine and non-binding transactions, offered an allegory for the ways in which a lawful society might be undermined by unscrupulous self-interest, perhaps even by liberty itself. Invoking the seducer and heroine of Richardson's most famous seduction novel, Nabby Smith's father, John Adams—who became second president of the United States—opined that "Democracy is Lovelace and the people are Clarissa."[1] Whether attributing danger to democratic unruliness or the sway of demagogues, the seduction trope as a post-Revolutionary national allegory only served to intensify its personal and private relevance for women, who had the most to lose should they prove vulnerable. In a society where virtue was highly valued in unmarried women, premarital relations might destroy a woman's reputation and opportunity for a respectable marriage—or any marriage at all.[2] As Nabby's mother, Abigail Adams, had written earlier to a young male relative in the same letter in which she critiqued Perez Morton, "America will not wear chains while her daughters are virtuous, but corrupt their morals by a general depravity, and believe me sir a state or nation is undone. Was not Adam safe whilst Eve was Innocent? If you render us wicked you inevitably bring ruin upon yourselves" (Appendix C2, pp. 244–45). Female virtue,

1 John Adams to William Cunningham, 15 Mar. 1804, qtd. in Fliegelman 237. On the broader political uses of this trope of the "tragic citizen," see Mercieca, ch. 3.

2 In early America, children born out of wedlock might result in charges of fornication being laid against both women and men. However, the decline in fornication charges over the eighteenth and early nineteenth centuries meant that increasingly women were held solely responsible for illegitimate births; see Friedman 16. On the gradual move to address premarital sexuality as a family matter, see Dayton, ch. 4. On the roles played by popular media in producing new gender ideology in the wake of these transformations, see Ryan, ch. 6.

in the Adams family's formulation, depends on male prudence; private gratification could undo public interest. Operating on such assumptions, the American novel—and American literature broadly conceived—came into existence as a primary tool for both creating and regulating sexual and economic desire, social and political ambition. Presenting the death of the heroine as inevitable, seduction novels painted a grim picture of the prospects of any woman who did not sufficiently guard her virtue, and of the consequences such behavior could have for extended families.[1]

"I think it is well worth the perusal of every Body": Authorship, Partisanship, and Gossip in the Literary Aftermath

Seduction fiction has most frequently been read by modern critics in the same terms *The Power of Sympathy* used on its title page: as warnings about the new nation's virtue imperiled. But what did these literary scandals mean to more local publics, made up of neighbors or political rivals, peers, young people, or other curious subordinates? Betsy Cranch's meditations on the nature of sympathy and Nabby Smith's on the economy of national virtue contrast with the interpretive responses of a third contemporary observer, much the same age, named Nathan Webb. A schoolteacher and songmaster born in 1767, Webb had been undergoing inoculation in a smallpox hospital when the Apthorp–Morton affair went public in the fall of 1788; his diary does not begin until October 1788, two months after Fanny's death. On his return to social life, Webb spent much of his time with friends, organizing a young people's singing club, attending church, courting, and thinking about marriage. Like young women his age he read fiction and poetry, and, like Betsy Cranch, he noted in his diary real-life examples of seduction, as in one entry about "a young girl ... found dead to day in the millpond drowned by accid/t," who was "said to be a girl of loos morals—."[2] The back pages of Webb's diary are filled with

1 Some critics have argued that the inevitability of death was especially true in American variations on the theme; see Braunschneider, ch. 5. Tennenhouse, ch. 3, argues that *The Power of Sympathy*, and the American seduction novel more broadly, uses the death of seduced maidens to render their fathers the ultimate victims, as marriage still functioned primarily as an economic relationship between men.

2 Nathan Webb, Diary, 23 Sept. 1790, MHS.

miscellaneous maxims and an admonition to young women, warning them against base young men.

If Betsy longed for exposure to metropolitan sociability and the culture of sensibility, Nathan Webb came closer to attaining these goals. The mobility opportunities for a young man were more expansive, to be sure, but another difference in these young people's experiences was the role of print in urban, as opposed to suburban, life. Cranch, who lived just outside Boston, does not mention newspapers in her diary. Some parents considered newspapers inappropriate reading for young women, but newspapers also didn't circulate quite as freely where she lived. For Webb, newspapers played a major role in his social, intellectual, and political life. He and his friends, when they were not singing or playing whist or accompanying young women home from church, spent a considerable amount of time reading and writing for the *Herald of Freedom*, which had dedicated so much space in its first issues to Fanny's suicide notes and continued to excoriate Morton over the coming months. Much of what else appeared in the *Herald of Freedom* was light satire consistent with sentiments expressed in *The Power of Sympathy*: a burlesque on a pretentious "Stockjobber's lackey" who thought it beneath him to dance at the same school where "reputable Mechanicks attend," a humorous description of a New England ball, or riddles and other puzzles based on the names of popular young women. Webb's role as a consumer and occasional producer of newspaper writing led him to become a regular subscriber to the *Herald* and to seek out the acquaintance of one of the paper's editors, Loring Andrews, who in turn introduced him in January 1789 to publisher Isaiah Thomas. Thomas apparently shared Andrews's desire to capitalize on the Morton scandal, perhaps for personal or political reasons but also, perhaps, simply to sell books. Noting in his diary his introduction to Thomas, Webb added that he had "heard there was a new novel in two Volumes coming out—the Characters are supposed to be P Morton—& a Miss Apthorp who lately made away with her self in this town & her Father &c." On 6 February he recorded what comes down to us as a very rare response to the novel from an ordinary reader: "Finished reading the Power of Sympathy, or the First American Novel lately published & printed by I. Thomas & Co. I think it is well worth the perusal of every Body. —"[1]

What kind of reader was Nathan Webb, and what made him, apparently, the ideal audience for the first American novel, despite

1 Nathan Webb, Diary, 6 Feb. 1789, MHS.

the fact that he was not one of "the Young Ladies of America"? What made the novel, in his mind, worthy of readership regardless of sex, class, or age? To begin with, we can note his attempt to trace connections from fictional characters to their real-life counterparts. Webb does not seem to have known Morton or Apthorp personally, as Cranch and Smith did, though he had at least heard of the scandal. The gossip he picked up at Thomas's shop emphasized the real-life correspondences. What seems to have mattered even more is the network of relations that led him to visit Thomas in the first place. Webb was not very different, in demographic terms, from William Hill Brown. He also had much in common with others who promoted the scandal both before and after *The Power of Sympathy* was published. Offering a window onto the *Herald of Freedom*'s readership and contributors, he suggests that the paper targeted polite, middling but upwardly mobile, younger, single, precocious readers like himself, young men who would want to be "in the know" when it came to political gossip, which could serve as a form of currency useful to their upward mobility. Perhaps Webb's disdain for Morton and his eager reception and recommendation of the novel stemmed from partisan bias, his friendship with Andrews, or his admiration of Thomas as a printer. But other motivations to resent Morton are apparent enough. Although Webb doesn't indicate knowledge of Brown or even that he was the novel's author, his preoccupations and sentiments coincide with several expressed by younger characters in Brown's novel. Webb's generational, class, and gender alignment with Brown and his protagonists would seem to suggest genuine resentment against their disreputable elders, some of whom occupied powerful social positions. Webb and Brown were people to whom a powerful libertine like Perez Morton represented a very specific threat—and a very different threat than the one he posed to old-guard republicans such as Samuel Adams or Mercy Otis Warren, or even their younger incarnation in Nabby Adams Smith—since Morton had targeted a member of the female social set within which they hoped to marry. What Webb found valuable in *The Power of Sympathy* seems to confirm the novel's own interpretive strategies for reading the Apthorp/Morton scandal. The young people—including William Hill Brown and Nathan Webb—who contributed to the literary afterlife of this scandal had warnings for their elders in return: founding fathers ought not to be trusted simply because their Revolutionary credentials were intact. *The Power of Sympathy* realizes such concerns, as the elder Harrington's illicit relationship imperils the happiness of his son, who inadvertently falls in love with his half-sister. The sins of the fathers, as the novel warns, might very well be passed to their children if young people do not remain vigilant. But bad fathers can be exposed or overthrown as well.

This moral may have been more important to Webb than the gossipy details themselves. While he clearly thought the novel deserved a wide audience, in the end *The Power of Sympathy* did not reveal much new information about the scandal, to the disappointment of some readers. The portion of the novel that was rooted in recent events, even though it claims pride of place in the opening illustration and promotional materials, is reduced to one of a series of seduction stories, though it does express a point of view on where readers' sympathies should be placed. Three letters (XXI–XXIII) from Harriot to Myra cover the affair, passed along as a story Harriot herself has received second-hand after witnessing and being perplexed by the distress of some of the principals. She prefaces her account of the affair with a moral, claiming it "exhibits a melancholy picture of the wickedness and depravity of the human heart" (p. 111). In the first of the three letters, Harriot describes for Myra the plot by "Martin" to seduce his younger sister-in-law, Ophelia, sacrificing her "innocence and virtue" simply to satisfy his "diabolical appetite" through this "incestuous connexion" (pp. 111–12). After she bears a child in the countryside, Ophelia suffers the wrath of her father, Shepherd, including alleged physical abuse. But she also receives only the "blackest ingratitude from her seducer," who is "the first to brand her with the disgraceful epithets, of undutiful and unchaste" (p. 112). Ophelia's hopes that Martin would leave her sister for her are dashed. Continuing to follow the Apthorp/Morton template quite faithfully, Shepherd calls a "meeting of the parties" over his daughter's protestation, but before it can take place Ophelia poisons herself. At this point, Harriot is forced to stop her narration and ends her letter to Myra, modeling the cult of sensibility as she is overcome with "sympathetick sorrow" (p. 114). The second letter in this series contains Harriot's paraphrase of the "writings [Ophelia] left" (p. 114), closely modeled on Fanny Apthorp's letters as circulated in manuscript copies and published in the *Herald of Freedom* the previous fall. The third letter focuses on the confrontation between Shepherd and Martin, including Martin's contention that Shepherd's "severe use of paternal power" (p. 116) drove Ophelia to suicide. (Shepherd, for his part, had "charged *Martin* with the seduction and murder of his daughter.") In her position as narrator, Harriot expresses her own sense that Martin must be held accountable as "the remote cause," though she also opines in her letter's conclusion, "Happy the parents, who have bestowed upon their children such an education, as will enable them, by a principle of mediocrity, to govern them without extorting obedience, and to reclaim them without exercising severity" (p. 117). Spoiler alert: Harriot will also be dead by the novel's end, having learned that her fiancé is actually her half-brother, news that drives him to suicide and her to be consumed by grief, as if to emphasize that an unfeeling father bears a heavy part of the blame in her case as well.

In her landmark reception history of *The Power of Sympathy*, Cathy Davidson suggests that contemporary readers responded to the novel along gendered lines, almost as if various commentators were not reading "the same novel" (170).[1] Davidson grounds this reading in an exchange between someone writing in the *Centinel* under the name Civil Spy and a respondent in the *Herald of Freedom* called Antonia. Civil Spy's review is generally negative: they express disappointment that the novel didn't offer more dirt on the Apthorp–Morton story and that the frame narratives with Harrington and Harriot or the elder Harrington and Maria weren't recognizably grounded in fact. Antonia's rejoinder defends the author of *Power of Sympathy* as an "amiable youth" and "a champion of feminine innocence, a promoter of religion and chastity, and a pleasing moniter of inexperienced minds," and imagines Civil Spy as either "an old snarling *misanthrope*, or a young, cynical *Fop*," in either case someone who is not "a friend to either women or virtue."[2] But the contrast between these two writers can't simply be reduced to the authors' apparent gender difference: categories of age, styles of manliness, and even contrasting views of human nature are invoked here, as well as one's patronage of competing newspapers. Consistent with the broader Perez Morton paper trail—from his own early literary and oratorical productions, through the several plays, poems, and newspaper debates his actions occasioned, to the novel and the debates surrounding its publication—this exchange about the novel invokes social divisions occasioned by, or at least informing, how one responded to these scandals. From whatever vantage point these constructions

---

1 For other studies of the novel's Boston reception, see Pendleton and Ellis, ch. 2; Walser, "Boston's Reception."

2 Civil Spy, "For the Centinel," *Massachusetts Centinel*, 7 Feb. 1789, [2]; Antonia, "For the Herald of Freedom," *Herald of Freedom*, 10 Feb. 1789, [2]. See the final sarcastic rebuttal in Civil Spy, "For the Centinel," *Massachusetts Centinel*, 18 Feb. 1789 [1].

arose or were received, they agreed on one thing: these Boston scandals show how rapidly members of the founding generation made the transition from "sons of liberty" to "founding fathers" and how much a range of Americans depended on ideas filtered through their reading of novels for their belief that national patriarchs needed to behave more prudently than Morton had.[1]

Critical consensus holds that *The Power of Sympathy*—even more so than the scandal that precipitated it—enjoyed a short shelf life. "Though the narrative was concerned with the popular subject of the evils of seduction," wrote Richard Walser in the early 1980s, "and though its serious intention was to contribute to the education of women, Brown's didactic novel, except for the ineffective outbursts of Perez Morton, caused but little stir." The novel's failure to sell out its first and only printing is evidenced by its appearance on booksellers' lists into the first decade of the nineteenth century.[2] This ephemeral quality of the first American novel may actually tell us something about how seduction stories worked: divorced from the immediacy of a local situation, any one story seemed able to stand for another; the repetition of basic plot structures suggests not only that seducers and victims of seduction were exposed as individuals but also that they represented general classes and structural relations; the accumulation of such accounts served as indictments (and possible reinforcements) of social relations as they were currently constituted.

While Nathan Webb and the rest of the general public may not have known who authored *The Power of Sympathy*, the Apthorp and Morton families almost certainly did.[3] In close proximity to

1 Although we are not focusing extensively on partisan representational strategies here—Boston's political landscape in the 1780s was too messy to allow for any simple dichotomization of such rhetoric—the process of abstracting national character from the actions of representative subjects is related to the cultural work of the constitutional debates, as described in Smith-Rosenberg, "Dis-Covering the Subject." Smith-Rosenberg further develops key portions of her argument in *This Violent Empire*.

2 After January 1789, Thomas didn't advertise the novel again in Boston until a full-page ad in his *Massachusetts Spy* (10 Dec. 1789, 3) included it among his available stock in his Worcester and Boston shops. The novel was regularly advertised for months or in some cases years in various other places, from Salem, Massachusetts, to New York and Philadelphia. The assertion by Brown's niece that Brown himself suppressed the novel seems unlikely; see Brayley.

3 A letter from Halifax, Nova Scotia, where some extended family members who were Loyalists settled, suggests that knowledge of Brown's authorship was circulated; see Byers.

the Morton household both geographically and socially, William Hill Brown was well poised to know—and reveal—their secrets. His father, Gawen Brown, was a respected clock- and watchmaker whose work adorned Boston's churches and fine homes; he ran a shop across the street from Apthorp House, where the Mortons lived. Two of Gawen Brown's marriages, one to Elizabeth Byles, the daughter of the Loyalist minister Mather Byles, and another to Elizabeth Hill, the widow of Samuel Adams's brother, linked young William to some of the city's most influential families. One of William's older brothers, Mather Brown (1761–1831), had cultivated notable talents as a poet and painter, apparently favorite family activities. Some of Mather's poems were submitted by an aunt to the *Boston Magazine* after he left home as a teenager to work as an itinerant artist. Eventually, Mather Brown studied under the famous American painter Benjamin West (1738–1820) in London (Evans 7–8).[1] Certainly the Anglophilic Apthorps knew who he was; they probably knew his younger brother as well. A year apart in age from Fanny Apthorp, William Hill Brown likely knew her socially. A story passed down in the Brown family may be apocryphal, but it does suggest that his authorship of the novel was an open secret; as Brown's niece, Rebecca Vollentine Thompson, relates, his mother discussed it with the mother of Sarah and Fanny. Mrs. Apthorp asked, "Oh, why did Willie do such a thing when we were such good friends?" "The names are fictitious," Mrs. Brown reassured her. "But," replied Mrs. Apthorp, "everyone knows whom he means" (see Brayley 232).

For a few years following his first novel's publication, Brown seemed poised to be a regular presence in Boston literary circles. Thomas clearly cultivated him as an author, promoting *The Power of Sympathy* and publishing additional work in the first volume of the *Massachusetts Magazine* and other local publications.[2] Brown contributed poetry to newspapers; along with his friend, the poet and editor Robert Treat Paine Jr., he even engaged in a poetic correspondence with Sarah Wentworth Apthorp Morton, who became increasingly well known as a poet under her pen name,

---

1 Six short poems by Mather Brown, apparently written when he was twelve years old, were published anonymously in *Boston Magazine* 3, Jan. 1786, 38. They were submitted by his aunt, Catherine (or Katherine) Byles, whose papers confirm his authorship. For her literary taste and likely influence on Mather and William Hill Brown, see Eamon.

2 A collection of his short writings is compiled in Brown, *Selected Poems*. The introduction is a useful guide to Brown's career.

Philenia.[1] Like the Mortons, Brown supported the movement in the early 1790s to legalize the theater in Boston; years later, a play Brown based on the story of Benedict Arnold would be posthumously produced. But by 1792, Brown had moved to North Carolina to live near a married sister and study law. His premature death in 1793, following a sudden illness, no doubt contributed to the lack of awareness of his oeuvre.

Even before his death, however, speculation about the novel's author was both abundant and misdirected. For decades, many believed that Sarah Wentworth Apthorp Morton herself was the novel's true author.[2] There were numerous reasons to suspect her, not the least of which were her own literary ambitions. The conventions of anonymous publication would also sustain a theory of her authorship. However, the fact that the book did not carry its author's name was hardly definitive proof of a motive; in republican print culture, works were often published anonymously and meant to serve the common good. Sarah Morton's first known published productions appeared under the pen name Philenia in 1788.[3] Many readers believed her to be the author of a poem on the subject of the seduction scandal that appeared in the *Massachusetts Centinel* on 27 September 1788—as attributed to her in the play *Occurrences of the Times*. Adding potential fuel to the fire was the fact that her first published volume, *Ouâbi; or, The Virtues of Nature, An Indian Tale*, also appeared from Isaiah Thomas's press—and just a year after *The Power of Sympathy*, suggesting she did not bear any ill will toward Thomas for his role in exposing her family's domestic tragedy.

---

1 Brown wrote as Pollio, while his friend Robert Treat Paine Jr. (1773–1811) wrote poems to Philenia under the name Menander. (Brown and Paine were six and fourteen years younger than Sarah Morton, respectively.) The exchange took place in the *Massachusetts Magazine* and *Massachusetts Mercury* during February and March 1793, after Brown was already in North Carolina. Brown may have selected Pollio as his pen name after Philenia addressed a poem to Pollio in the January 1793 issue of the *Massachusetts Magazine*. The Pollio to whom she addressed the poem that sparked the exchange, she later revealed, was the painter John Trumbull (1756–1843). See Shoulz 11. Paine continued to admire and promote Philenia despite his political opposition to Morton; see Clough 94.

2 This belief appears to have taken hold by the mid-nineteenth century. See manuscript note by Samuel Jemison, cited in Pendleton and Ellis 109–10.

3 Morton is said to have contributed to various publications before her marriage, but nothing definitive has been located. See Pendleton and Ellis 41.

If print conventions supported such a theory, so, too, would conventions of reading. Eighteenth-century readers wanted to believe that authors who wrote fictional versions of events had some inside knowledge.[1] Nearly a decade later, the anonymous publication of the much more popular novel *The Coquette*, written by "A Lady of Massachusetts," generated rumors that the author, Hannah Webster Foster (1758–1840), was related to the real-life inspiration, Elizabeth Whitman (whose story appears in Letter XI of Brown's novel, and a long accompanying footnote). Many readers believed that she must have had access to actual letters penned by Whitman. In part, the epistolary nature of novels like *The Power of Sympathy* and *The Coquette* lend themselves to such interpretations: letter writing was a familiar form in which readers actively participated. Anyone who had seen Fanny Apthorp's widely reprinted suicide notes would have recognized them as only gently altered in Brown's novel. Epistolary fiction and posthumously published "remains" of famous writers both depended not only on the familiarity of the letter form but on audiences' desires to eavesdrop on someone else's confidential correspondence. As readers modeled their own letters on examples drawn from letter-writing manuals and epistolary fiction alike, fact and fiction blurred, making the factual appear highly literary in its form and the fictional appear very real in its familiarity.

But the most compelling argument for Sarah Wentworth Apthorp Morton's authorship may have been human nature, specifically the desire for revenge, a motive raised in the poetic response to Fanny's death and echoed by subsequent readers and scholars. If she did write the poem of 27 September 1788, it invoked the goddess of revenge by name, while *Ouâbi* took revenge as one of its primary themes—along with adultery and extravagance, suicide and female melancholia. Readers who sympathized with her and those who condemned her as complicit or even herself adulterous—a charge leveled in *Occurrences*—might both plausibly believe she had authored the volume out of a desire to see her husband punished socially as he had not been legally.[2] Many of her early poems, appearing in the *Massachusetts Magazine* and other local outlets, created a persona for Philenia of a female genius wounded by life's sorrows. Engaging in poetic

1 For another approach to the "non-fictional novel" in the early United States, see Koenigs, esp. ch. 2.

2 Accusations of adultery against Sarah may have been unfounded at the time, but she did afterward have an affair with the dashing (*continued*)

correspondence with her under the pen name Pollio in the early 1790s, William Hill Brown certainly contributed to this construction of her literary character.[1] In reality, *Ouâbi* and some verses which appeared in her 1823 volume of autobiographical sketches and selected works—"Stanzas, to a Recently United Husband" and "Conciliation," for instance—appear to constitute her authentic literary response to this scandal.[2] As does the fact that after 1787, and following a very close succession of pregnancies for their entire marriage to that point, Sarah never bore another child.[3] But on the question of her authorship of the novel, the rumors were unfounded. Late nineteenth-century testimony by Brown's family, as well as subsequent archival research, has proven the fact of Brown's authorship beyond a doubt.[4]

The novel's ingredients, drawing on familiar structures and vocabularies of what was beginning to be known as "sentimental" literature, would have been as familiar to Morton as they were to Brown. "Sentimentalists" made up a substantial consumer demographic in the 1770s and 1780s and provided many avenues

---

Gouverneur Morris (1752–1816), American ambassador to France, as documented in his diaries. The affair was not a well-kept secret and may have been an act of revenge on her part, but it did not appear to injure her reputation; see Brookhiser 171. While Perez did not fulfill his early promise, Sarah has been described as the "most famous New England salonniere of her day," and as such she would have wielded significant influence both socially and politically, albeit behind the scenes; see Shields 311.

1 When Philenia responded to Menander's poems, Pollio sent a poem of congratulations on "hear[ing] THY PRAISES SOUNDED FROM BLEST PHILENIA'S LYRE!" It would be Menander's enviable lot to help ease Philenia's constant sorrow: "'Tis thine, sweet bard, to soothe the soul of grief, / To lend the wounded breast a healing balm; / 'Tis thine to give the sinking heart relief, / And the rude billow of distress to calm."

2 See Morton's selected poems in Appendix B of this volume. For ways in which *Ouâbi* may be read as a riposte to *The Power of Sympathy*, see Shoulz 61–64. The other poems mentioned can be found in Sarah Wentworth Apthorp Morton, *My Mind and Its Thoughts*.

3 Jane Kamensky has put forward the possibility that the couple's final child, Charlotte, born in the fall of 1787, to whom Sarah referred in her poetry as the child of her "sorrowing soul," may actually have been Fanny Apthorp's baby, silently adopted; see Kamensky, "Exchange Artist's Wife." Thanks to Kamensky for sharing this talk and many conversations about Fanny Apthorp's story.

4 See Brayley; Pendleton and Ellis 109–12; Walser, "North Carolina Sojourn," "More about the First American Novel," and "Fatal Effects of Seduction"; Byers.

through which gossip, newspapers, and novels themselves circulated. Signature works that had gone viral in Europe had also been imported for and marketed to American sentimentalists, including Laurence Sterne's *A Sentimental Journey through France and Italy* (1768), first published in London, whose title presented this populous subculture with the label they seemed to embrace, and Johann Wolfgang von Goethe's *The Sorrows of Young Werther* (1774), originally in German and first published in Leipzig, before being translated for English readers in 1779. Sterne's novel provides the characters in *The Power of Sympathy* with topics of discussion and models for their own sentimental expression; Goethe's *Werther* also makes a cameo in Brown's novel, when in the final pages it apparently provides a dangerous template for the increasingly unstable Thomas Harrington.[1] At stake were key questions about how to manage feelings—and the roles reading played in that effort.

A sentimentalist definition of sensibility is crucial to understanding the novel's framing not just of gender but also of race, especially as Brown provides his young, white, middling or upwardly mobile characters with opportunities to demonstrate their keen or refined capacity for feeling. The most striking example of this pattern comes in Letter XXXVI, Thomas Harrington's account of his encounter with an enslaved woman during a journey south. The woman's willingness to endure physical suffering to protect her child leads Harrington to rapturous praise, not only of her actions but also of her "heroic" verbal expression. Her appearance in the novel seems to function primarily, however, not as a critique of slavery but as an opportunity for the performance of Harrington's own sensibility. We would rightly consider his feelings to be rather shallow: he makes no movement, after all, to secure or argue for her freedom. (The anecdote was prompted by an incident that stirred him even more: Harriot's mistreatment by her employer, Mrs. Francis.) Shallow, misplaced, or otherwise, Harrington's sensibility on behalf of social inferiors would be viewed by some as dangerous. While he clearly believes the "sentimental" few are superior to "the vain, the giddy, and the proud" (p. 136), many contemporaries worried that if left unregulated, sensibility could carry one to dangerous extremes,

1 For more on Goethe's (1749–1832) influence on transatlantic sentimental reading practices—especially on the question of copycat suicides his novel was widely credited with inspiring—see Bell, *We Shall Be No More*, ch. 2.

as it had, perhaps, in Harrington and Harriot's case. Yet even their unfortunate deaths could teach readers how to experience and ultimately govern their feelings. As an observer in the novel puts it on one such occasion, "We consider thee as the dupe of Nature, and the sacrifice of Seduction" (p. 176). If seduction demanded brutal tribute, such sad cases could still serve the general good as reminders of the need to temper sympathy with reason, or sensibility with sense.[1]

Seeming to set aside traditional aversions to literary imagination, post-Revolutionary Bostonians found value in using fiction, drama, and poetry to comment on current events and create a feeling audience. *The Power of Sympathy* did not mark the limits of the Apthorp–Morton scandal's literary circulation. Although theater remained illegal in Boston until the mid-1790s, Boston writers had shown during the Revolution and most recently during the Sans Souci affair that closet dramas, intended to be read in private, were an apt mode for social commentary.[2] (The satirical closet drama as a genre had been taken up most notably during the Revolution by Mercy Otis Warren.) As some writers already had done during the earlier scandal, they used the dramatic genre to call attention to the artificiality of Morton's public persona and to frame him as one of the politically dangerous "designing men" feared by the framers of the new Constitution.[3] Who could trust leaders whose public performances were so much like play-acting? This broader lens rendered the artificial and designing Morton a potential seducer not just of young women but also of Boston's voting citizenry. Newspaper editorialists also drew on melodramatic language of sentiment and seduction to frame

---

1 For an argument that the novel advocates for the sentimentalism of Samuel Richardson (1689–1761) over the unruly sensibility of Laurence Sterne (1713–68), see Arner. For another attempt to schematize the novel's vocabulary of feeling, which also argues that its ultimate aim is to rein in or control strong emotions, see McClain.

2 An act passed by the General Court of Massachusetts outlawing playacting was passed in 1750. In 1792, a bill appeared before the Massachusetts legislature urging repeal of the law; an entrepreneurial group of citizens constructed a theater in anticipation, only to have it closed when the bill failed. On Boston's theater controversy of the 1790s, in which Morton was one of the theater's chief supporters and investors, see Milford, "Boston's Theater Controversy"; Nathans 65–68.

3 Massachusetts delegate Elbridge Gerry (1744–1814), for example, saw citizens as being "daily misled into the most baneful measures and opinions by the false reports circulated by designing men," language that echoes seduction fiction. Qtd. in Mercieca 96.

political events. In the same newspapers that contained spirited exchanges about *The Power of Sympathy* and other fallout of Morton's scandals, including an aborted duel with his brother-in-law in February, the language of seduction featured prominently in debates on federal and local elections and the ratification of the Constitution. The *Herald of Freedom* for 10 February 1789, for instance, included an attack on Morton by "By-Stander"—dubbing him "Proteus" and "Mr. Subterfuge"—as well as a long piece by "Marcus," who warned about "plans that are laid to enslave" Boston's voters by "private cabals" that by "artifice" would introduce "tyranny and despotism." Marcus targets what he claims to be a conspiracy to oust Governor John Hancock (1737–93), whom he frames as a benevolent father who "protects you from [the] ravages" of the "artful Lo heres or Lo theres, which are so cunningly contrived to seduce you."[1] Hancock's opponents had their own uses for seduction language, charging that the governor's debts, reaching back to the Revolution, made him susceptible to seduction by foreign powers.[2] The twists and turns of Boston's early partisan warfare were dense enough that the same issues of newspapers that included attacks on Morton—a Hancock supporter—also included contributors who attacked the opposition. The questions raised by Morton's domestic scandals, about the relationship between private and public character, were on the table in other cases. What happened in private could compromise one's virtue; but it could also slide effortlessly into conspiracy to seduce the general public, an accusation that partisans on all sides lobbed at their opponents.

All Politics Is Local: *Occurrences of the Times*

The Power of Sympathy may have assumed the form of a national allegory the farther it traveled from Boston, but at home, it and the other works the Morton scandals inspired were tied directly to local political scenes. During the first two weeks of February, nearly every copy of the *Centinel* and *Herald of Freedom* carried pieces about a spoiled duel between Morton and his brother-in-law, Charles Apthorp, with both coming in for severe criticism.

1 Marcus, "For the Herald of Freedom. To the People of Massachusetts," *Herald of Freedom*, 10 Feb. 1789, [1]. He's probably taking aim at Stephen Higginson, whose anti-Hancock "Laco" letters would appear in the *Centinel* over the coming weeks.

2 Laco [Stephen Higginson], *Massachusetts Centinel*, 18 Feb. 1789, [1].

During the second half of the month, Morton could have picked up any of the Boston papers and found advertisements for not just one but two farces making him out to be sententious at best or, at worst, a conniving villain—running his friends into debt and risking their reputations. Isaiah Thomas had meanwhile published another farce indicting the Mortons, a musical comedy called *The Better Sort, or the Girl of Spirit,* which featured eighteen original "Federal" songs that poked fun at their marital antics, though with some reserve.[1] Advertisements for the other farce, *Occurrences of the Times,* included the stanza printed on the play's title page:

> ——No longer by vain fear, or shame control'd
> In guilty amours, grown securely bold,
> Mocking rebuke, they brace it in our streets,
> And ******, even at noon, his mistress meets.
> So public in their crimes, so daring grown,
> They almost take a pride to have them known.[2]

Of the three publications to appear within a month of one another, *Occurrences of the Times* bore most directly on recognizable events. Often attributed to Brown, the play instead seems to have been published by E. Larkin, who would later print Hannah Webster Foster's novel *The Coquette.* Even if Brown or Thomas had nothing to do with it, however, the play effectively served as publicity for and a supplement to *The Power of Sympathy.* The novel's pending publication, in fact, provides the play's central dramatic tension.

---

1 Although Mr. and Mrs. Sententious in *The Better Sort* are consistent with other parodies of the Mortons, they are less cruel portraits than those found in *Occurrences of the Times* or *Sans Souci.* The plot of *The Better Sort* does not take the specifics of recent scandals as its model so much as a generalized satire of superficial social climbers and their extravagant spending.

2 *Occurrences of the Times* was advertised only in *The Herald of Freedom* (see 13, 20, and 27 Feb. 1789). *The Better Sort,* published by Isaiah Thomas, was advertised in the *Centinel,* the *Independent Chronicle,* and the *Herald of Freedom* through February. Both works have been attributed to Brown; some evidence exists for attributing *The Better Sort* to him. See Walser, "More about the First American Novel," 357. The lines in the advertisement and on the title page are taken from the English satirist Charles Churchill's (1732–64) poem "The Times" (1764), an attack on his political opponents, centering especially on accusations of sodomy. In Churchill's original, instead of "******" he offers the name "Lumley." For the poem in full, see Churchill.

In the farce, Mr. Sidney, Morton's avatar, has deftly avoided a duel with his brother-in-law, Lieutenant Harcourt, but is horrified that local papers have announced that a novel will soon be published "that will brand him a villain centuries to come" (p. 218). (His black servant, Debauchee, bungles the title—*The Trumpets of Nature*—in just the right way, with the malapropism suggesting that Sidney's "nature" will be proclaimed from the rooftops, or perhaps that humanity's sinful nature will inevitably find a way to announce itself.) Alarms sounded when Morton was rumored to attempt a suppression of the novel. Whether this actually happened, *Occurrences of the Times* alleges that it did, reinforcing the familiar perception of Morton's ongoing obsession with controlling his public reputation.[1] The play alleges as well that Mr. and Mrs. Sidney were both adulterers and that Sidney covered up the pregnancy and childbirth of his sister-in-law, "Ophelia"—the play uses the same pseudonym for Fanny as Brown's novel had—by relying on the services of a doctor whose own infidelity Sidney had helped to conceal, an apparent reference to Dr. Thomas Phipps, to whom Fanny had addressed one of her final letters. "Heavens defend us from such fathers" (p. 223), the doctor's wife declares at one point, sealing the point that Morton and others had failed in their patriarchal roles. The play also implies that the doctor's wife and her family had "lost thousands" of dollars through Sidney's "chicanery" (p. 223) and that the Sidneys' servants, who are represented through racist caricature as perpetually drunk and poorly supervised, had been bribed to help conceal their crimes. The link of moral depravity with economic and political corruption was made explicit by such charges. "[I]f he ever did any thing that was praise-worthy," the doctor's wife says of Sidney, "it was so long since that he has forgot it" (p. 223).[2]

As Nathan Webb had with *The Power of Sympathy*, Boston's readers matched characters with satirical details related to major

1 Walser, "Boston's Reception," makes a strong case that the novel was not actually suppressed. Its ready availability in booksellers' lists for many years afterward would indicate as much. *The American Herald and the Worcester Recorder*, 5 Feb. 1789, [4], includes one of the poems contained in *The Power of Sympathy* ("The Court of Vice: An Apologue"), and mentions in a headnote that the novel had "lately made its publick appearance in Boston; and ... has been the cause of much uneasiness, and some disturbance."

2 Bibliographers typically list Benjamin Russell as publisher and Brown as author, but the evidence for either seems more traditional than conclusive.

and minor characters in this farce. One reader literally filled in the blanks in a copy now owned by Harvard University, inserting names next to the printed Dramatis Personae: The Quaker, whom other characters implicate as the actual father of Mrs. Sidney's youngest child, was supposedly the merchant Joseph Russell (or, perhaps, his son). Dr. Harrangue was the Hancock associate Dr. Charles Jarvis. Worthy, who arrives just in time to prevent the duel, was supposed to be Suffolk County sheriff John Anderson. The miserable Peep, caught peeking in windows and enamored with spreading gossip about his neighbors, was the same James Hughes (c. 1758–99) who had been portrayed as Morton's friend Jemmy Satirist in *Sans Souci*. And Dr. Turncoat was Dr. Phipps, said here to have spirited away Fanny's newborn baby to a country town on a snowy night a year earlier. The farce's pseudonyms for Isaiah Thomas and Co.—Steady and Firm—suggests a disposition in favor of the printers (see Walser, "More about the First American Novel" 353–54). The farce comes close to exposing Brown by naming the "suspect for the author" as "*****" (p. 220) ("[I]f I can find out the author," Sidney fumes, "I'll blow his brains out" [p. 225]). Whether or not Brown authored this farce, as is commonly claimed, *Occurrences* was clearly familiar with the text of *The Power of Sympathy*; Fanny's character—whose "bustle enough in the great world" has turned Boston into "nothing but duels, and novels, and such nonsense" (p. 217)—is once again called Ophelia. But where *The Power of Sympathy*'s Martin refers to Ophelia as "a straying, but penitent child" (p. 116), Sidney in *Occurrences* maligns her: "the world believes the young lady in question to have been as pure as an angel," he tells an associate, "but their opinions are most egregiously erroneous" (p. 220).

Sarah Morton comes in for her own criticism in *Occurrences of the Times* and *The Better Sort*, as she had in *Sans Souci*. In *The Better Sort* she pressures her husband—here portrayed as a long-suffering republican and sentimentalist—to aid her in "be[ing] remarked for splendor" as she "ascend[s] to the pinnacle of politeness and the tip top of the bettermost genii" (10). Constantly misusing French terms, she confesses that she "do[es] not aspire to the honour of being a woman of *words*" but would prefer "the humble title of *a woman of letters*," a jab at her budding reputation as a poet (38). Meanwhile, Mrs. Sidney's servants in *Occurrences*—"[in]fected with the fate of the family" (p. 216)—recite the poem Morton had published in *The Centinel* accusing her parents of being unsympathetic to her plight following Fanny's death. The farce ends with Mrs. Sidney narrowly avoiding exposure of her affair with Quaker, and Mr. Sidney waiting to hear about his friends' efforts to suppress publication of the novel. Their situations remain precarious, and their crimes are in danger of being further amplified.

The farces and the novel all belonged to post-Revolutionary Boston's broader world of political print. Sympathies, fortified by gossip, were hardening into partisan affiliations. Each work incorporated text that had circulated first in newspapers; announced, advertised, and in some cases excerpted in these same papers, they were also debated there. The most pointed of the three—*Occurrences*—had specific partisan content that contemporary readers would have recognized. It also trafficked in anecdotes that were already circulating, such as Peep's unfortunate confrontation with an angry sleigh driver or his tumbling into a bucket of suds while attempting to spy on neighbors, or Sidney's artful avoidance of an actual duel with his brother-in-law, enlisting the sheriff's assistance. Dr. Harrangue's comments to Quaker, in which he indicates that Sidney has colluded with the sheriff to avoid the duel ("the gentlemen of the law have advantages superior to their neighbors") prefaces a comment that appears to be a specific reference to contemporary politics: "There is *Argue*, for instance; why there is no speaking a word for him in the house. But I am determined to oppose him with all my power" (p. 214). Whether or not Harrangue is, as at least one contemporary reader supposed, Dr. Charles Jarvis, the line, which isn't developed any further, suggests that readers would have known not only who Harrangue represented but also who *Argue*, Dr. Harrangue's target for political opposition, would be.[1] If the portrait in *Occurrences* were granted credit, the play might be seen as exposing the inner workings of Morton's network of powerful allies, from politicians like Dr. Jarvis to Sheriff Henderson to fellow members of the legal profession, such as James Hughes and perhaps William Wetmore. When Sidney frets about not having enough cash to suppress the novel's publication, his friend Dupe (supposedly based on Dr. John Warren, a member of Morton's Masonic lodge) wonders

---

1 On Dr. Charles Jarvis, see Thacher 313–16. He was known for being elegant and well spoken and had a fashionable clientele. Like Morton, he became a Jeffersonian in the 1790s and was an associate of John Hancock. For more on this controversy, which shares column space in the papers with commentary on Morton's behavior, see "Sketch of Business in the General Court. House of Representatives. Thurs., Jan 15. Support of Lieut. Governor," *Massachusetts Centinel*, 17 Jan. 1789, [2].

aloud whether "his Satannick Majesty" might "condescend to lend us a trifle" (p. 218), a probable reference to Governor John Hancock, who enjoyed the allegiance of Morton's political circle.[1] Whether or not these speculations about the dramatis personae were accurate, the farce clearly belongs to a broader political print discourse in which Morton's personal affairs were taken by many to have specific public consequences and implications. Seducers, speculators, and political conspirators were all versions of the same character type in "a world of masks and mirrors—of artifice" (Kamensky, *Exchange Artist* 45).

Did the literary works collected here have lasting local or national political repercussions? Yes and no. In the end, Morton suffered some setbacks and probably had to scale back his ambitions, but by no means was he driven from public life. Bostonians' attention was apparently as fleeting as it was initially furious: Morton would go on to become a speaker of the state House of Representatives and a state attorney general; Sarah, as was noted above, would become a renowned poet (see Vietto 111–12).[2] In the early 1790s, when Perez began his social ascent for the second or third time, John Adams wrote from Philadelphia to Abigail, in Braintree, with the latest gossip: "Well: Boston comes on: Mr. Morton is now to be its Leader: How changed in Reputation Since 1788[!]"[3] Adams's tone here is one of resignation, perhaps exasperation, though his sideline observation also reminds us that he was complicit in controlling the damage from Morton's affair that summer. Decades later he still counted Morton a friend, at least in polite correspondence.[4] Perhaps Adams was part of the problem people like Morton imposed—an enabler, an investor in

---

1 In the play, Turncoat hears the gossip about Sidney's near-duel while visiting "neighbour *Whitmore*" (p. 223), a possible reference to Morton's fellow barrister, William Wetmore. Again, no other reference or details about "Whitmore" seem to have been needed for informed contemporaries to understand who was being implicated.

2 Morton dedicated her first volume of poetry to James Bowdoin. A few months later yet another drama—this time a tragedy based on Fanny's suicide—was staged at a prep school in Vermont. Rather than fade, the scandal had not only assumed importance as a homegrown tragedy but also "gone viral" as a cautionary lesson about the dangers of trusting injudiciously. See Walser, "Fatal Effects of Seduction" 574–76.

3 John Adams to Abigail Adams, 17 May 1794, in Adams 474.

4 Sarah was friendly to the Adamses as well, sending them gift copies of her publications and even dedicating one long poem, *The Virtues of Society*, to Abigail in 1799. See John Adams's response, late in life, to

his repeatedly recuperated reputation. Perhaps, despite the condemnation heaped by his daughter, Adams helped Prospero ring true: "Ye all which [the globe] inherit, shall dissolve / And, like this insubstantial pageant faded, / Leave not a rack behind." Morton may have weathered the storms and continued to find a place in Massachusetts politics, but his longest-lasting legacy would come from the fact that he served as a prototype for one of *The Power of Sympathy*'s villains. "I cannot support it Sir," Morton's avatar, Sidney, exclaims in *Occurrences of the Times* at the prospect of becoming a character in that novel:

> only think of my situation; a family and connections that are dear to me; carry [the] ideas a little farther, and behold my son reading a book, where his father is branded with the opprobrious epithet of villain—Horrour is the thought—'tis more than man can bear. (p. 220)

One might say the punishment fit the crime.

Conclusion

A few weeks after Fanny Apthorp's letters had made an appearance in the *Pennsylvania Mercury*—the same paper to which the Philadelphia physician and moral reformer Benjamin Rush had contributed an account that fall of the unfortunate Elizabeth Whitman—Rush wrote, using the pseudonym "A Friend to the Union," to the editor of a new Philadelphia daily, *The Federal Gazette*, with a laundry list of advice on how to conduct a newspaper. "Avoid filling your paper with anecdotes of British vices and follies," he advised, hoping to establish the moral equivalence of three thousand miles distance from Europe. "What have the citizens of the United States to do with the duels, the elopements, the crim. cons. [criminal conversations, i.e., adulterous relations], the kept mistresses, the murders, the suicides, the thefts, the forgeries, the boxing matches, the wagers for eating, drinking and walking, &c. &c. of the people of Great Britain?" Such distractions, he warned, too readily reprinted in American papers, threatened

Perez Morton's request for assistance in publishing a legal treatise: "We have lived together for more than half a Century in fearful times—& in all the vicisstude of political flickerings & Conflicts—we have never been enemies." John Adams to Perez Morton, 7 Aug. 1824, Adams Family Papers, Letterbooks, MHS.

"the virtue of a young country." And even if such reprehensible acts themselves should be mimicked in the United States, Rush advised, "the less that is said about it the better."

Perez Morton himself was on Rush's mind as he wrote this piece, as he was surely on the gossiping lips and sharpened quills of many other well-informed Americans: "What have the citizens of Philadelphia to do," Rush asked, "with the criminal amours of Mr. M-----, of Boston?" Such a teaser brought Rush dangerously close to undermining his own advice to the *Federal Gazette*'s editor. Repeated exposure to the "frequent and minute histories of such gross vices," he warned, would gradually accustom readers to immoral behavior. The physician's sense of propriety outweighed any general impulse to expose the bad behavior of fellow citizens. "Never suffer your paper to be a vehicle of private scandal, or personal disputes," he advised the *Gazette*'s editor. "If the faults of public officers are to be exposed, let it be done with decency," but the "vices or follies of private citizens," he believed, have no place "in a newspaper." Freedom of the press, he stressed, should not extend to "lay[ing] open the secrets of families, and thereby wound[ing] female honor and delicacy." Rush underscored this point, that female readers were particularly at risk: "Never publish an article in your paper," he advised, "that you would not wish your wife and daughter (if you have any) should read or understand."[1]

Moral instruction, if not carefully regulated by patriarchal authority, could run against its own best intentions, Rush believed, especially where women's reading habits were concerned. His comments highlight the degree to which such conversations about how to regulate women's reading were often conducted between men. Rush was himself deeply distrustful of novels' capacity to generate emotional responses in readers. He worried they would become

1 A Friend to the Union [Benjamin Rush], "For the Federal Gazette," *Federal Gazette, and Philadelphia Evening Post,* 1 Oct. 1788, [2]. Repr. as "Directions for Conducting a Newspaper," in Runes. The editor's statement to the public in the same issue (the inaugural issue) coincides with Rush's sentiments for the most part. Promising to accept contributors regardless of political persuasion, the editor only reserved the right not to publish anything indecent. "The liberty of the press shall be inviolably preserved, but no considerations shall induce the editor to prostitute this paper to the unworthy purposes of personal malice, in which the liberty or happiness of the community are in no ways interested." See "To the Public," *Federal Gazette, and Philadelphia Evening Post,* 1 Oct. 1788, [1].

lost in books, unable to exercise real sympathy when appropriate situations arose. Addressing the young women of Philadelphia's first female academy, Rush decried in 1787 "[t]he abortive sympathy which is excited by the recital of imaginary distress, blunts the heart to that which is real." Invoking *The Sorrows of Werther*, the same novel Brown's hero would emulate in *The Power of Sympathy*, Rush warned his listeners against "instances of young ladies, who weep away a whole forenoon over the criminal sorrows of a fictitious Charlotte or Werther, turning with disdain at three o'clock from the sight of a beggar, who sollicits in feeble accents or signs, a small portion only of the crumbs which fall from their fathers' tables" (qtd. in Bell, "Moral Thermometer" 317).

In Boston, Isaiah Thomas claimed to operate on principles similar to Rush's. When he first published, that fall, proposals for his *Massachusetts Magazine*, he also declared that concern for "the ear of Chastity" would lead him "not to trespass on domestick happiness, or retail anecdotes of scandal."[1] But such pronouncements were soon put to the test by his commitment to publish Brown's novel, which clearly emerged in just such a context of domestic strife. The first issue of the *Massachusetts Magazine*, which promoted Thomas's interests in *The Power of Sympathy*, took scandal as a special topic in the first two columns by "The Reformer," an anonymous contributor often thought to be William Hill Brown. Clearly Thomas believed there was some value in "retail[ing]" the general topic. Whether or not Bostonians or Philadelphians needed to know the specifics of a case like Mr. M-----'s, clearly Thomas at least believed that their general outlines, sitting at the intersection of private and public affairs, might be effectively put to use in shaping private and public virtue—or at least in selling print.

Today we return to Brown's novel, as well as to *Sans Souci* and *Occurrences of the Times*, less for any moral or even documentary truths they might convey and more for their ability to teach us how contemporaries used literary forms and conventions to respond to their historical situations, with their attendant morals, anxieties, and aspirations. Especially in the context of our own awareness of political and cultural power's implication in systemic injustice and the exploitation of vulnerable or marginal subjects, we might pay close attention to what these works tell us about the ways in which

---

1 *Proposal of Isaiah Thomas and Company, for Publishing by Subscription, a New Periodical Work, to be entitled Massachusetts Magazine: or Monthly Museum of Knowledge and rational Entertainment*. Printed by Isaiah Thomas, Worcester, MA, 1788.

female agency and sexual autonomy continue to be politicized in public discourse. Kate Davies argues that the Sans Souci debate was a struggle over the meanings of gender and republicanism in the post-Revolutionary metropolis and usefully highlights the role gendered representations played in the formation of political ideologies and partisan divisions. This gendered understanding of politics, critics have argued, informs all three of the texts collected here. Anticipating, perhaps, the #MeToo movement that arose in the late 2010s, they call attention to the ways in which vulnerable young women are exploited by powerful older men. In the post-Revolutionary context, this situation established a parallel between innocent youth led astray and the uncertain future of the new nation, an association that ultimately could render female subjects even more powerless. Concomitantly, a host of critics have drawn attention to the way in which sympathy is presented as an ideal reading strategy for understanding and responding to characters who have failed to safeguard their virtue and thus are unable to expend it in the cause of the new nation. It is not merely that such failures present "teachable moments" in their negative examples but that the production of sympathy is a way to generate new usable emotional capital that can then help advance national virtues, and thus it has its own political efficacy.

This emphasis upon sympathy as emotional connection has led generations of critics to label *The Power of Sympathy* a sentimental novel, and it is one, but it is not a sentimentality of kittens, hearts, and flowers evacuated of politics, and to read it as such is to efface Brown's implicit critique of, and intervention in, the cultural politics of its era. If sentimentality might obscure politics absent the historical context, satire, as deployed in *Sans Souci* and *Occurrences of the Times*, serves to highlight the critique. And yet it is worth considering that in all three texts, sentimentality and satire serve the same function. *The Power of Sympathy*, *Sans Souci*, and *Occurrences of the Times* (along with other contemporary expressions of outrage and ridicule) all characterize the Mortons and their ilk—and, in many cases, the Apthorp parents as well—as lacking in self-regulation or as unfeeling. Importantly, these criticisms arise, especially in the novel's case, from a consideration of the victim's age. Satire and sentimentality, whether aiming to guide or vindicate the young or simply to indict the middle-aged, invited readers to align themselves against would-be social leaders who are superficial, selfish, and self-protective. The readers who readily participated in such responses—readers like Betsy Cranch, Nabby Adams Smith, or Nathan Webb—aligned themselves against such characters, their passions, and the behaviors they endorsed. In recognizing and condemning the same, virtuous readers could demonstrate that they were superior to such faults, capable of acting and feeling in ways that would advance a city or nation's public good instead of depleting it. This is, of course, the powerful rhetorical and emotional sway of literature. Writing in the wake of Revolution, Brown and his contemporaries remind us that literature has seductive force of its own, which made it both useful and, to those whose entrenched power was under threat, potentially dangerous.

William Hill Brown and the Morton Scandals: A Brief Chronology

1751 Perez Morton is born in Plymouth to James Morton, the keeper of Boston's White Horse Tavern, and Anna Bullock.

1759 Sarah Apthorp is born in Boston to James Apthorp and Sarah Wentworth.

1765 William Hill Brown is born in Boston to Gawen Brown, a clockmaker, and Elizabeth Hill Adams, a widow whose first husband, Joseph Adams, was brother of the Patriot leader Sam Adams.

1766 Frances Theodora Apthorp is born in Boston to James Apthorp and Sarah Wentworth.

1773 Mather Brown (b. 1761), William's older half-brother, begins to study with the painter Gilbert Stuart.

1776 Perez Morton delivers and publishes a celebrated oration to Freemasons on the reinterment of Gen. Joseph Warren.

1777 Perez Morton again addresses Freemasons, creating a mild newspaper scandal, by suggesting that women would never become Masons because they could not keep secrets.

1781 Sarah Apthorp and Perez Morton are married on 24 February. Sarah adopts her mother's maiden name, Wentworth, as a middle name.

1782 Mather Brown leaves for London to study with the American painter Benjamin West.

1784 Perez and Sarah Morton purchase, for a nominal sum, the Apthorp family mansion on State Street, preventing it from being seized and sold as Loyalist property. They also occupy the Apthorp family pew at King's Chapel, where Perez is a vestryman. They side against Sarah's parents in the church's transition from Anglicanism to Unitarianism.

1785 The Mortons are embroiled in the Sans Souci controversy, regarding a subscription social club to which they belonged. They are satirized in the play *Sans Souci, alias, Free and Easy*, published anonymously in late January.

1786	Six of Mather Brown's juvenile poems are published in *Boston Magazine*.
1786	Fanny Apthorp moves into the State Street home of Sarah and Perez Morton.
1787	Fanny Apthorp gives birth to a child, allegedly Perez Morton's, though the event is dealt with quietly and the baby is apparently removed to Rhode Island. (Some possibility exists that this child was raised by Sarah and Perez as their own daughter, Charlotte.)
1788	Fanny Apthorp dies by poison on 28 August. Her final letters appear in the *Herald of Freedom* on September 15. The Morton and Apthorp families agree to an independent inquest by John Adams and James Bowdoin. The Coroner's Jury returns a verdict on 23 September of suicide, but Adams and Bowdoin release their own decision that she was insane when she committed the act and therefore not guilty. Newspapers offer space for substantial debate about the case and these decisions. Fanny is buried in the Apthorp family's crypt at King's Chapel Burying Ground.
1789	*The Power of Sympathy* is announced in the *Herald of Freedom* on 16 January. An attempted duel that week between Morton and Fanny's brother, Charles Apthorp, is averted, as is a purported attempt to suppress the novel, which is published as planned by Isaiah Thomas and Company at the end of January. Excerpts appear in Thomas's *Massachusetts Magazine* for that month (actually published in February). Two farces, *Occurrences of the Times* and *The Better Sort*, are both published in February.
1790	Sarah Morton, writing under the pen name Philenia, publishes her first book-length poem, *Ouâbi; or, The Virtues of Nature: An Indian Tale in Four Cantos*. Published by Isaiah Thomas, the book is dedicated to James Bowdoin.
1791–93	Perez Morton helps to lead the movement to legalize the theater in Boston, whose end is finally achieved in 1794.
1792	William Hill Brown moves to Murfreesboro, North Carolina, to live with his sister, Eliza. He studies law with William Richardson Davie.

1793 Brown's sister dies in January. He engages in a poetic correspondence with Robert Treat Paine Jr. and Sarah Morton, all using pen names, in Boston publications. Brown dies in August, possibly from malaria.

1793 The Mortons support the successful repeal of a ban on dramatic performances in Massachusetts. Morton invests in the first theater to open the following year.

1797 Four years after his death, William Hill Brown's play *West Point Preserved* enjoys a brief run in Boston.

1807 Brown's second novel, *Ira and Isabella, Or, The Natural Children*, is posthumously published in Boston.

1810 Perez Morton serves as attorney general of Massachusetts until 1832.

1823 Sarah Wentworth Apthorp Morton publishes *My Mind and Its Thoughts, in Sketches, Fragments, and Essays*.

1837 Perez Morton dies at age eighty-five.

1846 Sarah Wentworth Apthorp Morton dies at age eighty-six.

A Note on the Texts

The Power of Sympathy: Or, the Triumph of Nature was published in two volumes by Isaiah Thomas and Company in Boston in early 1789. Thomas printed selections from the novel in his own *Massachusetts Magazine* for January 1789, but no additional printings or editions of the full work appeared for over a century. (The novel was regularly advertised in multiple cities through the early nineteenth century, leading modern scholars to believe that claims about its suppression at the hands of Perez Morton's allies or by William Hill Brown himself are inaccurate.) We follow the 1789 edition's spelling, punctuation, and use of ALL CAPS and *italics* in most cases, including an erratic use of dashes of varying length, which we take to approximate informal practices associated with epistolary writing. Where eighteenth-century printers often placed quotation marks at the beginning of each line of a block quotation, however, we have chosen only to use quotation marks at the opening and closing of a quotation. (See the quotation from Sterne in Letter VII for an example.)

Sans Souci, alias, Free and Easy: Or an Evening's Peep into a Polite Society was published in Boston by William Warden and Benjamin Russell, editors of the *Massachusetts Centinel*, in two separate 1785 editions. We have used the first edition as our copy text, though our footnotes account for any changes made in the subsequent edition. As in the text for *The Power of Sympathy*, we preserve original spelling and punctuation and attempt to mirror most typesetting conventions.

Occurrences of the Times. Or, the Transactions of Four Days was printed in Boston by E. Larkin in a single edition in February 1789, within weeks of Thomas's publication of *The Power of Sympathy*. As in the other texts included here, we retain original spelling, punctuation, and most typesetting conventions.

The material in the appendices follows the spelling and punctuation of the originals unless otherwise noted. In the case of Fanny Apthorp's letters (Appendix A), we use the first printed version, from the *Herald of Freedom*, 15 Sept. 1788, as our copy text, while noting variations that occur in the various scribal copies we have identified.

To better convey the print culture of the era, the original spelling and punctuation of personal letters has been preserved.

THE POWER OF SYMPATHY

PREFACE.

Novels have ever met with a ready reception into the Libraries of the Ladies, but this species of writing hath not been received with universal approbation: Futility is not the only charge brought against it. Any attempt, therefore, to make these studies more advantageous, has at least a claim upon the patience and candour of the publick.

In Novels which *expose* no particular Vice, and which *recommend* no particular Virtue, the fair Reader, though she may find amusement, must finish them without being impressed with any particular idea: So that if they are harmless, they are not beneficial.

Of the Letters before us, it is necessary to remark, that this errour on each side has been avoided—the dangerous Consequences of Seduction are exposed, and the Advantages of Female Education set forth and recommended.

THE POWER OF SYMPATHY, &C.

LETTER I. HARRINGTON *to* WORTHY.

BOSTON.

You may now felicitate me—I have had an interview with the charmer I informed you of. Alas! Where were the thoughtfulness and circumspection of my friend *Worthy?* I did not possess them, and am graceless enough to acknowledge it. He would have considered the consequences, before he had resolved upon the project. But you call me, with some degree of truth, a strange medley of contradiction—the moralist and the amoroso[1]—the sentiment and the sensibility—are interwoven in my constitution, so that nature and grace are at continual fisticuffs.———To the point:—

I PURSUED my determination of discovering the dwelling of my charmer, and have at length obtained access. You may behold my Rosebud,[2] but should you presume to place it in your bosom, expect the force of my wrath to be the infallible consequence.

I DECLARED the sincerity of my passion—the warmth of my affection—to the beautiful *Harriot*. Believe me, *Jack,* she did not seem inattentive. Her mien is elegant—her disposition inclining to the melancholy, and yet her temper is affable, and her manners easy. And as I poured my tender vows into the heart of my beloved, a crimson drop stole across her cheek, and thus I construe it in my own favour, as the sweet messenger of hope:—

"Do not wholly despair, my new friend; excuse the declaration of a poor artless female—you see I am not perfectly contented in my situation—[Observe, *Jack,* I have not the vanity to think this distress *altogether* upon my account]—Time therefore may

---

1 A man in love, enamored.

2 A generic term of endearment for a young woman, possibly recalling the 1648 poem by Robert Herrick, "To the Virgins, to Make Much of Time," which famously expresses the theme of carpe diem, or "seize the day," and begins:

> Gather ye Rose-buds while ye may,
>   Old Time is still a-flying:
> And this same flower that smiles to day,
>   To morrow will be dying.

disclose wonders, and perhaps more to your advantage than you imagine—do not despair then."

SUCH vulgar, uncongenial souls, as that which animates thy clay cold carcase, would have thought this crimson drop nothing more than an ordinary blush! Be far removed from my heart, such sordid, earth-born ideas: But come thou spirit of celestial language, that canst communicate by one affectionate look—one tender glance—more divine information to the soul of sensibility, than can be contained in myriads of volumes!

HAIL gentle God of Love! While thou rivetest the chains of thy *slaves,* how dost thou make them leap for joy, as with delicious *triumph.* Happy enthusiasm! that while it carries us away into captivity, can make the heart to dance as in the bosom of content. Hail gentle God of Love! Encircled as thou art with darts, torments, and ensigns of cruelty, still do we hail thee. How dost thou smooth over the roughness and asperities of present pain, with what thou seest in reversion! Thou banishest the *Stygian*[1] glooms of disquiet and suspense, by the hope of approaching *Elysium*[2]—Blessed infatuation!

I desire you will not hesitate to pronounce an *amen* to my Hymn to Love, as an unequivocal evidence of your wish for my success.

LETTER II.
WORTHY *to* HARRINGTON.

NEWYORK.

"WISH you success!"—In what? Who is this lady of whom you have been talking at such an inconsistent rate? But before you have leisure to reply to these inquiries, you may have forgotten there is such a person, as she whom you call *Harriot*—I have seen many juvenile heroes, during my pilgrimage of two and twenty years, easily inflamed with new objects—agitated and hurried away by the impetuosity of new desires—and at the same time they were by no means famous for solidity of judgment, or remarkable for the permanency of their resolutions. There is such

1 Relating to the River Styx, in Greek mythology the boundary between earth and the underworld; dark or foreboding.

2 In Greek mythology the paradise where heroes retired after receiving immortality.

a tumult—such an ebullition of the brain in these paroxisms of passion, that this new object is very superficially examined. These, added to partiality and prepossession, never fail to blind the eyes of the lover. Instead of weighing matters maturely, and stating the evidence fairly on both sides, in order to form a right judgment, every circumstance not perfectly coincident with your particular bias, comes not under consideration, because it does not flatter your vanity. "Ponder and pause"[1] just here, and tell me seriously whether you are in love, and whether you have sufficiently examined your heart to give a just answer.

DO you mean to insinuate that your declaration of love hath attracted the affection of the pensive *Harriot?* If this should be the case, I wish you would tell me what you design to do with her.

LETTER III.
HARRINGTON *to* WORTHY.

BOSTON.

I CANNOT but laugh at your dull sermons, and yet I find something in them not altogether displeasing; for this reason I permit you to prate on. "Weigh matters maturely!" Ha! ha! why art thou not arrayed in canonicals![2] "What do I design to do with her?" Upon my word, my sententious friend, you ask mighty odd questions. I see you aim a stroke at the foundation upon which the pillar of my new system is reared—and will you strive to batter down that pillar? If you entertain any idea of executing such a task, I foresee it will never succeed, and advise you timely to desist. What! dost thou think to topple down my scheme of pleasure? Thou mightest as well topple down the pike of *Teneriffe.*[3]

I SUPPOSE you will be ready to ask, why, if I love *Harriot,* I do not marry her—Your monitorial correspondence has so

---

1 A cliché, used in sermons and moral essays to call readers to reflection. See, for example, Edward Young's popular poem *The Complaint: or, Night Thoughts* (1742–45): "Here pause, and ponder—Was there death in heaven?"

2 A clergyman's robes or dress.

3 The largest of the Canary Islands, controlled by Spain, and site of Mount Teide, the highest point in Spain. The island, sometimes referred to as "Pike Teneriffe," was a major stopping point on European routes to colonies in the Americas and Australia. The first fleet to Botany Bay prison colony, in Australia, anchored at Santa Cruz de Tenerife in June 1787.

accustomed me to reproof, that I easily anticipate this piece of impertinence—But *who* shall I marry? That is the question. *Harriot* has no father—no mother—neither is there aunt, cousin, or kindred of any degree who claim any kind of relationship to her. She is companion to Mrs. *Francis,* and, as I understand, totally dependent on that lady. Now, Mr. *Worthy,* I must take the liberty to acquaint you, that I am not so much of a republican as formally to wed any person of this class. How laughable would my conduct appear, were I to trace over the same ground marked out by thy immaculate footsteps—To be heard openly acknowledging for my bosom companion, any daughter of the democratick empire of virtue!

To suppose a smart, beautiful girl, would continue as a companion to the best lady in Christendom, when she could raise herself to a more eligible situation, is to suppose a solecism[1]—She might as well be immured in a nunnery. Now, *Jack,* I will shew you my benevolent scheme; it is to take this beautiful sprig, and transplant it to a more favourable soil, where it shall flourish and blossom under my own auspices. In a word, I mean to remove this fine girl into an elegant apartment, of which she herself is to be the sole mistress. Is not this a proof of my humanity and goodness of heart? But I know the purport of your answer—So pray thee keep thy comments to thyself, and be sparing of your compliments on this part of my conduct—for I do not love flattery. A month has elapsed since my arrival in town. What will the revolution of another moon bring forth?

Your &c.

LETTER IV.

Miss HARRIOT FAWCET *to Miss* MYRA HARRINGTON.

BOSTON.

I HAVE somehow bewitched a new lover, my dear *Myra*—a smart, clever fellow too—and the youth expresses such fondness and passion that I begin to feel afraid even to pity him—for love will certainly follow. I own to you I *esteem* him very much, but must I go any farther? He is extremely generous—polite—gay—and I believe if you were to see him, your partiality in his favour would exceed mine.

---

1 A breach of manners.

I NEVER saw my poor swain[1] so seemingly disconcerted and abashed as he was a few days ago—he appeared to have something very particular to communicate, but his tongue faultered—ought not one to help out a modest youth in such cases?

Your &c.

LETTER V.

Miss MYRA HARRINGTON *to Mrs.* HOLMES.

BOSTON.

ARE the rural pleasures of *Belleview*, my dear friend, so engaging as to debar us of the pleasure of your company forever? Do your dear groves, and your books, still employ your meditating mind? Serious sentimentalist as you are, let me ask, whether a Ball, a Concert or Serenade, would not afford you the satisfaction of a contemplative walk in your garden, listening to the love tales of the melodious inhabitants of the air?

RAILLERY apart—when shall I take upon myself the honour to wait upon you here?—I want to advise with you on certain points of female conduct, and about my new dress—I have heard you say, lessons to a volatile mind should be fresh and fresh applied, because it either pretends to despise them, or has a tendency to degeneracy—Now you must know I am actually degenerating for want of some of your *Mentor*[2] like lessons of instruction. I have scarcely any opinion of my own, these fashions, changing about so often, are enough to vitiate the best taste in the world.

I FORGOT to tell you my brother has been at home this month; but, from certain indubitable symptoms, I suspect the young man to be in love.

HEIGHHO! What is become of *Worthy?* The time of my liberty steals away, for you know I was to have three or four months of liberty before I gave myself up to his authority, and relinquished all my right and title to the name of

HARRINGTON.

---

1 A suitor; the term invokes a rustic lover, the shepherd-hero of love poems.

2 The tutor and advisor of young Telemachus in Homer's *Odyssey*. The word "mentor" entered English in the mid-eighteenth century to mean a general teacher or counselor. Myra's punctuation suggests she has the classical reference in mind.

LETTER VI.
HARRINGTON *to* WORTHY.

BOSTON.

ABASHED—confounded—defeated—I waited upon my beloved with my head well furnished with ready made arguments, to prevail on her to acquiesce in my benevolent scheme—she never appeared so amiable—grace accompanied every word she uttered, and every action she performed. "Think, my love," said I, in a tone something between sighing and tears, and took her hand in a very cordial manner—"Think, my love, on your present, unhappy, menial situation, in the family of Mrs. *Francis.*" I enlarged on the violence of my passion—expatiated most metaphysically on our future happiness; and concluded by largely answering objections. "Shall we not," continued I, "obey the dictates of nature, rather than confine ourselves to the forced, unnatural rules of——— and—and shall the halcyon days of youth slip through our fingers unenjoyed?"

Do you think, *Worthy,* I said this to *Harriot?*—Not a syllable of it. It was impossible—my heart had the courage to dictate, but my rebellious tongue refused to utter a word—it faultered—stammered—hesitated.—

THERE is a language of the eyes—and we conversed in that language; and though I said not a word with my tongue, she seemed perfectly to understand my meaning—for she *looked*—(and I comprehended it as well as if she had *said*)——"Is the crime of dependence to be expiated by the sacrifice of virtue? And because I am a poor, unfortunate girl, must the little I have be taken from me?" "No, my love," answered I, passionately, "it shall not."

OF all those undescribable things which influence the mind, and which are most apt to persuade—none is so powerful an orator—so feelingly eloquent as beauty—I bow to the all-conquering force of *Harriot's* eloquence—and what is the consequence?—I am now determined to continue my addresses on a principle the most just, and the most honourable.

HOW amiable is that beauty which has its foundation in goodness! Reason cannot contemplate its power with indifference—Wisdom cannot refrain from enthusiasm—and the sneering exertions of Wit cannot render it ridiculous. There is a *dignity* in *conscious virtue* that all my impudence cannot bring me to despise—and if it be beauty that subdues my heart, it is *this* that completes the triumph—It is here my pompous parade, and all my flimsy subterfuges, appear to me in their proper light. In fine, I have *weighed matters maturely,* and the alternative is—*Harriot* must be mine, or I miserable without her.—I have so well weighed the matter that even this idea is a *flash* of joy to my heart—But, my friend, *after the lightning comes the thunder*—my father is mortally averse to my making any matrimonial engagement at so early a period—this is a bar in my way, but I must leap over it.

Adieu!

LETTER VII.

Mrs. HOLMES *to Miss* HARRINGTON.

BELLEVIEW.

ALTHOUGH my attachment to *Belleview* is not so romantick as your airy pen has described it, I think its quiet and amusements infinitely preferable to the bustle and parade with which you are surrounded.

THE improvements made here by my late husband (who inherited the virtues of his parents, who still protect me, and endeavour to console the anguish of his loss by the most tender affection) have rendered the charms of *Belleview* superiour in my estimation to every gilded scene of the gay world.

IT is almost vanity to pretend to give you a description of the beauty of the prospect[1]—the grandeur of the river that rolls through the meadow in front of the house, or any eulogium on rural elegance, because these scenes are common to most places in the country. Nature is every where liberal in dispensing her beauties and her variety—and I pity those who look round and declare they see neither.

A GREAT proportion of our happiness depends on our own choice—it offers itself to our taste, but it is the heart that gives it a relish—what at one time, for instance, we think to be humour, is at another disgustful or insipid—so, unless we carry our appetite with us to the treat, we shall vainly wish to make ourselves happy. "Was I in a desart," says *Sterne,* "I would find wherewith in it to call forth my affections—If I could do no better, I would fasten them on some sweet myrtle, or seek some melancholy cypress to connect myself to—I would court their shade and greet them kindly for their protection—If their leaves withered, I would teach

1 An extended view, especially one that is aesthetically pleasing.

myself to mourn, and when they rejoiced, I would rejoice along with them."[1]

I BELIEVE you could hardly find the way to the summer house, where we have enjoyed many happy hours together, and which you used to call "The TEMPLE of *Apollo.*" It is now more elegantly furnished than it formerly was, and is enriched with a considerable addition to the library and musick.

IN FRONT of the avenue that leads to this place, is a figure of CONTENT, pointing with one hand to the Temple, and with the other to an invitation, executed in such an antique style, that you would think it done either by the ancient inhabitants of the country, or by the hand of a Fairy—she is very particular in the characters she invites, but those whom she invites she heartily welcomes.

Rural Inscription.

COME ye who loath the horrid crest,
Who hate the fiery front of MARS;
Who scorn the mean—the sordid breast—
Who fly AMBITION'S guilty cares:
YE who are blest with peaceful souls,
Rest HERE: Enjoy the pleasures round;
HERE Fairies quaffe[2] their acorn bowls,
And lightly print the mazy ground.

THRICE welcome to this humble scene—
(TO YE alone such scenes belong)
PEACE smiles upon the fragrant green,
And here the woodland sisters throng,
And fair CONTENTMENT'S pleasing train,
Whilst in the Heav'n the stars advance,
With many a maid and many a swain,
Lead up the jocund, rural dance.

THRICE welcome to our calm retreat,
Where INNOCENCY oft hath strove,
With violet blue, and woodbine sweet,
To form the votive wreath to LOVE:
O! pardon then, our cautious pride—

1 From Laurence Sterne's 1768 novel *A Sentimental Journey through France and Italy*, which was published in a Boston edition within months of its appearance in London (see the Introduction, pp. 57–58).

2 Drink.

(CAUTION, a virtue rare, I ween)
For evils with the great abide,
Which dwell not in our sylvan scene.[1]

THESE are the scenes to which I have chosen to retreat; contented with the suffrage of the virtuous and the good, and inattentive to the contemptuous sneer of the giddy and the futile, for even *these* have the vanity to look with pity on those who voluntarily remove from whatever agrees with *their* ideas of pleasure. He who has no conception of the beauties of the mind, will contemn a person aukward or illfavoured; and one whose store of enjoyment is drawn from affluence and abundance, will be astonished at the conduct of him who finds cause to rejoice, though surrounded with inconvenience and penury. Hence we judge of the happiness of others by the standard of our own conduct and prejudices.

FROM this misjudging race I retire, without a sigh to mingle in their amusements, nor yet disgusted at whatever is thought of sufficient consequence to engage their pursuits. I fly from the tumult of the town—from scenes of boisterous pleasure and riot, to those of quietness and peace, "where every breeze breathes health, and every sound is the echo of tranquillity."[2]—On this subject I give my sentiments to you with freedom, from a conviction that I bear the world no spleen; at the same time with a degree of deference to the judgment of others, from a conviction that I may be a little prejudiced.

I HOPE to be with you soon—in the mean time continue to write.

ELIZA HOLMES.

LETTER VIII.
WORTHY *to* HARRINGTON.

NEWYORK.

I APPLAUD your change of sentiment: *Harriot* is a good girl, and your conduct is extremely praiseworthy and honourable. It

1 The poem is Brown's. It was reprinted in the Boston periodical *The Emerald*, in vol. 32, 6 Dec. 1806, 383.

2 From the introduction to Oliver Goldsmith's (1728–74) short-lived London periodical *The Bee, Being Essays on the Most Interesting Subjects* (6 Oct. 1759).

is what her virtues incontestibly merit.——But I advise you certainly to gain your father's approbation before you proceed so far as to be unable to return. A contrary step might terminate in the utter ruin of you both.———Direct to me at *Belleview*—for I intend to stop there in my return to *Boston.*

LETTER IX.
HARRINGTON *to* WORTHY.

BOSTON.

I have had a conversation with my father on the subject of early marriages, but to no purpose—I will not be certain whether he understood my drift, but all his arguments are applicable to my situation. One must be an adept to argue with him; and interested as he thinks himself in the result of the debate, he cannot be prevailed upon to relinquish his settled opinion. I am too much chagrined to write you even the heads of our conversation. I now stand upon my old ground.

Adieu!

LETTER X.
WORTHY *to* MYRA.

BELLEVIEW.

I AM very happy at present enjoying the sweets of *Belleview* with our excellent friend Mrs. *Holmes.* To dwell in this delightful retreat, and to be blest with the conversation of this amiable woman, cannot be called solitude. The charms of Nature are here beheld in the most luxuriant variety—it is here, diversified with a beautiful prospect, the late Mr. *Holmes* planned his garden; it is elegant, but simple. My time glides off my hands most happily—I am sometimes indulging my solitary reflections in contemplating the sublimity of the scenes around me—and sometimes in conversation with *Eliza* and the old people.

THE old gentleman is a man of a most benevolent heart; he continues to preach—is assiduous in the duties of his profession, and is the love and admiration of his flock. He prescribes for the health of the body, as well as that of the soul, and settles all the little disputes of his parish. They are contented with his judgment, and he is at once their parson, their lawyer, and their physician.——I often read in the little building that was finished by his son. He was a man of an excellent taste, and I have paid my tribute to his memory—It is the same place that you used to admire, and perhaps I improve more of my time in it on that very account.

Adieu!

LETTER XI.
Mrs. HOLMES to MYRA.

BELLEVIEW.

I SIT down to give you, my dear *Myra,* some account of the visitants of today, and their conversation. We are not always *distinguished* by such company, but perhaps it is sometimes necessary; and as it is a relaxation from thought, it serves to give us more pleasure in returning to the conversation of people of ideas.

MRS. *Bourn* assumes a higher rank in life than she pretended to seven years ago.—She then walked on foot—she now, by good fortune, rides in a chariot. Placed, however, in a situation with which her education does not altogether comport, she has nothing disagreeable but her over assiduity to please—this is sometimes disgusting, for one cannot feast heartily upon honey: It is an errour which a candid mind easily forgives. She sometimes appears solicitous to display her mental accomplishments, and desirous to improve those of her daughter; but it is merely apparent. Notwithstanding a temporary wish may arise towards the attainment of this point, a habitual vacancy nips it in the bud.

MISS *Bourn* is about the age of fourteen—genteel, with a tolerable share of beauty, but not striking—her dress was elegant, but might have been adjusted to more advantage—not altogether aukward in her manners, nor yet can she be called graceful—she has a peculiar air of *drollery* which takes her by fits, and for this reason, perhaps, does not avail herself of every opportunity of displaying the modesty of her sex—she has seen much company, but instead of polishing her manners, it has only increased her assurance.

THUS much of the characters of our *company.* After some small chat which passed as we took a turn in the garden, we entered the Temple.

"WHAT books would you recommend to put into the hands of my daughter?" said Mrs. *Bourn,* as she walked into the library—"it is a matter of some importance."

"IT is a matter of *more* importance," answered *Worthy,* "than is generally imagined, for unless a proper selection is made, one would do better never to read at all:—Now, Madam, as much depends on the choice of books, care should be taken not to put those in the way of young persons, which might leave on their minds any disagreeable prejudices, or which has a tendency to corrupt their morals."—"As obvious as your remark is," added Mr. *Holmes,* "it is evidently overlooked in the common course of education. We wisely exclude those persons from our conversation, whose characters are bad, whose manners are depraved, or whose morals are impure; but if they are excluded from an apprehension of contaminating our minds, how much more dangerous is the company of those books, where the strokes aimed at virtue are redoubled, and the poison of vice, by repeatedly reading the same thing, indelibly distains the young mind?"

"WE all agree," rejoined *Worthy,* "that it is as great a matter of virtue and prudence to be circumspect in the selection of our books, as in the choice of our company.—But, Sir, the best things may be subverted to an ill use. Hence we may possibly trace the cause of the ill tendency of many of the Novels extant."

"MOST of the Novels," interrupted my father, "with which our female libraries are overrun, are built on a foundation not always placed on strict morality, and in the pursuit of objects not always probable or praiseworthy.—Novels, not regulated on the chaste principles of true friendship, rational love, and connubial[1] duty, appear to me totally unfit to form the minds of women, of friends, or of wives."

"BUT, as most young people read," says Mrs. *Bourn*—"what rule can be *hit upon* to make study always terminate to advantage?"

"IMPOSSIBLE," cried Miss, "for I read as much as any body, and though it may afford amusement, while I am employed, I do not remember a single word, when I lay down the book."

"THIS confirms what I say of Novels," cried Mr. *Holmes,* addressing *Worthy* in a jocular manner, "just calculated to kill time—to attract the attention of the reader for an hour, but leave not one idea on the mind."

"I AM far from condemning every production in the gross," replied *Worthy;* "general satire against any particular class, or order of men, may be viewed in the same light as a satire against the species—it is the same with books—If there are corrupt or mortified members, it is hardly fair to destroy the whole

1 Marital.

body. Now I grant some Novels have a bad tendency, yet there are many which contain excellent sentiments—let these receive their deserved reward—let those be discountenanced; and if it is impossible 'to smite them with an apoplexy, there is a moral certainty of their dying of a consumption.'[1]——But, as Mrs. *Bourn* observes, most young persons read, I will therefore recommend to those who wish to mingle instruction with entertainment, method and regularity in reading. To *dip* into *any book* burthens the mind with unnecessary lumber, and may rather be called a disadvantage, than a benefit—The record of memory is so scrawled and blotted with imperfect ideas, that not one legible character can be traced."

"WERE I to throw my thoughts on this subject," said my good father-in-law, as he began to enter more warmly into the debate—drawing his chair opposite *Worthy,* and raising his hand with a poetical enthusiasm—"Were I to throw my thoughts on this subject into an Allegory, I would describe the human mind as an extensive plain, and knowledge as the river that should water it. If the course of the river be properly directed, the plain will be fertilized and cultivated to advantage; but if books, which are the sources that feed this river, rush into it from every quarter, it will overflow its banks, and the plain will become inundated: When, therefore, knowledge flows on in its proper channel, this extensive and valuable field, the mind, instead of being covered with stagnant waters, is cultivated to the utmost advantage, and blooms luxuriantly into a general efflorescence—for a river properly restricted by high banks, is necessarily progressive."

THE old gentleman brought down his hand with great solemnity, and we complimented him on his poetical exertion. "I cannot comprehend the meaning of this matter," said the penetrative Miss *Bourn.* "I will explain it to you, my little dear," said he, with great good nature—"If you read with any design to improve your mind in virtue and every amiable accomplishment, you should be careful to read methodically, which will enable you to form an estimate of the various topicks discussed in company, and to bear a part in all those conversations which belong to your sex—you see, therefore, how necessary general knowledge is—what would you think of a woman advanced in life, who has no other store of knowledge, than what she has obtained from experience?"

1 Source unknown. *Apoplexy*: a cerebral hemorrhage or stroke; *consumption*: pulmonary tuberculosis, or, colloquially, any wasting disease.

"I THINK she would have a sorry time of it;" answered Miss.

"To prevent it in yourself," said Mrs. *Bourn* to her daughter, "be assiduous to lay in a good stock of this knowledge, while your mind is yet free from prejudice and care."

"How shall I *go to work,* Madam," enquired the delicate daughter.

MRS. *Bourn* turned towards Mr. *Holmes,* which was hint enough for the good old man to proceed.

"There is a medium to be observed," continued he, "in a lady's reading; she is not to receive every thing she finds, even in the best books, as invariable lessons of conduct; in books written in an easy, flowing style, which excel in description and the luxuriance of fancy, the imagination is apt to get heated—she ought, therefore, to discern with an eye of judgment, between the superficial and the penetrating—the elegant and the tawdry—what may be merely amusing, and what may be useful. General reading will not teach her a true knowledge of the world.

"IN books she finds recorded the faithfulness of friendship—the constancy of *true love,* and even that honesty is the best policy. If virtue is represented carrying its reward with it, she too easily persuades herself that mankind have adopted this plan: Thus she finds, when, perhaps, it is too late, that she has entertained wrong notions of human nature; that her friends are deceitful—her lovers false—and that men consult interest oftener than honesty.

"A YOUNG young lady who has imbibed her ideas of the world from desultory reading, and placed confidence in the virtue of others, will bring back disappointment, when she expected gratitude. Unsuspicious of deceit, she is easily deceived—from the purity of her own thoughts, she trusts the faith of mankind, until experience convinces her of her errour—she falls a sacrifice to her credulity, and her only consolation is the simplicity and goodness of her heart.

"THE story of Miss *Whitman**[1] is an emphatical illustration of

---

1 [Brown's note:] *THIS young lady was of a reputable family in *Connecticut.* In her youth she was admired for beauty and good sense. She was a great reader of novels and romances, and having imbibed her ideas of *the characters of men,* from those fallacious sources, became vain and coquetish, and rejected several offers of marriage, in expectation of receiving one more agreeable to her fanciful idea. Disappointed in her *Fairy* hope, and finding her train of admirers less solicitous for the honour of her hand, in proportion as the roses of youth decayed, she was the more easily persuaded to relinquish that *stability* which is the honour and happiness of the sex. The consequences of her amour becoming

the truth of these observations. An inflated fancy, not restricted by judgment, leads too often to *disappointment* and repentance. Such will be the fate of those who become (to use her own words)

---

visible, she acquainted her lover of her situation, and a *husband* was proposed for her, who was to receive a considerable sum for preserving the reputation of the lady; but, having received security for the payment, he immediately withdrew. She then left her friends, and travelled in the stage as far as *Watertown,* where she hired a young man to conduct her in a chaise to *Salem.* Here she wandered alone and friendless, and at length repaired to the *Bell-Tavern, in Danvers,* where she was delivered of a lifeless child, and in about a fortnight after (in *July,* 1788) died of a puerperal fever, aged about 35 years.

Before her death she amused herself with reading, writing and needlework, and though in a state of anxiety, preserved a cheerfulness, not so much the effect of insensibility, as of patience and fortitude. She was sensible of her approaching fate, as appears from the following letter, which was written in characters.

"MUST I die alone? Shall I never see you more? I know that you will come, but you will come too late: This is, I fear, my last ability. Tears fall so, I know not how to write. Why did you leave me in so much distress? But I will not reproach you: All that was dear I left for you; but do not regret it.—May God forgive in both what was amiss: When I go from hence, I will leave you some way to find me; if I die, will you come and drop a tear over my grave?"

In the following Poem, she, like the dying *Swan,* sings her own Elegy, and it is here added, as a sorrowful instance, how often the best, and most pleasing talents, not accompanied by virtue and prudence, operate the destruction of their possessor.

The description of her unfortunate passion, will remind the critical reader of the famous ode of *Sappho.* In genius and in misfortune, these poetical ladies were similar.

"DISAPPOINTMENT.

"WITH fond impatience all the tedious day
I sigh'd, and wish'd the lingering hours away;
For when bright *Hesper* led the starry train,
My shepherd swore to meet me on the plain;
With eager haste to that dear spot I flew,
And linger'd long, and then with tears withdrew:
Alone, abandon'd to love's tenderest woes,
Down my pale cheeks the tide of sorrow flows;
Dead to all joys that fortune can bestow,
In vain for me her useless bounties flow;
Take back each envied gift, ye pow'rs divine,
And only let me call FIDELIO mine.

"Ah, wretch! what anguish yet thy soul must prove, (*continued*)

'Lost in the magick of that sweet employ,
To build *gay scenes* and fashion *future joy*'

"WITH a good heart she possessed a poetical imagination, and an unbounded thirst for novelty; but these airy talents, not

---

Ere thou canst hope to lose thy care in love;
And when FIDELIO meets thy tearful eye,
Pale fear and cold despair his presence fly;
With pensive steps, I sought thy walks again,
And kiss'd thy token on the verdant plain;
With fondest hope, thro' many a blissful bow'r,
We gave the soul to fancy's pleasing pow'r;
Lost in the magick of that sweet employ,
To build gay scenes, and fashion future joy,
We saw mild peace o'er fair *Canäan,* rise,
And show'r her blessings from benignant skies;
On airy hills our happy mansion rose,
Built but for joy, no room for future woes;
Sweet as the sleep of innocence, the day,
(By transports measur'd) lightly danc'd away;
To love, to bliss, the union'd soul was given,
And each! too happy, ask'd no brighter heaven.
"And must the hours in ceaseless anguish roll?
Will no soft sunshine cheer my clouded soul?
Can this dear earth no transient joy supply?
Is it my doom to hope, despair and die?
Oh! come, once more, with soft endearments come,
Burst the cold prison of the sullen tomb;
Through favour'd walks, thy chosen maid attend,
Where well known shades their pleasing branches bend.
Shed the soft poison from thy speaking eye,
And look those raptures lifeless words deny;
Still be, though late, reheard what ne'er could tire,
But, told each eve, fresh pleasures would inspire;
Still hope those scenes which love and fancy drew;
But, drawn a thousand times, were ever new.
"Can fancy paint, can words express;
Can aught on earth my woes redress;
E'en thy soft smiles can ceaseless prove
Thy truth, thy tenderness and love.
Once thou couldst every bliss inspire,
Transporting joy, and gay desire:
Now cold despair her banner rears,
And pleasure flies when she appears;
Fond hope within my bosom dies,
And agony her place supplies:
O, thou! for whose dear sake I bear,

counterposed with judgment, or perhaps serious reflection, instead of adding to her happiness, were the cause of her ruin."[1]

"I CONCLUDE from your reasoning," said I, "and it is, besides, my own opinion, that many fine girls have been ruined by reading Novels."

"AND I believe," added Mrs. *Bourn,* "we may trace from hence the causes of spleen[2] in many persons advanced in life."

"YOU mean old maids, Madam," cried the sagacious Miss, "like my aunt *Deborah*—she calls all the men deceitful, and most women, with her, are no better than they should be."

"WELL said!" exclaimed *Worthy,* "the recollection of chagrin and former disappointment, sours one's temper and mortifies the heart—disappointment will be more or less severe in proportion as we elevate our expectations; for the most *sanguine*

A doom so dreadful, so severe,
May happy fates thy footsteps guide,
And o'er thy *peaceful* home preside;
Nor let ELIZA'S early tomb
Infect thee, with its baleful gloom."

1 Brown's account of Elizabeth Whitman's death draws on several newspaper sources. A letter from the Boston minister Jeremy Belknap (1744–98) to the Philadelphia physician and reformer Benjamin Rush (1746–1813) was excerpted anonymously as "Extract of a Letter from Boston," *Pensylvania Mercury and Universal Advertiser,* 23 Aug. 1788, [4], and was reprinted in several newspapers before it returned to Boston as "Extract of a Letter from Boston," in *Boston's Independent Chronicle and Universal Advertiser,* 11 Sept. 1788, [3], citing a New York newspaper as its source. This account was supplemented by a correspondent calling himself "Curiosos," who wrote to the *Massachusetts Centinel* on 24 Sept. 1788, enclosing the poem "Disappointment" as well as "A Letter in Characters Decyphered," both of which Brown includes in his footnote. Curiosos's account aimed to set the record straight after the poem had been attributed to Fanny Apthorp in another Boston paper, *The Herald of Freedom and Federal Advertiser,* 18 Sept. 1788, [6]. The most substantial difference between Brown's account and those previously circulated in newspapers is the salacious detail that her family sought to procure a husband for Whitman in order to preserve her reputation. Brown is also original in his comparison of Whitman's poetry to that of the Greek poet Sappho (630–580 BCE).

2 Ill-nature. In humoral theory, which dated to the Greek physician Hippocrates (third–fourth century BCE) and dominated popular medical imagination through the eighteenth century, the production of black bile by the spleen gave people of that dominant humor a sour or melancholic temper. Old maids and sometimes bachelors were popularly associated with splenetic temperaments.

tempers[1] are the soonest discouraged; as the highest building is in the most danger of falling."

"IT appears from what I have said," resumed Mr. *Holmes,* "that those books which teach us a knowledge of the world are useful to form the minds of females, and ought therefore to be studied."

I MENTIONED *Rochefoucault's* maxims.[2]—

"DO they not degrade human nature?" enquired my father.

"This little book," answered *Worthy,* "contains much truth—and those short sketches traced by the hand of judgment, present to us the leading features of mankind." "But," replied my father, "that *interest should assume all shapes,* is a doctrine, which, in my mind, represents a caricature rather than a living picture."[3] "It is the duty of a painter to produce a likeness," said *Worthy.*—"And a skilful one," cried my father, continuing the metaphor, "will bring the amiable qualities of the heart to light; and throw those which disgrace humanity into the shade." "I doubt," rejoined *Worthy,* "whether this flattery will answer the purpose you aim to accomplish—You entertain a high opinion of *the dignity of human nature,* and are displeased at the author who advances any thing derogatory to that dignity. *Swift,* in speaking of these maxims, in one of his best poems, affirms,

'They argue no corrupted mind
In him—the fault is in mankind.'"[4]

"As I began this subject," added I, "it shall be ended by one observation—As these maxims give us an idea of the manners and characters of men, among whom a young person is soon to appear; and as it is necessary to her security and happiness that she be made acquainted with them—they may be read to advantage."

---

1 This optimistic or cheerful temperament was related popularly to another of the body's four humors and related to the blood and heart.

2 François VI, Duc de La Rochefoucauld (1613–80), published several editions of his famous volume *Réflexions ou sentences et maximes morales* beginning in 1665.

3 Mr. Holmes refers to Rochefoucauld's Maxim 39: "Interest speaks all sorts of tongues and plays all sorts of characters; even that of disinterestedness."

4 The closing quotation mark is missing in the original edition. The quotation comes from Jonathan Swift's "Verses on the Death of Dr. S[wift], D.S.P.D., Occasioned by Reading a Maxim in Rochefoucault" (1739), in which he defends Rochefoucauld's *Maxims* (and, implicitly, his own role as satirist).

"THERE is another medium,"[1] said Mr. *Holmes,* assenting to my observation, "to be noticed in the study of a lady—she takes up a book, either for instruction or entertainment; the medium lies in knowing when to put it down. Constant application becomes labour—it sours the temper—gives an air of thoughtfulness, and frequently of absence. By *immoderate reading* we hoard up opinions and become insensibly attached to them; this miserly conduct sinks us to affectation, and disgustful pedantry; *conversation* only can remedy this dangerous evil, strengthen the judgment, and make reading really useful. They mutually depend upon, and assist each other.

"A KNOWLEDGE of HISTORY[2] which exhibits to us in one view the rise, progress and decay of nations—which points out the advancement of the mind in society, and the improvements in the arts which adorn human nature, comes with propriety under the notice of a lady. To observe the origin of civilization—the gradual progress of society, and the refinements of manners, policy, morality and religion—to observe the progression of mankind from simplicity to luxury, from luxury to effeminacy, and the gradual steps of the decline of empire, and the dissolution of states and kingdoms, must blend that happy union of instruction and entertainment, which never fails to win our attention to the pursuit of all subjects.

"POETRY claims her due from the ladies, poetry enlarges and strengthens the mind, refines the taste and improves the judgment. It has been asserted that women have no business with *satire*[3]—now satire is but a branch of poetry. I acknowledge, however, much false wit is sent into the world, under this general title; but no critick with whom I am acquainted ever called satire false wit—for as long as vice and folly continue to predominate in the human heart, the satirist will be considered as a useful member of society. I believe *Addison* calls him an auxiliary to the pulpit.[4]

---

1 A position of moderation or compromise, as in a happy medium.

2 Most eighteenth-century thinkers privileged historical writing over fiction and often held them in opposition, especially when prescribing appropriate reading for women. See esp. Phillips, ch. 4.

3 The idea that satire should be the province of male readers and writers was a common misogynist refrain in the eighteenth century, especially as the number of prominent women poets expanded. Many of them were capable satirists.

4 Joseph Addison (1762–19), the famous London periodical writer, in *Spectator* no. 34 (9 Apr. 1711), described "the great Use this Paper [*The Spectator*] might be of to the Publick, by reprehending those (*continued*)

Suffer me to enlarge on this *new idea*. Satire is the correction of the vices and follies of the human heart; a woman may, therefore, read it to advantage. What I mean by enforcing this point, is, to impress the minds of females with a principle of self correction; for among all kinds of knowledge which arise from reading, the duty of self knowledge is a very eminent one; and is at the same time, the most useful and important.

"OUR ordinary intercourse with the world, will present to us in a very clear point of view, the fallacious ideas we sometimes entertain of our own self knowledge.—We are blinded by pride and self love, and will not observe our own imperfections, which we blame with the greatest acrimony in other people, and seem to detest with the greatest abhorrence; so that it often happens, while we are branding our neighbour for some foible, or vanity, we ourselves are equally guilty.

"RIDICULOUS as this conduct must appear in the eyes of all judicious people, it is too frequently practised to escape observation.

"I WILL drop this piece of morality, with a charge to the fair reader, that whenever she discovers a satire, ridiculing or recriminating the follies or crimes of mankind, that she look into her own heart, and compare the strictures on the conduct of others with her own feelings."

LETTER XII.
Mrs. HOLMES *to* MYRA.
In Continuation.

MY good father-in-law being so strenuous in proving the eligibility of reading satire, had spun out, what he called his *new idea*, to such a metaphysical nicety, that he unhappily diminished the number of his hearers; for Mrs. *Bourn*, to whom he directed his discourse, had taken down a book and was reading to herself, and Miss was diverting herself with the cuts in *Gay's* Fables.[1]

A CONSIDERABLE silence ensued, which *Worthy* first broke, by asking Mrs. *Bourn* what book she had in her hand. Every one's attention was alarmed at this important enquiry. Mrs. *Bourn*,

Vices which are too trivial for the Chastisement of the Law, and too fantastical for the Cognizance of the Pulpit."

1 John Gay, *The Fables* (London, 1727). *Cuts*: the book's woodcut illustrations.

with little difficulty, found the title page, and began to read, "*A Sentimental Journey through France and Italy, by Mr.* Yorick."[1]

"I DO not like the *title,*" said Miss *Bourn.*

"WHY, my dear!" apostrophized the mother, "you are mistaken—it is a very famous book."

"WHY, my dear!" retorted the daughter, "It is sentimental—I abominate every thing that is sentimental—it is so unfashionable too."

"I NEVER knew before," said Mr. *Holmes,* "that wit was subject to the caprice of fashion."

"Why 'Squire *Billy,*" returned Miss, "who is just arrived from the centre of politeness and fashion, says the bettermost genii[2] never read any sentimental books—so you see sentiment is out of date."

The company rose to go out.—

"SENTIMENT out of date!" cries *Worthy,* repeating the words of Miss *Bourn,* and taking the book from her mother, as she walked towards the door—"Sentiment out of date—alas! poor *Yorick*—may thy pages never be soiled by the fingers of prejudice." He continued his address to the book, as they went out, in the same *Shandean*[3] tone—"These antisentimentalists would banish thee from the society of all books! Unto what a pitiful size are the race of *readers* dwindled! Surely these *antis* have no more to do with thee, than the gods of the *Canaanites*[4]—In character and understanding they are alike—eyes have *they,* but they see not—ears have *they,* but they hear not, neither is there any knowledge to be

---

1 Sterne, *A Sentimental Journey* (1768), whose narrator is the Reverend Mr. Yorick.

2 Geniuses, or the fashionable literary elite. Esquire Billy has presumably just returned from London.

3 After the manner of Tristram Shandy, the hero of Laurence Sterne's nine-volume novel *The Life and Opinions of Tristram Shandy, Gentleman* (London, 1759–67). The adjective "Shandean" gained popular usage to indicate someone light-hearted, clever, and prone to humorous wordplay. Worthy's exclamation—"alas! Poor Yorick"—refers simultaneously to the narrator of Sterne's *Sentimental Journey* and to a character in *Tristram Shandy* whose grave is marked using lines from Shakespeare's *Hamlet* (5.1), in which Hamlet addresses the skull of his father's deceased court jester.

4 In biblical terms, an idolatrous and polytheistic people whose lands were delivered to the Israelites as their Promised Land. Worthy says that the anti-sentimentalists, who have turned against reading, would have as little to do with Sterne's books as the gods of the Canaanites would have to do with the Israelites, or the chosen people.

found in them."[1] "It is hardly worth while to beat it into them," said my father-in-law, "so let us follow the company."

WE did so—they walked towards the house, and *Worthy* and myself brought up the rear.

I COULD not but remark, as we went on, that Miss *Bourn* had spoken the sentiments of many of her sex;—"and whence," said I to *Worthy*, "arises this detestation of books in *some* of us females, and why are *they* enemies to any thing that may be called sentiment and conversation: I grant it often happens there is such rapidity of *speeches* that one may be at a loss to distinguish the speakers; but why is there such a calm silence, should an unfortunate sentiment inadvertantly—"[2]

"I WILL tell you," interrupted he, "You all read, and it is from the books which engage your attention, that you generally imbibe your ideas of the principal subjects discussed in company—now, the books which employ your hours of study, happen to be Novels; and the *subjects* contained in these Novels are commonly confined to *dress, balls, visiting,* and the like *edifying* topicks; does it not follow, that these must be the subjects of your conversation? I will not dispute whether the Novel makes the woman, or the woman makes the Novel; or whether they are written to engage your attention, or flatter your vanity. I believe the result will shew they depend, in some measure, upon each other; and an uninformed woman, by reading them, only augments the number of her futile ideas. *The female mind,* notwithstanding, *is competent to any task,* and the accomplishments of an elegant woman depend on a proper cultivation of her intelligent powers; a barrenness—a sterility of conversation—immediately discovers where this cultivation is wanting."

"GIVE me leave," answered I, "to espouse the cause of this class of females. Tell me candidly, Mr. *Worthy,* whether that insipid flattery, perhaps sacrificed at the expense of truth, does not misguide many of us into erroneous paths? You declare we are handsome—and your conduct demonstrates you to be more solicitous for the possession of *beautiful,* than of *mental* charms. Hence is the deluded female persuaded of the force of her fascinating powers, and vainly imagines one glance of her eye sufficient to reduce a

---

1 Jer. 5:21: "Hear now this, O foolish people, and without understanding; which have eyes, and see not; which have ears, and hear not" (KJV), a prophetic utterance prefacing a call to repentance. Similar ideas and phrasing are found in Isa. 6:9; Matt. 13:13–14.

2 The closing quotation mark is missing in the original edition.

million of hearts whenever she chooses: Her aims, therefore, are confined to the decoration of her person, and her views centre solely in finishing herself in those attractive, allpowerful graces, with which you declare yourselves to be enchanted. How then are they to be censured for neglecting to improve, and to adorn the mind, when your adulation diverts their attention to an external object?"

"I join with you," replied *Worthy*, "in calling it insipid flattery—and the vain coxcomb, the powdered beau, the insignificant *petit maitre*,[1] are those who make use of it. Will women of real merit, and sound sense, believe, what is said by *them* to be *their* real sentiments?—No—There must be a congeniality in the minds of those who give and receive flattery—Has not the vain coquette as much inclination to be thought a goddess, as the empty admirer to declare her so?

"FLATTERY is become a kind of epidemical distemper; many run into it, perhaps, without designing it, or only through civility. There are some women who expect it—who dress to be admired—and who deem it a mark of impoliteness and rudeness in men, who do not pay them the tribute of compliment and adulation. A man of, sense *may* comply with their expectation—he will still think them agreeable *playthings*, to divert him at an hour of relaxation; but I cannot suppose he will entertain any serious thoughts of *a more permanent connexion*.

"MAY we not conclude these things to be productive of many evils that happen in society—do they not frighten all sentiment from conversation—introduce affectation—pride—envy—clandestine marriages—elopements—division of families—and ultimately terminate in the *ruin* of very many innocent, but inconsiderate females?"

BY this time we had got into the house, and our company soon after departed, leaving us at full leisure to contemplate on the many wrong ideas entertained, and fallacious steps pursued by the generality of mankind, in the sentimental part of female education.

Adieu!

---

1 From French: literally, "little master." Used to indicate a dandy, fop, or coxcomb, all terms, like "powdered beau," used to indicate a young man who is overly invested in his fashionable appearance.

LETTER XIII.
WORTHY *to* MYRA.

BELLEVIEW.

A PEACEFUL, recluse life, is suited to my temper—there is something in the soft breath of Nature—in the delicacy of smiling meadows and cultivated fields—in the sublimity of an aged wood—of broken rocks—of rivers pouring along their lucid waves, to which the heart always gives a ready reception—there is something within us congenial to these scenes; they impress the mind with ideas similar to what we feel in beholding one whom we tenderly esteem.

I WAS making this observation to Mrs. *Holmes,* and she told me I was in love—"These are the very scenes," said she, "which your beloved *Myra* used to praise and admire, and for which you, by a secret sympathy, entertain the same predilection. The piece of embroidery which she worked at an early age, and which ornaments the Temple, I have seen you gaze upon several times—you seem to trace perfection in every part of it, because it was executed by the hand of *Myra.*"

I ACKNOWLEDGE I have often *gazed* upon it (as Mrs. *Holmes* terms it) but did not recollect it to be a piece of your work. I stole an opportunity to revisit it by myself, and I instantly remembered it—I remembered when you finished it, and all the happy, inoffensive scenes of our childhood, returned fresh upon my heart.

IT is the work of *Myra,* said I to myself—Did not her fingers trace these beautiful, expanding flowers?—Did not she give to this carnation its animated glow, and to this opening rose its languishing grace? Removed as I am—continued I in a certain interiour language that every son of nature possesses—Removed as I am, from the amiable object of my tenderest affection, I have nothing to do but to admire this offspring of industry and art—It shall yield more fragrance to my soul than all the *boquets* in the universe.

I DID not care to pursue the thought—it touched a delicate string—at first, however, I flattered myself I should gain some consolation—but I lost in every reflection.

I CONSIDERED the work as coming from your hand, and was delighted the more with it. A piece of steel that has been rubbed with a loadstone, retains the power of attracting small bodies of iron: So the beauties of this embroidery, springing from your hands, continue to draw my attention, and fill the mind with ideas of the artist.

Farewel!

LETTER XIV.
HARRINGTON *to* WORTHY.

BOSTON.

HOW incompetent is the force of words to express some peculiar sensations! Expression is feeble when emotions are exquisite.

I WISH you could be here to see with what ease and dignity every thing comes from the hand of *Harriot*—I cannot give a description equivalent to the great idea I wish to convey—You will tell me I am in love—What is love? I have been trying to investigate its nature—to strip it of its mere term, and consider it as it may be supported by principle—I might as well search for the philosopher's stone.[1]

EVERY one is ready to praise his mistress—she is always described in her "native simplicity," as "an angel" with a "placid mien"[2] "mild, animated" "altogether captivating," and at length the task of description is given up as altogether "undescribable." Are not all these in themselves bare insignificant words? The world has so long been accustomed to hear the sound of them, that the idea is lost. But to the question—What is love? Unless it is answered now, perhaps it never will be. Is it not an infinitude of graces that accompany every thing said by *Harriot?* That adorn all she does? They must not be taken severally[3]—they cannot be contemplated in the abstract.—If you proceed to a chymical[4] analysis, their tenuous essence will evaporate—they are in themselves nothing, but the aggregate is love.

WHEN an army composed of a great number of men, moves slowly on at a distance, nobody thinks of considering a single soldier.

Adieu!

---

1 In alchemical lore, a substance that turns other metals into gold, sometimes assumed to confer immortality on its bearer.

2 A person's look, taken to indicate inward disposition or character. A *placid mien* is an indication of calm temperament.

3 Separately or individually.

4 I.e., chemical. Subjected to scientific scrutiny, Harriot's individual graces will evaporate, but compounded they form love.

LETTER XV.
HARRINGTON *to* WORTHY.

BOSTON.

AM I to believe my eyes—my ears—my heart!—and yet I cannot be deceived.—We are generally most stupid and incredulous in what most materially concerns us. We find the greatest difficulty, in persuading ourselves of the attainment of what we most ardently desire—She loves!—I say to myself, *Harriot* loves me, and I reverence myself.

I THINK I may now take upon me some share of happiness—I may say I have not lived in vain—for all my heart holds dear is mine—joy and love encompass me—peace and tranquillity are before me; the prospect is fair and promising as the gilded dawn of a summer's day—There is none to supplant me in her affection—I dread no rival, for our tempers are similar, and our hearts beat in unison together.

Adieu!

LETTER XVI.
HARRINGTON *to* WORTHY.

BOSTON.

LOVE softens and refines the manners—polishes the asperities of aukwardness, and fits us for the society of gentle beings. It goes further, it mends the heart, and makes us better men—it gives the faint-hearted an extraordinary strength of soul, and renders them equal and frequently superiour to danger and distress.

MY passions you know are quick, my prejudices sometimes obstinate—She tells me these things are wrong—This gentle reprimand is so tempered with love that I think she commends me. I however promise a reform, and am much pleased with my improvement. *Harriot* moulds my heart into what form she chooses.

A LITTLE party is proposed tomorrow evening, and I shall attend *Harriot.* These elegant relaxations prevent the degeneracy of human nature, exhilerate the spirits, and wind up this machine of ours for another revolution of business.

LETTER XVII.
HARRINGTON *to* WORTHY.

BOSTON.

OUR little party was overthrown by a strange piece of folly. A Miss P—— was introduced, a young lady of beauty and elegant accomplishments. The whole company were beginning to be cheerful—business and care were disgusted at the sight of so many happy countenances, and had gone out from among us. Jollity and good humour bade us prepare for the dance—unhappily at this juncture a lady and gentleman were engaged in a conversation concerning Miss P——, and one of them repeated the words "a mechanick's daughter"[1]—it is supposed the word "mechanick" was repeated scornfully—She heard it—thought herself insulted—and indignantly retired—Disorder and confusion immediately took place, and the amusement was put an end to for the evening.

I WISH people would consider how little time they have to frolick here—that they would improve it to more advantage, and not dispute for any precedence or superiority but in good nature and sociability—"a mechanick"—and pray whence this distinction!

INEQUALITY among mankind is a foe to our happiness—it even affects our little parties of pleasure—Such is the fate of the human race, one order of men lords it over another; but upon what grounds its right is founded I could never yet be satisfied.

FOR this reason, I like a democratical better than any other kind of government; and were I a *Lycurgus*[2] no distinction of rank should be found in my commonwealth.

IN my tour through the United States, I had an opportunity of examining and comparing the different manners and dispositions of the inhabitants of the several republicks.[3] Those of the southern states, accustomed to a habit of domineering over their slaves, are haughtier, more tenacious of honour, and indeed possess more of an aristocratick temper than their sisters of the confederacy. As we travel to the northward, the nature of the constitution seems to operate on the minds of the people—slavery is abolished—all men are declared free and equal, and their tempers are open, generous

---

1 The daughter of an artisan; though a member of polite society, she encounters here some prejudice against her father's occupation.

2 Lycurgus (800–730 BCE), a Spartan reformer, lawgiver, and proponent of equal rights among citizens.

3 I.e., the separate states.

and communicative. It is the same in all those countries where the people enjoy independence and equal liberty. Why then should those distinctions arise which are inimical to domestick quietude? Or why should the noisy voice of those who seek distinction, so loudly reecho in the ears of peace and jollity, as to deafen the sound of the musick? For while we are disputing who shall lead off the dance, behold! the instrument gets out of tune—a string snaps—and where is our chance for dancing?

Adieu!

LETTER XVIII.
HARRINGTON *to* WORTHY.

BOSTON.

MY beloved has left me for a while—she has attended Mrs. *Francis* in a journey to *Rhodeisland*—and here am I —anxious—solitary—alone!—

NO thoughts, but thoughts of *Harriot,* are permitted to agitate me. She is in my view all the day long, and when I retire to rest my imagination is still possessed with ideas of *Harriot.*

Adieu!

LETTER XIX.
HARRINGTON *to* HARRIOT.

BOSTON.

IF a wish, arising from the most tender affection, could transport me to the object of my love, I persuade myself that you would not be troubled with reading this letter.

YOU must expect nothing like wit or humour, or even common sense, from me; wit and humour are flown with you, and your return only can restore them. I am sometimes willing to persuade myself that this is the case—I think I hear the well known voice, I look around me with the ecstacy of *Orpheus,* but that look breaks the charm, I find myself alone, and my *Eurydice* vanished to the shades.[1]

---

1 In the Greek legend, Orpheus descends to the underworld to rescue his wife Eurydice from death. Having charmed Hades with his musical

I HOPE you will not permit yourself to grow envious of the beauties of *Rhodeisland.* Of the force of their charms I am experimentally acquainted. Whereever fortune has thrown me, it has been my happiness to imagine myself in love with some divine creature or other; and after all it is but truth to declare that the passion was seated more in fancy than the heart; and it is justice to acknowledge to you that I am now more provident of my passion, and never suffer the excursion of fancy, except when I am so liberal as to admit the united *beauty* of the *Rhodeisland* ladies in competition with yours.

WHERE there are handsome women there will necessarily be fine gentlemen, and should they be smitten with your *external graces,* I cannot but lament their deplorable situation, when they discover how egregiously they have been cheated. What must be his disappointment, who thought himself fascinated by beauty, when he finds he has unknowingly been charmed by reason and virtue!

BUT this you will say contains a sentiment of jealousy, and is but a transcript of my apprehensions and gloomy anxieties: When will your presence, like the return of the sun in the spring, which dispels glooms, and reanimates the face of nature, quiet these apprehensions. If it be not in a short time, I shall proceed on a journey to find you out; until then I commit you to the care of your guardian angel.

LETTER XX.
HARRINGTON *to* HARRIOT.

BOSTON.

LAST night I went on a visit to your house: It was an adventure that would have done honour to the Knight of *La Mancha.*[1]

---

abilities, Orpheus is granted the right to retrieve Eurydice on the condition that he not look back to see whether she is following him. Unable to hear her steps, he looks back, causing her to remain forever among the dead.

1 Don Quixote, hero of the novel by Miguel de Cervantes, *The Ingenious Nobleman Sir Quixote of La Mancha* (Madrid, 1605 and 1615). The first English translation was published in London (1612 and 1620). By the late eighteenth century, the term "quixotic" was used as a synonym for "romantic," with a connotation of extravagant imagination. Opponents of novel reading used the term to mean someone who was lost in romance, like Cervantes's hero.

The moon ascended a clear, serene sky, the air was still, the bells sounded the solemn hour of midnight—I sighed—and the reason of it I need not tell you. This was, indeed, a pilgrimage; and no *Musselman* ever travelled barefooted to *Mecca*[1] with more sincere devotion.

YOUR absence would cause an insufferable *ennui* in your friends, were it not for the art we have in making it turn to our amusement. Instead of wishing you were of our party, you are the goddess to whose honour we perform innumerable *Heathenish* rites. Libations of wine are poured out, but not a guest presumes to taste it, until they implore the name of *Harriot;* we hail the new divinity in songs, and strew around the flowers of poetry. You need not, however, take to yourself any extraordinary addition of vanity on this occasion, as your absence will not cause any repining:

"HARRIOT, our goddess and our grief no more."

BUT to give you *my* opinion on this important matter, I must descend to plain truth, and acknowledge I had rather adore you a *present* mortal, than an *absent* divinity; and therefore wish for your return with more religious ardour than a devout disciple of the false prophet for the company of the *Houri.*[2]

THANKS to the power of imagination for one fanciful interview. Methought I somewhere unexpectedly met you—but I was soon undeceived of my imaginary happiness, and I awoke, repeating these verses:—

THOUGH sleep her sable pinions[3] spread,
    My thoughts still run on you;
And visions hovering o'er my head,
    Present you to my view.
By FANCY'S magick pencil drest,
    I saw my *Delia*[4] move;
I clasp'd her to my anxious breast,
    With tears of joy and love.

---

1 *Musselman*: Muslim; *Mecca*: a city in the Arabian Peninsula, the birthplace of the Prophet Mohammed and of Islam; also, the destination of the Hajj, an annual pilgrimage of devout Muslims.
2 Beautiful young virgins, said in the Qur'an to greet believers as they enter paradise.
3 The outer part of a bird's wing.
4 A common cognomen in the eighteenth century for a female lover, especially when addressed in song or poetry.

Methought she said—"Why thus forlorn?—
  Be all thy care resign'd:"—
I 'woke and found my *Delia* gone,
  But still the TEAR behind.[1]

LETTER XXI.
HARRIOT *to* MYRA.

RHODEISLAND.

WE arrived here in safety, but our journey is not without incident—an incident which exhibits a melancholy picture of the wickedness and depravity of the human heart.

WHEN we came to the house of Mrs. *Martin,* who, I suppose you know is cousin to Mrs. *Francis,* we were not a little astonished at the evident traces of distress in her countenance; all her actions were accompanied with an air of solemnity, and her former gaiety of heart was exchanged for sad, serious thoughtfulness: She, however, put on a face of vivacity upon our being introduced, but her cheerfulness was foreign to the feelings of her heart.

MR. *Martin* was equally agitated; he endeavoured to dispossess himself of an *uncommon* weight of remorse, but in vain—all his dissimulation could not conceal his emotion, nor his art abate the continual upbradings of conscious guilt.

MRS. *Francis* was anxious to enquire the cause of this extraordinary change, but wisely forebore adding to the distress of her friend, by desiring her to explain it, in a manner too precipitate. She was in a short time made acquainted with the particulars of the story—which is not more melancholy than uncommon.[2]

SOMETIME after the marriage of *Martin,* the beautiful *Ophelia,* sister to Mrs. *Martin,* returned from an *European* visit, to her friends in *Rhodeisland.* Upon her arrival, she received a polite offer from her brother-in-law of an elegant apartment at his house in town, which was cheerfully accepted—Fatal acceptation! He had conceived a passion for *Ophelia* and was plotting to gratify it. By

1 The poem is Brown's.

2 The story that follows closely reflects the outline of the Apthorp–Morton affair, which played out in public during the six months prior to publication of Brown's novel. Martin is Perez Morton, Mrs. Martin is Sarah Wentworth Apthorp Morton, Ophelia is Fanny Apthorp, Shepherd is James Apthorp, and Mrs. Shepherd is Sarah Wentworth Apthorp.

a series of the most artful attentions, suggested by a diabolical appetite, he insinuated himself into her affection—he prevailed upon the heart of the unsuspicious *Ophelia,* and triumphed over her innocence and virtue.

THIS incestuous connexion[1] has secretly subsisted until the present time—it was interrupted by a symptom[2] which rendered it necessary for *Ophelia* to retire into the country, where she was delivered of a child, at once the son and nephew of *Martin.*

THIS event was a severe mortification to the proud spirit of *Shepherd,* the father of *Ophelia.* His resentment to his daughter was implacable, and his revenge of the injury from *Martin* not to be satiated. The blaze of family dispute raged with unquenchable fury—and poor *Ophelia* received other punishment from the hand of a vindictive father than bare recrimination.

THE affection of *Martin* now became changed to the vilest hatred.

THUS doomed to suffer the blackest ingratitude from her seducer on the one hand, and to experience the severity of paternal vengeance on the other—and before her the gloomy prospect of a blasted reputation—what must be the situation of the hapless *Ophelia!* Hope, the last resort of the wretched, was forever shut out. There was no one whom she durst implore by the tender name of father, and he who had seduced her from her duty and her virtue, was the first to brand her with the disgraceful epithets, of undutiful and unchaste.

PERHAPS it was only at this time, that she became fully sensible of her danger; the flattery and dissimulation of *Martin* might have banished the idea of detection, and glossed over that of criminality; but now she awoke from her dream of insensibility, she was like one who had been deluded by an *ignis fatuus*[3] to the brink of a precipice, and there abandoned to his reflection to contemplate the horrours of the sea beneath him, into which he was about to plunge.

WHETHER from the promises of *Martin,* or the flattery of her own fancy, is unknown, but it is said she expected to become his wife, and made use of many expedients to obtain a divorcement of *Martin* from her sister: But this is the breath of rumour. Allowing it to be truth, it appears to be the last attempt of despair; for such

1 Incestuous because Ophelia is, in marital law, Martin's sister.

2 I.e., her pregnancy.

3 A phosphorescent light hovering over a swamp or marsh at night; used colloquially to mean an illusion that might lead one astray.

unnatural exertions, with the compunction attending them, represent a gloomy picture of the struggle between sisterly affection and declining honour. They however proved unavailable, and her efforts to that end, may with propriety be deemed a wretched subterfuge.

In the mean while the rage of *Shepherd* was augmenting. Time, instead of allaying, kindled the flame of revenge in the breast of the old man. A sense of the wounded honour of his family, became every day more exquisite; he resolved to call a meeting of the parties, in which the whole mystery should be developed—that *Ophelia* should confront her seducer, and a thorough enquiry and explication be brought about.

Ophelia exercised all her powers to prevent it; she intreated her father to consent to her desire, but her tears and intreaties were vain. To this earnest desire of his daughter, *Shepherd* opposed the honour of his family. She replied that such a procedure would publish its disgrace and be subversive of his intention: That she hoped to live retired from the world, and it was in his power to accept her happy repentance: In extenuating, she wished not to vindicate her errours, but declared herself to be penetrated with a melancholy sense of her misconduct, and hoped her penitence might expiate her guilt: She now beheld in the most glaring colours, the dangers to which she had been exposed, and acknowledged the effects of her temerity had impressed her mind with sincere contrition: All persons, continued she, are not blest with the like happiness of resisting temptation; she intreated her father, therefore, to believe her misfortunes proceeded from credulity and not from an abandoned principle—that they arose more from situation than a depraved heart: In asking to be restored to the favour and protection of a parent, she protested she was not influenced by any other motive, than a wish to demonstrate the sincerity of her repentance, and to establish the peace and harmony of the family.

Ophelia now became melancholy, and her intentions visibly bent on the *manner of her death*. As the time drew nigh, her sensibility became more exquisite: What was before distress, she now averred to be horrour: Her conduct bordered upon insanity.

The day was appointed to bring to a settlement this unhappy business—the time of hearing arrived—the parties met—the presence of *Ophelia* was necessary—she was missing—the unfortunate *Ophelia* died by her own hand.

Mrs. *Shepherd* entered the apartment of her daughter—she beheld her pale and trembling—she saw the vial, and the cup with the remains of the poison—she embraced her lost child—"My *Ophelia!* my daughter! return—return to life."

AT this crisis entered the father—he was mute—he beheld his daughter struggling with the pangs of dissolution—he was dumb with grief and astonishment.

THE dying *Ophelia* was conscious of the distress of her parents, and of her own situation—she clasped her mother's hand, and raising her eye to heaven, was only heard to articulate "LET MY CRIME BE FORGOTTEN WITH MY NAME.—O FATAL! FATAL POISON!"

ADIEU! my dear *Myra*—this unhappy affair has worked me into a fit of melancholy. I can write no more. I will give you a few particulars in my next. It is impossible to behold the effects of this horrid catastrophe and not be impressed with feelings of sympathetick sorrow.

LETTER XXII.
HARRIOT *to* MYRA.

RHODEISLAND.

HOW frail is the heart! How dim is human foresight! We behold the gilded bait of temptation, and know not until taught by experience, that the admission of one errour is but the introduction of calamity. One mistake imperceptibly leads to another—but the consequences of the whole bursting suddenly on the devoted head of an unfortunate wanderer, becomes intolerable. How acute must be that torture, which seeks an asylum in suicide! O SEDUCTION! how many and how miserable are the victims of thy unrelenting vengeance. Some crimes, indeed, cease to afflict when they cease to exist, but SEDUCTION opens the door to a dismal train of innumerable miseries.

YOU can better imagine the situation of the friends of the unfortunate *Ophelia* than I can describe it.

THE writings she left[1] were expressive of contrition for her past transaction, and an awful sense of the deed she was about to execute. Her miserable life was insupportable, there was no oblation but in death—she welcomed death, therefore, as the

1 Fanny Apthorp's letters, collectively constituting a suicide note, appeared in newspapers beginning with the first issue of the *Herald of Freedom,* 15 Sept. 1788. Harriot's letter paraphrases these closely. For the letters' full text, see Appendix A.

pleasing harbinger of relief to the unfortunate. She remembered her once loved seducer with pity, and bequeathed him her forgiveness—To say she felt no agitation was not just, but that she experienced a calmness unknown to a criminal was certain. She hoped the rashness of her conduct would not be construed to her disadvantage—for she died in charity with the world. She felt like a poor wanderer about to return to a tender parent, and flattered herself with the hopes of a welcome, though unbidden to return. She owned the way was dark and intricate, but lamented she had no friend to enlighten her understanding, or unravel the mysteries of futurity. She knew there was a God who will reward and punish: She acknowledged she had offended him, and confessed her repentance. She expatiated on the miserable life she had *suffered*, not that she feared detection, that was impossible; but that she had been doing an injury to a sister who was all kindness to her; she prayed her sister's forgiveness—even as she herself forgave her seducer; and that her crime might not be called ingratitude, because she was always sensible of her obligation to that sister. She requested her parents to pardon her, and acknowledged she felt the pangs of a bleeding heart at the shock which must be given to the most feeling of mothers. She intreated her sisters to think of her with pity, and died with assurance that her friends would so far revere her memory as to take up one thing or another, and say this belonged to poor *Ophelia*.

O MY friend! what scenes of anguish are here unfolded to the survivours. The unhappy *Shepherd* charged *Martin* with the seduction and murder of his daughter.[1] What the termination of this most horrible affair will be, is not easy to foresee.

Adieu!

---

1 Public debate in the aftermath of Fanny Apthorp's suicide centered on whether she, her father, or Morton should be held accountable for the "crime" of her suicide. A Coroner's Jury convicted her of the crime; John Adams (1735–1826) and James Bowdoin (1726–90), conducting their own inquiry by agreement of Apthorp and Morton, determined Fanny was insane when she made the decision to end her life, removing the blame from either Morton or James Apthorp and encouraging them to let the matter drop (for information on the Adams–Bowdoin inquest, see the Introduction, pp. 23–28).

LETTER XXIII.
HARRIOT *to* MYRA.

RHODEISLAND.

WHATEVER may be the other causes (if there were any besides her seduction) which drove the unhappy *Ophelia,* temerariously to end her existence, it certainly becomes us, my dear friend, to attend to them—and to draw such morals and lessons of instruction from each side of the question, as will be a mirrour by which we may regulate our conduct and amend our lives. A prudent pilot will shun those rocks upon which others have been dashed to pieces, and take example from the conduct of others less fortunate than himself: It is the duty of the moralist, then, to deduce his observations from preceding facts in such a manner as may directly improve the mind and promote the economy of human life.

THIS may be an apology for sending you the arguments of *Martin* in answer to *Shepherd,* who in his rage and grief had called him the murderer of his child.

HE reminded *Shepherd* of his obstinacy in *persisting* in an explanatory meeting, and refusing to grant *Ophelia's* request in suffering the affair to subside—"Your proud spirit," said he, "would not hearken to the gentle remonstrance of your daughter—your heart was closed to every conciliatory proposition. Though she expressed a propensity to fly from the eye of the world, she had hitherto appeared lulled in a kind of happy insensibility; yet the approaching time of explanation was terrible, it renewed the story and torture of all her misfortunes, and the idea filled her with grief and dismay. Had you been as willing to receive her, as she to return to you, happy would it have been for both; but your pride was the cause of additional calamities—when the time arrived—But why shall we harrow up our souls with the reiteration of her sorrowful exit?——

"FROM these circumstances," said *Martin,* "you cannot accuse me as the *immediate* cause of *Ophelia's* death; the facts are as I have stated them—and thus was a straying, but penitent child, driven to despair and suicide by a severe use of paternal power, and a vain attempt to resent an injury, for which it was impossible the accused party could make compensation."

NOTWITHSTANDING the plausibility of *Martin's* plea, I have little hesitation in my mind to charge him with the *remote cause* of the miserable end of *Ophelia.*[1]

HOW far parental authority may be extended, is a question which I shall not determine; I must however think it depends upon the combination of circumstances. The duty of a child to her parents will be in proportion to the attention paid to her education. If, instead of the usual pains bestowed by many partial parents, upon the vain parade of forming the manners of a child, and burthening the mind with the *necessity* of the douceurs and the graces, would it not often be happier for both, to take a small share of thought to kindle *one spark of grace* in the heart?

HAPPY the parents, who have bestowed upon their children such an education, as will enable them, by a principle of mediocrity,[2] to govern them without extorting obedience, and to reclaim them without exercising severity.

Farewel!

LETTER XXIV.
HARRIOT *to* MYRA.

RHODEISLAND.

MRS. *Francis* is not altogether satisfied with her journey to this part of the country—She does not delight to brood over sorrow—She flies from the house of mourning, to scenes of dissipation, congenial to her temper and disposition—and, like the rest of the world, bears the misfortunes of her friends with a most christian fortitude: The melancholy aspect of affairs here, will therefore shorten our visit—so you may expect us at *Boston* in a few days.

MY faithful lover (with whom I will certainly make you acquainted in a short time) continues to write to me in very passionate and sentimental strains. His last letter proves him to be a *tolerable maker of rhymes,* and I inclose it[3] for your *entertainment.*

I am, my dear,

Your most affectionate Friend.

---

1 I.e., Harriot holds Martin at least partially responsible (a "remote" if not the "immediate" cause) for Ophelia's death.

2 Moderation.

3 [Brown's note:] See Letter XX.

LETTER XXV.
MYRA *to* HARRIOT.

(*Written before she had received the preceding.*)

BOSTON.

YOUR sorrowful little history has infected me with grief. Surely there is no human vice of so black a die—so fatal in its consequences—or which causes a more general calamity, than that of *seducing* a female, from the path of honour. This idea has been improved by my brother, on the hint of your favour—as an acknowledgment for which I inclose you his production.

[The Inclosed.]
The Court of Vice.
An APOLOGUE.[1]

VICE "on a solemn night of state,
In all her pomp of terrour sate,"[2]
Her voice in deep, tremendous tone,
Thus issu'd from her ebon throne:
"This night at our infernal court,
Let all our ministers resort;
Who most annoys the human race,
At our right hand shall take his place,
Rais'd on a throne—advanc'd in fame—
Ye crimes now vindicate your claim."

Eager for praise, the hideous host,
All spake, aspiring to the post.

---

1 I.e., a moral fable. The poem is Brown's. Preceding the novel's publication by a few weeks, this poem appeared in the *Herald of Freedom*, 23 Jan. 1789.

2 Lines qtd. from John Gay's poem "The Court of Death," included in his book *The Fables* (1727). See p. 100, note 1, above. Brown models his poem (supposed to be Harrington's in the novel) closely on Gay's, responding to the original's survey of causes of death with a survey of vicious behavior. Gay takes aim at intemperance—unrestrained drinking—as the most notorious cause of death; Brown makes seduction the most notorious vice.

PRIDE said, to gain his private ends,
He sacrific'd his dearest friends;
Insulted all with manners rude,
And introduc'd ingratitude.
'Twas he infus'd *domestick* hate,
And party spirit in the *state;*
Hop'd they'd observe his mystick plan,
Destroy'd all confidence in man;
And justify'd his high pretentions,
By causing envy and dissentions.

INTEMP'RANCE loud, demands the place,
He'd long deceiv'd the human race;
None could such right as he maintain,
Disease and death were in his train.

THEFT next appears to claim the station,
E'er constant in his dark vocation;
He thought the place might well repay,
The *crime* who labour'd night and day.

FRAUD own'd (tho' loth to speak his praise)
He gain'd his point by secret ways;
His voice in cities had been heard,
And oft in senates been preferr'd!
Yet much derision had he borne,
Treated by honest fools with scorn;
His influence on the western shore
Was not so great as heretofore:
He own'd each side alike assail'd,
Complain'd how sadly he was rail'd,
Curst by the name in ev'ry street,
Of Paper, Tendry, Rogue and Cheat:
Yet if some honour should requite
His labour—things might still go right.

MURDER before the footstool stood,
With tatter'd robe distain'd in blood.
"And who," he cry'd, with daring face,
"Denies my title to the place?
My watchful eyes mankind survey,
And single out the midnight prey;
Not cowardlike I meet the foe,

With footsteps insecure and slow,
Or cause his death by languid strife—
Boldly this dagger ends his life.
Give back, ye crimes, your claims resign,
For I demand the post as mine."

AV'RICE declar'd his love of gold;
His nation, or himself he sold;
He taught the sin of PRIDE betimes;
Was foster-father of all *crimes:*
He pawn'd his life; he stak'd his soul,
And found employment for the whole:
Acknowledg'd that he gain'd his wealth,
By FRAUD, by MURDER and by STEALTH:
On one so useful in her cause,
VICE well might lavish due applause.

The hagger'd host bow low the head,
The *Monster* rose, and thus she said:
"Ye *ministers* of VICE, draw near,
For fame no longer persevere;
No more your various parts disclose,
Men *see, and hate you all as foes.*
One yet remains among your crew,
Then rise, SEDUCTION! claim your due.
Your baleful presence quickly parts
The tie that holds the happiest hearts;
You *rob*—what *wealth* can ne'er repay;
Like *Judas* with a kiss *betray:*[1]
Hence come the starving, trembling train,
Who prostitute themselves for gain,
Whose languid visages impart
A smile, while anguish knaws the heart;
Whose steps decoy unwary youth,
From honour, honesty, and truth,
Which follow'd 'till too late to mend,
In ruin, and the gallows end—
Be thine the post. Besides, who knows
Where all thy consequences close?

---

1 Jesus' apostle Judas betrayed him to soldiers by marking him with a kiss in public. Used generally to denote betrayal by one who pretends to be a friend.

With thee, SEDUCTION! are ally'd
HORROUR, DESPAIR and SUICIDE.
YOU wound—but the *devoted* heart
Feels not alone—the poignant smart:
YOU wound—th' electrick pain extends
To fathers, mothers, sisters, friends.
MURDER may yet delight in blood,
And deluge round the crimson flood;
But sure his merits rank above,
Who murders in the mask of love."

LETTER XXVI.
MYRA *to Mrs.* HOLMES.

BOSTON.

IN one of my former letters I acquainted you that I suspected my brother to be in love, and now, Madam, I am enabled to tell you with whom—the amiable *Harriot.*

HARRIOT attended Mrs. *Francis* in her journey to *Rhodeisland,* and our young hero has, in her absence, been dreaming of his mistress; and, in a letter to her has written a description of his visionary interview. *Harriot,* with whom I maintain a constant correspondence, and who keeps no secret from me, inclosed the verses in her last, when lo! the hand writing of Master *Harrington.*

I WAS a little mortified that the young man had kept me in ignorance of his amour all this time, and this morning determined upon a little innocent revenge—*"Tommy,"* said I, as he entered the room, "here is a piece of poetry, written by an acquaintance of mine—I want your judgment on it"—"Poetry or rhyme," answered he, advancing towards me, and casting his eye on it—He took the letter and began to read——"Why do you blush, young man?" said I, *"Harriot* is a fine girl."——

THIS produced an *eclaircissement,*[1] and as the matter must remain secret, for a certain weighty reason, I am to be the *confidante.*

I MUST acknowledge to you, Mrs. *Holmes,* there is a certain *je ne sçais quoi*[2] in my amiable friend, that has always interested

1 A clarifying explanation of something that had previously been inexplicable.

2 French, "I can't say what": an indescribable but attractive quality.

me in her favour—I have an affection for her which comes from the heart—an affection which I do not pretend to account for—Her dependance[1] on Mrs. *Francis* hurts me—I do not think this lady is the gentle, complaisant being, that she appears to be in company—To behold so fine a girl in so disagreeable a situation, might at first attract my commiseration and esteem, and a more intimate knowledge of her virtues might have ripened them into love. Certain it is, however, that whom I admire as a friend, I could love as a sister. In the feelings of the heart there can be no dissimulation.

PLEASE to tell Mr. *Worthy,* he may continue to write, and that I will condescend to read his letters.

Farewel!

LETTER XXVII.
WORTHY *to* MYRA.

BELLEVIEW.

I AM just returned from a melancholy excursion with *Eliza.* I will give you the history of it—We generally walk out together, but we this time went further than usual—The morning was calm and serene—all Nature was flourishing, and its universal harmony conspired to deceive us in the length of the way.

While we were pursuing our walk, our ears were struck with a plaintive, musical voice, singing a melancholy tune.—"This," said Mrs. *Holmes,* "must be *Fidelia. The* poor distracted girl was carried off by a ruffian a few days before her intended marriage, and her lover, in despair, threw himself into the river"—*Eliza* could say no more—for *Fidelia* resumed her melancholy strain in the following words:—[2]

TALL rose the lily's slender frame,
It shed a glad perfume;
But ah! the cruel spoiler came,
And nipt its opening bloom.
Curse on the cruel spoiler's hand
That stole thy bloom and fled—
Curse on his hand—for thy true love

1 I.e., financial dependence.
2 Brown's original poem.

Is number'd with the dead.
Poor maiden! like the lily frail,
'Twas all in vain you strove;
You heard the stranger's tender tale—
But where was thy true love?
Thou wast unkind and false to him,
But he did constant prove;
He plunged headlong in the stream—
Farewel, farewel, my love!
'Twas where the river rolls along,
The youth all trembling stood,
Opprest with grief—he cast himself
Amidst the cruel flood.
White o'er his head the billows foam,
And circling eddies move;
Ah! there he finds a watery tomb—
Farewel, farewel, my love!

WE advanced towards the place from whence the sound issued, and *Fidelia,* who heard our approach, immediately rose from the ground; "I was tired," said she, "and sat down here to rest myself."

SHE was dressed in a long white robe, tied about the waist with a pink ribband; her fine brown hair flowed loosely round her shoulders—In her hand she held a number of wild flowers and weeds, which she had been gathering. "These," she cried, "are to make a nosegay for my love." "He hath no occasion for it," said *Eliza.* "Yes! where he lives," cried *Fidelia,* "there are plenty—and flowers that never fade too—I will throw them into the river, and they will swim to him—they will go straight to him"—"And what will he do with them?" I asked. "O!" said the poor girl as she looked wistfully on them, and sorted them in her hand, "he loves every thing that comes from me—he told me so"—"He will be happy to receive them," cried *Eliza*—"Where he is," said *Fidelia,* "is happiness—and happy are the flowers that bloom there—and happy shall I be, when I go to him—alas! I am very ill now"—"He will love you again," said *Eliza,* "when you find him out"—"O he was very kind," cried she, tenderly, "he delighted to walk with me over all these fields—but now, I am obliged to walk alone." *Fidelia* drew her hand across her cheek, and we wept with her.—"I must go," she said, "I must go," and turned abruptly from us, and left us with great precipitation.

Farewel!

LETTER XXVIII.
WORTHY *to* MYRA.

BELLEVIEW.

MY melancholy meditations led me yesterday to the same place where I had seen the distracted *Fidelia*, and walking down the hill I again beheld her by the side of a beautiful spring—Before I could come up to the place, she was gone—she went hastily over the field—I followed her—after a few minutes walk, I overtook her, and we both went on together towards a small, neat, farm house. An old man was sitting at the door—he gave a sigh as she passed by him to go in—I asked him if she was his daughter—"Alas!" said he, "my poor child—she has been in this state of affliction for near a twelve month." I inquired what cause produced the loss of her senses—He looked down sorrowfully—the question awakened the gloomy sensations of past evils, the recollection of which was painful, and opened wounds afresh that were not yet healed. "She has lost her lover," cried the old man—"the youth was the son of one of our neighbours—their infancy was marked by a peculiar attachment to each other. When the young people danced together, *Fidelia* was always the partner of *Henry*—as they grew up their mutual tenderness ripened into passionate affection. They were engaged to each other, and *Henry* saved all his little stock of money to begin the world by himself. All the town beheld them with pleasure—they wished them success and happiness—and from their knowledge of both their characters, were led to hope they would one day become good members of society—but these hopes are blasted, and they now bestow the bitterest curses on the wretch who hath crushed their expectations—who hath deprived *Fidelia* of her senses, and caused the death of her lover.

"The gay *Williams* comes among us, and participates in our domestick pastimes—he singles out *Fidelia,* and is assiduous in his attentions to her—her little heart is lifted up—but her prudence rises superiour to her vanity. *Henry* observes the operations of *Williams* and thinks he sees in him a powerful rival—the unhappy youth becomes melancholy—he sickens with jealousy—the pleasures of our country are forgotten by him—his thoughts are continually employed on his *Fidelia.*—To complete the measure of his promised happiness he wishes to call her his own—he declares the desire of his soul—*Fidelia* pledges her faith. He now sees the accomplishment of all his wishes in reversion—his heart leaps for joy—but—as the little paraphernalia is preparing, the ruffian hand of the Seducer dashes the cup of joy from their lips—*Fidelia* suddenly disappears—*Williams*—the ungrateful *Williams*—betrays her to a carriage he had prepared, and she is hurried off. *Henry* stands astonished—wild with grief and dismay, he appears senseless and confounded.

"WHEN the heart is elevated by strong expectation—disappointment and misfortune come with redoubled force—To receive pain, when we look for pleasure, penetrates the very soul with accumulated anguish."

THE old man paused—He endeavoured to hide a tear that was stealing down his cheek—and to check the violence of his passion.

I ASKED him how long his daughter was missing—"Not long," he answered—"the young men, enraged at the insult, arm themselves and pursue the robber—they overtake him—*Williams* is wounded in the scuffle, and is carried away bleeding, by his servant—My daughter is regained—we thank Heaven for her restoration. She enquires for her *Henry*—alas! *Henry* is no more! The object of his love had flown from him, and with her, all the light of his soul—Darkness and grief had encompassed him—he had no resource, no consolation, no hope—she whom his soul loved was stolen—was wrested from his embrace. Who was there to administer relief?—Who was there to supply her loss?—Not one.—The light of his reason now became clouded—he is seized by despair, and urged forward by the torments of disappointed love, he plunges into the river—to close his sorrows with his life.

"THE loss of *Fidelia's* senses followed this tragical event.

"SHE hears the fate of her lover and becomes petrified—the idea of her sorrows—her own agitation and care for her person, are lost in the reflection of her lover's death.—A while she raved—but is now somewhat restored, and, as you see, the poor maniack strays about the fields harmless and inoffensive."

THE old man proceeded to inform me of the death of his wife—the idea of one misfortune aroused in him that of another—or rather there was a gradual progression in them, and consequently a connexion—He told me she did not long survive the death of *Henry*. "O *Charlotte!*" he cried, "thou wast kind and cheerful—very pleasant hast thou been unto me. I will not cease to regret thy loss, till I meet thee in a better world."

"OUR hearts," continued the old man, addressing me, "are loosened from their attachment to this world by repeated strokes of misfortune. Wisely is it ordered thus. Every calamity severs a string from the heart—until one scene of sorrow on the back of another, matures us for eternity—Thus are our affections estranged from this scene of misery. The cord that detains the bird is severed in two—and it flies away.

"FORMERLY as I sat in this place—in the mild shade of the evening—when I had returned from my labour and took *Fidelia* on my knee, how often have I rendered thanks to Heaven for the happiness I enjoyed, and implored his power to make my child such another as *Charlotte*—This sweet remembrance yet swells and agitates my heart, and in the midst of the distress which surrounds me, I feel a consolation in tracing to you a feeble sketch of the happy times that are passed."

THE old man was sensibly affected—he delighted to dwell on what his child had been—he thought of those times—and he sighed when he contrasted them with the present.

"IN her disordered state," continued he, "she knows me not as a father—I spread my morsel before her, and she flies from it—she forgets the sound of my voice—she is no longer unto me as a daughter. She who hath so often said, she would support me with her arm, and lead me about, when I should be old and decriped[1]—to her I call, but she returns me no answer. Is not the cause of my woe, a melancholy instance of the baleful art of the SEDUCER?—She is deprived of her reason, and knows not the weight of her misery; and I am doubly burdened with her affliction, and the accumulated misfortune of immature decripitude."

"SEDUCTION is a crime," I observed, "that nothing can be said to palliate or excuse."

"AND woe to him," added the old man, "who shall endeavour to extenuate it—*They have taken away my staff"*—continued he, raising a look of imploring mercy to Heaven, while a trembling tear rolled from his swollen eye, *"They have taken away my staff in my old age."*

FREELY did my heart share in the sorrows of the good old man—when I left him, I prayed Heaven to compassionate his distress—and as I bent my pensive step towards *Belleview,* I had leisure to animadvert on the fatal tendency of SEDUCTION.

Adieu!

END OF VOL. I.

---

1 Decrepit.

THE
POWER of SYMPATHY, *&c.*

LETTER XXIX.
Mrs. HOLMES *to* MYRA.

BELLEVIEW.

I AM sometimes mortified to find the books which I recommend to your perusal, are not always applicable to the situation of an *American* lady. The general observations of some *English* books are the most useful things contained in them; the principal parts being chiefly filled with local descriptions, which a young woman here is frequently at a loss to understand.

I send you a little work, entitled *"A Lady of Quality's Advice to her Children"*[1] which, though not altogether free from this exception, is highly worthy of your attention. A parent who is represented struggling with the distress of a lingering illness, bequeaths a system of education to her offspring. I do not recommend it to you as a Novel, but as a work that speaks the language of the heart and that inculcates the duty we owe to ourselves, to society and the Deity.

DIDACTICK essays are not always capable of engaging the attention of young ladies. We fly from the laboured precepts of the essayist, to the sprightly narrative of the novelist. Habituate your mind to remark the difference between truth and fiction. You will then always be enabled to judge of the propriety and justness of a thought; and never be misled to form wrong opinions, by the meretricious *dress* of a pleasing tale. You will then be capable of deducing the most profitable lessons of instruction, and the design of your *reading* will be fully accomplished.——

HENCE you will be provided with a key to the characters of men: To unlock these curious cabinets is a very useful, as well as entertaining employment. Of those insidious gentlemen, who

1 Generally attributed to Marquis Louis-Antoine Caraccioli (1721–1803), a prolific French author of didactic religious literature, *Advice from a Lady of Quality to Her Children, in the Last Stage of a Lingering Illness* was published in France in 1769 and translated into English by Samuel Glasse, with multiple editions in London and Boston beginning in 1778.

plan their advances towards us on the *Chesterfieldian* system,[1] let me advise you to beware. A prudent commander would place a double watch, if he apprehended the enemy were more disposed to take the fort by secresy and undermining, than by an open assault.

I CANNOT but smile sometimes, to observe the ridiculous figure of some of our young gentlemen, who affect to square their conduct by his Lordship's principles of politeness—they never tell a story unless it be very short—they talk of decorum and the *etiquette*—they detest every thing vulgar or common—they are on the rack if an old man should let fall a proverb—and a thousand more trifling affectations, the ridicule of which arises, not so much from their putting on this foreign dress, as from their ignorance or vanity in pretending to imitate those rules which were designed for an English nobleman—Unless, therefore, they have a prospect of being called by Congress to execute some foreign negociation, they ought certainly to be minding their business.

THIS affectation of fine breeding is destructive to morals. Dissimulation and insincerity are connected with its tenets; and are mutually inculcated with the art of pleasing.

A PERSON of this character grounds his motives for pleasing on the most selfish principle—He is polite, not for the honour of obliging you, as he endeavours to make you believe, but that he himself might be obliged. Suspect him, therefore, of insincerity and treachery, who sacrifices truth to complaisance, and advises you to the pursuit of an object, which would tend to his advantage.

ALWAYS distinguish the man of sense from the coxcomb. Mr. *Worthy* is possessed of a good understanding, and an exact judgment. If you are united with him, let it be the study of your life to preserve his love and esteem. His amiable character is adorned with modesty and a disposition to virtue and sobriety. I never anticipate your future happiness, but I contemplate this part of his character with pleasure. But remember the fidelity of a wife alone,

---

1 Philip Dormer Stanhope, 4th Earl of Chesterfield (1694–1773), popularly known as Lord Chesterfield, author of the posthumously published *Letters to His Son on the Art of Becoming a Man of the World and a Gentleman* (London, 1774). The book was extraordinarily popular—if controversial—on both sides of the Atlantic. Critics of the "Chesterfieldian system" pointed to his endorsement of flattery, insincerity, and even dissimulation as avenues to social success and also to his demeaning comments on women in general, whom he portrays as generally susceptible to flattery and seduction (see the Introduction, pp. 32–33).

will not always secure the esteem of a husband; when her personal attractions do not continue to delight his eye, she will flatter his judgment. I think you are enabled to perform this, because you are solicitous to supply your mind with those amiable qualities which are more durable than beauty. When you are no longer surrounded with a flattering circle of young men, and the world shall cease to call you beautiful, your company will be courted by men of sense, who know the value of your conversation.

I AM pleased with the conduct of some agreeable girls, and the return of civility and attention they often make to the conceited compliments of a certain class of beaux. These ladies wisely consider them as the butterflies of a day, and therefore generally scorn *to break them on a wheel!*[1]

WHEN you are in company, where the vain and thoughtless endeavour to shew their ingenuity by ridiculing particular orders of men, your prudence will dictate to you not to countenance their abuse—The book I have just mentioned, intimates, that "there are a great many things done and said in company which a woman of virtue will neither see nor hear."[2]—To discountenance levity, is a sure way to guard against the encroachment of temptation; to participate in the mirth of a buffoon, is to render yourself equally ridiculous. We owe to ourselves a *detestation* of folly, and to the world, the appearance of it. I would have you avoid coquetry and affectation, and the observance of my maxims will never make you a prude—Pretend, therefore, should a vain youth throw out illiberal sarcasms against Mechanicks, Lawyers, Ministers, Virtue, Religion, or any serious subject, not to comprehend the point of his wit.

I HAVE seldom spoken to you on the importance of Religion, and the veneration due to the characters of the Clergy. I always supposed your good sense capable of suggesting their necessity and eligibility. The Ministers of no nation are more remarkable for learning and piety than those of this country. The fool may pretend to scorn, and the irreligious to contemn, but every person of sense and reflection must admire that sacred order, whose business is to inform the understanding, and regulate the passions of mankind. Surely, therefore, that class of men, will continue to merit our esteem and affection, while virtue remains upon earth.

---

1 I.e., they are too delicate to be worth "breaking" or training.

2 A loose paraphrase of a passage from "Conference X" in *Advice from a Lady of Quality to Her Children,* in which women are encouraged to be silent and modest in the face of unseemly behavior in company.

I AM always pleased with the reasonable and amiable light in which the Clergy are placed by the author of the *Guardian*[1]—"The light," says he, "in which these points should be exposed to the view of one who is prejudiced against the names, *Religion, Church, Priest,* or the like, is to consider the Clergy as so many Philosophers, the Churches as Schools, and their Sermons as Lectures for the improvement and information of the audience. How would the heart of *Tully*[2] or *Socrates*[3] have rejoiced, had they lived in a nation where the law had made provision for philosophers to read lectures of philosophy, every seventh day, in several thousands of schools, erected at the publick charge, throughout the whole country, at which lectures, all ranks and sexes, without distinction, were obliged to be present, for their general improvement?"

YOU may, perhaps, think this letter too serious, but remember that virtue and religion are the foundation of education.

Adieu!

LETTER XXX.
Mrs. HOLMES *to* MYRA.

BELLEVIEW.

YOU will observe, my dear friend, that most of the letters I have written to you of late, on female education, are confined to the subject of study. I am sensible of the ridicule sometimes levelled at those who are called learned ladies. Either these ladies must be uncommonly pedantick, or those who ridicule them, uncommonly ignorant—Do not be apprehensive of acquiring that title, or sharing the ridicule, but remember that the knowledge which I wish you to acquire, is necessary to adorn your many virtues and amiable qualifications. This ridicule[4] is evidently a *transatlantick* idea, and must have been imbibed from the source of some *English* Novel or Magazine—The *American* ladies of this class, who come within our knowledge, we know to be justly celebrated

1 *The Guardian*, Richard Steele's successor periodical to *The Spectator*, no. 130, Mon. 10 Aug. 1713. In a modern edition, see J.C. Stephens 433.

2 Roman statesman and orator Marcus Tullius Cicero (106–43 BCE).

3 The famous Greek philosopher (470–399 BCE).

4 I.e., the ridicule of female education, which Mrs. Holmes attributes to England, not America.

as ornaments to society, and an honour to the sex. When it is considered how many of our countrywomen are capable of the task, it is a matter of regret that *American* literature boasts so few productions from the pens of the ladies.

SELF complacency is a most necessary acquirement—for the value of a woman will always be commensurate to the opinion she entertains of herself. A celebrated *European* wit, in a letter to a lady, concenters much good advice in one short rule of conduct: "REVERENCE THYSELF."[1]

I was this morning reading *Swift's* letter to a very young lady, on her marriage.[2] Although this famous writer is not celebrated for delicacy or respect towards us, yet I wish some of his observations contained less truth—If you are in company, says this writer, when the conversation turns on the manners and customs of remote nations, or on books in verse or prose, or on the nature and limits of virtue and vice, it is a shame for a lady not to relish such discourses, not to improve by them, and endeavour by reading and information, to have her share in those entertainments, rather than turn aside, as is the usual custom, and consult with the woman who sits next her, about a new cargo of fans.

HE then descends to particulars, and insists on the necessity of orthography. Is it not a little hard, continues he, that not one gentleman's daughter in a thousand should be brought to read or understand her own natural tongue, or be judge of the easiest books that are written in it; as any one may find, who can have the patience to hear them mangle a Play or a Novel?

IF there be any of your acquaintance to whom this passage is applicable, I hope you will recommend the study of Mr. *Webster's* Grammatical Institute,[3] as the best work in our language to facilitate the knowledge of Grammar. I cannot but think Mr. *Webster* intended his valuable book for the benefit of his countrywomen: For while he delivers his *rules* in a pure, precise, and elegant style,

---

1 Laurence Sterne, *Letters from Yorick to Eliza* (London, 1775), Letter X. These were letters, published after Sterne's death, to a married friend, Eliza Draper. His *Journal to Eliza* was published in 1904, after more of the correspondence came to light. Sterne's narrator mentions Eliza in his *Sentimental Journey*.

2 Jonathan Swift, "A Letter to a Young Lady, on Her Marriage," *Miscellanies in Prose and Verse*, vol. 2 (London, 1727), was frequently reprinted throughout the eighteenth century.

3 Noah Webster, *A Grammatical Institute, of the English Language, Comprising an Easy, Concise, and Systematic Method of Education, Designed for the Use of English Schools in America* (Hartford, 1784).

he *explains* his meaning by *examples* which are calculated to inspire the female mind with a thirst for emulation, and a desire of virtue.

NO subject has been more exhausted than that of education. Many *Utopian* schemes have been delineated, and much speculation employed. When I peruse these labours, and am persuaded the intention of their authors is to promote our welfare, I feel myself prompted to a prudent and amiable demeanour; and I suppose every woman of reason and reflection feels the same inclination to virtue, and the same sensations of gratitude, in reading the works of those writers, the characteristicks of whom, are sentiment, morality and benevolence.

WHAT books do you read, my dear? We are now finishing *Barlow's* Vision of *Columbus,*[1] and shall begin upon *Dwight's* Conquest of *Canaan*[2] in a few days. It is very agreeable to read with one, who points out the beauties of the author as we proceed. Such an one is *Worthy.*—Sometimes Mr. *Holmes* makes one of our party, and his notes and references to the ancient poets are very entertaining. *Worthy* is delighted with the ease and freedom with which we live here. We have little concerts, we walk, we ride, we read, we have good company—this is *Belleview* in all its glory!

ADIEU, my dear—I shall continue this subject no longer, though I flatter myself you would receive my hints with satisfaction, because you must be persuaded I love you, and so interest myself in your welfare—I need not add that I think your conduct worthy of you. You are such a good girl that I know not in what to direct you; for you leave me no room for advice—continue to anticipate the desires of my heart, and to secure the high opinion you have there obtained.

YOUR friend forever!

---

1 Joel Barlow, *The Vision of Columbus: A Poem in Nine Books* (Hartford, 1787).

2 Timothy Dwight, *The Conquest of Canaan: A Poem in Eleven Books* (Hartford, 1785).

LETTER XXXI.
Mrs. HOLMES *to* MYRA.

BELLEVIEW.

IF the affair of your brother and *Harriot* be serious, and matrimony is really on the tapis,[1] do not fail to make me *previously* acquainted with it——I very much doubt the evidence of the verses—they weigh little in my mind—and he is easily excused for sending them to so fine a girl, as *Harriot.*

YOUR observations on her dependence on Mrs. *Francis* do honour to your heart—virtue does not consist in affluence and independence—nor can it be reflected on us by the glory of our connexions—those who pride themselves on it, make but an indifferent figure; for in the estimation of all sensible people—true merit is personal.

HOWEVER, my dear friend, as one who wishes for your welfare and the happiness of your family, I advise you to discourage the proposed connexion—and if you cannot undertake this disagreeable task with a *certainty of success,* do not fail to acquaint me of it *speedily.*

Adieu!

LETTER XXXII.
HARRINGTON *to* WORTHY.

BOSTON.

What ails my heart? I feel a void here—and yet I verge towards my happiness—for a few days makes *Harriot* mine—*Myra* says I had *better not marry her.* What could prompt her to use such an expression? *Better not marry her.* She has repeated it several times—and with too much eagerness—I give no heed to it—and yet why should it affect me in this manner? Is it an artifice to fathom the depth of my love? Such schemes are my utter aversion—it disturbs me—I hate such artifice—You cannot imagine how it touches my heart.

Adieu!

1 On the carpet, or under discussion.

LETTER XXXIII.
Mrs. HOLMES *to* MYRA.

BELLEVIEW.

IT is the duty of friends to be interested in all the concerns of one another—to join in their joys and to avert the stroke of danger. It is the duty of a centinel to give the alarm at the approach of what he may think such—and if the result does not prove to be a real evil—he has but performed his duty, and the action is meritorious.

IF your exertions to countermine the connexion of your brother with *Harriot* should prove ineffectual (and do not fail to acquaint me with it either way) I HAVE A TALE TO UNFOLD which may possibly forbid the bans.[1]

LETTER XXXIV.
HARRINGTON *to* WORTHY.

BOSTON.

I FIND my temper grow extremely irritable—my sensibility is wounded at the slightest neglect—I am very tenacious of every thing, and of every body.

A PARTY was made yesterday to go on the water; I was omitted, and the neglect hurt me. I inquired the cause, and what think you is the answer? "I am no company—I am asked a question and return nothing to the point—I am absent—I am strangely altered within a few days—I am thinking of a different subject when I ought to be employed in conversation—I am extravagant in my observations—I am no company."

THEY would persuade me that I am little better than a mad man—I have no patience with their nonsensical replies—Such wiseacres do not deserve my pity.

Farewel!

1 Public notice of a contract; marriage banns were the public announcement of an engagement.

LETTER XXXV.
MYRA *to Mrs.* HOLMES.

BOSTON.

YOUR letter is filled with such ambiguous expressions, that I am utterly at a loss to discover your meaning.

I HAVE, however, sounded him on the article of marriage, and the result is—he loves *Harriot* most passionately—and on account of my father's aversion to early marriages, will marry her privately in a few days.

THE oftener I read your letter, the more I am perplexed and astonished: "YOU HAVE A TALE TO UNFOLD"—For Heaven's sake then unfold it, before it be too late—and as you dread the consequence of keeping it secret, by disclosing it to me, you will prevent the mischief, you so much deprecate——I am all impatience.

Adieu!

LETTER XXXVI.
HARRINGTON *to* WORTHY.

BOSTON.

I HAVE just left *Harriot*—but how have I left her? In tears. I wish I had not gone. Mrs. *Francis* had intrusted *Harriot* with some trifling commission—It was not done—she had not had time to perform it. *Harriot* was reprimanded—Yes! by Heaven—this Mrs. *Francis* had the insolence to reprimand *Harriot* in my presence—I was mortified—I walked to the window—my heart was on fire—my blood boiled in my veins—it is impossible to form an idea of the disorder of my nerves—*Harriot's* were equally agitated—Mrs. *Francis* saw our confusion and retired—she left me so completely out of temper that I was forced to follow her example. I kissed away the tear from the cheek of *Harriot* and withdrew to my chamber.

HERE let me forget what has passed—my irritability will not permit it—my feelings are too easily set in motion to enjoy long quietness—my nerves are delicately strung; they are now out of tune, and it is a hard matter to harmonize them.

I FEEL that I have a soul—and every man of sensibility feels it within himself. I will relate a circumstance I met with in my late travels through *Southcarolina*—I was always susceptible of *touches of nature.*

I HAD often remarked a female slave pass by my window to a spring to fetch water. She had something in her air superiour to those of her situation—a fire that the damps of slavery had not extinguished.

As I was one day, walking behind her, the wind blew her tattered handkerchief from her neck and exposed it to my sight—I asked her the cause of the scar on her shoulder—She answered composedly, and with an earnestness that proved she was not ashamed to declare it—"It is the mark of the whip," said she, and went on with the history of it, without my desiring her to proceed—"my boy, of about ten years old, was unlucky enough to break a glass tumbler—this crime was immediately inquired into—I trembled for the fate of my child, and was thought to be guilty. I did not deny the charge, and was tied up. My former good character availed nothing. Under every affliction, we may receive consolation; and during the smart of the whip, I rejoiced—because I shielded with my body the lash from my child; and I rendered thanks to the best of beings that I was allowed to suffer for him."

"Heroically spoken!" said I, "may he whom you call the best of beings continue you in the same sentiments—may thy soul be ever disposed to sympathize with thy children, and with thy brethren and sisters in calamity—then shalt thou feel every circumstance of thy life afford thee satisfaction; and repining and melancholy shall fly from thy bosom—all thy labours will become easy—all thy burdens light, and the yoke of slavery will never gall thy neck."

I WAS sensibly relieved as I pronounced these words, and I felt my heart glow with feelings of exquisite delight, as I anticipated the happy time when the sighs of the slave shall no longer expire in the air of freedom. What delightful sensations are those in which the heart is interested! In which it stoops to enter into the little concerns of the most remote ramification of Nature! Let the vain, the giddy, and the proud pass on without deigning to notice them—let them cheat themselves of happiness—these are circumstances which are important only to a sentimental traveller.

HAIL *Sensibility!* Sweetener of the joys of life! Heaven has implanted thee in the breasts of his children—to soothe the sorrows of the afflicted—to mitigate the wounds of the stranger who falleth in our way. *Thou* regardest with an eye of pity, those whom *wealth* and *ambition* treat in terms of reproach. Away, ye seekers of power—ye boasters of wealth—ye are the *Levite* and the *Pharisee,* who restrain the hand of charity from the indigent, and turn with indignation from the wayworn son of misery:—But *Sensibility* is the good *Samaritan*,[1] who taketh him by the hand, and consoleth him, and poureth wine and oil into his wounds. Thou art a pleasant companion—a grateful friend—and a *neighbour* to those who are destitute of shelter.——

From thee! Author of Nature! from thee, thou inexhaustible spring of love supreme, floweth this tide of affection and sympathy—thou whose tender care extendeth to the least of thy creation—and whose eye is not inattentive even though a sparrow fall to the ground.

LETTER XXXVII.
Mrs. HOLMES *to* MYRA.

BELLEVIEW, *12 o'clock at night.*

I CANNOT rest—this affair lies so heavy on my mind, that sleep flies from my eye-lids. Your brother *must* discontinue his addresses to *Harriot*——with what should I not have to upbraid myself, if, through my remissness—your brother marries his sister!

GREAT God! of what materials hast thou compounded the hearts of thy creatures! admire, O my friend! the operation of NATURE—and the power of SYMPATHY!

HARRIOT IS YOUR SISTER! I dispatch the bearer at this late hour to confide in your bosom the important secret.

Adieu!

LETTER XXXVIII.
MYRA *to Mrs.* HOLMES.

BOSTON.

ACCEPT my warmest acknowledgment, my good friend, for your kindness—Your letter sufficiently explains your former anxiety—it has removed all ambiguities.

YOUR servant entered hastily with the letter—and gave it me

1 In the Parable of the Good Samaritan (Luke 10:25–37), Jesus describes a traveler beaten and left to die who is passed over by various religious figures—a Levite and a Pharisee—before being assisted by a Samaritan. Because Samaritans and Jews generally held one another in antipathy, his benevolence is especially pronounced.

with evident tokens of its containing a matter of importance.—My father was present—I broke it open, not without agitation—I read it—but the shock was too severe—it fell from my hands, and I sunk into the chair.

My fainting was not of any duration. I opened my eyes and found my father supporting me—but the idea of *Harriot* was still engraven deeply in my heart—I inquired for my sister—the tear rolled down his cheek—it was a sufficient answer to my inquiry—He said nothing—there was no necessity of his saying a word.

Could I ask him to explain your letter? No—my heart anticipated his feelings—the impropriety struck me at once. *"You have a tale to unfold."* Do not delay to unfold it.

Adieu!

LETTER XXXIX.
Mrs. HOLMES *to* MYRA.

BELLEVIEW.

I readily undertake to give you a sketch of the history of *Harriot*. Her mother's name was *Maria Fawcet;* her person I yet recollect, and forgive me if I drop a tear of pity at the recital of her misfortunes.

My mother and Mrs. *Holmes* were remarkable friends, and the intimacy, you know, was maintained between the two families. I was on a visit with my mother when the destiny of *Maria* led her to *Belleview*. I was frequently there during her illness—and was with her in her last moments.

It was the custom of Mrs. *Holmes* to walk in the garden towards the close of the day. She was once indulging her usual walk, when she was alarmed by the complaints of a woman which came from the road. Pity and humanity were ever peculiar characteristicks of my amiable parent—She hastened to the place from whence the sound issued, and beheld a young woman, bathed in tears, sitting upon the ground. She inquired the cause of her distress, with that eager solicitude to relieve, which a sight so uncommon would naturally occasion. It was sometime before the distressed woman could return an intelligible answer, and then she with difficulty proceeded: "Your goodness, Madam, is unmerited—you behold a stranger, without home—without friends—and whose misery bears her down to an untimely grave—Life, truly is a blessing—but my life is become burthensome, and were the Almighty this moment to command me to the world of spirits, methinks I could gladly obey the summons, and rejoice in the stroke which bade me depart from sorrow and the world." "Moderate your grief, my dear woman, repine not at the will of Providence, nor suffer yourself to despair, however severe your misfortunes."[1]

THE unfortunate woman was at length prevailed on to accompany Mrs. *Holmes* into the house, she partook of some refreshment and retired to sleep. In a few days she appeared to be better; but it was a temporary recovery; she then told her story, with frequent interruptions, in substance as follows:——

History of Maria.

"I DATE the rise of my misfortunes," said *Maria,* "at the beginning of my acquaintance with the Honourable Mr. *Harrington.*—But for his solicitations I might still have lived in peace—a sister would not have had occasion to blush at the sound of my name—nor had a mother's pillow been steeped in tears, too fondly prone to remember a graceless but repenting child—We lived happily together in the days of my father, but when it pleased Providence to remove him, we no longer asserted our pretentions to that rank of life which our straitened finances were unable to continue—A young woman in no eligible circumstances, has much to apprehend from the solicitations of a man of affluence. I am now better persuaded of this truth, than I ever was before—for this was my unhappy situation—I always entertained a predilection for Mr. *Harrington*—he urged his passion with protestations of sincerity and affection—he found my heart too slightly guarded—he strove—he triumphed.

"—MUST I proceed!—

"A SMILING female was the offspring of our illicit connexion—Ah! my little *Harriot!*" continued *Maria,* as she wiped away a tear from her eye, "mayest thou enjoy that happiness which is denied to thy mother.

"OUR amour was not fated to last long—I discovered his gay temper to be materially altered—he was oftentimes thoughtful and melancholy, and his visits became suddenly shorter, and less frequent.

"I AFTERWARDS thought this change of conduct owing to jealousy—for he once asked me if a gentleman had called upon

---

1 The closing quotation mark is missing in the original edition.

me—I persisted in avowing my abhorrence of his ungenerous suspicion—He left me abruptly, and I saw nothing of him after.

"A STROKE so unexpected fell heavy on my heart—it awakened me to the state of misery into which my imprudence had hurried me.—What recompense could I expect from my Seducer?—He had been married two years—From the inflexibility of his temper I had little to hope, and I formed a determination of leaving town, for I had now indubitable testimony of his affection being estranged from me—half frantick, I immediately set out—but whither I knew not—I walked with precipitation until Providence directed me to your hospitable door: To your goodness, Madam, I am indebted for prolonging my existence a *few days:* For amidst the kindness and civilities of those around me, I feel myself rapidly verging towards the grave. I prepare myself for my approaching fate—and daily wait the stroke of death with trembling expectation."

SHE wrote to Mr. *Harrington* about a week before her decease—I transcribe the Letter:——

"*The Hon. Mr.* HARRINGTON.

"To the man for whom my bleeding heart yet retains its wonted affection, though the author of my guilt and misery, do I address my feeble complaint—O! *Harrington,* I am verging to a long eternity—and it is with difficulty I support myself while my trembling hand traces the dictates of my heart. Indisposed as I am—and unable as I feel to prosecute this task—I however collect all my powers to bid you a long—a final farewel.

"OH! *Harrington,* I am about to depart—for why should I tarry here? In bitter tears of sorrow do I weep away the night, and the returning day but augments the anguish of my heart, by recalling to view the sad sight of my misfortunes. And have I not cause for this severe anguish, at once the sorrow and disgrace of my family?—Alas! my poor mother!—Death shall expiate the crime of thy daughter, nor longer raise the blush of indignation on thy glowing cheek.—Ought I not, therefore, to welcome the hand of death?

"BUT what will become of my poor helpless infant, when its mother lies forgotten in the grave? Wilt thou direct its feet in the path of virtue and rectitude?—Wilt thou shelter from the rude blasts of penury and want?—Open your heart to the solicitude of a mother—of a mother agonizing for the future welfare of her child. Let me intreat you to perform this request—by the love which you professed for thy *Maria*—by her life which you have sacrificed.

"AND wilt thou not drop a tear of pity in the grave of thy *Maria?*—I know thy soul is a soul of sensibility; but my departure shall not grieve thee—no, my *Harrington,* it shall not wrest a sigh from thy bosom—rather let me live, and defy the malice and misery of the world—But can tenderness—can love atone for the sacrifices I have made?—Will it blot out my errours from the book of memory? Will love be an excuse for my crime, or hide me from the eye of the malignant—No, my *Harrington,* it will not. The passion is unwarrantable. Be it thine, gentle *Amelia*—be it thine to check the obtruding sigh, and wipe away the tear from his face—for thou art his wife, and thy soul is the seat of compassion—But—for me——

"Farewel—farewel forever!

Maria."

SHE survived but a short time—and frequently expressed a concern for her child—but Mrs. *Holmes* quieted her fears by promising to protect it. She accordingly made inquiry after it—and it is the same *Harriot* who was educated by her order, and whom she afterwards placed in the family of Mrs. *Francis.*

The assurances of my mother were like balm to the broken hearted *Maria*—"I shall now," said she, "die in peace."

The following is a copy of a letter written by the Rev. Mr. *Holmes* to the Hon. Mr. *Harrington:*—

"BELLEVIEW.

"SIR,

"WE have a scene of distress at our house peculiarly pathetick and affecting, and of which you, perhaps, are the sole author—You have had a criminal connexion with Miss *Fawcet*—you have turned her upon the world inhumanly—but chance—rather let me say Providence, hath directed her footsteps to my dwelling, where she is kindly entertained, and will be so, as long as she remains in this wilderness world, which is to be, I fear, but a short time—And shall she not, though she hath been decoyed from the road that leadeth to peace, long life and happiness—shall she not, if she return with tears of repentance and contrition, be entitled to our love and charity? Yes—this is my doctrine—If I behold any child of human nature distressed and forlorn, and in real want of the necessities of life, must I restrain or withhold the hand of charity—must I cease to recal the departing spirit of them that are ready to perish, until I make diligent inquiry into their circumstances and character? Surely, my friend, it is a duty incumbent on us by the ties of humanity and fellow feeling, and by the duty imposed on us by our holy religion, equally to extend the hand of relief to *all the necessitous*—however they may be circumstanced in the great family of mankind.

"THE crime of *Maria* is not the blackest in the annals of human turpitude; but however guilty she might have been, the tears of penitence do certainly make atonement therefor.

"THUS much have I thought proper to say in vindication of my conduct—in sheltering under my roof a poor wanderer—who hath strayed, but not wantonly, and who hath now happily returned.

"ONE would imagine, there was little necessity of making such a vindication to you; but my sentiments always flow from the abundance of my heart, and I am willing the whole world should judge of those which influence my conduct—Now, though some men, whose charity is contracted, and who may be denominated *prudes in virtue,* might deem wrongfully of my attention to the calamity of this frail woman—yet let me appeal to the hearts and understandings of all men, and these in particular, if I have erred, whether it be not an errour on the side of humanity. Would to God such amiable errours were more frequent!—In as much, my friend, as there is joy in heaven over one sinner that repenteth, I may say with assurance that I have felt an emanation of this heavenly joy animate my heart, in beholding this woman delighting to steer her course heavenward.

"FROM the unhappy condition of *Maria,* I have been led to reflect on the mischievous tendency of SEDUCTION. Methinks I view the distressing picture in all its horrid colours.——

"BEHOLD the youthful virgin arrayed in all the delightful charms of vivacity, modesty and sprightliness—Behold even while she is rising in beauty and dignity, like a lily of the valley, in the full blossom of her graces, she is cut off suddenly by the rude hand of the Seducer. Unacquainted with his baseness and treachery, and too ready to repose confidence in him—she is deluded by the promises and flattery of the man who professes the greatest love and tenderness for her welfare:—But did she understand the secret villainy of his intentions—would she appear thus elate and joyous? Would she assent to her ruin? Would she subscribe her name to the catalogue of infamy? Would she kiss the hand of the atrocious dastard, already raised to give the final wound to her reputation and peace?

"O! WHY is there not an adequate punishment for this crime,

when that of a common traitor is marked with its deserved iniquity and abhorrence!

"Is it necessary to depicture the state of this deluded young creature after her fall from virtue? Stung with remorse, and frantick with despair, does she not fly from the face of day, and secrete her conscious head in the bosom of eternal forgetfulness? Melancholy and guilt transfix her heart, and she sighs out her miserable existence—the prey of poverty, ignominy and reproach! Lost to the world, to her friends, and to herself, she blesses the approach of death in whatever shape he may appear, that terminates a life, no longer a blessing to its possessour, or a joy to those around her.

"BEHOLD her stretched upon the mournful bier!—Behold her silently descend to the grave!—Soon the wild weeds spring afresh round the *little hillock,* as if to shelter the remains of betrayed innocence—and the friends of her youth shun even the spot which conceals her relicks.

"SUCH is the consequence of SEDUCTION, but it is not the only consequence. Peace and happiness fly the nuptial couch[1] which is unattended by love and fidelity. The mind no longer enjoys its quiet, while it ceases to cherish sentiments of truth and gratitude. The sacred *ties* of connubial duty are not to be violated with impunity; for though a violation of those *ties* may be overlooked by the eye of justice, the heart shall supply a *monitor,* who will not fail to correct those, who are hardy enough to burst them asunder.—I am, &c.

"W. Holmes."

To this Letter, Mr. *Harrington* returned the following Answer.

Hon. Mr. HARRINGTON *to the Rev. Mr.* HOLMES.

"PERMIT me, my ever honoured friend, to return you thanks for your late favours—need I add—an acknowledgment for your liberality? No—your heart supplies a source of pleasure which is constantly nourished by your goodness and universal charity.——

"THE picture you have exhibited of a ruined female is undoubtedly just, but that the *rude spoiler* has his share of remorse is equally so—The conclusion of your letter is a real picture of the situation of my heart.

"PERHAPS you was always ignorant of the real motives that

1 Marital bed.

influenced me, and gave a particular bias to my conduct—At an early period of my life, I adopted a maxim, that *the most necessary learning was a knowledge of the world,* the pursuit of which, quadrating with a volatility of disposition, presented a variety of scenes to my heated imagination. The *eclat*[1] of my companions gratifying my vanity and increasing the gale of passion, I became insensibly hurried down the stream of dissipation. Here I saw mankind in every point of view—from the acme of the most consummate refinement, to the most abject stage of degradation. I soon became a ready proficient in the great school of the world—but an alteration of conduct was soon after necessary—I was compelled to it, not so much from the world's abhorrence of a dissolute course of life, as the dictates of my own heart—It was, indeed, my policy to flatter the world, and exhibit a fair outside—for I was in love with *Amelia*—My licentious amour[2] with *Maria* was secret—she was affectionate and tender—her manners were pleasing, but still I was unhappy.——

"MY career of dissipation, however alluring it struck my vitiated fancy, left little satisfaction on the mind—Reflection had its turn—and the happiness I had promised myself in a connexion with the amiable *Amelia,* I fully enjoyed in our marriage. A course of uninterrupted tranquillity ensued, but it was of short duration. The volatility of my temper, and the solicitude of my old associates, induced me at subsequent periods to fall again into my old vagaries. The taverns frequently found me engaged in meannesses derogatory to the character of a gentleman. These things I perceived affected the soul of *Amelia*—she was all meekness, gentleness and compassion, and she never once upbraided me with my illiberal conduct;

> But let concealment, like a worm in the bud,
> Feed on her damask cheek.[3]

"BLESSED be that power who has implanted within us that consciousness of reproach, which springs from gentleness and love!—Hail sensibility! Ye eloquent *tears* of *beauty!* that add dignity to human nature by correcting its foibles—it was *these* that corrected my faults when recrimination would have failed of success—it was

1 From French, meaning a flash of brilliance. Used to indicate a showy or dazzling effect.

2 Extramarital affair.

3 From Shakespeare, *Twelfth Night*, 2.4.111–12 (1602).

these that opened every avenue of contrition in my heart, when *words* would have dammed up every sluice of repentance.

"IT was now I appeared fully sensible that my conduct had hitherto been a course of disorder, and that systems of reformation, however well planned, had been overturned by the breath of adulation, before they had been thoroughly carried into execution—that I had been drifting upon a sea of inconsistency, without exercising my judgment; like a ship without a rudder, buffetted on the bosom of the ocean, the sport of winds and waves.

"THE criminality of my connexion with *Maria* appeared with the most aggravated circumstances; it stung me with remorse—and I instantly determined, however severe the conflict, to tear her from my bosom—to see her no more.—But how was I to inform her of it?—In what manner was I to bring about such a task?—*Maria* must be sacrificed to the happiness of *Amelia*. This was all I had to perform—it was a short lesson, but it was a hard one for me to execute.

"WITH this determination, however, I entered the apartment of *Maria*—Duty to *Amelia* and gratitude to *Maria* interchangeably agitated me—the contention was dubious—but duty prevailed, and I adhered to my former resolution—yet how was I to tell her *this would be the last visit?*—Conscious she had ever acted in conformity to my wishes—how could I accuse her, without accusing myself?—I threw out a few inconsiderate, and ungrateful hints of jealousy, and left the room abruptly. The feelings of *Maria* must have been injured—but however her sensibility was affected, mine was doubly so; I felt for her—I felt for our infant, and these feelings were added to the afflictions which had already burst upon my devoted head. A few days consideration, however, convinced me of the impropriety and ingratitude of my behaviour to *Maria*—I hastened to tell her of it—to place her in a situation that should screen her from penury and malice—and to make provision for the child—but, she was not to be found. I was informed that she had suddenly disappeared, and that a countryman had, by her order, called and taken away the child but a few hours before. This information burst upon my head like the voice of sudden thunder—I stood motionless, but my agitation was too violent to be of any long duration.——

A natural tear I shed, but wip'd it soon.[1]

---

1 Paraphrasing John Milton, *Paradise Lost*, 12.64 (1667), on Adam and Eve's expulsion from the Garden of Eden.

"IT was your goodness, and the humanity of your family, that sheltered the wretched *Maria,* and provided for the helpless *Harriot*—Your feelings are your reward.

"FROM all the variegated scenes of my past life, I daily learn some new lesson of humanity. Experience hath been my tutor—I now take a retrospect of my past conduct with deliberation, but not without some serious reflection: Like a sailor, escaped from shipwreck, who sits safely on the shore and views the horrours of the tempest; but as the gale subsides, and the waves hide their heads in the bosom of the deep, he beholds with greater concern the mischief of the storm, and the dangers he hath escaped. From what innate principle does this arise, but from the *God within the mind!*—I assert it for the honour of human nature, that no man, however dissolute, but comes back to the hour of reflection and solemn thoughtfulness—when the actions that are passed return upon the mind, and this *internal monitor* sits in judgment upon them, and gives her verdict of approbation or dislike.

"HE who listens to its call, views his character in its proper light—I have attended to its cry, and I see my deformity—I recal my mispent time, but in vain—I reflect on the misery of *Maria,* and I curse my temerity—I reflect on the state into which I have plunged a once happy female, and am eager to apply a speedy remedy, but this is vain also: Can I restore her that virtue—that innocence—that peace, of which I have unmanfully robbed her?——Let us leave the melancholy subject.——

"I WILL not so far supersede the fruit of your benevolence, as to presume to offer you any other recompense, than my sincere prayers for your happiness.

"I have the honour to be,

"With respect,

"Your &c.

"J. HARRINGTON."

THE disorder of *Maria* was fatal and rapid—but I hasten to the last scene of her life—it has, though I was young, made an impression on my mind that time cannot efface. I went to her, as she was seated on the bed—virtue and harmony were blended in her aspect—she was serene and composed—and her mien, while it expressed a consciousness of superiour worth and dignity, exhibited in one view, a striking picture of the grandeur of the human soul—patient, though afflicted—of a spirit broken, and borne down by severe distress, yet striving to surmount all, and aspire to heaven. In what words shall I paint to you, my dear *Myra,* her heroism and greatness of mind? "Weep not for me," said she, perceiving my emotion—"Death has nothing shocking to me—I have familiarized myself to his terrours—I feel the gradual decay of mortality; and waiting with confidence in the father of mercy, I am prepared to resign this mortal breath—I resign it in firm assurance of the soul's blessed immortality—Death I view as freeing me from a world which has lost its relish—as opening new scenes of happiness——But a few moments," continued she, clasping my hand, "and the scene of life is closed forever—Heaven opens on my soul—I go where all tears shall be wiped away—I welcome death as the angel of peace."——She uttered these words with a placid smile of resignation—her head sunk down on the pillow—and the next minute she was an angel.

"SOUL of the universe!" exclaimed my father-in-law—"there flew the gentlest spirit that ever animated human dust—Great were thy temptations—sincere thy repentance. If some human infirmity fell to thy lot, thy tears, dear shade, have washed out thy guilt forever!"

LETTER XL.
Mrs. HOLMES to MYRA.

BELLEVIEW.

HAVING presented you with several observations on Seduction, I think it will not be *mal apropos*[1] to consider the question in another point of view, and discover how a woman may be accessary to her own ruin—It is hardly worth while to contend about the difference between the meaning of the terms *accessary* and *principal.* The difference, in fact, is small; but when a woman, by her imprudence, exposes herself, she is *accessary;* for though her heart may be pure, her conduct is a tacit invitation to the Seducer.

EDUCATED in the school of luxury and pride, the female heart grows gradually torpid to the fine feelings of sensibility—the blush of modesty wears off—the charms of elegant simplicity fade by degrees—and the continual hurry of dissipation, supersedes the improvement of serious reflection. Reflection is a kind of relaxation from frolicking—it encourages the progress of virtue, and upholds the heart from sinking to depravity.

WE may lay it down as a principle, that *that conduct which will*

---

1 Inappropriate.

bear the test of reflection, and which creates a pleasure in the mind from a consciousness of acting right, is virtuous: And she whose conduct will not bear this test, is necessarily degenerating, and she is assenting to her destruction.

LET a lady be liberal or even magnificent, according to her circumstances or situation in life; but let the heart remain uncorrupt, let her not be contaminated by wealth, ambition or splendour. She may then take a happy retrospect of her conduct—her heart cannot upbraid her—and the suffrage of her own mind is a convincing proof that she has not strayed from the path of virtue.

HAPPY they who can thus reflect—who can recal to view the scenes that are passed, and behold their actions with reiterated satisfaction—they become ambitious of excelling in every thing virtuous, because they are certain of securing a continual reward: For as a mighty river fertilizes the country through which it passes and encreases in magnitude and force until it empty itself into the ocean: So virtue fertilizes or improves the heart, and gathers strength and vigour by continual progression, until it centre in the consummation of its desires.

DAZZLED by the glitter of splendour, and unmindful of the real charms of economy and simplicity, the female heart sighs for the enjoyment of fashion, and flutters to join the motley train of pleasure. But how is it deluded by empty deceptions! Like the fruit which sprang up in the infernal regions, beautiful to the eye, but which left upon the taste bitter ashes,[1] and was followed by repentance—A great quantity of this kind of fruit presents itself to my rashly judging sex; and it frequently happens that their hearts have as little inclination to resist the temptation, as our general parent[2] to refuse the fatal apple.

WE do not rouse to our aid fortitude to enable us to surmount the temptation, but yield ourselves to a kind of voluntary slavery. Hence it is observable, that a woman is often unhappy in the midst of pleasures—and petulent without cause—that she is trifling in matters of the highest importance; and the most momentous concern is considered futile, as whim and caprice may chance to dictate.

THE progress of female luxury, however slow it may appear, unless timely checked, works with infallible and destructive advances. The rule we at first adopted might perhaps answer this check; for by the examination there recommended, we behold the

---

1 Cf. Milton, *Paradise Lost,* 10.565–67.

2 Eve.

dangers of a continuation of such conduct—Ruin and contempt, the invariable concommitants of vice and immorality, proclaim their denunciations on a prosecution of it.

LET us examine the gradual steps, and the consequence of female luxury.—A desire to be admired is the first. Behold a woman surrounded by her worshippers, receiving the sacrifice of adulation—what was given her at first as compliment, she now demands as her due. She finds herself disappointed, and is mortified. The first desire still predominating, she attaches herself to the votaries of pride, who direct their feet in the paths of extravagance and irreligion. Thus sunk into effeminacy and meanness, *she forfeits her virtue rather than her pride*. Thus terminates the career of a woman, whose mind is debilitated, and whose life is expended in the pursuit of vanity.

IT is said of some species of *American* serpents, that they have the power of charming birds and small animals, which they destine for their prey. The serpent is stretched underneath a tree—it looks stedfastly on the bird—their eyes meet to separate no more—the charm begins to operate—the fascinated bird flutters and hops from limb to limb, till unable any longer to extend its wings, it falls into the voracious jaws of its enemy: This is no ill emblem of the fascinating power of pleasure. Surrounded with temptation, and embarrassed in her circumstances, a woman of dissipation becomes less tenacious of her honour—and falls an easy prey to the fascinating power of the SEDUCER.

HAVING traced to you, my dear *Myra,* the rise, advancement and termination of pleasure and pride in the female heart, it appears almost unnecessary to remark that this conduct cannot bear the test of reflection and serious examination. We may, however, observe on the contrary, that a woman who advances a few steps, often hurries on still further to prevent thought. This bars the way to a return to that conduct which *can* give pleasure on recollection. She behaves to herself as the populace did formerly to women suspected of witchcraft—they were tied neck and heels and thrown into the river; if they swam they were hung for witches—if they sank they were acquitted of the crime, but drowned in the experiment: So when we only suspect our hearts of an errour, we plunge still deeper into the sea of dissipation, to prevent the trial of that conduct which impartial reason and judgment would approve.

NOTWITHSTANDING I give this instance as an encouragement for virtue; yet in all those I have mentioned is a woman *accessary* to her ruin.

DO not imagine, my dear *Myra,* that I mean to argue against all pleasure—Many of us set out on a principle of false delicacy and destructive rivalship; we cannot behold a fine woman without wishing to appear finer. A laudable emulation in the conduct of all women is extremely praiseworthy—it stimulates them in the line of their duty—increases vivacity and good humour; and ambition, thus directed and pursued, I beg leave to designate a female virtue, because it is productive of the most happy consequences.

BUT it sometimes happens that particular virtues loose themselves in their neighbouring vices, and this laudable emulation degenerates into destructive rivalship.

A GENTEEL, handsome woman, deservedly shares the esteem and admiration of all men; but why should this esteem and admiration, justly paid to merit, give us disquiet? the answer is ready. That desire to be admired, so predominant in all females, by degrees works itself into the ruling passion, and precludes from the mind the particular virtue of emulation; for why a woman who merits the love of the world, should draw on her the disapprobation of many of her own sex, can be accounted for, by no other principle, than the mean, pitiful passion of envy.

THIS may possibly give rise to defamation. It is astonishing how this practice prevails among a *few* persons—because it is known by experience, to prove subversive of its very intention.—The arrows of envy recoil upon herself.

HOW foolish must that woman appear who depreciates the merit of another, that she may appear unrivalled! She raises up the dykes of ill nature, and inundates the land with a flood of scandal, but unhappily drowns herself in the event.

I LEAVE it to the result of your observation, my dear *Myra,* whether the woman who is first to develope her stores of defamation, and through false emulation, the first to traduce a woman of real merit and virtue, is not also the first who becomes a scandal to herself, and consequently the first that is contemned.

HOW opposite are the pursuits and rewards of her who participates in every rational enjoyment of life, without mixing in those scenes of indiscretion which give pain on recollection!—Whose chymical genius[1] leads her to extract the poison from the most luxuriant flowers, and to draw honey even from the weeds of society. She mixes with the world seemingly indiscriminately—and because she would secure to herself that satisfaction which arises from a consciousness of acting right, she views her conduct with

1 I.e., an almost scientific skill for understanding social propriety.

an eye of scrutiny. Though her temper is free and unrestrained, her heart is previously secured by the precepts of prudence—for prudence is but another name for virtue. Her manners are unruffled, and her disposition calm, temperate and dispassionate, however she may be surrounded by the temptations of the world.

Adieu!

LETTER XLI.
HARRINGTON *to* WORTHY.

BOSTON.

PRAY that the sun of Thursday may rise propitious—that it may gild the face of nature with joy. It is the day that beholds thy friend united in the indissoluble bands of *Hymen.*[1]

> Let this auspicious day be ever sacred,
> No mourning, no misfortune happen on it;
> Let it be marked for triumphs and rejoicings,
> Let happy lovers ever keep it holy,
> Choose it to bless their hopes and crown their wishes.[2]

IT is the day that gives me Harriot forever.

Adieu!

LETTER XLII.
The Hon. Mr. HARRINGTON *to the Rev. Mr.* HOLMES.

BOSTON.

YOU very well know of my amour with *Maria,* and that a daughter was the offspring of that illicit connexion—That sixteen years have elapsed since, by your goodness, she has lived with Mrs. *Francis,* and let me add, daily improving in beauty and every amiable accomplishment—But how shall we be able—how shall we pretend to investigate the great springs by which we are

1 The Greek god of marriage; *bands of Hymen*: marital bonds.
2 These are the opening lines from Nicholas Rowe, *The Fair Penitent* (1703). For the line "This happy day, that gives me my Calista," Brown substitutes Harrington's line about Harriot.

actuated, or account for the operation of sympathy—my son, who has been at home about eight weeks, has accidentally seen her, and to complete the triumph of nature—has loved her. He is now even upon the point of marrying—shall I proceed!—*of marrying his Sister!*—A circumstance seemingly fortuitous has discovered this important affair—I fly to prevent incest—Do not upbraid me with being the author of my own misfortunes,—"This comes of your libertinism," you will say, "this comes of your adultery!"—Spare your reflections, my friend—my heart is monitor enough—I am strangely agitated!

Adieu!

LETTER XLIII.

The Hon. Mr. HARRINGTON *to the Rev. Mr.* HOLMES.

BOSTON.

MY heart failed me! twenty times have I attempted to break the matter to my son—and twenty times have I returned from the task—I have engaged a friend to acquaint him how nearly connected he already is with the object of his love. This is a new, and to me a sorrowful instance of the force of SYMPATHY—My grief is insupportable—my affliction is greater than I can bear—it will bring down my grey hairs with sorrow to the grave.

Farewel!

LETTER XLIV.

HARRINGTON *to* WORTHY.

BOSTON.

ALL my airy schemes of love and happiness are vanished like a dream. Read this, and pity your unfortunate friend.

To Mr. T. HARRINGTON.

"SIR,

"YOU are about to marry a young lady of great beauty and accomplishments—I beg you to bestow a few serious thoughts on this important business—Let me claim your attention, while I disclose an affair, which materially concerns you—*Harriot* must not be your wife—You know your father is averse to your early connecting yourself in marriage with any woman—The duty we owe a parent is sacred, but this is not the only barrier to your marriage—the ties of consanguinity[1] prevent it—She is your SISTER——Your father, or Miss *Harrington,* will inform you more particularly—It is sufficient for me to have hinted it in time.——I am, with the most perfect esteem, and sincere wishes for your happiness, your

"UNKNOWN FRIEND, &c."

(In CONTINUATION.)

THE gloom of melancholy in the faces of the family but too well corroborated this intelligence—so I asked no questions—they read in my countenance that I had received the letter, and my sister put into my hand *The History of Maria*—I concealed my emotion while I read the account—"It is a pitiful tale," said I, as I returned it—and walked out of the room to give vent to the agitation of my heart.

I HAVE not yet seen *Harriot—Myra* has run to greet her with the new title of *sister.* Adieu! my friend—little happiness is left for me in this world.

LETTER XLV.
MYRA *to Mrs.* HOLMES.

BOSTON.

IN what words shall I describe to you, my dear friend, the misery that has suddenly overwhelmed us! It is impossible to communicate the distressed situation of *Harriot*—Expression is inadequate to give you an idea of our meeting—I called her my friend—my sister—She always loved me—but joy and affection gave way to passion—Her speech refused its office—

Sorrow in all its pomp was there,
Mute and magnificent without a tear.[2]

---

1 Blood relations.

2 An adaptation of lines from John Dryden's funeral poem for King Charles II, "Threnodia Augustalis" (1685).

SHE had gained a sister—she had lost a lover—a burst of joy would suddenly break from her, but it was of short duration—and was succeeded by pangs of exquisite distress—nature was unable to support it, and she fainted under the weight of the severe conflict. Her constitution at best is feeble; her present illness is therefore attended with more danger—Unless a speedy alteration should take place, the physician has little hopes of her recovery.——Heaven preserve us!

Farewel!

LETTER XLVI.
HARRINGTON *to* WORTHY.

BOSTON.

I have seen her—I prest her to my heart—I called her my Love—my *Sister.* Tenderness and sorrow were in her eyes—How am I guilty, my friend—How is this transport a crime? My love is the most pure, the most holy—*Harriot* beheld me with tears of the most tender affection—"Why," said she, "why, my friend, my dear *Harrington,* have I loved! but in what manner have I been culpable? HOW WAS I TO KNOW YOU WERE MY BROTHER?—Yes! I might have known it—how else could you have been so kind—so tender—so affectionate!"—Here was all the horrour of conflicting passions, expressed by gloomy silence—by stifled cries—by convulsions—by sudden floods of tears—The scene was too much for my heart to bear—I bade her adieu—my heart was breaking—I tore myself from her and retired.

WHAT is human happiness? The prize for which all strive, and so few obtain; the more eagerly we pursue it, the farther we stray from the object: Wherefore I have determined within myself that we increase in misery as we increase in age—and if there are any happy they are those of thoughtless childhood.

I THEN viewed the world at a distance in perspective. I thought mankind appeared happy in the midst of pleasures that flowed round them. I now find it a deception, and am tempted sometimes to wish myself a child again. Happy are the dreams of infancy, and happy their harmless pursuits! I saw the *ignis fatuus,* and have been running after it, but now I return from the search. I return and bring back disappointment. As I reflect on these scenes of infantine ignorance, I feel my heart interested, and become sensibly affected—and however futile these feelings may appear as I communicate them to you—they are feelings I venture to assert which every one must have experienced who is possessed of a heart of sensibility.

Adieu!

LETTER XLVII.
HARRINGTON *to* WORTHY.

BOSTON.

I NO longer receive satisfaction from the enjoyments of the world—society is distasteful to me—my favourite authors I have entirely relinquished—In vain I try to forget myself, or seek for consolation—my repose is interrupted by distressing visions of the night—my thoughts are broken—I cannot even think regularly.

HARRIOT is very weak—there is no hope of her life.

Adieu!

LETTER XLVIII.
HARRINGTON *to* WORTHY.

BOSTON.

MY dear friend, I have a great desire to see you—I wish you could come home speedily—I must be short—I have some serious business to do.

Farewel!

P.S. THEY say life is a blessing and it is our duty to improve and enjoy it; but when life becomes insupportable and we find no blessing in it—have we not a right to resign it?

Farewel!

LETTER XLIX.

The Hon. Mr. HARRINGTON *to the Rev. Mr.* HOLMES.

BOSTON.

ACCUMULATED sorrows continue to break over my devoted head. *Harriot* is at times deprived of her reason, and we have no expectation of her recovery—my son is deeply affected—he seems strangely disordered.

REVOLVING in my mind all these things, and the unhappy affair that led to them, the whole train of my past life returned fresh upon my mind. Pained with the disagreeable picture, and oppressed with the weight of my affliction, I sunk down to sleep: These circumstances had so strongly impressed my imagination that they produced the following Dream—My blood is chilled with horrour as I write.

METHOUGHT I suddenly found myself in a large, open field, waste and uncultivated—here I wandered in a solitary manner for some time—grief seized my heart at the awful appearance of the place, and I cried aloud—"How long shall I travel here, alone and friendless—a dusky mist swims before my sight, and the obscure horizon seems only to inclose this dismal wild!" Having advanced a few steps, I thought a light at a distance appeared to my doubtful view. Faint with fatigue, I approached it, and had the satisfaction to behold a person of the most benign aspect—a quiet serenity was painted on his brow, and happiness ineffable beamed from his divine countenance—Joy leaped in my bosom, and in the ecstacy of passion I endeavoured to clasp the blessed spirit to my heart; but it vanished in my embrace.

"TEACH me, blessed shade," said I, with a trembling voice—"teach me to find the habitations of men—What do I here?—Why am I doomed to explore the barren bosom of this baleful desert?" *"This,"* returned the spirit, in a voice, which, while it commanded veneration and love; struck awe and terrour into my soul—*"This* is not the habitation of the sons of mortality—it is the place appointed to receive the souls of all men, after they have resigned the bodies they animated on earth. Those who have violated the laws of reason, humanity, religion, and have dishonoured their God, here meet the punishment due to their crimes.

"ATTEND me, therefore, and view the condition of those thoughtless souls, who, a few days ago, were upon earth immersed in pleasure, luxury and vice—Regardless of futurity, and unprepared for their eternal summons to another world—and who persisted in the delight of their own eyes in opposition to the divine law, and deaf to the voice of reclaiming virtue. These, the sons of folly and riot, are smitten by the angel of death, while they are yet drinking of the bowl of vice—while the words of blasphemy yet dwell upon their tongues. And when their unhappy spirits sink to these infernal regions, their surviving companions rehearse their funeral panegyricks[1]—the praise of one is, that he could drink the longest—the merit of another, that he could sing a good song—a third secures his fame by being excellent in mimickry and buffoonery—How unhappy must he be, who leaves no other testimony of his usefulness behind him!

"How different is the fate of the good man: While upon earth his life is employed in the cause of virtue—The happiness he bestows on those around him is reflected back with tenfold reward; and when he takes rank in that happy place, where there is fulness of joy, and leaves the world of mankind, what numbers are joined in the general concern for his loss—The aged, while they prepare for the same journey, delight to dwell on his good actions—the virgin strews flowers on his grave, and the poet consumes the midnight oil to celebrate his virtues."

There was so much benignity in every word and action of my attendant, that I found myself imperceptibly attached to him. My attention to his discourse had prevented me from observing the progress we had made—for we had arrived at a place encircled with high walls—a great gate, at the command of my guide, instantly flew open—"Follow me," said he—I tremblingly obeyed.——

My ears were instantaneously filled with the faint cries of those here doomed to receive the rewards of their demerits. Looking earnestly forward, I beheld a group of unhappy wretches—I observed a person who was continually tormenting them—he held in one hand a whip, the lashes of which were composed of adders, and the stings of scorpions; and in the other a large mirrour, which, when he held up to the faces of the tormented, exhibited their crimes in the most flagrant colours, and forced them to acknowledge the justness of their punishment. "These," said my guide, "who are scourged with a whip of scorpions, and who start with horrour at the reflection of their deeds upon earth, are the souls of the Gambler—the Prodigal—the Duelist, and the Ingrate.

"Those whom you see yonder," continued he, "those wasted, emaciated spirits, are the souls of the Envious—they are doomed

1 Orations honoring the deceased.

to view the most beautiful fruit, which they can never taste, and behold pleasures which they can never enjoy. This punishment is adjudged them because most of those vile passions, by which men suffer themselves to be ruled, bring real evil, for promised good.

"For this reason the allwise Judge hath ordered the same passions still to inflame those ghosts, with which they were possessed on earth—Observe yon despicable crew!—behold the sin of Avarice!—those sordid ghosts are the souls of Misers—Lo! they eye their delightful bags with horrid pleasure; and with a ghastly smile, brood over their imaginary riches. Unable to carry their wealth about with them, they are confined to one spot, and in one position. This infernal joy is the source of their tortures, for behold them start at every sound, and tremble at the flitting of a shade. Thus are they doomed to be their own tormentors—to pore over their gold with immortal fear, apprehension, and jealousy, and to guard their ideal wealth with the tears of care, and the eyes of eternal watchfulness.

"Behold here," continued my guide, "the miserable division of Suicides!"—"Unhappy they!" added I, "who, repining at the ills of life, raised the sacrilegious steel against their own bosoms! How vain the reiterated wish to again animate the breathless clay—to breathe the vital air—and to behold the cheering luminary of Heaven!"—"Upbraid me not—O my father!" cried a voice—I looked up, and thought my son appeared among them—but immediately turning from so shocking a spectacle, I suddenly beheld my once loved *Maria*—"O delight of my youth! do I behold thee once more!—Let me hide my sorrows in thy friendly bosom." I advanced towards her—but she flew from me with scorn and indignation—"O speak! *Maria!* speak to me!" She pointed with her finger to a group of spirits, and was out of sight in a moment.

"Let me," said my conductor, "prepare you for a more dreadful sight." The increasing melancholy, and affecting gloom of the situation, forboded something terrifying to my soul—I looked toward the place where *Maria* had pointed, and saw a number of souls remote from any division of the unhappy. In their countenances were depicted more anguish, sorrow and despair—I turned my head immediately from this dreadful sight, without distinguishing the nature of their torments. Quivering with horrour, I inquired who they were—"These," answered my guide, with a sigh, "are the miserable race of SEDUCERS.—Repentance and shame drive them far from the rest of the accursed. Even the damned look on them with horrour, and thank fate their crimes are not of so deep a die."

HE had hardly finished, when a demon took hold of me, and furiously hurried me in the midst of this unhappy group—I was so terrified that it immediately roused me from my sleep.——

EVEN now, while I write to you, my good friend, my hand trembles with fear at the painful remembrance—Yet

——'Twas but a dream, but then
So terrible, it shakes my very soul.——[1]

Farewel!

LETTER L.
HARRIOT *to* HARRINGTON.

BOSTON.

MUST I then forget the endearments of the lover, and call you by the name of brother? But does our friendship remain upon this foundation? Is this all that unites us? And has there subsisted nothing more tender—a sentiment more voluntary in our hearts? My feelings affirm that there has. At the hour of our first interview I felt the passion kindle in my breast: Insensible of my own weakness, I indulged its increasing violence and delighted in the flame that fired my reason and my senses. Do you remember our walks, our conversations, our diversions?—The remembrance of these things fill my mind with inconceivable torture—they seem to reproach me with unmerited criminality—I deprecate, I detest all these scenes of gaity and frivolity—yet I have preserved my innocence and my virtue—what then have I to deprecate, what have I to detest?

ALAS! how have we been forming schemes of happiness, and mocking our hearts with unsubstantial joys. Farewel! farewel! ye gilded scenes of imagination. How have we been deluded by visionary prospects, and idly dwelt upon that happiness which was never to arrive. How fleeting have been the days that were thus employed!—when anticipation threw open the gates of happiness, and we vainly contemplated the approach of bliss;—when we beheld in reversion, the pleasures of life, and fondly promised ourselves, one day to participate in them;—when we beheld in the magick mirrour of futurity, the lively group of loves that sport

1 From Colley Cibber's adaptation of Shakespeare's *Richard III* (1699), popular throughout the eighteenth century.

in the train of joy. We observed in transports of delight the dear delusion, and saw them, as it were, in bodily form pass in review before us; as the fabled hero views the region of preexistant spirits, and beholds a race of men yet to be born.

SUCH was our hope, but even this fairy anticipation was not irrational. We were happy in idea, nor was the reality far behind. And why is the vision vanished? O! I sink, I die, when I reflect—when I find in my *Harrington* a brother—I am penetrated with inexpressible grief—I experience uncommon sensations—I start with horrour at the idea of incest—of ruin—of perdition.

HOW do I lament this fatal discovery, that includes the termination of a faithful love! I think of him to whom I have resolved to be eternally constant—and ah! how often have I resolved it in my heart. I indulge, in idea, the recollection of his caresses—of his protestations, and of his truth and sincerity—I become lost in a wilderness, and still I travel on, and find myself no nearer an escape. I cherish the dear idea of a lover—I see the danger and do not wish to shun it, because, to avoid it, is to forget it—And can I, at one stroke, erase from my mind the remembrance of all in which my heart used to delight? Ah! I have not the fortitude—I have not the virtue, to "forget myself to marble."[1] On the contrary, I strive no longer to remember our present connexion. I endeavour to forget—I curse the idea of a brother—my hand refuses to trace the word, and yet

——The name appears
Already written; blot it out my tears![2]

AH, whence this sorrow that invests my soul! This gloom that darkens—this fire of impassioned grief, that involves all my thoughts! why do I rave, and why do I again abandon myself to despair! Come, O *Harrington!* be a friend, a protector, a brother—be him, on whom I could never yet call by the tender, the endearing title of *parent.* I will reverence him in whom all the charities of life are united—I will be dutiful and affectionate to you, and you shall be unto me as a father—I will bend on the knee of respect and love, and will receive your blessing.

WHY did you go away so soon? Why leave me when I was

1 I.e., to imagine oneself a statue or monument to grief. Cf. Milton, *Il Penseroso* (1645), l. 42.

2 Alexander Pope, "Eloisa to Abelard" (1717), ll. 13–14. Pope's poem retells a famous story of forbidden love.

incapable of bidding you adieu? When you pressed my cheek with the kiss of love, of fraternal affection, what meant its conscious glow? What meant the ebullition of my veins, the disorder of my nerves, the intoxication of my brain, the blood that mantled in my heart? My hand trembled, and every object seemed to swim before my doubtful view—Amidst the struggle of passion, how could I pronounce the word—how could I call you by the title of brother. True—I attempted to articulate the sound, but it died upon my tongue, and I sank motionless into your arms.

——ALLIED by birth, and in mind, and similar in age—and in thought still more intimately connected, the sympathy which bound our souls together, at first sight, is less extraordinary. Shall we any longer wonder at its irresistible impulse?—Shall we strive to oppose the *link of nature* that draws us to each other? When I reflect on this, I relapse into weakness and tenderness, and become a prey to warring passions. I view you in two distinct characters: If I indulge the idea of one, the other becomes annihilated, and I vainly imagine I have my choice of a brother or———

I AM for a while calm—but alas! how momentary is that calmness; I dwell with rapture on what fancy has represented; but is the choice regulated by virtue? Is it prompted by reason? I recollect myself, and endeavour to rouse my prudence and fortitude; I abhor my conduct, and wish for obscurity and forgetfulness. Who can bear the torment of fluctuating passion? How deplorable is the contest? The head and the heart are at variance, but when Nature pleads, how feeble is the voice of Reason? Yet, when Reason is heard in her turn, how criminal appears every wish of my heart? What remorse do I experience? What horrours surround me? Will my feeble frame, already wasted by a lingering decline, support these evils? Will the shattered, frail bark outride the tempest, and will the waves of affliction beat in vain? Virtue, whose precepts I have not forgotten, will assist me—if not to *surmount*, at least to *suffer* with fortitude and patience.

OH! I fear, I fear my decaying health—If I must depart, let me beseech you to forget me—I know the strength of your passion, and I dread the fatal consequences my departure may occasion you.

ONCE more let me intreat you, my dear friend, to arm yourself with every virtue which is capable of sustaining the heaviest calamity. Let the impetuosity of the lover's passion be forgotten in the undisturbed quietness of the brother's affection, and may all the blessings that life can supply be yours—Seek for content, and you will find it, even though we should never meet again in this world.

Adieu!

LETTER LI.
MYRA *to Mrs.* HOLMES.

BOSTON.

THE curtain is dropped, and the scene of life is forever closed—THE LOVELY *HARRIOT* IS NO MORE.

SHE is fit to appear in Heaven, for her life was a scene of purity and innocence—If there is any consolation to be felt by a survivor, it is in the reflection of the amiable qualities of the deceased. My heart shall not cease to cherish her idea, for she was beautiful without artifice, and virtuous without affectation.

See! there all pale and dead she lies;
Forever flow my streaming eyes——
There dwelt the fairest—lovliest mind,
Faith, sweetness, wit together join'd.
Dwelt faith and wit and sweetness there?
O! view the change, and drop a tear.[1]

MY brother is exceedingly agitated—He will never support this disastrous stroke—Nothing can attract his attention—nothing allay his grief—but it is the affliction of reason and not of weakness——God grant that it prove not fatal to him.

Adieu!—Adieu!—

LETTER LII.
HARRINGTON *to* WORTHY.

BOSTON.

SHE is gone—she is dead—she who was the most charming, the most gentle, is gone—You may come—you may desire to behold all that was lovely—but your eyes will not see her.

---

1 Brown adapts these lines from "On the Death of a Beloved Wife, Written by Her Husband," which dates at least to its appearance in *Miscellaneœ Curiosœ: or, Entertainments for the Ingenious of Both Sexes* (London, 1734–35) and was reprinted as "On the Death of Mrs. BIRCH, Written by Her Husband upon Her Coffin," attributed to Thomas Birch, in *Gentleman's Magazine*, vol. 6, Mar. 1736. The poem was frequently excerpted and reprinted through the century. The popular writer and poet Elizabeth Rowe quotes this passage, beginning in 1738, in her *Friendship in Death*,

YES! I raved—I was distracted—but now I am calm and dispassionate—I am smooth as the surface of a lake—I shall see her again.

WHEN our spirits are disencumbered of this load of mortality, and they wing their flight to the celestial regions, shall we not then know those who were dear to us in this world? Shall we not delight in their society, as we have done in this state of existence? Yes—certainly we shall—we shall find them out in Heaven—there alone is happiness—there shall I meet her—there our love will not be a crime—Let me indulge this thought—it gives a momentary joy to my heart—it removes the dark mist that swims before my eyes—it restores tranquillity; but the more I reflect on this thought—the more I long to be there—the more I detest this world and all it contains. I sigh to fly away from it.

LETTER LIII.
HARRINGTON *to* WORTHY.

BOSTON.

INGRATITUDE is a predominant principle in the conduct of man. The perfidious ——, who owes to me his reputation and fortune, and with whom I intrusted a great part of my property, has deceived me. This affair will materially retard my business.

TO be unfortunate in trade is not worth a sigh—to receive inattention and incivility does not merit a frown; but *Ingratitude*—it is this that cuts to the quick. Yet I freely give him my pity; for what man, who considered for a moment the inconsistency of the human heart, would hurl the thunderbolt of indignation at the head of an ingrate? What an important little thing is man! he contrives to overreach his neighbour, and mount to the enjoyment of riches, ambition and splendour; but remembers not the period of enjoyment—that his life is a day, and his space a point!

NATURALISTS inform us of insects whose term of existence is confined to a few hours—What is the business and importance of such a life?

WOULD not a being, whose *circle of living* is immensity of ages, inquire with equal propriety, "What is the importance

---

in Twenty Letters from the Dead to the Living. It also appears at the close of an anonymously published novel, *Fatal Friendship* (London, 1771). Brown's adaptation had a life of its own: it appears on the headstone of Mrs. Martha Thurston, of Bradford, Massachusetts, who died in 1799.

of *man*—What actions can he perform—What happiness can he enjoy, whose insignificant life is circumscribed to seventy years?"——In this point of view I behold the tinsel, the vanity and noise of the world, and the little plots and cunning artifices of mankind to cheat and ruin one another.

INGRATITUDE, then, is constitutional, and inseparable from human nature, but it ought not to fill us with surprize, because it is no new discovery—It has ever been invariably the characteristick of man. Is not the page of antiquity distained[1] with the blood of those who ought to have received honour and adoration? Behold the brilliant race of the world's benefactors: Consider their benevolent actions, and regard their ungrateful return—these benefactors, who have been sent from heaven to inform and entertain mankind, to defend the world from the arm of tyranny, and to open the gates of salvation, have been despised, and banished, and poisoned and crucified.

BEHOLD the support of the *Roman* power, the invincible *Belisarius!*[2] who protected his country from the ravage of the *Huns,* and displayed the *Roman* eagle in every quarter of the globe! Behold him fall a sacrifice to malice, to faction and ingratitude! Behold him cast out by the country he had defended, and for which he had wasted his life to protect and honour, and left alone to deplore his unfortunate condition, when he was old, and blind, and naked and miserable!

UNFORTUNATE is the man who trusts his happiness to the precarious friendship of the world—I every day become more of a misanthrope, and see nothing to increase my desire of living, but your esteem and affection. I want advice, but am too proud to let the world know I am weak enough to be under obligation to any one else.

THAT you may never want friends or advice, is the sincere prayer of

Your &c.

---

1 Stained.

2 Favius Belisarius (c. 500–565), a renowned Byzantine general. Brown may have had in mind the version of his story told in Jean-François Marmontel's novel *Bélisaire* (Paris, 1767), which had been translated into English as *Belisarius* (London, 1767) and published as *The History of Belisarius* in Philadelphia in 1770. Marmontel popularized a legend in which Belisarius is betrayed by the Emperor Justinian, whose empire he had helped to extend, and left to die a blind beggar.

LETTER LIV.
HARRINGTON *to* WORTHY.

BOSTON.

ALL the scenes of my past life return fresh upon my memory. I examine every circumstance as they pass in review before me—I see nothing to cause any disagreeable or unwelcome sensations—no terrour upbraids me—no reproaching conscience stings my bosom as I reflect on the actions that are past. With her I expected happiness—I have expected a vain thing—for there is none—She is gone—gone to a far country—she is preparing a place for me—a place of unutterable bliss—But ah! an immeasurable gulph lies between us—Who can tell the distance that separates us? What labour—what toil—what pain must be endured in traversing the thorny paths that lead to her blessed abode?—And will she not receive me into those happy regions with as much joy—with as sincere a welcome—if I cut short my journey?—And will not the Eternal Dispenser of Good, pardon the awful deed that frees me from this world of misery—the deed by which I obtrude myself into his divine presence?

WHY must I wait the lingering hand of the grisly messenger to summon me to the world above?

LETTER LV.
HARRINGTON *to* WORTHY.

BOSTON.

Am I a child that I should weep?—I have been meditating on the cause of my calamities—Why did my father love *Maria*—or rather, why did I love their *Harriot?* Curse on this tyrant custom that dooms such helpless children to oblivion or infamy! Had I known her to have been my sister, my love would have been regular—I should have loved her as a sister—I should have marked her beauty—I should have delighted in protecting it. I should have observed her growing virtues—I should have been happy in cherishing their growth. But alas! She is gone——and I cannot stay—I stand on the threshold of a vast eternity.

LETTER LVI.
HARRINGTON *to* WORTHY.

BOSTON.

I AM determined to quit this life. I feel much easier since my determination. The step must not be taken with rashness. I must be steady—calm—collected—I will endeavour to be so.——

HER eager solicitation—the anxiety she always expressed for me————When I think she is no more, it wrings my heart with grief, and fills my eyes with tears——

——I MUST go——

THE idea chills me—I am frozen with horrour—cold damps hang on my trembling body—My soul is filled with a thousand troubled sensations—I must depart—it must be so—My love for thee, O *Harriot!* is dearer than life—Thou hast first sat out—and I am to follow.—

WERE it possible that I *could live* with her, should I be happy? Would her presence restore peace and tranquillity to my disordered mind? Ah no! it never would *here*—it *never* would. I will fly to the place where she is gone—our love will there be refined—it will be freed from all criminality—I will lay my sorrows before her—and she shall wipe away all tears from my eyes.

WHEN the disembodied spirit flies above—when it leaves behind the senseless clay, and wings its flight—it matters not with me what they do with his remains.

> Cover his head with a clod or a stone,
> It is all one—it is all one!——[1]

LETTER LVII.
HARRINGTON *to* WORTHY.

BOSTON.

THE longer I live, and the more I see of the misery of life—the more my desire of living is extinguished. What I formerly esteemed trifles, and would not deign to term misfortunes, now appear with a formidable aspect—though I once thought them

---

1 See William Coombe's *Original Letters of the Late Reverend Mr. Laurence Sterne* (1788).

harmless, and innoxious[1] to my peace, they assume new terrours every day.—But is not this observation general? It is—It is thus every son of human nature, gradually wishes for death, and neglects to seek for, and improve those comforts, which by diligent search there is a possibility of attaining.

AM I to reason from analogy? I know what has been—the afflictions I have felt; but what is the prospect before me? The path is darkened by mists—

> Puzzled in mazes, and perplex'd with errours—[2]

Who is there hardy enough to try its difficulties? Is not the view horrible! My pains and anxieties have been severe—those, which, if I live, I shall suffer, may be yet more so—This idea sinks me to despair.

As a thing becomes irksome to us, our detestation is always encreased—Whatever object is disagreeable, we pine and sicken until it is moved out of sight. Life growing upon one in this manner—increasing in horrour—with continual apprehension of death—a certainty of surviving every enjoyment, and no prospect of being delivered from suspense—it is intolerable—he will assuredly be tempted to terminate the business with his own hand.

LETTER LVIII.
WORTHY *to* HARRINGTON.

BELLEVIEW.

YOU argue as if your reason were perverted—Let your mind be employed, and time will wear out these gloomy ideas; for it is certainly a truth, that *the love of life increases with age*—Your letters, therefore, are predicated on the most erroneous principles.

REMEMBER the story of the old man, who had been buried in a dungeon the greater part of his life, and who was liberated at an advanced age. He viewed, once more, the light of the sun, and the habitations of men—he had come into a new order of beings, but found their manners distasteful—In the midst of the sunshine of the world, he remembered the prison, where he had

---

1 Unharmful.

2 From Joseph Addison, *Cato, a Tragedy* (1713), 1.1: "The ways of heaven are dark and intricate; / Puzzled in mazes, and perplex'd with errors."

wasted his life, and he sighed to be again immured within its walls.

SUCH is our passion for life; we love it because we know it; and our attachment becomes the more riveted, the longer we are acquainted with it—Our prison grows familiar—we contemplate its horrours—but however gloomy the walls that surround us, there is not one but sets a full value on his dreary existence—there is not one but finds his partiality for his dungeon increase, in proportion to the time he hath occupied it—for among the race of human beings confined to this narrow spot—how few are they who are hardy enough to break their prison?

LET us watch over all we do with an eye of scrutiny—the world will not examine the causes that give birth to our actions—they do not weigh the motives of them—they do not consider those things which influence our conduct—but as that conduct is more or less advantageous to society, they deem it madness or wisdom, or folly or prudence—Remember this——

Adieu!

LETTER LIX.
HARRINGTON *to* WORTHY.

BOSTON.

You are egregiously mistaken, argue as you will.—My perceptions are as clear as any one's—The burden that is at first heavy and inconvenient, galls us as we proceed—it soon becomes intolerable, we sink under its weight, and lie gasping in the publick way long before night.

As to the world—who strives to please it, will be deservedly rewarded—he will reap his labour for his pains—Let it judge of my conduct. I despise its opinion—*Independency of spirit* is my motto—I think for myself.

LETTER LX.
HARRINGTON *to* WORTHY.

BOSTON.

HOW vain is the wish that sighs for the enjoyment of worldly happiness. Our imagination dresses up a phantom to impose on our reason: As *Pygmalion*[1] loved the work of his own hand—so do we fall in love with the offspring of our brain. But our work illudes[2] our embrace—we find no substance in it—and then fall a weeping and complain of disappointment. Miserable reasoners are we all.

WHY should I mourn the loss of *Harriot* any longer? Such is my situation—in the midst of anxiety and distress, I complain of what cannot be remedied.—I lament the loss of that which is irretrievable: So on the sea-beat shore, the hopeless maid, unmindful of the storm, bewails her drowned lover.

LETTER LXI.
WORTHY *to* HARRINGTON.

BELLEVIEW.

I THANK you for your letters, but I wish you had something better for the subject of them—the sad repetition of your feelings and sorrows, pains me exceedingly—I promise to be with you soon—perhaps before you can receive this letter.

WHATEVER concerns my friend, most sensibly affects me—You, *Harrington,* are the friend of my heart, and nothing has so much grieved me as the story of your misfortunes.

IT is a maxim well received, and seems to be admitted an article in the moral creed of mankind, "that the enjoyments of life do not compensate the miseries."[3] Since, then, we are born to suffer, and pain must attend us in all the stages of our journey, let us philosophically welcome our companion. The most

1 In Ovid's *Metamorphoses,* a Cyprian sculptor who falls in love with a statue of his own creation, which is then granted life by the goddess Aphrodite.

2 Eludes.

3 See, e.g., Matthew Prior, preface to "Solomon on the Vanity of the World," in *Poems on Several Occasions* (London, 1718).

eligible plan we can adopt, is to be contented in the condition that Providence hath assigned us. Let us trust that our burden will not be heavier than we can bear—When we adopt this plan, and are sensible we have this trust, our lesson is complete—we have learned all—we are arrived to the perfection of sublunary happiness.

DO not think I am preaching to you a mere sermon of morality—let me impress your mind with the folly of repining, and the blessing of a contented mind.

LET me intreat you not to puzzle your brain with vain speculations—if you are disposed to argue, do not put foolish cases that never existed—take the light of facts, and reason from them.

WHEN we are surrounded with the miseries of life—the baseness of false friends—the malice of enemies—when we are inveloped in those anxious fears, the result of too much sensibility, human nature feels a degree of oppression, which, without a manly exertion of reason and this practical philosophy, would be intolerable. I have heard you mention *St. Evremond,*[1] as a philosopher of this kind. Arm yourself with his prudence and fortitude—he, though in exile—though reduced almost to penury, and labouring under the disadvantages of a bad constitution, lived to be a very old man; he established a course of rational pleasures—for when the mind is employed, we regret the loss of time—we become avaricious of life.

WHEN misfortunes come upon us without these consolations, it is hard, I acknowledge, to buffet the storm—it is then human frailty is most apparent—there is nothing left to hope—Reason is taken from the helm of life—and Nature—helpless, debilitated Nature—lost to herself, and every social duty, splits upon the rocks of despair and suicide. We have seen several examples of this—By exploring, and therefore shunning the causes, let us avoid the catastrophe.

THE pensive and melancholy will muse over the ordinary accidents of life, and swell them, by the power of imagination, to the heaviest calamities. Hence we find a treacherous friend will sensibly affect some men, and a capricious mistress will destroy a real lover: Hence people in misfortune frequently construe the slightest inattention into neglect and insult, and deem their best friends

1 Charles de Marguetel de Saint-Denis, seigneur de Saint-Évremond (1613–1703), a French soldier and essayist who lived in exile in England after running afoul of governmental authority for his criticism of state policy.

false and ungrateful. The sting of ingratitude deeply pierces the heart of sensibility.

THE passions and affections which govern mankind are very inconsistent. Men, confined to the humble walks of life, sigh for the enjoyment of wealth and power, which, when obtained, become loathsome—The mind unaccustomed to such an easy situation, is discontented, and longs to be employed in those things in which it was formerly exercised.

THE greatest rulers and potentates become unhappy—they wish for the charms of solitude and retirement, which, when attained, become more irksome than their former condition—*Charles* the Fifth, of *Spain,*[1] resolved to taste the pleasures of a recluse life, by abdicating the throne—he soon found his imagination had deceived him, and repented of the step he had taken. This lazy life, when compared to the business and grandeur of a court, became tasteless and insipid.—"The day," says a historian, "he resigned his crown to his son, was the very day in which he repented making him such a present."[2]

It is a great art to learn to be happy in the state in which we are placed—I advise you to mingle in the concerns of your acquaintances—be cheerful and undisturbed, nor give yourself up to those gloomy ideas, which tend only to make you more wretched—If such obtrude themselves, avoid being alone—I had rather be a dupe to my imagination than sacrifice an hour's easiness to my sensibility or understanding. Determine to be happy, and you will be so——

God be with you!

LETTER LXII.
HARRINGTON *to* WORTHY.

BOSTON.

WHEN we seek for diversion in any place, and there is nothing to be found that we wish, it is certainly time to depart.

TOMORROW I go—There is nothing here that can calm the

1 Charles V (1500–58), King of Spain, abdicated multiple European thrones before retiring to the monastery of St. Just, where he died.

2 A version of this anecdote circulated in Gregorio Leti's *Life of Pope Sixtus the Fifth* (1779): "Charles V. resigned his crown in the morning and repented of it in the evening."

tumult of my soul—I fly from the sight of the human countenance—I fly from the face of day—I fly from books—Books that could always cheer me in a melancholy moment, are now terrifying—They recal scenes to my recollection that are past—pleasant scenes that I am never more to enjoy. They present pictures of futurity—of gloomy futurity—I just opened a book, and these are the words that I read:—"The time of my fading is near, and the blast that shall scatter my leaves. Tomorrow shall the traveller come, he that saw me in my beauty shall come; his eyes will search the field, but they will not find me."[1]

THESE words pierce me to the quick—they are a dismal prospect of my approaching fate.

TOMORROW I shall go—But ah! whither?——

O! MY friend, when we find nothing we desire in this world, it is time to depart. To live is a disgrace—to die is a duty.

Farewel!

LETTER LXIII.
WORTHY *to Mrs.* HOLMES.

BOSTON.

I ARRIVED in town last evening—you desired me to write you a statement of affairs as I should find them here—and of my marriage with the amiable *Myra*—I promised to obey—but how little do we know of the termination or consequence of the most probable event!

I SAW my beloved—her eyes were yet heavy and smarting with weeping for the death of *Harriot*—and *this,* once the house of joy and cheerfulness, is turned into the house of mourning. My unfortunate friend had just then fallen into a calm sleep, and it was impossible to see him—it was what I very much desired—but it was the wish of the family that I should desist for the present—he had not slept the evening before—he had been heard walking

---

1 James Macpherson, "Berrathon: A Poem," in *Fingal, An Ancient Epic Poem, in Six Books* (London, 1762). In the 1760s, Macpherson (1736–96) published several poems he claimed were translations of a Gaelic bard named Ossian. This and related poems were translated into German by Johann Wolfgang von Goethe (1749–1832) and included in his popular novel *The Sorrows of Young Werther* (1774). Werther quotes these lines from Ossian as he descends into madness. See p. 57 in the Introduction.

across his chamber all the night, with little intermission, oftentimes talking to himself in a passionate tone of voice.

THIS melancholy account deeply affected me—and I parted from my beloved, praying Heaven to give her consolation, and to be the support of my disordered friend.

IT is with difficulty I bring myself to the serious and painful employment of being the informer of unwelcome tidings—my heart feels the wound—vainly it tells me my friend is no more—my hand reluctantly traces—my friend—my *Harrington* is no more.

EARLY this morning I was surprised with a visit from a gentleman, whom I had formerly seen at *Myra's*—it was the same neighbour who informed *Harrington* of his affinity to *Harriot*—he found a difficulty in his utterance—he told me, with trembling lips, my young friend *Harrington* was dead—"He has killed himself," said I—he asked me if I had heard the news—I told him my heart presaged it.

WHEN any uncommon event happens to us, we often have a presentiment of it—The circumstances of his death are these:—At midnight the gentleman heard the report of the pistol, and went into the house—he found the unhappy youth weltering in his blood—few signs of life remained—the ball had entered his brain—the surgeon came, but in a few hours he was cold. A few friends were requested to attend—and this gentleman had called upon me, by desire of *Myra.*

IT is not possible to describe the distress of the family and connexions—I shall leave it to your imagination.

A letter that he had written for me, laid unsealed upon the table, and *The Sorrows of Werter*[1] was found lying by its side. I send you the letter—it appears to have been written at intervals, and expresses the disorder and agitation of his mind.

Adieu!

1 See the previous note. Goethe's novel was translated into English (London, 1779). American editions followed in Philadelphia (1784) and Litchfield, Connecticut (1789). *Werther,* which ends in its hero's suicide, was infamous for inspiring copycat suicides.

LETTER LXIV.
HARRINGTON *to* WORTHY.

HARRIOT is dead—and the world to me is a dreary desert—I prepare to leave it—the fatal pistol is charged—it lies on the table by me, ready to perform its duty—but that duty is delayed till I take my last farewel of the best of friends.

YOUR letter is written with the impetuosity of an honest heart; it expresses great sincerity and tenderness.

I THANK you for all your good advice—it comes too late—O *Worthy!* she is dead—she is gone—never to return, never again to cheer my heart with her smiles and her amiable manners—her image is always before me—and can I forget her?—No!—She is continually haunting my mind, impressing the imagination with ideas of excellence—but she is dead—all that delighted me is become torpid—is descended into the cold grave.

> - - - - With thee
> Certain my resolution is to die;
> How can I live without thee—how forego
> Thy converse sweet, and love so dearly join'd,
> To live again in these wild woods forlorn?
> -
> - - - - loss of thee
> Will never from my heart—no! no!—I feel
> The link of nature draw me.
> - - - - From thy state
> Mine never shall be parted, bliss or woe.[1]

THOU hast sat out on a long journey—but you shall not go alone—I hasten to overtake thee. My resolution is not to be diverted—is not to be shaken—I will not be afraid—I am inexorable——

——I HAVE just seen my father—he is dejected—sullen grief is fixed on his brow—he tells me I am very ill—I looked at *Myra*—she wiped her face with her handkerchief—perhaps they did not imagine this was the last time they were to behold me.

SHE mentioned the name of *Worthy,* but my thoughts were differently engaged. She repeated your name, but I took no heed of

---

1 These lines are fragments of a passage from Book IX of Milton's *Paradise Lost,* 9.907–16, in which Adam responds to Eve's account of her sin in eating the forbidden fruit.

it.——Take her, my *Worthy*—*Myra* is a good girl—take her—comfort her. Let not my departure interrupt your happiness—perhaps it may for a short time. When the grass is grown over my grave, lead her to it, in your pensive walks—point to the spot where my ashes are deposited—drop one tear on the remembrance of a friend, of a brother—but I cannot allow you to be grieved—grieve for me! Wretch that I am—why do I delay—

——I WISH I could be buried by the side of her, then should the passenger who knows the history of our unfortunate loves, say—"Here lies *Harrington* and his *Harriot*—in their lives they loved, but were unhappy—in death they sleep undivided."—Guardian[1] spirits will protect the tomb which conceals her body—the body where every virtue delighted to inhabit.——

DO not judge too rashly of my conduct—let me pray you to be candid—I have taken advantage of a quiet moment, and written an Epitaph—If my body were laid by her's, the inscription would be pertinent. Let no one concerned be offended at the moral I have chosen to draw from our unfortunate story.

——MY heart sinks within me—the instrument of death is before me—farewel! farewel!—My soul sighs to be freed from its confinement—Eternal Father! accept my spirit——Let the tears of sorrow blot out my guilt from the book of thy wrath.

LETTER LXV.
WORTHY *to Mrs.* HOLMES.

BOSTON.

WE have surmounted the performance of the last scene of our tragedy, with less difficulty and distress than I imagined. Great numbers crouded to see the body of poor *Harrington;* they were impressed with various emotions, for their sympathizing sorrow could not be concealed—Indeed a man without sensibility exhibits no sign of a soul. I was struck with admiration at the observations of the populace, and the justness of the character they drew of the deceased. "Alas!" said one—"poor youth, thou art gone. Thou wast of a promising genius, of violent passions, thou wast possessed of a too nice sensibility, and a dread of shame. It is only such an one who would take the trouble to kill himself. Ah! poor well natured, warm hearted, hot headed youth—how my heart

1 An apparent error, "Gaurdian," in the original has been corrected here.

bleeds for you! We consider thee as the dupe of Nature, and the sacrifice of Seduction."—The old father hears this, and becomes overwhelmed with shame and sorrow.

THE jury which sat upon the body of our friend, after mature consideration, brought in their verdict SUICIDE. The rigour of the law[1] was not executed—the body was privately taken away, and I saw it deposited by the side of his faithful *Harriot.*

I SEND you inclosed a copy of the Monumental Inscription, as written by *Harrington.* I found it with many loose papers. It contains the story of our unfortunate friends, and a profitable moral is deduced from it.

THOUGH a few weeks begin to spread a calm over our passions, yet the recollection of our misfortunes will sometimes cause a momentary agitation, as the ocean retains its swell, after the storm subsides.

Adieu!

MONUMENTAL INSCRIPTION[2]

THOU who shalt wander o'er these humble plains,
Where one kind grave their hapless dust contains,
O pass not on—if merit claim a tear,
Or dying virtue cause a sigh sincere.
Here rest their heads, consign'd to parent earth,
Who to one common father ow'd their birth;
Unknown this union—Nature still presides,
And Sympathy unites, whom Fate divides.
They see—they love—but heav'n their passion tries,
Their *love* sustains it, but their *mortal* dies.
Stranger! contemplate well before you part,
And take this serious counsel to thy heart:
Does some fair female of unspotted fame,
Salute thee, smiling, with a father's name,

1 Throughout the eighteenth century, coroner's juries in Massachusetts—the bodies of citizens assembled to rule on such cases—were increasingly reluctant to enforce full penalties even when they found the deceased guilty of the crime of suicide. Such penalties might have included the confiscation of property or a refusal to allow burial in a churchyard or public cemetery, leaving friends of the deceased to resort to "highway burial." Although the Coroner's Jury has ruled against Harrington here, they chose not to confiscate his property or prevent him from being buried alongside Harriot.

2 Brown's original poem.

Bid her detest the fell Seducer's wiles,
Who smiles to win—and murders as he smiles.
If ever wandering near this dark recess,
Where guardian spirits round the ether press;
Where, on their urn, celestial care descends,
Two lovers come, whom fair success attends,
"O'er the pale marble shall they join their heads,
And drink the falling tears each other sheds,
Then sadly say, with mutual pity mov'd,
O! may we never love as these have lov'd."

The END.

SANS SOUCI, ALIAS, FREE AND EASY

DRAMATIS PERSONÆ.[1]

MEN.

Mr. IMPORTANCE,
JEMMY SATIRIST,
Doctor GALLANT,
Mr. BON TON,
YOUNG FORWARD,
LITTLE PERT.
Waiter, Servants, &c.

WOMEN.

Madam IMPORTANCE,
Madam BRILLIANT,
REBUBLICAN HEROINE,
Mrs. W—N.

SCENE—*The Metropolis of the Massachusetts.*

---

1 Handwritten annotations in copies of the play held at the Boston Athenæum and American Antiquarian Society agree on several points when matching characters with historical counterparts: Perez Morton and Sarah Wentworth Apthorp Morton as Mr. and Madam Importance; Dr. [Oliver?] Smith as Dr. Gallant; Isaac Winslow (1743–93) as Little Pert. Jemmy Satirist was identified by John Quincy Adams in a 19 September 1785 letter to his mother as James Hughes, a lawyer and (at least by the end of the decade) acting justice of the Supreme Court. For more discussion, see pp. 33–38 in the Introduction to this volume ("The Sans Souci Scandal"). See also Warren.

SANS SOUCI, &c.

ACT I. SCENE. I.

The HALL.[1]

YOUNG FORWARD, and *LITTLE PERT*.[2]

YOUNG FORWARD.

SANS SOUCI—free and easy![3] This is high bon ton[4]—Ante-revolution days[5]—routs[6]—drums, &c. This would do for my Lord *Paxton*,[7] that essence of Chesterfield:[8] We want some of that *Sans Souci* air and address, which were so conspicuous in that great character; but however we practice very well in the school of politeness, and a few years will produce many a Beau Nash[9] in our modern circles.

---

1 The Concert Hall, built in 1752, at the corner of Hanover and Queen streets, hosted public and private functions ranging from concerts to meetings of Freemasons to dancing lessons. A public dancing assembly had met regularly in Boston for years; the Sans Souci club, also meeting at the Concert Hall, competed with the more established and socially sanctioned assembly. During the British occupation of Boston (1768–76), officers established a subscription assembly for dancing and theatricals that was shunned by many Patriots, who instead instituted a "Liberty Assembly."

2 Both characters' names indicate youth and impertinence.

3 French for "carefree" or "without worry," *Sanssouci* was also the name of a summer palace in Potsdam, Germany, of Frederick the Great (r. 1740–86), king of Prussia, built in the 1740s.

4 French for "good tone," the term, sometimes shortened to "the ton," indicates the world of fashion and polite manners, the upper crust. The term entered English in the mid-eighteenth century.

5 I.e., comparable to Boston's society prior to the Revolution.

6 Fashionable gatherings.

7 Charles Paxton (1708–88), a colonial British customs official in Boston with a reputation for an extravagant lifestyle and courtly manners, had been hung in effigy at the Liberty Tree in 1767.

8 Philip Dormer Stanhope, 4th Earl of Chesterfield (1694–1773), popularly known as Lord Chesterfield, author of the posthumously published *Letters to His Son on the Art of Becoming a Man of the World and a Gentleman* (London, 1774). Chesterfield's *Letters*, popular but controversial on both sides of the Atlantic, offered advice on how to behave in polite society in order to advance socially.

9 Richard Nash (1674–1761), an English barrister and social leader in Bath who was infamous as a dandy and a gambler.

LITTLE PERT.

D—n[1] the old musty rules of decency and decorum—national characters—Spartan virtues—republican principles[2]—they are all calculated for rigid manners, and Cromwelian[3] days;—they are as disgusting as old orthodoxy:—Fashion and etiquette are more agreeable to my ideas of life—this is the independence I aim at—the free and easy air which so distinguishes the man of fashion, from the self formal[4] republican—the court stile[5]—the *jê ne scai quoi*[6]—give me but this and away with all your buckram of Presbeterianism.[7]

YOUNG FORWARD.

I find, my good friend, you have a genuine idea of taste.—From the many starched sentiments which some of our Old Dons[8] have endeavoured to instil among us by their resolves—town-meetings, &c. I expected we should all, at the close of the war,[9] be obliged to be confined to our closets to learn political creeds, and read political disquisitions—and instead of balls, concerts and card-parties, we should be employed in writing dissertations on government:—Happy reverse! We have now worn off those old

---

1 The word *damn*, censored to protect the sensibility of delicate readers.

2 "National," "Spartan," and "republican" are used as synonyms here and indicate republican ideology often attributed to classical democracies of ancient Greece. The term "Spartan" also carries connotations of austerity, frugality, or generally forgoing luxury.

3 Characterized by Oliver Cromwell (1599–1658), Puritan, military leader during the English Civil War, and Lord Protector of the Commonwealth of England, Scotland, and Ireland following the execution of Charles I (r. 1625–49). "Cromwelian" suggests both Puritanism and republicanism.

4 Self-made and -regulated instead of following social forms or mandates.

5 Courtly, following the fawning manners of a monarch's immediate circle.

6 French, meaning literally "I don't know what." An unnamable but attractive quality or characteristic.

7 Buckram is a stiff fabric, also used to indicate a stiffness of manners. Used here to indicate the rigidity of Congregationalist manners but especially prohibitions on fine clothing. The spelling of Presbyterian is found in the play's first edition; the second edition has an obvious typesetting error: "Presberianism."

8 Preceptors or teachers, used to indicate heads of colleges at Oxford or Cambridge universities; more generally suggesting the conservative leaders of a prior generation.

9 The American Revolution ended with the signing of the Treaty of Paris on 3 September 1783.

fashion sentiments, and can breathe the free air of gallantry[1] and etiquette.[2]

LITTLE PERT.

Can any prospect be more pleasing than the brilliant appearance of this Hall?—What a fine arrangement!—Let me see—twenty card-tables,—Behold those agreeable ladies!—what animated countenances!—How the chance of play gives new vivacity to their eyes!—How charming this assemblage of flowers in this garden of beauty!—What a beautiful variety adorns this parterre![3]—This is an improvement of Eden, there only *one fruit* tempted our first parents,[4] but here they hang in such clusters, that we are surrounded in the circle of temptations.

YOUNG FORWARD.

Not only the ladies, but I think the gentlemen appear with a particular grace.—We have the happy faculty of blending business and amusements—I hate those *tare* and *tret* fellows[5] in London, that can only make a figure in a *compting house*,[6] and walk athrawt[7] a room as clumsy as *gross hundreds*,[8] meer *avoirdupois* weight;[9]—I like to see a man throw aside his professional character, and enter a polite circle with the *Sans Souci* air of a petit maitre[10]—and instead

---

1 Carefully prescribed manners.

2 Chivalry, especially toward women, but by the end of the eighteenth century used by critics to signify artificial or exaggerated deference.

3 A careful arrangement of flower beds in an ornamental garden; also, perhaps, punning on the term's use in theater architecture, meaning the seated area just behind the orchestra (synonymous with parquet circle).

4 I.e., in the original sin of Adam and Eve, which led to their expulsion from Paradise.

5 Accountants. *Tare* and *tret* are accounting terms. The former indicates the weight of a shipping container, deducted in order to calculate the net weight of goods; the latter indicates an allowance for the weight of dust or other waste accumulated during shipping.

6 Counting house, or accounting offices. To make a figure is a pun indicating both an accountant's numbers and a notable public appearance.

7 Possibly an amalgamation of the words "athwart," or across from side to side, and "thrawt," or awry. To walk across a room awkwardly, in other words. The second edition spells this word "a-thrawt."

8 In accounting terms, a gross hundred is 120.

9 A standard set of measurements for weight in shipping common goods, in pounds and ounces, developed in Great Britain. "Meer" is an alternative spelling of *mere*.

10 French, literally translated as "little master"; used here with approbation, but typically a derisive term meaning dandy or fop.

of plodding in a *Ledger* over Dr. and Cr.[1] I like to see him versed in all the tender stile of a billet doux[2]—not calculated solely to *ballance accounts*, but to decide with precission the arrangements of a lady's toilette.[3]

LITTLE PERT.

When I was at New-York, among the British, I was ashamed to acknowledge myself a Bostonian—we had such a particular character—we were always pictured as a set of canting[4] presbeterians, who began Sundays before sun set on Saturday, and held out praying until Monday morning at sunrise—that all our diversions were singing psalms, and going to Thursday-Lectures:[5]—But thank Heaven we can now hold up our heads amidst the most polite circle at Raneleigh,[6] or join with full eclat[7] the brilliant assembly at Vauxhall.[8]

YOUNG FORWARD.

For the present we will seperate as our extacies may possibly be observed by the company.

Exeunt.

1 In double-entry accounting, debit and credit, respectively.
2 From French for "sweet notes," or love letters.
3 The rituals attending fashionable appearance.
4 Sanctimoniously, often hypocritically, preaching in a whining tone.
5 Mid-week lectures or sermons had been a significant part of Boston public life since the 1630s. Typically delivered by ministers, they veered toward social or political topics, especially during the Revolution.
6 Ranelagh Gardens, in Chelsea, outside London, was a fashionable site of public amusement, partly owned by a syndicate of London's major theaters, in the late eighteenth century. Activities included romantic walks and open-air musical performance.
7 Flair, style, with dramatic effect.
8 Vauxhall Gardens, across the Thames from London and accessible by boat, was established in the 1660s and was the city's most famous pleasure gardens in the eighteenth century. The Gardens hosted a variety of entertainments, including hot-air balloons, musical performances, and fireworks.

SCENE II.
The DRAWING-ROOM.

Enter *Madam IMPORTANCE* and *Madam BRILLIANT*.

Madam IMPORTANCE.

PRAY waiter are there much company this evening?

WAITER.

A great deal, Madam.

Madam BRILLIANT.

Are they very brilliant in their dress?

WAITER.

Very much so, Madam.

Madam BRILLIANT.

I am sorry the ladies have been so attentive to their dress, as I am afraid this will occasion the breaking up this entertainment—as the gentlemen will by and bye make this a plea,[1] after they find it is attended with so great expence.

Madam IMPORTANCE.

Don't be apprehensive on this account—this is the very thing I was in hopes would take place—this will serve to *sift down families*,[2] and will be the most effectual means to establish a *precedency*[3]—we have for a long while been too much on a level—once a fortnight a publick assembly, will for a long time, keep up this *equality*—but the oftner we meet, those which cannot keep pace, will be obliged to resign their pretensions to high life, and leave a few of *us* to enjoy the field—for my own part, I conceive it to be the happiest plan that could have been adopted—it ensnares people in their own trap, which you know, Madam, is the most effectual method to ensure their destruction.

Madam BRILLIANT.

If those are your intentions, Madam, we must carry it much further, and instead of a few shillings, which I suppose the

1 I.e., raise an objection.

2 I.e., to separate families of means as socially superior.

3 A social hierarchy.

generality will play for, we must establish at our own table the rubbers of ten guineas[1] at least.

Enter *Mr. IMPORTANCE* and *Dr. GALLANT.*

Doct. GALLANT.

Ladies, your servant.

LADIES.

Your servant, Gentlemen.

Mr. IMPORTANCE.

Ladies, shall I be permitted to hand you[2] into the Hall?—You will be *monstrously* pleased with the appearance.

Madam BRILLIANT.

Are all the tables full?

Doct. GALLANT.

Mostly Madam,—but a few are reserved for certain ladies—not to be taken up by the company, until we know whether certain characters will be of the company for the evening.

Madam IMPORTANCE.

Very right—I am glad you have thought to make this reserve—as distinctions in all companies are necessary.

Exeunt.

SCENE III.
The HALL.

Enter *Mr. IMPORTANCE, JEMMY SATIRIST,* and *Doctor GALLANT.*

JEMMY SATIRIST.

WHAT most surprises me, is, that the plan was so readily consented to—the parade of the card-table has been so long out of

---

1 In whist, the card game characters are likely to play, a "rubber" is a series of odd-numbered matches, usually three, in which the winner takes the majority (e.g., "best two of three"). Ten guineas would be the minimum win in the scenario Madam Brilliant proposes.

2 Escort.

fashion—I did not think they would with so much alacrity,[1] have introduced it into a publick assembly—however, we are fond[2] of novelty, and the fascinating charms of high life have too many allurements to be resisted.—We have made a notable caveat—not to play beyond one shilling and six pence upon our HONOUR! there's the rub—Gaming is like a coy mistress, whose meer smiles we at first think a happiness—but when those become familiar, we urge forward to more *substantial* joys.

Mr. IMPORTANCE.

We have in our *professional character*, a mighty influence in carrying any plans we wish to adopt—for my own part, I endeavour to inforce every thing with the prerogative of the of the *black robes*,[3] and dressed in the *sable livery*,[4] can establish doctrines of etiquette, with equal decision, as our bretheren[5] of the pulpit can their articles of faith.

Doct. GALLANT.

Well it is quite right—professional characters must be supported with dignity—otherways, all distinctions will be lost in the levelling[6] spirit of republicanism—therefore, if we expect to support taste and stile, we must keep up this parade, and by assuming an appearance above the commonality, we may stamp on our characters a *superiority* of rank—This may appear a new doctrine—*that in order to promote distinction, we must introduce all into one society*—but depend upon it, a particular *deportment*[7] observed at such times, more effectually secures preeminence, than shutting ones self up from the crowd.

1 Eagerness.
2 The second edition silently corrects "found," an obvious error in the first.
3 Ministry.
4 The term would generally refer to a minister's vestments, but here it refers to the long black robes worn by Boston's barristers, the highest-ranking attorneys and the only lawyers allowed to appear before the justices of the State Judicial Supreme Court. Perez Morton had been admitted as a barrister in 1784. Mr. Importance, in his pun, pits the office and authority of barrister against the traditional authority of the clergy in setting social norms.
5 "Brethering" in the second edition.
6 Democratic, leveling social classes or distinctions.
7 Display of manners.

Mr. IMPORTANCE.

Upon my word, Doctor, you have improved on Chesterfield—I have ever thought that keeping aloof, and only appearing at times, when some important questions were agitated, would be most likely to secure my importance—a town-meeting harangue,[1] (for instance) I conceived would produce wonderful effects—and then retiring with a peculiar easy air of consequence, would secure the respectful complaisance of the whole assembly.

JEMMY SATIRIST.

No person can dispute with brother *Importance* his right of station in the beau monde[2]—he soon threw off all incumbrances, and like a true disciple, forsook ALL—he had no notion of mounting the mere *shadow of Pegasus,*[3] but chose rather to prance among the Muses[4] with the nag fully caparisoned[5]—however brother, not to be too severe—but we gentlemen of the ——— sometimes take the liberty to abuse each other, as well as our C——s[6]—Indulgencies![7]—Indulgencies, brother!—But let us hasten among the company, as the tables begin to be filled.

Exeunt.

---

1 Political speech.
2 From French, literally meaning "fine world"; high or fashionable society.
3 In Greek myth, the winged horse, offspring of the god Poseidon and the Gorgon Medusa. Pegasus was said to strike the rocks on Mount Helicon so forcefully that the Hippocrene spring erupted there, a spot sacred to the Muses and often associated with poetry. For this reason, writers at least as early as the eighteenth century used Pegasus as a figure for fame, particularly literary or poetic fame. Most likely, given the context, the phrase "shadow of Pegasus" refers to Pegasus unbridled or without other riding accoutrements.
4 In Greek myth, nine goddesses who inspire poetry, song, and other arts.
5 With ornamental cloth covering the saddle, merely for show.
6 The meaning here is unclear. If "gentlemen of the ________" refers to members of the court (the characters here are supposed to be based on an acting justice and a barrister of the Supreme Judicial Court), the first blank could signify "gentlemen of the bar" and the second (our C_____s) could mean "our Clients" or "our Courts."
7 Favors or privileges. In eighteenth-century New England, the term might have resonated in multiple ways. Anti-Catholic prejudice among New England Calvinists held that "indulgences" were granted to Catholics to absolve them of sins committed or yet to be committed. The term was also used for privileges or exemptions granted by a monarch in exchange for faithful service.

ACT II.

SCENE I.

Enter *The REPUBLICAN HEROINE* and *Mrs. W—N.*[1]

REPUBLICAN HEROINE.

I HAVE been complimented with a Card for a new Entertainment called Sans Souci.

Mrs. W—N.

Have you attended?

REP. HEROINE.

Upon my word, Madam, I was a long while considering whether it was a real or imaginary compliment; I could scarcely believe it possible, that this country particularly this town, whose name stands foremost in the annals of America, should so early plunge into the utmost excesses of dissipation:[2] How will such an account read among the friends of America in Europe. I could hardly refrain from tears when I entered the Hall, to see the respectable inhabitants of this metropolis, so wantonly introducing a custom of publick card playing, even at so early a period after the war. Forgive me, Madam my expressing my sentiments so freely; but believe me I have hitherto indulged such pleasing ideas respecting this country, from their publick proceedings during the war, that when I find those sentiments of their virtue turn out mere chimeras[3] of my own imagination, I cannot but lament my disappointment. The respect that has been shewn me since my arrival, I most gratefully acknowledge, but often on my retiring from the parade of their entertainments, I cannot but pity their delusion. I did not carry my enthusiasm so far as to expect to find the rigid Spartan principles[4] practised; but I did conceive to be introduced into societies of frugality and

---

1 Understood by contemporaries to represent the English historian Catharine Macaulay (1731–91), who visited Boston during the Sans Souci controversy, and Mercy Otis Warren, American poet, playwright, and historian (1728–1814). See the Introduction, pp. 34–37, for further detail.

2 Debauchery.

3 In Greek myth, fire-breathing female monsters with the head of a lion, body of a goat, and tail of a serpent; in common usage, a fantasy or illusion that vanishes on close inspection.

4 Extreme frugality or simplicity; see p. 184, note 2.

œconomy:[1] I did expect to find a cultivation of manners somewhat similar to their[2] publick resolves; but again pardon me, Madam, when I inform you I am greatly disappointed. British gewgaws[3]—etiquette and parade, are too prevailing to be easily eradicated, unless some immediate exertions are made to turn this destructive current: As a stranger, I cannot with propriety set up to give examples, but on ladies of established characters in the country, much ought to be expected from them.

Mrs. W—N.

I am very unhappy to find your observations are so just. I cannot but acknowledge we have too far copied the vices of that nation which we have so lately opposed: But however, I do not think this late entertainment will be long continued; there are many respectable characters among them, who I am persuaded when they consider the dangerous tendency of this assembly will readily discountenance it. We must be convinced how dangerous to the morals of youth—how destructive to the happiness of families and individuals, an introduction of card parties has ever been; therefore though they have become of the party, which from inattention, rather than from inclination to promote a spirit of dissipation they at first engaged in it; they will readily give up the entertainment, and even discountenance the promoters of it.

REP. HEROINE.

I wish sincerely you may not be disappointed in your hopes; but, my dear Madam,

'*Vice is a monster of so frightful mein*,' &c.[4]

Exeunt.

---

1 Careful management of resources, especially financial.
2 Changed to "the" in the second edition.
3 Gaudy ornaments or playthings.
4 *Mien*: appearance or expression. From Alexander Pope, "An Essay on Man," Epistle II (1733):

> Vice is a monster of so frightful mien
> As, to be hated, needs but to be seen;
> Yet seen too oft, familiar with her face,
> We first endure, then pity, then embrace.

SCENE II.

YOUNG FORWARD and *LITTLE PERT*.

YOUNG FORWARD.

I HAVE been to all the Booksellers in town to purchase *Hoyle*;[1] but find they have been all bought up—There are proposals in the Drawing Room for a new edition with improvements; also there is to be kept a minute Book for remarks on the game of whist, as many particular cases may take place in the course of play which will render it a valuable collection, as an appendix to this new edition; the whole are to be revised by our D-r-ct—s,[2] and dedicated to them.

LITTLE PERT.

A good proposal! Let me see the subscription:[3]—To promote the work I will subscribe for 100 books. However, we are so d—d[4] contracted in this town, we shall never come to a full improvement in the polite arts.—The present card party is a mere burlesque on the institution!—How ridiculous we appear!—A guinea a corner alarms one half of them:—There are but few tables here that dare hazard.—I almost scar'd one fellow into panicks, and a lady into hystericks, by offering to bet ten guineas on the rubber: They made answer they did not play so high.—Was there any thing ever so laughable? What the devil do they come here for? Do they come merely to shuffle a pack of cards? We might as well be in a private party;—let us be something or nothing:—*A card party gingling*[5] *shillings and six pences*; Ha, ha, ha.—The circle of etiquette with purses of silver;—this would sound high at BROOK's;[6]—A republican card party; quite a political phænomenon. However never mind it, Rome was not built in a day;—*free and easy* is our motto, and we are fond of consistency—perseverando.[7]

---

1 Edmond Hoyle, *A Short Treatise on the Game of Whist* (London, 1742), frequently reprinted and pirated. An American edition of *Hoyle's Games Improved*, which included instruction in backgammon and other games as well, was printed in Boston in 1796.

2 Directors.

3 I.e., the list of subscribers. Publishers often circulated subscription lists as a way to gauge interest, raise funds, and advertise new works prior to publication.

4 Damned (censored).

5 Jingling.

6 A London gentlemen's club, founded in 1764, notorious for gambling.

7 Latin, persevering.

YOUNG FORWARD.

We are often bemoaning the want of plays in this town;[1] this will be a considerable introduction to this entertainment; we can with the greatest propriety ask permission for a theatre after we have been indulged with a card party; for of two evils, plays must be considered the least;—so that we have nothing to do, but to resign for a season our card amusements until we can get a theatre erected, and after that we can return to our present entertainment by pleading *precedents*; for we must hold precedents as tenacious in the polite circle as we lawyers do *authorities* in our profession.

LITTLE PERT.

But one essential matter I am afraid we shall be deprived of;—Graham[2]—the celebrated Doctor Graham;—the celestial bed; hah![3]—here the Cupids would nestle on the downy pillows: Lectures on love;—these are Evening Lectures worth attending to: I dare say he would have a thronged assembly; a full congregation—zealots—enthusiasts—high orthodoxy—this would be a hopeful school of good breeding—all well versed in the principles of galantry—no[4] awkward modesty, and shame-face'd diffidence—but full confidence—polite amours;—never be afraid, we shall soon pave the way for this amusement—lectures surely cannot be disapproved—who can object to lectures?—We could blind one half the old women in town, by telling them the

---

1 Although occupying British forces staged theatricals during the war, theaters remained illegal until 1794. Many of the strongest proponents for legalizing the theater were affiliated with the Sans Souci circle. An exception is Harrison Grey Otis (1765–1848), a key defender of Sans Souci and supposed to be the prototype for Young Forward, but who opposed the theater's legalization in the following decade.

2 Catharine Macaulay created a scandal when she married William Graham (1757–1845). (She was forty-seven; he was twenty-one.) He traveled with her to the United States in May 1784, where they stayed for over a year. Graham, described in contemporary documents as a "surgeon's mate," was the brother of James Graham (1745–94), a controversial Scottish physician and reformer, but little else is known about him.

3 James Graham, the older brother of Macaulay's husband, was best known as the inventor of an electrified, magnetic, musical "Celestial Bed," which was designed to maximize both sexual pleasure and the chances of conception for his patients. Graham also delivered public lectures on sex and reproduction. By the mid-1780s his practice had gone under and he had retreated to Edinburgh.

4 "Now" in first edition, corrected in the second.

celebrated Doctor Graham intended to deliver evening lectures on various subjects—they would at least think him a second Whitfield.[1]

YOUNG FORWARD.

You have a happy faculty at anticipation—but however let us be going, for while I attend to your rhapsody, I am losing the present amusement.

Exeunt.

SCENE III.
The DRAWING-ROOM.

Enter *Madam IMPORTANCE* and *Madam BRILLIANT.*

Madam IMPORTANCE.

WHAT an awkward piece of business this is! I am really tired.—The foreign lady[2] who was at our table, alarmed some of our circle, by laying down a purse of ten guineas. As our assembly was somewhat similar to those in England—she (I suppose) thought we did in some degree practice playing at least to the amount of so triffling a sum—we all stared at each other—for my own part I did not like to tell her we did not play so high, or to inform her of our resolution to the contrary, as we should make but an indifferent appearance to her, if we supposed such a sum were extravagant—however, as it was late, I pretended to be fatigued, and threw up my hand, with an apology that I was indisposed;—she even seemed surprised at my indisposition and exclaimed—*indisposed at a card table!* I therefore found my complaints were intirely foreign from etiquette—however, I still persisted in my indisposition, and the lady observing my embarrassment, politely declined urging me any further.

1 George Whitefield (1714–70), celebrated English evangelist who achieved extraordinary popularity preaching in the colonies during the Great Awakening in the 1730s and 1740s. He returned to North America several more times and died in Newburyport, Massachusetts, in 1770.

2 [Note in original publication:] This is not pointed at any particular foreign character now among us, but what is likely may happen in future.

Madam BRILLIANT.

This is a circumstance of which I was not aware, as we may in time expect foreigners among us, they will naturally suppose from so polite a circle, they may *bet* as at assemblies they have frequented in Europe—and being from our stations, introduced to their tables, we shall often be put to the disagreeable necessity of pleading indisposition—and indisposition may in time, become a cant[1] term among the polite circle for declining a bet:—Free and easy therefore is not very applicable to our present situation.

Madam IMPORTANCE.

To-morrow we will talk over this affair at our leisure.

Exeunt.

ACT III. SCENE. I.
The HALL.

Enter *Mr. IMPORTANCE*, *JEMMY SATIRIST*, and *Doctor GALLANT*.

Mr. IMPORTANCE.

How we can divert ourselves through the several rooms?—In one circle we can observe the most agreeable parties of ladies, seated at the several tables, which look like an assembly of Goddesses! The Graces seem here to have taken up their residence—such a beautiful variety displayed in the arrangement of their dress, adds to the redundancy of their charms: Within this Hall, I would risque the reputation we have already acquired, of having as fine a collection of ladies in our assembly, as any the world can produce.—However, sometimes I can see a little anxiety in a countenance—it is a pity to sully one lustre[2] amid such a cluster of charms—but taste and etiquette must be complied with, however fatal the consequences may be to beauty.

JEMMY SATIRIST.

This is a pretty harangue, brother *Importance*, one would almost suppose you was fee'd[3]. by the ladies—but I am sensible you have

1 Slang.

2 To reduce in brightness or beauty; to stain. In this case, to besmirch reputation.

3 Hired, in this case as a lawyer.

a good cause, and may be sure of a verdict in your favour. It is a pity you had not always spoke your mind with so much safety, for nothing is more fatal to a man of fashion than doing any thing reflecting on the ladies—it was rather unfortunate in your first appearing on the publick stage, to have such a hue and cry after you[1]—but however, not to call to mind things past—I wish the ladies had heard this late panegyrick.[2]

Doct. GALLANT.

While you are attending to the appearance of their persons, you do not observe the gracefulness of their dancing—T———r[3] has a most happy faculty at teaching—like a limner,[4] he *draws every grace of gentility, and blends ease and address in every feature*—however, let us leave this subject, and talk on some other.—Pray have you seen Doctor Price's[5] new publication?

Mr. IMPORTANCE.

Yes.

Doct. GALLANT.

Well, what do you think of it?

---

1 In the winter of 1777–78, Perez Morton had created a mild stir in local newspapers when he suggested, in a lecture to an audience of Freemasons and their wives, that women were not admitted as Masons because they could not keep secrets.

2 A public speech in praise of something.

3 William Turner (1745–92), a celebrated dancing master and owner, from 1769 to 1789, of the Concert Hall, where this play is set. See p. 183, note 1.

4 Portrait artist.

5 Richard Price (1723–91), famous English moral philosopher, republican, and supporter of the American Revolution. The publication referred to is *Observations on the Importance of the American Revolution* (1784), in which he asserts that American independence is second only to the introduction of Christianity in "the progressive course of human improvement" and issues an abundance of warnings to the new nation: "Should they lose those virtuous and simple manners by which alone Republics can long subsist—Should false refinement, luxury, and irreligion spread among them; excessive jealousy distract their governments; and clashing interests, subject to no strong control, break the federal union—The consequence will be, that the fairest experiment ever tried in human affairs will miscarry."

Mr. IMPORTANCE.

The Doctor would do to live in Carthage, Sparta, or Rome[1] in the most rigid times; but now those sentiments are wholly imaginary ideas of a Republican's brain[2]—they are too antiquated—modern republicanism is of a very different complexion, as contrasted as the severe countenance of Cromwell, and the pretty smooth face of a petit maitre—those of the Doctor's[3] are principles of republicanism of the uncivilized kind—but now we soften them down in the school of politeness, and make them wear a more pleasing garb—the antient republican[4] spirit is like the old principles of religion—staunch Calvinism—but now we have modernized them,[5] and united them with the court stile of taste and fashion.

JEMMY SATIRIST.

The Doctor's sentiments did well enough in war times, when we were under the influence of whig[6] principles—this mercury did very well in our political thermometer—but now we have no occasion for this blood heat[7]—they were pleasing doctrines to preach up at that time, but now, why are we to be ding'd[8] with national manners—national debts—œconomy—industry and

---

1 Ancient republics.

2 This word appears as "oran" in the first edition and "bran" in second, but "brain" seems most likely, given the context.

3 I.e., Dr. Price's republican principles.

4 Both editions spell this "rebublican," which seems to be a typesetting error, corrected here.

5 Morton attended King's Chapel, founded in 1686 as New England's first Anglican church. The church sat largely empty during the Revolution. In the 1780s it controversially adopted a Unitarian theology, including a revised Book of Common Prayer to which Perez Morton contributed. James Apthorp, Morton's father-in-law, was among those members of the congregation who publicly dissented from these developments as "unscriptural and heretical" (*Independent Chronicle*, 22 Nov. 1787). Morton was a vestryman at King's Chapel from 1783 to 1788 and occupied the pew that had formerly belonged to Charles Paxton (see p. 183, note 7). It's possible that he lost his position as vestryman following the scandal of Fanny Apthorp's pregnancy and suicide that year.

6 In British politics, the party that endorsed the supremacy of Parliament; in Revolutionary American politics, a supporter of independence from Britain.

7 In humoral medicine, which retained a hold in popular culture through the late eighteenth century, a sanguinary temper was governed by forceful heat and circulation of the blood.

8 Beaten repeatedly with heavy blows.

such disagreeable subjects?—Independence in the original is my idea—high court independence—independent of every restraint which can mar the pleasures and amusements of life.

Doct. GALLANT.

I know the old Dons lift up their eyes with horror, when they see what they call the *old principles* subsiding—they are as tenacious of their *old sentiments*, as they are of their white wigs[1]—but we know better—we act on the *benevolent* plan—why should we ever keep up a d—n[2] distinction between whig and tory?[3]—For my own part, I wish to embrace ALL, and this very assembly is one means of introducing to a *sociability* the several parties which have been distinct through the war—let all political distinctions be buried, and let us with fraternal affection embrace every one, whatever may have been his principles during the war, or however inimical his conduct—these are genuine sentiments and agreeable to our modern republicanism—We must desist from our political observations for the present.

Exeunt.

SCENE II.
The ENTRY.—SERVANTS.[4]

Cuffy.[5] WAT clok Jack?

---

1 Powdered wigs for men were already a declining fashion in the 1780s and by the turn of the century had largely been discarded.

2 Damn (censored).

3 In British politics, a member of the conservative party, defenders of the monarchy and established Anglican Church; in Revolutionary American politics, a Loyalist and opponent of American independence. Most Tories or Loyalists had been driven from Boston following the end of British occupation; the Banishment Act of the State of Massachusetts, passed in September 1778, named over three hundred people prevented by law from returning. Many of these had already fled, returning to Britain or moving to Nova Scotia, their land confiscated by the new government.

4 The dialogue in this scene is supposed to represent phonetically the dialect of African servants or enslaved people. Slavery was at least theoretically abolished in Massachusetts in 1783, when Quock Walker sued his owner for his freedom and won. In 1788, following a highly publicized incident in which six free black people were kidnapped and sent to Martinique as slaves, the slave trade was formally outlawed.

5 In both editions, the typesetting changes for this brief scene, with the characters' names appearing in the left margin (rather than centered) and their lines following directly.

Jack. Pass twelbe clok.

Cuffy. Dis be no lik ole Massa tims—ten clok, go bed—de gate shot—go prarrs—all de serbants go bed—Massa put out de fire.

Jack. Yesse Cuffe—but you be ole fello—I like bery vel dis setin up—Massa and Misse brod—gate open all nite—why you fool, what optunty for serbants? But when Massa and Misse kep hom all de ebning, go bed ten clok, what time for poor serbants frolik.

Cuffy. Massa and Messe come home twelbe clok, scold and hangry—poor serbants pay for all—find falt wid ebery ting—noting rite.

Jack. You neber been Ningland[1] Cuffe—dar fin tims—presenly Bosson lik it—masserades[2]—pantons[3]—no litle Cornshort-Hal[4] for gentry—presenly panton—tea-trays—flambeaux[5]—no dribe wid one poor hosse and sha—but tree serbants—no one poor deble lik youself—but libry serbants.[6]

Cuffy. Me be owl felo Jack—but I frad too tru—me here notin now but Sam and Susy[7]—me dont no wat day meen—but me here dem say, we go Sam and Susy to night—d——n baboon.[8]

Jack. Baboon—Cuffe wat you say?—Balloon you mean.[9]

Cuffy. Hah, balloon—wel no mater for dat.

---

1 In England.

2 Masquerades.

3 Bon Tons, or high society.

4 Concert hall.

5 From French, a torch or candlestick with several branches, but perhaps a cheeky malapropism here if Jack is commenting on "beaux," or single young men.

6 Livery servants, uniformed and trained to drive and care for horses. Drivers.

7 Cuffy mistakes "Sans Souci" for "Sam and Susy."

8 Unclear what Cuffy means by this reference to a "damn baboon," whether he is using the term to refer to someone or whether he is repeating a racist epithet his master and mistress have applied to him.

9 In the 1780s, a hot-air balloon craze took hold in France and spread to England and eventually to North America. A former Boston physician, Dr. John Jeffries (1745–1819), who had fled as a Loyalist, was on the first manned balloon to cross the English Channel the same month this

SCENE III.
The HALL.—A Card Table.

Mr. BON TON, Madam IMPORTANCE, Madam BRILLIANT, and *Dr. GALLANT.*

Madam BRILLIANT.

A DIAMOND led,[1] Mr. Bon Ton.

Mr. BON TON.

I beg pardon, Madam—but there is so much laughing, whispering and talking in the room, that I am quite embarrassed in my play.

Madam IMPORTANCE.

I believe, Sir, you have not been used to play in a social circle—but rather in places where every idea is absorb'd in the game.

Mr. BON TON.

Why truly, Madam, I have imbibed the manners of Europe so far, that I cannot have ears to attend to conversation, and eyes to observe the variety of objects around me, and at the same time

---

play was published. The previous summer, the *Massachusetts Centinel* had reported that "[t]he taste for Air Balloon matters has grown so much to an extraordinary pitch, that nothing can pretend to have any intrinsic value in it, unless it has this *name* as an appendage. The gentlemen and ladies upon *bon ton* are not the only objects that can boast of this aerial bombastic insignia to their ornaments; as a countryman was heard to say one day last week,—'*Fine balloon String Beans!*'" (14 July 1784). The Boston *American Herald* for 3 January 1785 carried a letter from London, describing "a thing, puffed up like a bladder, and as big again as our village church; this they call the balloon," which had carried a cat and dog into the air at the Pantheon public gardens. The *Centinel* for 15 January 1785, which also carried the first advertisement for this play, included a celebratory poem titled "The Progress of Balloons" that imagined future air travel between Boston and New York as well as the balloon's uses in wartime. By 2 February, the *Centinel* was reporting that a subscription had been launched in New York to fund construction of a hot-air balloon, and on 30 March the same paper declared that "[t]he advancement of philosophy will most assuredly receive the assistance and applause of every friend of science" and that local "enterprising geniuses" would enter the field in order to "do honor to the invention, and add reputation to the town."

1 She calls attention to the game of cards they are playing, nudging Mr. Bon Ton to take his turn.

pay so great attention to the play as to know the disposition of the cards.

Madam IMPORTANCE.

I find, Sir, you practice wholly on the strictest principles of whist;[1]—but we endeavour to make this game only an evening's amusement.

Mr. BONTON.

Amusement, Madam, is not the principle in Europe; possibly the first institutions of this kind were established on these principles and suppose the sums to be play'd for, were limited, as among us;—but the company which now visit those places of publick resort, do not go for amusement solely, but to pursue a regular branch of business.—They have no idea of playing to pass away a few leisure hours, but to improve the moments for their profit—they are their busy hours—the time on which depends their future prospects. Therefore no conversation while at play is admitted but what is on the subject of the game, and a person would appear equally as ridiculous to be speaking at that time on any other subject, as to be talking of Hoyle at the tabernacle.[2]

Madam BRILLIANT.

You have quite forgot your play, by your lengthy observations.—Hearts are trumps.

Mr. BONTON.

And have been so, Madam, ever since you entered the room.

Madam BRILLIANT.

I suppose compliments are agreeable to the rules laid down by Hoyle?

Mr. BONTON.

Yes, Madam, and are often played to great advantage.

Madam IMPORTANCE.

I always suspect a gentleman's hand when he begins to compliment the lady he plays against.

---

1 A trick-taking card game made popular in eighteenth-century England; it takes its name from the need for players to be silent and attentive.

2 Church.

Mr. BONTON.

I suppose, Madam, you conceive it a *finesse*;[1]—at least for the *odd trick*.[2]

Madam BRILLIANT.

I suppose you calculate by the table of chances?[3]

Mr. BONTON.

I do, Madam, but my success depends on your smiles.

Doctor GALLANT.

Pray how are we for game?

Mr. BONTON.

Nine.

Madam BRILLIANT.

Well, Sir, we will for the present be whist,[4] and endeavour to finish before 12 o'clock.

Mr. BONTON.

The hours pass most rapidly;—but however, Madam, we must not find fault with time, for in your company *eternity* can be the only measure of our happiness.

Madam BRILLIANT.

I shall not answer you at present, as it is time to withdraw.

Exeunt omnes.

---

1 An intricate and refined delicacy; also, in whist, a strategy by which one attempts to take a trick with a card that is not sure to win.

2 In whist, each side scores a point for each "odd trick" (a trick over and above six).

3 She asks if he is playing scientifically.

4 Silent.

OCCURRENCES OF THE TIMES

FARCE.

OCCURRENCES OF THE TIMES.

OR, THE

TRANSACTIONS

OF

FOUR DAYS.

[Viz. — From FRIDAY the 16th, to MONDAY the 19th *January*, 1789.

A

FARCE

IN TWO ACTS.

" — No longer by vain fear, or shame control'd
In guilty amours, grown securely bold,
Mocking rebuke, they brave it on our streets,
*And ******, even at noon, his mistress meets.*
So public in their crimes, so daring grown,
They almost take a pride to have them known."[1]

PRINTED for the PURCHASERS.

---

1 The epigraph is extracted and adapted from the English satirist Charles Churchill's poem "The Times" (1764). In the original, instead of "******," Churchill offers the name "Lumley." By redacting the name, *Occurrences* both ambiguously applies the verse to "Morton" and also associates Boston's alleged immorality with that of London. For the poem in full, which explicitly levels charges of sexual depravity against several contemporary politicians, see Churchill. See p. 60, note 2 in the Introduction.

DRAMATIS PERSONÆ.[1]

MEN.	WOMEN.
MR. SIDNEY.	MRS. SIDNEY.
QUAKER.	MRS. TURNCOAT.
DR. HARRANGUE.	MARTHA.
WORTHY.	TIPSY.
POSITIVE.	
FRIENDLY.	
PEEP.	
DUPE.	
HARCOURT.	
TURNCOAT.	
STEADY and FIRM.	
IMPARTIALIST.	
DRBAUCHEE.[2]	

SCENE—BOSTON, *and a neighbouring Town.*

---

1 A copy of the play in the Houghton Library at Harvard University includes handwritten notes in which a contemporary reader attempts to identify these characters with Morton's allies. Sidney is identified as Morton; Quaker as Joseph Russell, merchant; Harrangue as Dr. Charles Jarvis, physician and politician; Worthy as "Sheriff Anderson," a misspelling of Henderson; Positive as James Lovell, a customs official; Friendly as Johannes, a bank employee; Peep as James Hughes, attorney; Dupe as John Warren, a member of Morton's Masonic lodge; Harcourt as Charles Apthorp; Turncoat as Dr. Thomas Phipps, a Quincy physician. Steady and Firm, though not identified in this copy, is Isaiah Thomas and Co. For more on these identifications, see Walser, "More about the First American Novel," esp. p. 353.

2 The name appears to include a typo but could also be a pun (Dr. for "doctor"). Elsewhere in the play, the name is rendered as Debauchee, or abbreviations of that word, which in French refers to a person routinely given to sensual excess.

A
FARCE.

ACT I.

SCENE I.

A Room in Sidney's *House.*

Mrs. SIDNEY.

BLESS me Mr. *Sidney,* why you are early up: What takes you out so soon; the clock has but this moment struck six.

Mr. *Sidney.* Why I am to meet that dam'd puppy[1] *Harcourt.* I believe he has courage; but I'm determined to conduct in such a manner, as to prevent any attack.

Mrs. *Sidney.* That is easily done: I'll send a note to *Worthy*: You protract the meeting 'till you think *Worthy* is near the ground; and the matter is up.

Mr. *Sidney.* We must have an eye to appearances, or the *finesse*[2] will take air.

Mrs. *Sidney.* Your address will secure you.

Mr. *Sidney.* But where is *Dupe,* he has promised to stand by me. *Debauchee* must go too; he is a tried friend.

SCENE II.

A Room in Dr. *Harrangue's* House.

Enter *Quaker.*

Quak. Good morning Doctor.

Doct. Good morning, good morning, Sir, how do you do—what news.

Quaker. News with a vengeance, faith—*Sidney* and *Harcourt* have had a tilting bout[3] this morning; and poor Mrs. *Sidney* is in the horrors, through fear, that it may become a serious matter: Not that I think there is the least danger of that; for tho'

1 Intended as an insult or slur, a synonym for "curr," which was used as an insult with connotations of ill-breeding.

2 Colloquial, for artifice or stratagem; sometimes applied in the context of card playing, a gamble that is not a sure bet.

3 A duel.

Harcourt is a brave fellow, *Sidney* will find avenues enough to escape thro'.

Dr. *Harr.* That is very true; but I am anxious to hear how it terminates. Suppose we call on Mrs. *Sidney.* Pray, did you hear who he took with him.

Quak. Dupe and *Debauchee* were his escorts. I heard of it by accident; and flew immediately to *condole* with Mrs. *Sidney.* I found her more calm than I expected. She mentioned the ground on which she founded her hopes—From thence I drew the conclusion I mentioned.

Dr. *Harr.* And a very rational one: the gentlemen of the law have advantages superior to their neighbours. There is *Argue,* for instance; why there is no speaking a word for him in the house.[1] But I am determined to oppose him with all my power.

SCENE III.

A Scene *in* Sidney's *house, at a kitchen fire.*

Tipsy *drunk.*

Enter Martha.

Mar. Well *Tipsy,* how are you all: how is Mrs. *Sidney.*

---

1 Whether or not Harrangue is, as at least one contemporary reader supposed, Dr. Charles Jarvis, the line, which isn't developed any further, suggests that readers would have known not just who Harrangue represented but also who *Argue,* Dr. Harrangue's target for political opposition, would be. Jarvis, a close associate of John Hancock, was known for being elegant and well spoken and had a fashionable clientele. He was nominated by the Massachusetts House in 1788 to be one of Massachusetts's first two US senators but was opposed by the state Senate. In January 1789, Jarvis led opposition to Benjamin Lincoln, lieutenant governor, being appointed Captain of the Castle as a way for him to boost his salary. (This office was traditional, going back to British days.) Governor Hancock sided with Jarvis. Lengthy debates were noted in newspapers; Lincoln's defenders included Christopher Gore, a likely prototype for Argue. See "Sketch of Business in the General Court. House of Representatives. Thurs., Jan 15. Support of Lieut. Governor," *Massachusetts Centinel,* 17 Jan. 1789, 144. Whether or not these speculations about the dramatis personae were accurate, the farce clearly belongs to a broader political print discourse in which Morton's personal affairs were taken by many to have public consequences and his political connections to Hancock—glibly invoked in the play as "his Satannick Majesty"—also made him a target.

Tip. How—how are we—all in confusion. The very de—devil's to pay—and—and my head's turn'd—Don't you see how I talk. all's in gumbustion[1]—I can't do any thing, I'm in such trouble.

Mar. Why, what now, any thing new.

Tip. No, but its—I—I shall come too presently—but—here's Debushe—he—he'll tell you.

Enter Debauchee.

Debau. Ah—Missy *Marta.*—Here is terribe tings—did you eber see de like—My massa and I went to fite.

Mar. What—say—what do you mean.

Deb. Ah! dat is—we didn't fite—Twixt you and I massa he no courage. Misser *Harcort* he say—shentlemen preas to measur;[2] and my massa say—shentlemen you no de law.[3]

Tip. Well, if they do—ont, he does. For I say, he has la—lawd us all out of our senses,[4] I think.

Mar. Do hold your tongue, *Tipsy,* I want to hear.

Deb. Well and so we didn't do any ting—and so he was beat, I tink, and den we come home.

Mar. Such devilish work, I don't believe was ever seen before. I wish they were all safe in heaven; turning every body's head topsy turvy, with their deviltry. I wish to the Lord *Ophelia's* ghost[5] would come and scare them all to death.

Deb. Do you tink it will.

Mar. Yes: and you black son of satan, will be sent neck and heels to the lowest pit of misery; and your master too, for his deceit and duplicity. He with his intriges has made me commit more sin than I can ever answer for—and if he is the guilty man, I hope he will be brought out.

---

1 A malapropism that invokes both combustion and confusion. The author follows a convention that gives servants comedic dialogue in which wrong words sometimes hit the mark quite effectively.

2 Please to measure, an invitation from Harcourt to mark off the distances for the duel.

3 You know the law. Dueling had been illegal in Massachusetts since the early eighteenth century. Later in the play another character suggests that Sidney had the sheriff, Worthy, intervene to stop the duel.

4 I.e., invoked legal terminology until the people around him are driven mad.

5 Like William Hill Brown in *The Power of Sympathy,* the author uses the name Ophelia for the character based on Fanny Morton. The reference to Shakespeare's *Hamlet* suggests a young woman driven mad, torn between or mistreated by her father and her lover.

Tip. Ah—and so—and so do I. And it will be soon; for he owes me; and I can't get my money; and if he can't pay me, he can't bribe any more.[1]

Mar. Well I know he never brib'd me.—I knew nothing; and what I did know, I declared. Why *Tipsy* you are asleep.

Tip. No—no—I an't.

Deb. And he made me clare[2] more than what I know, for he made me clare I know what an oaf[3] was.

Tip. He—he—says its a parcel of words put together, to—to I forgot what—I can't talk as he does, for he talks high flow'd.

Mar. Well; If Mrs. *Sidney* had softened matters a little with her mother, things would never have come to this; but she has acted in this affair as she does in all others, making the world believe she was an angel, when at the same time, her heart was foreign to every virtuous action.—Do you remember *Tipsy* the piece of potry[4] there was in the newspapers.

Tip. Ah, that I do, and I'll peat it.

Mar. No, no, let me; you an't fit *Tipsy*.

Tip. Yes, yes; I am fit; I tell you I've been fected[5] with the fate of the famly—

"Where, where ———

Mar. Hold, hold, I tell you.

Deb. Come *Martha*, do you try.

Mar. *"Where is the father fled, with raptur'd breast;*
"Where the fond mother, in her offspring blest."

[*Sidney* calls *Debauchee*.]

Deb. Comin masser—Lordy what fine oration I lost.

Tip. Why its potry. [*Exit* Deb.

---

1 In a paternalistic and patriarchal culture, Sidney is responsible for the members of his household, including servants. Here, his servants indict him by acknowledging that he has bribed them to break the law on multiple occasions.

2 Declare

3 Oath; Deb's malapropism delivers a nice pun.

4 Poetry, perhaps also invoking the image of a poem as pottery. Tipsy and Martha proceed to attempt a recitation of a newspaper poem generally attributed to Sarah Wentworth Morton. See Appendix B2.

5 Seems to be conflating "affected" with "infected," the idea being that the family's emotional turmoil extends to the servants and has been facilitated in part by the literary performances it has inspired.

Mar. I have forgot the other part of it—But Lord, what will be done; they have wore me to death among them.

Tip. I must cook my dinner.

Mar. What, at four o'clock.

Tip. Yes—why we don't go to market till three.

Mar. O, mighty—such doings—this is living—I'll go into the parlour, and see Mrs. *Sidney.*

Tip. You better not, for she—she has got *Comfort* with her now—and there—therefore your company will be unwelcome.

Mar. Ah, who is it?

Tip. O the *Quaker,* to be sure.

Mar. Then she is happy—But how comes it about that Mr *Sidney* will have that black dog *Deb.* with him in all his frolics.

Tip. I don't know—Why he was Mr. *Sidney's* second;[1] and I'll tell you as how too—If Mr. *Harcourt* had shut Mr. *Sidney's* brains out, I—I take it *Deb.* would have shut out Mr. *Harcourt's.*

[*Re enter* Debauchee.]

Deb. O, Lord—O, Lord—shuch work—poor masser I pity him—He is swaring and taring, and says dam you madam to my misse, you are calm—and dare is, he says, a *Nobel* coming out nes week, cal'd the *Trumpets of Nature,*[2] and he be dam'd if he don't blow ebery body's brains out.

Mar. I think he had better blow his own brains out.

Deb. And he says its a scrilous[3] piece, and he will fascinate[4] de man in de dark, and be de deth of him; and he says, dem dam'd puppys *Tedy* and *Fum,*[5] de printers, have put a graf in de papers; and so we shall see it nes week.

---

1 Debauchee was Sidney's second, or backup, in the duel.

2 The novel coming out next week, *The Trumpets of Nature,* invokes "The Triumph of Nature," the subtitle of *The Power of Sympathy.* Sidney has just learned that the book will be published. The subtle change from "Triumph" to "Trumpets" may be a malapropism but certainly suggests the novel's capacity to publicize Sidney's sins. See also Luke 12:3 (KJV): "Therefore whatsoever ye have spoken in darkness shall be heard in the light; and that which ye have spoken in the ear in closets shall be proclaimed upon the housetops."

3 Scurrilous, or spreading rumors with the intention of damaging someone's reputation.

4 He means "assassinate"—i.e., Sidney threatens to kill the novel's author.

5 Steady and Firm, the name the play uses for Isaiah Thomas and Co., the novel's publisher. The play's author seems to make them heroes for following through with the publication despite threats made against them.

Mar. Well, every thing is beyond account, *Ophelia,* poor soul, has made bustle enough in the great world; there is nothing but duels, and novels, and such like nonsense.

Tip. You say, *Deb.* its the *Trumpets* of *Natur.*

Deb. Yes, or de *Scrimtons*[1]—I forgot wich; but I mus go to Mr. *Positive,* for my masser want him. [*Exit.*

Mar. O, when I look round this house, and see the change in this family, I am amazed—and pity *Sidney,* tho I withhold my reasons.

Tip. For why, my dear.

Mar. Because I have *reasons*—But I must see Mrs. *Sidney.*

SCENE IV.

The Street.

Positive *and* Dupe *meet.*

Dupe. Mr. *Positive,* well met; I have been in pursuit of you.

Pos. So I hear. *Debauchee* informed me there was warm work at home, and that *Sidney* wanted to see me.

Dupe. Yes, there is work enough cut out for him, and with all his faults I pity him—He must be more than man to sustain such a complicated load of misfortunes.

Pos. And those dam'd scoundrels *Steady* and *Firm,* are printing a Novel, that will brand him a villain centuries to come.——It must not be, Sir; some measures must be adopted to suppress the publication, and that immediately—I hear it is to come out next week.

Dupe. That's the very thing I wanted to talk to you about; *Sidney* is impatient to see you; money must be raised to suppress it—but without his Satannick Majesty[2] should condescend to lend us a trifle, I believe we shall fall short there.

Pos. You was with *Sidney* in the mall, I am told; how was it; I have not been able to come at the truth.

Dupe. I was present; but you must not expect information from me; as I disliked the manœuvres, I must beg to be silent on the subject.

---

1 Unclear, but it may be a combination of "scrimp"—or miserly—and "Mortons," though the play does not otherwise invoke the family's actual name.

2 Probably John Hancock.

SCENE V.

A Room in Peep's *house*—Peep *discovered reading a Letter.*

——This will do, by Heavens; this is glorious news; a royal subject for defamation; What a capital opportunity I shall have to gratify the idly curious—to spread dissention and discord—draw a tear from the eye of sensibility—or raise a blush of indignation on the cheek of candour; For tho my friend enjoyed the strictest secrecy, and has informed me if the affair should transpire, an amiable family would be involved in irretrievable misery and disgrace, yet I can never conquer my propensity to scandal so far, as to conceal it intirely, I can throw out a few insinuations—give a significant shrug or two, and the infection[1] will fly like wild fire; I am impatient to get out.

[*As he goes out, he meets* Debauchee.]

Peep. What news *Debauchee*? your looks are interesting.

Debau. Yes, Sir, me be in a great flury; my masser is in shuch a passion, dat I run very hard to fine you, Sir, for I tink, may be, you will be able to pease[2] him.

Peep. Why, what's the matter, I can't conceive; what has raised such a breeze now; don't you know *Debauchee*, you was in his confidence; you have been serviceable to him. How is it with the *disguises*, the *cakes*, the *milk,* and some other matters—you understand me *Debauchee.*

Deb. Yes, Sir, I stand you; but masser made me take an oaf; I don't know what that is; masser say "*me don't know any ting;*" now so I forget all bout it; but I hope, Sir, you will go to our house; masser want to see you bery much.

Peep. Directly, but ca'nt you give me a hint what's the matter.

Deb. Yes, Sir, masser and me went and fite dis morning.

Peep. Your master and you fight, that's surprising indeed.

Deb. No, Sir, you don't stand[3] me, misser *Harcoat* and my masser fite; I went to stand by him, long masser *Dupe*; I shoud fite if masser wod begin; but masser wont do noting;[4] so misser *Harcoat* went away; but dat an't all, masser want to see you, for

1 Gossip or scandal is figured here as viral or infectious, or as wildfire.

2 Appease.

3 Understand.

4 I.e., Sidney refused to duel.

Mr. *Tedy* and *Fum* has got a book, and dey going to publick it—and masser want you to help press it—I tink he say.

Peep. Suppress it you mean, honest *Debauchee;* this is news indeed; I will be with him in two minutes.

ACT II.

SCENE I.

Mr. Impartialist's *House.*

Enter Sidney.

Sid. Mr. *Impartialist,* good morning; I am fortunate in finding you at home; I wish to consult you upon a damn'd scurrilous Performance, that I hear is now in the booksellers hands; I would fain suppress it, if possible; I have been to the Printers, and have given them a damn'd warm dose; but for fear it should not take effect, I wish to solicit your assistance, in tracing the author of this infernal book, and try what can be done with him; for by my maker I swear, some of us must die; I cannot support it Sir; only think of my situation; a family and connections that are dear to me; carry your ideas a little farther, and behold my son reading a book, where his father is branded with the opprobrious epithet of villain—Horrour is in the thought—'tis more than man can bear—the cord is already stretched to its utmost limits—'twill soon break—and some victim must bleed, to expiate the crime.

Imp. Well, Sir, I am willing to give you all the assistance in my power; though I don't see any probability of suppressing the publication. Is there any person in particular that you suspect for the author?

Sid. Yes, Sir, *****[1]—I suspect him to be the author, but wish to be convinced before I proceed to extremities; You can have no adequate conceptions, Sir, of my sufferings; I am witheld, by *extreme delicacy,* from investigating the whole affair, and proving my innocence; the world believes the young lady in question to have been as pure as an angel; but their opinions are most egregiously erroneous—However, I shall wait until your return, before I make up my mind upon this cursed business.

[*Exeunt.*

1 The five asterisks indicate the five letters in Brown's name.

SCENE II.

Worthy's *House*. *Enter* Friendly.

Friend. Mr. *Worthy,* I hope I see you well.

Wor. Very well Sir; no bad news I hope has procured me the honor of a visit.

Friend. No, Sir, the affair seems to rest where you left it. I did myself the honor to call on you, to satisfy myself of some circumstances that took place this morning. There appeared some ambiguity in your traceing us. May I ask if your interference was solicited?

Wor. You may ask [*smiling significantly*] but I presume you are not ignorant, that it is not my office to betray a trust reposed in me, if that was the case.

Friend. True, Sir, I only wished to know for my own private satisfaction, as I concluded magic had no hand in transporting you to the spot *designed for action.*

Wor. I shall ever esteem myself happy in having it in my power to prevent the effusion of human blood; and I think *Sidney's* family and connections must be so completely miserable, that it would be the utmost stretch of inhumanity to augment it.

Friend. I think so too; and I exhausted all my rhetoric to divert *Harcourt* from the attempt; but it was in vain—for tho he is as worthy a fellow as wears the King of England's livery, his passions are too quick to be controuled by reason at all times; and in this case you may suppose he felt himself keenly injured.

Wor. Undoubtedly; but admitting the whole catalogue of crimes alledged to *Sidney* to be true, *Harcourt,* nor the family, in my opinion, cannot inflict a worse punishment on the wretched *Sidney* than his own reflections.

Friend. Well Sir, I have an appointment, and must take my leave. I know an apology is necessary for the motive of this visit—but your candor will speak one for me, or fame is not just in the encomiums she pays you.

Wor. Whatever may be the motive, I shall always be happy to see you: Mr. *Friendly's* established character will ever secure him a welcome. [*Exit.*

SCENE III.

Sidney's *Kitchen*—Tipsy *sitting.*

Enter Debauchee.

Debau. Tipsy—Tipsy—where be you—pray give me som ting to eat, for I'm most tarv'd—run about al day—cal misser *Postiv*—cal misser *Peep*—cal dis one—cal todder one—I hope if masser go for to cisnate de printer to night, he wont call me, for I most dead now.

Tip. Well you ought to have some trouble: you have half the honor[1]—Who have you been for now.

Debau. I ben for misser Peep; but he cant com now, he met shuch a luck littel vile ago; I laf til I cry; you member de time he went to peep in foks windows, and fall down in de sellar in de tub of shuds; jus so he look to day; he saucy to one man dribing his sled, misser *Peep* run again him sled, and damnd de man; de man dam him; by and by he saucy; de man put him down de gutter; poor misser *Peep* skulk heself, and now gorn home to get clene tocking, for he cant get any sasfactshen.[2]

Tip. I am glad of it with all my soul, for he is always poking his nose in every body's house, where they will let him tell lies, and talk about people; for my part, I hate the sight of him; but you did'nt tell me the story about his falling down cellar; I heard of it then, but never heard the petiklers.

Debau. Why de maid was geting seper, she had her hed up de gimny gorner—she heard a deble of a noise—som ting com splash down in de tub of suds; she hollow and run—de folks come, and dare dey find misser *Peep*—He say he com too close de cellar dor, so fall down, but somebody see him all de time he shulk his self; de folks good to him for all dat; dey give him some vinnegar and paper to dress his broken shins.

Tip. Hold your tongue; somebody calls.

[*Exit servants*

---

1 Tipsy suggests that because a duel is an "affair of honor," Debauchee as second shares half the honor.

2 Debauchee seems to convey a well-known anecdote by which Peep gained his name, when he was peeping in someone's window and ended up falling into a cellar. He compares that story to one in which Peep assails a driver only to end up beaten and in the gutter.

SCENE IV.

Turncoat's *house. Mrs.* Turncoat *discovered heading her breakfast table.*

Enter Turncoat.

Turn. Have you waited for me, my dear.

Mrs. *Turn.* Waited, yes; I have waited till I am faint for my breakfast; but it is nothing new, you always serve me so, when I am impatient to get things cleared away, that I may see after my family; for somebody must see to it, or we shall have nothing to eat; but that is the least of your concern; if you are fed no matter who finds it.

Turn. Why what a touse[1] you make about nothing; I only stept in to neighbour *Whitmore's* to hear if he brought any news from town last night; and I am glad I went, notwithstanding the clamor you make about it; and I am a good mind not tell you, since you have made such a fuss, tho I know you would give your ears to hear it, because it relates to your friend *Sidney.*

Mrs. *Turn.* He my friend; yes, my friendship for him is so great, that I don't care how soon he is hang'd, to keep him out of mischief. I am sure my family have lost thousands by his chicanery. But what do they say of him; they can't say any good of him, for if he ever did any thing that was praise-worthy, it was so long since that he has forgot it.

Turn. Why, they say *Harcourt* has called him to an account for some of the most notorious parts of his conduct.

Mrs. *Turn.* Bless me, then they have fought a duel; well, that's good; I hope he had his head shot off.

Turn. Not so quick, my dear, *Sidney* was too artful for him; he planned matters so well, that *Worthy* interposed his authority and parted them. I am glad I was not in the way. I should like to know which party gains the most applause; and to tell you the truth, I am sorry I assisted him in *any* of his manœuvres.

Mrs. *Turn.* If you had taken my advice, you would have saved yourself a great deal of trouble that you have had on his account; there was the jaunt you took of five and twenty miles, in a snow storm, set out at midnight too, to bring a poor infant, new-born from its mother—Heavens defend us from such fathers—monsters in human shape; but it seems gratitude was your motive; he had screened you from the punishment which some of your

1 A pull or tear.

libidinous conduct richly merited, and you undertook to return the obligation in the same style.

Turn. Heavens! what a blast! I'll hear no more of it this time, however. [*Exit.*

SCENE V.

Sidney's *house.* *Mrs.* Sidney *Solus.*

Great heaven, what will come next; sure Pandora's box has been empted on my devoted head; turn which way I will, I am wretched.

Enter Dr. Harrangue *and* Quaker.

Quak. My dear Mrs. *Sidney*; what alone—I expected to find Mr. *Sidney* here; you have seen him, I hope, since the morning.

Mrs. *Sidney.* Yes, he has been in, and I find the affair has ended better than I expected; but now he is in a violent passion about a Novel, that *Steady* and *Firm* have printed, and he is said to be the principal character in the Drama—he says he will suppress the publication if possible; for my own part, I am less solicitous about that, than I was about the duel: To have had my brother, or my husband fallen by the sword of the other would have been insupportable.

Doc. Har. Make yourself easy, madam, you have nothing to fear from that quarter; Mr. *Sidney* understands himself too well to trifle away his existence.

Quak. It would be the part of a madman, not to set the highest value on life, when he has so fine a woman to enjoy with. [Bowing.]

Enter Positive *and* Dupe.

Pos. Mrs. *Sidney,* and gentlemen, your most obedient—Pray, madam, is Mr. *Sidney* within, I understand he wants to see me.

Mrs. *Sidney.* He is very earnest to see you, and will be here in a few minutes.

Enter Sidney.

Sid. There never was a poor devil so harass'd since the flood, as I am: How do you do gentlemen, I am glad to see you, though I hardly know where I am. *Positive,* you must set off for *Planting*

Grove[1] to morrow morning, to see what can be done with the head of this dam'd company; by Heavens, if I can find out the author, I'll blow his brains out.

Mrs. *Sid.* You had better let it alone, I think, you will only render yourself more conspicuously infamous.

Mr. *Sid.* You have no feelings madam—thus calmly to support such misery and wretchedness.

Enter Peep.

Peep. Mr. *Sidney,* I hope you will forgive my not coming sooner, I assure you I have met with ill luck; a scoundrel of a truckman plumpt me into the gutter, because I happened to stand in his way.

[Ha—ha—ha—all laugh.]

Quak. Why *Peep,* you meet with trouble, 'tis not long since you had a ducking in a tub of suds.

Pos. Oh, that's an old story; but I would advise you, Mr. *Peep,* to take more care next time you attempt to look into people's windows.

Dr. *Harr.* And my young friend, look well about you, when next you borrow, unsolicited, from your neighbour at the Franklin's head[2]—the story of the *black negro* won't do.

Peep. Upon my word gentlemen, you are quite merry at my expence—I little thought of pleasantry in this place, at this particular moment—*Debauchee* informed me that Mr. *Sidney* was very unhappy, and I came to offer my services; if there is any thing that I can do, I hope Mr. *Sidney* will command me.

Sid. I am much obliged to you, Sir, I shall have business for all my friends at this rate;—But *Positive,* you have not told me whether you will go.

Pos. You could not doubt my readiness to go, Sir; and I will bring them to terms, or lose my arm in the attempt.

Sid. Take *Dupe* with you, my friend, you will find him very serviceable.

Pos. What time shall we go; to night or in the morning.

Sid. 'Tis too late now; you must get away by ten to-morrow,

---

1 Worcester.

2 The Franklin's Head, Court Street, was the location of a bookstore and publisher. The specific reference here, about Positive's attempt to borrow from a proprietor, may have been recognizable to contemporaries.

and exert yourselves, my friends; try what you can do for me, for by heavens, if this publication comes out, I shall go distracted: Don't you think the scoundrels had the assurance to tell me, with the most provoking calmness, that when the books were ready, I should have a set[1] as soon as any gentlemen in town.——Damn their impudence

Pos. You may depend on my exertions: *Dupe,* you will be ready, I hope.

Dupe. Certainly—as soon as you please.

Pos. Madam your most obedient—gentlemen your humble servant.

[*Exit* Pos. Dupe *and* Peep.

Dr. *Harr.* I would advice you Mr. *Sidney,* not to take any more notice of the affair; the best of us, don't escape the lash; you may talk to all eternity, and it will not alter the opinions of people, already prejudiced against you.

Sid. I am surprised, Dr. to hear you so warmly recommend taciturnity, that practice it so little when insulted.

Dr. *Harr.* I conceive a wide difference in passing by a personal attack, or one levelled at the community at large—then it is impossible for a man to be silent, *who has the good of his country at heart.* When we see men initiated into power, whose abilities are unquestionably inadequate for the office, they are to fill, I think it dastardly to be silent, and thus defeat the very purposes for which we are honoured with the suffrages of our grateful countrymen.

Sid. But there are some persons you never will concur with, let them propose what they will.

Dr. *Harr.* Then let the persons you allude to, solicit my concurrence, when they want it, or I never will hold up my hand for them,[2] let the consequences be what they may.

Quak. Mr. *Sidney,* you have not told us of yesterday's adventure; I was exceedingly alarmed when I heard *Harcourt* had called you out; and though I knew you had it in your power to extricate yourself if you thought proper; yet I was fearful *Harcourt's* impetuosity would throw you off your guard.

Dr. *Harr.* He is an enterprising youth, I have heard, and don't want spirit; I wonder how you managed to keep him at a proper distance.

---

1 *The Power of Sympathy* was originally published in two small volumes.

2 Vote for them.

Sid. O, admirably; he found I was determined to stand only on the defensive; had he attacked me in that situation, he knew the consequences.

Qua. Well gentlemen; shall we call another subject; we have been out of tune some time; let us banish such disagreeable topicks; and endeavour to harmonize each other, by more sprightly notes,—Where is the little one, I have not seen it to day.

[*Mrs.* Sidney *rings.* *Enter Servant.*

Mrs. *Sid.* Tell *Tipsy* to bring the child in.

[*Exit Servant.*

[*Enter* Tipsy *with the child.*]

Quak. Give it to me *Tipsy*—Come here you pretty creature—Why its a fine child as ever I saw, and very handsome too.

Tip. I do—dont wonder you—you think so, Sir, for it looks for all the world like you—It has got—it has got a–a–a nose—a mouth just like yours, as two peas—and sweet eyes, and red face—its the image of you.[1]

Mrs. *Sid.* What's the matter with the creature; how she talks.

Mr. *Sidney.* Drunk as the devil—Send her off.

Dr. *Harr.* I have business, gentlemen, to attend to, and shall leave you for the present. I congratulate you Madam, that your fears are hush'd in peace for this time.

Mrs. *Sidney.* I thank you Sir, I wish *all* my fears were as happily subsided, as the one you allude to. [*Exit Dr. Harr.*

Qua. Mr. Sidney, if there is any thing in my power that I can assist you in, let me know—you will find me ready to serve you.

Sid. I don't doubt it Sir, and I shall trouble you enough, I dare say, and all my friends; but I cannot determine on any thing, till I hear from Planting Grove.

Qua. Well, command me when you want—You know where to find me, and will find me ever ready and willing to befriend you—I wish you both a very good night. [*Exit Qua.*

FINIS.

---

1 Without realizing it, Tipsy implies here that Quaker is the child's actual father.

Appendix A: Fanny Apthorp's Final Letters

[The letters Fanny Apthorp wrote in the final week of her life circulated in handwritten copies and were widely reprinted in newspapers (see p. 20, note 1 in the Introduction). We have chosen to use the first newspaper printing for our copy text here, on the assumption that this version had the broadest popular audience. Our footnotes indicate any substantial differences between the newspaper versions and four manuscript copies of which we are aware: three versions in the collections of the Massachusetts Historical Society and one located at the Arthur and Elizabeth Schlesinger Library on the History of Women in America, Radcliffe Institute for Advanced Study, Harvard University.[1]]

Herald of Freedom, 15 Sept. 1788

Messrs. PRINTERS,

Reports respecting a late unhappy suicide, are now circulating with rapidity through the country, and a number of letters are handed about, said to be wrote by Miss F——— T——— A———, previous to her exit. As every transaction in matters of such a nature are generally exaggerated, to the detriment of one or other of the parties concerned, I send you the following, copied from the letters, said to be wrote by Miss

1 The copy filed as Misc. Bound MS, 20–27 Aug. 1788, Massachusetts Historical Society, has often been taken to be the "original" but is likely a case of scribal publication, copied and circulated by hand; on the outer leaf it says the note was "[f]ound in a book bought in a second-hand bookstore, New York," and was given to the MHS by Harry Walter Roett on 9 September 1897 (hereafter cited as MHS1 in these notes). One telling detail that suggests MHS1 is not the original: the apparently mistaken appearance of "Geo. W," who in all other manuscripts and print is named as "Gov. W," as in Governor Wentworth, a relative. Another copy at MHS is filed as MS N-2199 in Box 2, 1763–1788 of the Price-Osgood-Valentine Papers (hereafter cited as MHS2). This version is hand-titled "Copies of Papers Written by the Unfortunate Francis Theodore Apthorp, the last weeks of her life." The copy in the Price-Osgood-Valentine Papers includes a note in pencil on the reverse, probably written at a later date, explaining (*continued*)

A———. My intention for this procedure, is not to awaken the pangs of grief, or to add to the wounds of the afflicted breast–but only to place the matter in that point of view in which it is received by many. If mistaken ideas are entertained and propagated, there is room for an appeal to the impartial publick. Relying on your candour, Gentlemen, and that of your readers, I request you will give them a place in your first publication. J.

To *D———r* and *Mrs. P———s.*[1]

A WEEK ago I thought the world would not have persuaded me to have forgiven you, but the thoughts of leaving the world has made me give up all other considerations. To you do I partly owe my death.—Think of this; but I forgive you both. Perhaps when I am dead you will think it of no use to own what you never should have denied—But remember the dying request of a person, is of some consequence, and that the day is not far distant when you must give an account of every thing good and bad.—That you may think seriously of this, is the last request of

F——— T——— A———.

WHO is as wretched as myself? Innocent I am in this—nothing but that would make me own my guilt—yet I have no proof—I have no money to make those who know the whole truth declare it. Before long I shall be condemned in a Court of Justice!—O Lord God, thou knowest that my once loved M———[2] is the first and the last man I ever knew!—What is Justice?—most readily do I resign myself into the hands of the true and only God, who gave it.—If it pleases him, I wish to die at the bar with the truth in my

---

that Fanny "was put in the care of Miss Elizabeth Price when the latter returned to America in 1783. Miss Price was not pleased with her behavior on board the ship with the officers and would never have her visit her." A third version is filed as MS N-1720 in the Thomas Wallcut Papers (hereafter cited as MHS3). A fourth manuscript version is filed as "Frances Theodora Apthorp Letter," A/A652, Schlesinger Library, Radcliffe Institute, Harvard University. We are indebted to Cassandra Barney for finding the second and third versions at MHS and to Jane Kamensky for alerting us to the discovery of the version at the Schlesinger.

1 In the manuscript versions, this letter is addressed to "Doctor & Mrs Phipps" and dated 27 August 1788. The signatures are sometimes spelled out in full but most often rendered simply as initials (F.T.A.).

2 In the manuscript versions, "Morton" is spelled out here. They also begin with the address "To Mr. Morton," except for MHS2, which begins "This is to Morton."

mouth.—My *guilty innocence* cannot save me.—There is no oblation but in death! Come, come, then, *pleasing death*, and relieve the too unfortunate

F——— T——— A———.

N.B.[1] In the name of heaven let not my sweet infant[2] suffer—take care of it, unhappy M———,[3] if you ever lov'd its mother,—or, by a stronger tie, for you know in the sight of heaven, you are the father of it. F——— T——— A———.

YESTERDAY[4] I saw the unhappy M——— possessed with the rage of a madman—he had my pity; but he entered my chamber with a calmness[5] that made me feel a tenderness[6] for him.—I gave him my letters—I took them from him again.—He was soft and mild.—It was, unhappily, by the place in which I once shewed him a letter from Governour Wentworth;[7] I remember it yet;—for a moment I lov'd him.—When he left me, he was a madman; but something, I cannot tell what, prevented my being angry with him.[8]—I went to bed early—slept quietly—had pleasing dreams of him—remember in my sleep where he stood—it was impressed

---

1 Nota bene, or "mark well." In the manuscript versions, this postscript is dated "Thursday Noon," and in the Schlesinger version this entry is marked "No 2." It is possible the *Herald*'s publishers mistook the numbering for the abbreviation "N.B.," which is unique to the print version.

2 The MHS manuscript versions all have some version of the phrase "innocent infant" here. In MHS1 the adjective is struck through. The Schlesinger version omits the adjective altogether.

3 In the manuscript versions, Morton's name is spelled out in full.

4 In the manuscript versions, this letter is dated Friday morning; MHS2, MHS3, and the version at Schlesinger all add the date, 21 August, as well.

5 The manuscript version at the Schlesinger has "coldness" here instead.

6 In MHS1, the phrase "a tenderness" is struck out.

7 In MHS1, this name appears as "Geo. W," which leads us to the conclusion that this version is not, in fact, the original. Instead, this seems to be a scribal error. "Governor Wentworth" most likely refers to Sir John Wentworth (1737–1820), a cousin of Sarah Wentworth Morton's mother, who had been royal governor of New Hampshire during the American Revolution and was the subject of his own scandals, along with his wife, Frances Deering Wentworth, who was also Fanny Apthorp's namesake. The couple lived in Nova Scotia following the Revolution. All other versions of the letter point to Wentworth instead of "Geo. W."

8 In MHS1, the previous sentence does not appear. The other manuscript versions include it.

on my mind; but I do not now love him. I forgive him and pity him.

F——T——A——.

To say I feel no agitation this day,[1] is not just; but that I feel a calmness no criminal ever did, is certain. To morrow I mean to prove my *guilty innocence* (for I can give it no other name). It will be called by some a rash step—yet a thing which has not been out of my mind for a fortnight, cannot be called sudden. It may be for the Interest of some to call it Lunacy—yet consult any physicians;[2] ask them whether distraction was ever consistent. I felt, from the first, that this matter would go against me; I resolved not to live after it had. I feel like one that has been on a long visit, yet a most uncomfortable one. *I feel like a poor wanderer, about to return to a tender parent, tho unasked yet welcome.* The way I fear is dark—I have no one to shew it me. I know there is a God, who will reward and punish—I fear *that* God,[3] for him I have offended; yet from my heart I repent. I never have been happy—not that I feared detection, because I was persuaded that was impossible. I knew I was doing an injury to one who had been all kindness to me. I now pray her to forgive me, as I forgive them who have done me nothing but injury. I request her not to place this crime to that of black ingratitude; for I am sensible of the obligation I was under to her. This is the last time I shall write; therefore I must now pray for the forgiveness of my father and mother. My heart bleeds at the shock I must give the most feeling of mothers. I entreat my sister[4] sometimes to think of me with pity. I die with the assurance that my four tender friends, whom I leave behind, will often take up one thing or another, and say, this, and this, and this, was poor F——'s—and sometimes may drop a tear.——O God! forgive my many great faults and have mercy on my soul; and when it pleases thee, prove more fully than *this* can, the Innocence of a repenting sinner. F—— T—— A ——.

---

1 In the MHS manuscripts, this letter is dated Wednesday 27 August 1788. While the *Herald of Freedom* chose to close with this letter, the manuscript copies all place the letter to Dr. and Mrs. Phipps last.

2 In MHS1, she writes "consulting my Physicians."

3 In MHS1, the part of this sentence that reads "who will reward and punish—I fear *that* God" does not appear. MHS2 and the Schlesinger version both have "who will reward and punish crimes."

4 In MHS1 and the Schlesinger version, this reads "sisters," plural.

Appendix B: Sarah Morton's and Related Poetry

[The poetry that follows is attributed to Sarah Morton. While we can be certain Morton is the author of the works that appeared in her volume, the newspaper publications rely on other forms of identification. As many female poets used pseudonyms, it cannot be determined with certainty that she is the author of all works, particularly the poem of 4 December 1788.]

1. "ELEGY on a late melancholy Event," *Herald of Freedom* (25 September 1788)

Ah, FANNY! shall no tear be shed for thee,
   No pitying sigh the pensive bosom heave;
Shall no kind pen present the candid plea,
   And generously thy injur'd fame retrieve?

Ah, no! the unfeeling crowd unmov'd relate—
   The unfeeling crowd unmov'd the story hear;
Forget each pang that urg'd thee to thy fate,
   Indignant smile, "and wink away a tear."

Yet on the heart which sympathy controuls,
   Thy woes shall be by pity's plume portray'd;
We'll rise superior to those stoick souls,
   Which own of virtue nothing but the shade.

Oft at the silent hour of sober Eve,
   When the dim moon emits her faintest ray,
Each circle gay, each giddy joy we'll leave;
   And o'er thy grave one mournful tribute pay.

2. *Massachusetts Centinel* (27 September 1788)

The following appears to be written "warm from the heart, and true to all its fires,"—The occurrences which suggested the ideas are perhaps better conceived than related—The feeling heart cannot but commiserate the exquisite sensations on which the energetick complaint is founded.[1]

Where is the father fled, with raptur'd breast!
Where the fond mother, in her offspring blest!
Ah wretched child! no friends thy grief controul,
No melting parent sooths thy anguish'd soul;
No father's cares the bolts of fate defy,
No mother's fondness wipes the streaming eye;
But lost in grief, that loathes the tedious day,
The *hapless sufferer* mourns her life away.
What powers of **Até* could a parent move
To blast the child who claim'd his tenderest love!
Relenting stop! nor urge thy swelling rage
To crush the prop that rais'd thy sinking age;
Let pity's balm o'er reckless hatred flow,
And spare the helpless family of woe—
The lovely offspring from dishonour save,
And wrest thy drooping daughter from the grave.
*The Goddess of Revenge

3. *Massachusetts Centinel* (4 October 1788)

TO THE PRINTER

SIR—*The pompous verses in your last Saturday's paper, which should have had ATÉ for their signature, are destitute of the great essential TRUTH—which does not* "vindicate the line." *How can parents soothe or console, when one is* forbidden *the house with execration, and the other drove from it with approbrous language, when maternal affection was the sole cause of the visit?*

4. "*On the* SEDUCTION of VIRGINS and MARRIED WOMEN," *Herald of Freedom* (4 December 1788)

AND you, with pamper'd pride, and pomp elate,
Whose birth and wealth alone proclaim you great!
If humbler blessings, humbler minds enjoy,
Oh, triumph not, that little to destroy;
Nor think that wealth and eloquence were giv'n,
To banish peace from earth, or spurn at Heav'n.

---

1 Original headnote.

Oh! If thou bear'st a father's, husband's name—
If soft humanity be still thy claim;
Mark the sad mother—hear her wailings wild;
She beats her breast, and mourns her *darling child.*
Lur'd from her humble hearth, and fond embrace,
A slave to *lust obscene*, and *riot base*;
Doom'd in disease and guilt to waste her bloom,
Then sink, *with want and anguish, to her tomb!*
  But who is he, whose eye-balls widely roll,
And speak the mighty horrors of his soul!
See in his arms, his infants fondly press'd—
And now he drops a tear, and spurns them from his breast.
Dear innocents! whom *once* I lov'd as mine,
Cease your gay sports, nor round me smiling twine;
Mourn not your much lov'd mother's long delay,
Nor ask what keeps her ling'ring steps away.
O never may your peaceful bosoms know
The plaintive story of your father's woe!
Curs'd be the wretch, whose wealth and winning art,
Tore your lov'd mother from my bleeding heart;
And curs'd that greatness which its pow'r employs,
To poison all the spring of social joys.

5. Selected Poems from Sarah Wentworth Morton, *My Mind and Its Thoughts, in Sketches, Fragments, and Essays* (1823)

a. "Stanzas, to a Recently United Husband"

IN VAIN, upon that hand reclined,
    I call each plighted worth my own,
Or rising to thy sovereign mind,
    Say that it reigns for me alone.

Since, subject to its ardent sway,
    How many hearts were left to weep,
To find the granted wish decay,
    And the triumphant passion sleep?

Such were, of love the transient flame,
    Which by the kindling senses led,
To every new attraction came,
    And from the known endearment fled.

Unlike the gentle care that flows,
With all the blessed affections give,
Unlike the generous hope that knows
But for a kinder self to live.

Was theirs the tender glance to speak
Timid, through many a sparkling tear,
The ever changing hue of cheek,
Its flush of joy—its chill of fear.

Or theirs the full expanded thought,
By taste and moral sense refined—
Each moment with instruction fraught,
The tutored elegance of mind?

Be mine the sacred truth that dwells
On ONE, the kindred virtues known,
And mine, the chastened glance, which tells
That sacred truth to HIM alone.

No sordid hope's insidious guise,
No venal pleasure's serpent twine,
Invite those soul-illumined eyes,
And blend this feeling heart with thine.

b. "Conciliation"

GRACED be the hour, when severed friends unite
And loved the voice, whose softened tones endear,
Where the eye, melting in its morning light,
Dispels the cloud, and glistens through a tear.

When the heart freed from doubt's entangling wile,
Nor joys, nor sorrows, but with pensive care,
Speaks to the wedded heart, in sigh, or smile,
And feels its questioned kindness answer there.

While the regretful silence seems to plead,
No more the timid hand its pledge denies,
No more shall hurried steps, in scorn proceed,
Nor anger flash from quick averted eyes.

Steeled was the breast, that with a felon's heart,
Could, of confiding truth, its hope bereave;
Bid those whom heaven had joined, in madness part,
Grieving to live—and living but to grieve.

Reproach, with flushing cheek, and phrenzied brow,
Sullen suspicion's cold, regardless stare,
Whence is thy sway—and where that midnight now,
Which search'd the soul and struck its horrors there.

TRUTH came—and as the Saviour's glance adored,
Fell on the sealed eye, with opening ray;
Her guiding light on darkest error poured,
Gives mind to man and clears its gloom away.

Gives him to know, in blessing, to be blessed,
ONE friend, his joys—his portioned griefs to share,
To find his refuge, in ONE sheltering breast,
Source of his hope—and partner of his care.

Appendix C: Revolutionary American Women on "Chesterfieldian Politeness," Gender Relations, and National Virtue

1. Mercy Otis Warren to Winslow Warren, December 1779, as printed in the *Independent Chronicle* [Boston] (18 January 1781)

[The following letter from the historian, poet, and playwright Mercy Otis Warren (1728–1814) to her twenty-year-old son, Winslow (1759–1791), was circulated in manuscript among her approving friends before one of them, Abigail Adams, submitted it to the Boston *Independent Chronicle* just a year after it was written. Among the most famous Revolutionary-era responses to Lord Chesterfield's *Letters to His Son*, the letter was reprinted in the *Boston Magazine* in June 1784, just before the Sans Souci controversy took hold, and in the *Massachusetts Magazine* in January 1790, in the wake of the Apthorp–Morton scandals. Readers understood it as an attack on the excesses of polite masculinity that could lead young men to treat female counterparts with disregard or contempt. (Winslow Warren was a contemporary of William Hill Brown and Fanny Apthorp.) The original manuscript, which varies in places from the version printed in Boston magazines and newspapers, is in Warren's papers at the Massachusetts Historical Society. A transcription is published in Richards and Harris 120–23. For additional context, see Hayes. We have chosen to use the first newspaper printing here.]

MR. WILLIS, The enclosed letter was written by a Lady, born and educated in this State, whose friends have repeatedly ventured offending her delicacy by obliging the public with some of her ingenious and e[l]egant productions. Your readers of taste will discover how justly another Lady speaks of this performance, when writing to a friend, she says: "I embrace this opportunity to enclose to you, the copy of a letter which I have some time wished to see published. The writer is well known to you, and the letter stands not in need of any encomium of mine. The publication may in some measure serve as an antidote to the poison so profusely administered by a late celebrated letter writer. His Lordship has certainly laid himself open to the utmost severity of female pens; but you will find in this letter, an elegance of stile, a solidity of judgment, a discernment and penetration which would do honour to either sex, but which peculiarly distinguish this Lady." Your's, A. B.

MY DEAR SON,

I Perceive by your last you are enraptured with Lord Chesterfield,[1] nor do I wonder at it; I should have no opinion of your taste, if you was not charmed with the correct stile, the elegant diction, the harmony of language, the thousand beauties of expression that run parrallel with the knowledge of the world, and the arts of life, through this compleat system of refinement.—This masterly writer has furnished the present generation with a code of politeness, which, perhaps, surpasses any thing of the kind in the English language. But when he sacrifices truth to convenience, probity to pleasure, virtue to the graces, generosity, gratitude, and all the finer feelings of the soul, to a momentary gratification, we cannot but pity the man, as much as we admire the author; and I never see this fascinating collection of letters, taken up by the youthful reader, but I tremble, least the honey'd poison, that lurks beneath the fairest flowers of fancy and Rhetoric, should leave a deeper tincture on the mind, than, even his documents for an external decency and the semblance of Morality.

I have no quarrel with the graces; I love the *Deuceurs*[2] of civility, the placid manners, the *L-amiable*,[3] and all the innocent arts of engaging the esteem, and alluring the affections of mankind.—The passion is laudable, and may be indulged to the highest pitch, consistent with the eternal law of rectitude; but I love better that frankness and sincerity, which bespeak a soul above dissimulation; that generous, resolute, manly fortitude, that equally despises and resists the temptations to vice in the Purlieu's[4] of the Brothel, or the anti chamber of the Princess,

1 Warren refers to Philip Dormer Stanhope, 4th Earl of Chesterfield (1694–1773), whose posthumous *Letters to His Son on the Art of Becoming a Man of the World and a Gentleman* (1774), filled with advice on how to navigate polite society to one's personal advantage, was popular in Revolutionary America.

2 "Douceurs," French for sweets.

3 French, indicating friendly society.

4 French, the confines or surrounding area.

in the arms of the emaciated, distemper'd prostitute, or beneath the smiles of the painted Courtezan, who decorates her guilty charms even with the blandishments of honour. And however ennobled by birth, dignify'd by rank, or justly admired for his literary productions, I must beg leave to differ from his Lordship, and think it, by no means, necessary that a gentleman, in order to be initiated into the science of good breeding, should drop his humanity; or to acquire a courtly mien and become an adept in politeness, that he should renounce the moral feelings; or to be master of the graces, that his life should be a contrast to every precept of Christianity.

Can there be a portrait more unnatural and deformed, or an object more completely ridiculous, than that of a father exerting all the powers of brilliant talents, aided by the chicanery of subtle politicians, the false reasonings of the infidel tribe, and the vulgar witticisms of all the voluptuaries from Julius Caesar to Borgia,[1] to arouse the corrupt passions in the bosom of his son, to enflame the desires, and to urge those loose gratifications, which it has been the work of ages to connteract, by all the arguments of reason, religion, and philosophy. And, if in the pangs of paternal anxiety, he had sometimes omitted the consonant S.[2] and inculcated on his votary of pleasure, the necessity of a spark of *grace* in the heart, however exploded by *Les Beaux Esprit*,[3] it might have produced a brighter embellishment of manners in the person, than all his Lordship's studied rules, his labour'd maxims, his machiavilian politicks,[4] improved in the religious school of Voltaire,[5] or supported by all the advocates for simulation, and dissimulation,

---

1 Warren invokes famous rulers who notoriously regarded women as sexual or political objects. Caesar ruled Rome in the first century BCE; Cesare Borgia was a fifteenth-century Italian nobleman and military leader whose drive for power inspired Niccolò Machiavelli (1469–1527) to write *The Prince* (1532), a political treatise written as an instruction manual for rulers.

2 I.e., if he had inculcated *grace* instead of the *graces*, or politeness.

3 French, literally meaning "beautiful spirits," but meant colloquially to indicate clever or polite society. The beautiful people.

4 Another reference to Machiavelli's *The Prince*. Machiavellian politics would be one in which the ends of power justify the means of acquiring and maintaining it.

5 The pen name of François-Marie Arouet (1694–1778), French *philosophe* known for his criticism of organized and state-sponsored religion. A Deist, Voltaire believed in a god, but one who did not intervene in the world of his creation.

that have lived since the Augustan age,[1] when luxury was in its Zenith, till the more perfect model of education, exhibited by the noble Lord Chesterfield,—But I admire his sermon on *Suaviter in modo fortiter in re*;[2] yet, believe these happy emanations are, much oftener, the effects of a conscious moral principle, than the result of that finished turpitude, held up under a flimsy veil of deception, and urged on Mr. Stanhope as the point of perfection; and I am persuaded, had the same brilliancy of thought, and the many masterly strokes of genius been played off, with a view to some higher motives of action; had his L[o]rdship laid a little more stress on purity of sentiment, and less on the efficacy of intrigue and gallantry, it might have corrected the errors of his raw traveller, and, perhaps, sooner have rubbed off the awkwardness inherent to his character, than *Un gout vif*[3] about which the careful parent is so solicitous.—His Lordship's severity to the ladies only reminds me of the fable of the lion and the man: I think his trite, hackney'd, vulgar observations, the contempt he affects to pour on so fair a part of the creation, are as much beneath the resentment of a woman of education and reflection, as derogatory to the candor and generosity of a writer of his acknowledged abilities and fame; and I believe in this age of refinement and philosophy, few men indulge a peculiar asperity with regard to the sex in general, but such as have been unfortunate in their acquaintance, unsuccessful in their address, or sowered from repeated disappointments; and however practicable, this connoiseur in the spirit of intrigue, might announce the conquest of the whole sex, it has been asserted by one of his biographers, that he was never known to be successful in any of his gallantries, but that which brought Mr. Stanhope into the world. I ever considered human nature as the same in both sexes, nor perhaps is the soul very differently modified by the vehicle in which it is placed; the foibles, the passions, the vices, and the virtues, appear to spring from the same scource, and under similar advantages, frequently reach the same degree of perfection, or sink to the same stages of pravity which so often stamp disgrace on the human form; yet custom in most countries has branded licentious manners in female life with peculiar marks of infamy; but we live in days happily adroit in the

1 The period in Roman history, 31 BCE to 14 CE, when Augustus was ruler. In the early eighteenth century, British writers self-consciously staged an Augustan revival.

2 Latin: "Pleasantly in manner, powerfully in deed."

3 French, a strong, fresh, or sparkling taste.

arts of removing every impediment to pleasure, when the bars of rectitude are systematically reasoned down, and no other distinction is necessary but a dextrous talent at concealment.

It may, perhaps, be deemed presumption for a woman to speak thus freely of so celebrated a work as Dormer's advice; but I shall yet venture to say more, as I have read his letters with attention, much more with a view to the happiness of some I love, than for my own pleasure or advantage—I think them crowded with the repetition of the most trifling injunctions, replete with observations, rules and precepts, exceedingly advantageous for the conduct of younger life, but marked with the most atrocious licence of thought, and stained with insinuations subversive of every moral and religious principle; the utile is so studiously blended with the vile, that in some of his letters one would mistake Lord Chesterfield for a saint, was not his cloven step[1] discovered by its precipitance to procure an arrangement for his noviciate.

I am happy in having a son, to whom I can disclose the full flow of sentiment and the mixture of indignation, that arises in the maternal bosom, when surveying such a specious digest of mischief, so artfully adapted to lead into error the most valuable part of society, the youth, adorn'd with native grace, and the rudiments of every excellence implanted in his heart.—I feel inexpressible pleasure in believing you to be a reader capable of investigating truth, while charm'd with the easy numbers sportively rang'd to disguise it; and though you admire the painted evil, the polished address, and melodious stile, you cannot be a proselyte of the modern Clodius.[2]

It is the race of fops and fribbles, the half learn'd sceptic, the disciples of Hume and Bolingbroke,[3] who are the devotees of a man, bold enough to avow himself the champion of every species of vice, only cloathing it decently, that will subserve the guilty pleasure of the accomplished debauchee. Had I not made my letter so lengthy, I would add an observation or two from the celebrated Mr. Addison,[4] who did more to the improvement of the

---

1 Footprints made by the devil's hooves.

2 Publius Clodius Pulcher, another political figure from first-century BCE Rome whose scandalous reputation and sordid affairs led to an untimely death.

3 David Hume (1711–76) and Henry St. John, 1st Viscount Bolingbroke (1678–1751), both Enlightenment philosophers and political thinkers whose views were considered anti-religious.

4 Joseph Addison (1672–1719), an English essayist and moralist.

English language, and to correct the stile of the age, than, perhaps, any other man; and was a parrellel justly run, with regard to taste, manners, and even the graces, so far as they can be taught by letters, I believe Lord Chesterfield would drop in the comparison.

I expect the pleasure of seeing you here daily, but if you are prevented, you will answer some of my letters, as you are rather in arrears; when you recollect that circumstance, you will not be so deficient in *Les Bienseances*,[1] as to neglect a point of politeness to a Lady, as well as duty to a most affectionate Mother.

2. Abigail Adams to John Thaxter, 21 July 1780

[The following letter from Abigail Adams (1744–1818), the wife of Massachusetts politician and second president of the United States, John Adams, to John Thaxter Jr., a first cousin who was roughly a decade younger than she was, also falls into the category of admonitory letter or letter of advice. A shrewd political observer and advisor in her own right, Abigail Adams managed household and financial affairs during her husband's diplomatic absences in the 1770s and 1780s. Thaxter served as private secretary to John Adams during his travels to Europe between 1779 and 1783. He also served as a tutor to the Adamses' sons, Thomas and John Quincy, who traveled with their father. Abigail Adams writes to Thaxter in this wartime letter about the alignment between gender relations and the prospect of national virtue, a topic that would come to the fore during the scandals surrounding Perez Morton and family after the war ended. She also mentions the Mortons' engagement.]

My dear Sir — July 21 [1780]

Your agreable favour[2] of March 15 reachd me yesterday. I most sincerely thank you for every token of remembrance. You have been puntual to your word.

I have constantly replied to your favours but whether they have ever reachd you, I know not. So bad has our communication been, where it ought to have been best, that not a single opportunity has offerd, for a direct conveyance since your absence now 8

1 *Les Bienseances* or *les bienséances*: standards of propriety, manners, etiquette.

2 Another term for a letter, since correspondence could be considered acts of kindness or special preference.

months. If this is sound policy, I lay no claim to a share in it. Our packets[1] have lain still in our Harbours at the same expence to the continent, as if they had been passing and repassing. I believe I shall be in favour of Monarchy soon. We have so many wheels within wheels, and such Master workmen, it is next to impossible to set them all at work, the right way at once, so one runs against the other and Crash goes the whole fabrick at once.[2] Some move so slow that they never accomplish their journey, but there is no danger of their suffering from rapidity of motion.

I want an Energetick force that will draw forth our resources, put them in motion with vigor and lead on decisively. The present mode would undoe Peru.[3]

Will you go, and will you go? from day to day. "We will give you a thousand dollors bounty, 40 shillings per Month hard money, and a Bushel of corn per day till you return: or the value there of" is sufficient to bring ruin upon the richest Country upon the Globe, and puts an Everlasting bar against procuring a standing Army.—Should you not Grieve for such a stain upon the page of History? Well then, tell it not then to the Abbe Reynal.[4] Yet virtue exists, and publick spirit lives—lives in the Bosoms of the Fair Daughters of America, who blushing for the Languid Spirit, and halting Step, unite their Efforts to reward the patriotick, to stimulate the Brave, to alleviate the burden of war, and to shew that they are not dismayed by defeats or misfortunes. Read the Pensilvana papers, and see the Spirit catching from state to state.[5]

America will not wear chains while her daughters are virtuous, but corrupt their morals by a general depravity, and believe me sir a state or nation is undone. Was not Adam safe whilst Eve was

---

1 A term that refers both to small bundles of letters and to ships that transported mail.

2 As discussed in the Introduction (pp. 30, 39, note 1), the image comes from Shakespeare's *The Tempest* (4.1.148–56).

3 I.e., lead to ongoing colonial rule. Peru had been under Spanish rule since the sixteenth century, despite a series of failed rebellions.

4 Guillaume Thomas François Raynal (1713–96)—widely known as the Abbé Raynal, despite having left behind his ordination as a priest—was a French writer and historian, most famous at this juncture for his *Histoire des deux Indes* (1770), a history of European colonization. Raynal is credited by some as popularizing the image of American colonists as virtuous republicans.

5 American women who supported the Patriot cause were responsible for a number of economic initiatives instrumental to resisting British power. Here Adams refers to an effort, started in Pennsylvania, to sell expensive jewelry and clothing to raise money to support the Continental army.

Innocent? If you render us wicked you inevitably bring ruin upon yourselves.

I thank you sir for the agreable account you have given me of your Visit to the Abbe Reynal. I venerate the character of that Celebrated Historian and wish to become acquainted with his Works. Write me from time to time, every thing you meet with, entertaining and improveing.

The Ladies to whom you desired me to distribute your Love, are so eager to share it, and there are so many who lay claim to it, that divided and subdivided as it is, not one of them I fear will be warmed with its influence. They even fear that the Parissian Ladies will rob them of their favorite American. But we have so few Gentlemen at this day whose morals and principals are so pure and unimpeachable, that I own, I should be loth that some worthy Girl in my own Country should not monopolize a Heart unhacknyed in Gallantries. It is a *rara avis*[1] in these days of Modern refinement and Chesterfieldian politeness,[2] but the Devotees to his Lordships sentiments, must excuse me if I observe, that with all his Graces and politeness he has exhibited a peculiar Asperity against the Sex, inconsistant with that boasted refinement of sentiment upon which he lays so great stress, and Marks him in my mind a wretched votarie of vice, a voluptuary whose soul was debased by his dissolute connexions, a habit which vitiates the purest taste; and excludes all that refined and tender Friendship, that sweet consent of souls in unison, that Harmony of minds congenial to each other

> "Where thought meets thought e'er from the Lips it part
> And each pure wish springs mutual from the Heart"[3]

1 From the Latin, literally "a rare bird." Used here to indicate that something is rare or scarce.

2 Adams refers to Philip Dormer Stanhope, 4th Earl of Chesterfield, whose posthumous *Letters to His Son on the Art of Becoming a Man of the World and a Gentleman* (1774), filled with advice on how to navigate polite society to one's personal advantage, was popular in Revolutionary America. Chesterfield's comments on women aroused the indignation of female intellectuals on both sides of the Atlantic, including Adams and her friend Mercy Otis Warren.

3 The lines come from Alexander Pope's 1717 poem "Eloisa to Abelard." Here Eloisa remembers the period of her secret marriage to Abelard, her much older teacher, before her family forced their separation. The two entered monastic orders only to rekindle their feelings for each other in a series of letters. Pope's poem imagines one such piece of their correspondence.

and without which it is in vain to look for happiness in that Indisoluble union which Nought but death Dissolves. The Heart must be engaged to reap the genuine fruits of tenderness; contemptibly low must that commerce be in which the mind has no share. Love is an intellectual pleasure, and even the senses will be weakly affected where the Heart does not participate.

Believe me my young Friend, I say this to you in a firm belief and with a view to your persevering in that purity of sentiment which has always distinguished you in my mind; those persuits only are worth a reasonable Mans attention which will neither disgust by possession, nor sting with remorse; such you will find a soft and tender Friendship, enlivened by taste, refined by sentiment, which time instead of destroying, will render every hour more dear and interesting.

I cannot close this Letter without mentioning to you a connexion soon to take place between a Brother of your profession and a celebrated Lady who resides some times here and some times at B[osto]n.[1] You know who publickly affronted the whole Sex, and you know what Lady had refused such a Gentleman and such a Gentleman—for a Gambling Rake. Can a Bosom of Sensibility and Innocence, accept a Heart hardned by a commerce with the most profligate of the Sex?[2] a Constitution enfeabled, the fine feelings of the soul obliterated? What but disgust, suspicion, coldness, and depravity of taste, can be the consequence?

But I must close a Letter already long enough for a trial of your patience, but not till I have assured you of the affectionate and Maternal regard of

Portia[3]

---

1 Adams refers here to the engagement of Perez Morton and Sarah Wentworth Apthorp. The editors of the *Adams Family Correspondence* remained uncertain on this point, but they missed the clue in her phrase "publickly affronted the whole Sex," which refers to Morton's disparaging comments about women's capacity for keeping secrets in an oration he delivered to Boston Freemasons. See the Introduction to this volume (pp. 30–32) for more details on this episode.

2 The meaning here is somewhat ambiguous. If Adams means the "most profligate of the [male] Sex," she may be referring to Morton's association with gamblers; if she means "most profligate of the [female] Sex," she may be implying that he had known relations with prostitutes.

3 Literary cognomens were common among eighteenth-century letter writers. "Portia" is the name Adams had long since adopted in her personal correspondence.

Works Cited and Recommended Reading

Archival Holdings

Adams Family Papers, Letterbooks, Massachusetts Historical Society.

Apthorp, Frances T. Letter to Perez Morton, 20–27 Aug. 1788, Misc. Bound MSS, Massachusetts Historical Society.

Belknap, Jeremy. Sermon dated 21 Sept. 1788, manuscript sermon book for 1788, Belknap Papers, Massachusetts Historical Society.

"Bill of James Prince of inquest and burial costs for Theodora Apthorp," Suffolk County: Coroner's Inquisitions, Adlow Collection Selected Documents, MS Adl. C (33)—Suffolk Co., Mass. Coroner, Boston Public Library Rare Books and Manuscripts.

"Copies of Papers Written by the Unfortunate Francis Theodore Apthorp, the last weeks of her life," Price-Osgood-Valentine Papers, 1588–1910, Box 2 (1763–1788), Folder 1786–1788, Massachusetts Historical Society.

"Frances Theodora Apthorp Letter," A/A652, Schlesinger Library, Radcliffe Institute, Harvard University.

Norton, Elizabeth Cranch. Diary, 19–26 Aug. 1788, Jacob Norton Papers, Massachusetts Historical Society.

Wallcut, Thomas. Papers, MS N-1720 (microfilm P-391, reel 2), Massachusetts Historical Society.

Webb, Nathan. Diary, 23 Sept. 1790, Massachusetts Historical Society.

Published Materials

Adams, Charles Francis, editor. *The works of John Adams, second President of the United States*. Vol. 1, Little, Brown, 1856.

Arner, Robert D. "Sentiment and Sensibility: The Role of Emotion and William Hill Brown's *The Power of Sympathy*." *Studies in American Fiction*, vol. 1, no. 2, 1973, pp. 121–32.

Barker-Benfield, G.J. *Abigail and John Adams: The Americanization of Sensibility*. U of Chicago P, 2010.

Barnes, Elizabeth. *States of Sympathy: Seduction and Democracy*. Columbia UP, 1997.

The Beauties of Sterne: Including All His Pathetic Tales, & Most Distinguished Observations on Life. Selected for the Heart of Sensibility. Printed for T. Davies et al., 1782.

"The Beauties of 'The Power of Sympathy.'" *Massachusetts Magazine*, Jan. 1789, pp. 50–53.

Bell, Richard. "The Moral Thermometer: Rush, Republicanism, and Suicide." *Early American Studies*, vol. 15, no. 2, 2017, pp. 308–31.

——. *We Shall Be No More: Suicide and Self-Government in the Newly United States*. Harvard UP, 2012.

Braunschneider, Theresa. *Our Coquettes: Capacious Desire in the Eighteenth Century*. U of Virginia P, 2009.

Brayley, Arthur W. "The Real Author of *The Power of Sympathy*." *Bostonian*, vol. 1, no. 3, 1894, pp. 224–33.

Brookhiser, Richard. *Gentleman Revolutionary: Gouverneur Morris, the Rake Who Wrote the Constitution*. Free Press, 2008.

Brown, William Hill. *The Better Sort, or the Girl of Spirit*. Printed by Isaiah Thomas and Company, 1789.

——. *Selected Poems and Verse Fables, 1784–1793*. Edited by Richard G. Walser, U of Delaware P, 1982.

Buckingham, Joseph T. *Specimens of Newspaper Literature: with personal memoirs, anecdotes, and reminiscences*. Redding and Co., 1852. 2 vols.

Bullock, Steven C. *Revolutionary Brotherhood: Freemasonry and the Transformation of the American Social Order, 1730–1840*. U of North Carolina P for Omohundro Institute of Early American History and Culture, 1998.

Burstein, Andrew. "The Political Character of Sympathy." *Journal of the Early Republic*, vol. 21, no. 4, 2001, pp. 601–32.

Butterfield, Lyman H., et al., editors. *Adams Family Correspondence*. Harvard UP for the Massachusetts Historical Society, 1963–2021. 15 vols.

Byers, John R., Jr. "Further Verification of the Authorship of *The Power of Sympathy*." *American Literature*, vol. 43, no. 3, 1971, pp. 421–27.

Carr-Frobose, Jacqueline. *A Cultural History of Boston in the Revolutionary Era, 1775–1795*. U of California P, 1998.

Churchill, Charles. "The Times." *The Poetical Works of Charles Churchill*, edited by Douglas Grant, Clarendon Press, 1956, pp. 389–409.

Clough, Ruth Thorndike. *A Study of the Life and Works of Robert Treat Paine, Jr.* 1930. U of Maine, MA thesis.

Davidson, Cathy N. *Revolution and the Word: The Rise of the Novel in America*. Rev. ed., Oxford UP, 2004.

Davies, Kate. *Catharine Macaulay and Mercy Otis Warren: The Revolutionary Atlantic and the Politics of Gender*. Oxford UP, 2005.

Dayton, Cornelia Hughes. *Women before the Bar: Gender, Law, and Society in Connecticut, 1639–1789*. U of North Carolina P for Omohundro Institute of Early American History and Culture, 1995.

Debes, Remy. "Adam Smith and the Sympathetic Imagination." *Adam Smith: His Life, Thought, and Legacy*, edited by Ryan Patrick Hanley, Princeton UP, 2016, pp. 192–207.

Eamon, Michael J. "'Don't Speak to me, but Write on this': The Childhood Almanacs of Mary and Katherine Byles." *New England Quarterly*, vol. 85, no. 2, 2012, pp. 335–52.

Evans, Dorinda. *Mather Brown: Early American Artist in England*. Wesleyan UP, 1982.

Fliegelman, Jay. *Prodigals and Pilgrims: The American Revolution against Patriarchal Authority, 1750–1800*. Cambridge UP, 1982.

Foster, Hannah Webster. *The Coquette* and *The Boarding School*. Edited by Jennifer Harris and Bryan Waterman, Norton, 2013.

Friedman, Lawrence M. "Notes toward a History of American Justice." *American Law and the Constitutional Order: Historical Perspectives*, edited by Lawrence Meir Friedman and Harry N. Scheiber, Harvard UP, 1998, pp. 13–26.

Hayes, Edmund M. "Mercy Otis Warren vs. Lord Chesterfield, 1779." *William and Mary Quarterly*, vol. 40, no. 4, 1983, pp. 616–21.

Kamensky, Jane. *The Exchange Artist: A Tale of High-Flying Speculation and America's First Banking Collapse*. Viking, 2008.

——. "The Exchange Artist's Wife." Capitalism by Gaslight Conference, 7 June 2022, presented at the McNeil Center for Early American Studies and Library Company of Philadelphia. Keynote address.

Koenigs, Thomas. *Founded in Fiction: The Uses of Fiction in the Early United States*. Princeton UP, 2021.

Lyons, Clare A. *Sex among the Rabble: An Intimate History of Gender and Power in the Age of Revolution, Philadelphia, 1730–1830*. U of North Carolina P for Omohundro Institute of Early American History and Culture, 2006.

McClain, Dana C. "Regulating Feeling in the First American Novel: Sympathy, Sensibility, and Sentiment in William Hill Brown's *The Power of Sympathy*." *Studies in American Fiction*, vol. 45, no. 2, 2018, pp. 143–64.

Mercieca, Jennifer R. *Founding Fictions*. U of Alabama P, 2010.

Milford, T.A. "Boston's Theater Controversy and Liberal Notions of Advantage." *New England Quarterly*, vol. 72, no. 1, 1999, pp. 61–88.

——. *The Gardiners of Massachusetts: Provincial Ambition and the British-American Career*. U of New Hampshire P, 2005.

More, Hannah. *Poems by Miss Hannah More. To Wit, Sensibility, and Reflections of King Hezekiah*. Young, Stewart, and M'Culloch, 1785.

——. *Sensibility: a poetical epistle to the Hon. Mrs. Boscawen*. Meigs, Bowen and Dana, 1785.

Morton, Perez. *An oration; delivered at the King's-Chapel in Boston, April 8, 1776, on the re-interment of the remains of the late most worshipful Grand-Master Joseph Warren, Esquire*. J. Gill, 1776.

Morton, Sarah Wentworth Apthorp. *My Mind and Its Thoughts, in Sketches, Fragments, and Essays*. Wells and Lilly, 1823.

Nathans, Heather S. *Early American Theater from the Revolution to Thomas Jefferson: Into the Hands of the People*. Cambridge UP, 2003.

Occurrences of the Times. Or, the Transactions of Four Days. Viz.—from Friday the 16th, to Monday the 19th January, 1789. A Farce. In Two Acts. Printed for the purchasers, 1789.

Pasley, Jeffrey L. *The Tyranny of Printers: Newspaper Politics in the Early American Republic*. U of Virginia P, 2001.

Pendleton, Emily, and Milton Ellis. *Philenia: The Life and Works of Sarah Wentworth Morton, 1759–1846*. U of Maine P, 1931.

Phillips, Mark Salber. *Society and Sentiment: Genres of Historical Writing in Britain, 1740–1820*. Princeton UP, 2000.

Porter, Roy. *Health for Sale: Quackery in England, 1660–1850*. Manchester UP, 1989.

Pratt, Samuel Jackson. *Liberal Opinions, Upon Man, Animals and Providence*. Printed for G. Robinson and J. Bew, and sold by J. Walter, 1775–77. 6 vols.

Richards, Jeffrey H., and Sharon M. Harris, editors. *Mercy Otis Warren: Selected Letters*. U of Georgia P, 2009.

Rush, Benjamin. "Directions for Conducting a Newspaper." *The Selected Writings of Benjamin Rush*, edited by Dagobert D. Runes, Philosophical Library, 1947, pp. 396–98.

Ryan, Kelly A. *Regulating Passion: Sexuality and Patriarchal Rule in Massachusetts, 1700–1830*. Oxford UP, 2014.

Sans Souci, alias, Free and Easy, or an Evening's Peep into a Polite Social Circle. Warden and Russell, 1785. The second edition was also published in 1785.

Shields, David S. *Civil Tongues and Polite Letters in British America*. U of North Carolina P, 1997.

Shipton, Clifford K. *Sibley's Harvard Graduates*. Vol. 17, Massachusetts Historical Society, 1975.

Shoultz, Amy Elizabeth. *A Revolutionary Idea: Gilbert Stuart Paints Sarah Morton as the First Woman of Ideas in American Art*. 2008. U of Texas–Austin, PhD dissertation.

Smith-Rosenberg, Carroll. "Dis-Covering the Subject of the 'Great Constitutional Discussion,' 1786–1789." *Journal of American History*, 1992, pp. 841–73.

——. *This Violent Empire: The Birth of an American National Identity*. U of North Carolina P for Omohundro Institute of Early American History and Culture, 2010.

Stanhope, Philip Dormer, 4th Earl of Chesterfield. *Letters to His Son on the Art of Becoming a Man of the World and a Gentleman*. J. Dodsley, 1774–75. 2 vols.

Stephens, John Calhoun, editor. *The Guardian*. UP of Kentucky, 1982.

Stephens, Mitchell. *Beyond News: The Future of Journalism*. Columbia UP, 2014.

Tennenhouse, Leonard. *The Importance of Feeling English: American Literature and the British Diaspora, 1750–1850*. Princeton UP, 2009.

Thacher, James. *American Medical Biography, Or, Memoirs of Eminent Physicians Who Have Flourished in America*. Vol. 1, Richardson & Lord and Cottons & Barnard, 1828.

Vietto, Angela. *Women and Authorship in Revolutionary America*. Ashgate, 2006.

Walser, Richard. "Boston's Reception of the First American Novel." *Early American Literature*, vol. 17, 1982, pp. 65–74.

——. "The Fatal Effects of Seduction (1789)." *Modern Language Notes*, 1954, pp. 574–76.

——. "More about the First American Novel." *American Literature*, 1952, pp. 352–57.

——. "The North Carolina Sojourn of the First American Novelist." *North Carolina Historical Review*, 1951, pp. 138–55.

Warner, William B. *Protocols of Liberty: Communication Innovation and the American Revolution*. U of Chicago P, 2013.

Warren, Charles. "Samuel Adams and the Sans Souci Club in 1785." *Proceedings of the Massachusetts Historical Society*, vol. 60, 1927, pp. 318–44.

Waterman, Bryan. "Elizabeth Whitman's Disappearance and Her 'Disappointment.'" *William and Mary Quarterly*, vol. 66, no. 2, 2009, pp. 325–64.

——. "'Heaven defend us from such fathers': Perez Morton and the Politics of Seduction." *Atlantic Worlds in the Long Eighteenth Century: Seduction and Sentiment*, edited by Toni Bowers and Tita Chico, Palgrave Macmillan, 2012, pp. 49–64.

About the Publisher

The word "broadview" expresses a good deal of the philosophy behind our company. Our focus is very much on the humanities and social sciences—especially literature, writing, and philosophy—but within these fields we are open to a broad range of academic approaches and political viewpoints. We strive in particular to produce high-quality, pedagogically useful books for higher education classrooms—anthologies, editions, sourcebooks, surveys of particular academic fields and subfields, and also course texts for subjects such as composition, business communication, and critical thinking. We welcome the perspectives of authors from marginalized and underrepresented groups, and we have a strong commitment to the environment. We publish English-language works and translations from many parts of the world, and our books are available world-wide; we also publish a select list of titles with a specifically Canadian emphasis.

broadview press

This book is made of paper from well-managed FSC® - certified forests, recycled materials, and other controlled sources.